SHELF LIFE

Fantastic Stories Celebrating Bookstores

Other Books Edited by Greg Ketter

Temporary Walls: An Anthology of Moral Fantasy
(with Robert Garcia)

SHELF LIFE

Fantastic Stories Celebrating Bookstores

Edited by Greg Ketter

PRIME BOOKS

SHELF LIFE
Fantastic Stories Celebrating Bookstores

Trade Paperback: October 2012

ACKNOWLEDGEMENTS

"Introduction: Four Bookshops" Copyright © 2002 Neil Gaiman.
"From the Cradle" Copyright © 2002 Gene Wolfe.
"A Book, By Its Cover" Copyright © 2002 P.D. Cacek.
"The Hemingway Kittens" Copyright © 2002 A.R. Morlan.
"Lost Books" Copyright © 2002 John J. Miller.
"One Copy Only" Copyright © 2002 Ramsey Campbell.
"Pixel Pixies" was first published as a complimentary limited edition chapbook in an
    edition of 200 by Triskell Press, 2001. Copyright © 2001 by Charles de Lint.
    Reprinted by permission of the author.
"Blind Stamped" Copyright © 2002 Lisa Morton.
"Shakespeare & Co." Copyright © 2002 Jack Williamson.
"Ballard's Books" Copyright © 2002 Gerard Hoarurner.
"Books" Copyright © 2002 David Bischoff.
"Escapes" Copyright © 2002 Nina Kiriki Hoffman.
" 'I Am Looking for a Book. . .' " Copyright © 2002 Patrick Weekes.
"The Glutton" Copyright © 2002 Melanie Tem.
"In the Bookshadow" Copyright © 2002 Marianne de Pierres.
"Non-Returnable" Copyright © 2002 Rick Hautala.
"The Cheese Stands Alone" by Harlan Ellison. Copyright © 1981 The Kilimanjaro
    Corporation. Reprinted by arrangement with, and permission of, the Author and
    the Author's agent, Richard Curtis Associates, Inc., New York. All rights reserved.

Published by
Prime Books
www.prime-books.com

Book Design by
Robert T. Garcia / Garcia Publishing Services
919 Tappan St. Woodstock, Illinois, 60098
www.gpsdesign.net

ISBN 978-1-60701-358-7

To my parents, Robert and Lorraine Ketter,
for their help, their encouragement and their love.
Mom, I wish you could have seen it . . .

TABLE OF CONTENTS

FOREWORD

This is my baby. It took 25 years to deliver but it's a keeper.

I first opened my bookstore on April 1, 1977; my April Fools joke on the world. But the joke was on me. I remember that I opened a store mostly because I wanted to get my own books less expensively. I found that if I bought three copies of something, then sold two, I could keep one for free! A true Fool's Paradise. I started selling books when I was barely into my teens and then later began the work of opening my own store while I was still a teenager. And now, 25 years later, I'm fortunate enough to still operate an independent bookstore, and publish books by people whose work I like.

When I realized that I was approaching the milestone of 25 years, I decided to put together a collection of stories — science fiction, fantasy and horror — in which the bookstore was a character, a major component of the story, a true motivating factor. I solicited work from over 100 writers, many of whom I've become friends over the years, figuring twenty or so would actually have time to do stories. Word got out and I received over 400 stories of various kind and quality. Many were simply set in a bookstore because I was editing a "bookstore anthology"; those were easy to eliminate. Some were book oriented but the bookstore element just wasn't strong enough. Those were eliminated too, but with more deliberation and reluctance. And some were exactly what I was looking for . . .

Bookstores have always been special to me. I might go into a second hand bookstore looking for one book and come out with five more I had never heard of. Searching through dusty stacks of old books became my regular Saturday afternoon adventure as soon as I was old enough to scour our city by myself. Now, when I visit anywhere in the world, I seek out bookstores. I find them comforting and fulfilling. I see wonderful books, meet interesting people, and learn of things I never could dream without help. I am home.

This is a true labor of love — a love of books and bookstores. Books have been such a major part of my life for so long, I simply can't imagine a world without books or bookstores. Maybe - someone should do that story; to me, that would be the most frightening story ever written.

Greg Ketter
September 5, 2002

INTRODUCTION: FOUR BOOKSHOPS

i

These are the bookshops that made me who I am. They are none of them there, not any longer.

The first, the best, the most wonderful, the most magical because it was the most insubstantial, was a travelling bookshop.

From the ages of nine to thirteen I attended a local boarding school, as a day boy. Like all such schools, it was a world in itself, which meant that it had its own "tuck shop", its own weekly barbering facilities, and, once a term, it had its own bookshop. Up until then my bookbuying fortunes would rise or fall with what was for sale in my local W. H. Smiths — the Puffin books and Armada Paperbacks that I'd save up for, only from the children's shelves, as I had never thought to explore further. Nor had I the money to explore if I wanted to. School libraries were my friends, as was the local library. But at that age I was limited by my means and by what was on the shelves.

And then, when I was nine, the travelling bookshop came. It set up its shelves and stock in a large empty room in the old music school, and, this was the best bit, you didn't need any money. If you bought books, it went onto your school bill. It was like magic. I could buy four or five books a term, secure in the knowledge it would wind up in the miscellaneous bit of the school bill, down with the haircuts and the double bass lessons, and I'd never be discovered.

I bought Ray Bradbury's *The Silver Locusts* (a collection similar to, although not exactly the same as *The Martian Chronicles*). I loved it, especially "Usher II", Ray's tribute to Poe. I did not know who Poe was. I bought *The Screwtape Letters*, because anything the bloke that wrote Narnia did had to be good. I bought *Diamonds Are Forever* by Ian Fleming, the cover proclaiming that it was soon to be a major motion picture. And I bought *The Day of the Triffids*, and *I, Robot*. (The shop was very big on Wyndham and Bradbury and Asimov.)

There were few enough children's books there. That was the good thing, and the smart thing. The books they sold, when they came to town, were, in the main, rattling good reads — the kind of books that would be read. Nothing that would be controversial or confiscated (the first book of mine that was confiscated was a copy of "*. . . And To My Nephew Albert I Leave The Island What I Won Off Fatty Hagen In A Poker Game*", because it had an artistically naked female body on the cover. I got it back from the Headmaster by claiming that it was my father's book, which I'm pretty certain wasn't true). Horror was fine though — like most of my year I was a ten year old Dennis Wheatley Addict, and loved (although rarely bought) the Pan Books of Horror Stories. More Bradbury — much more, in the wonderful Pan covers — and Asimov and Arthur C. Clarke.

It didn't last for long. A year or so, no more — perhaps too many parents read their school bills and complained. But I didn't mind. I had moved on.

ii

In 1971, the United Kingdom went over to Decimal Currency. The familiar sixpences and shillings that I'd grown up with suddenly became New Pence. An old shilling was now five New Pence. And although we were assured it would make no real difference to the cost of things, it soon became obvious, even to a ten going on eleven-year old, that it had. Prices went up, and they went up fast. Books which had been two shillings and sixpence (er, 12_ new pence) were soon thirty new pence, or forty new pence.

I wanted books. But, on my pocket money, I could barely afford them. But there was a bookshop . . .

The Wilmington Bookshop was not a long walk from my house. They did not have the best selection of books, being also an art supply shop and even, for a while, a post office, but what they did have, I learned soon, were a lot of paperbacks that were waiting to sell. Not, in those days, the cavalier tearing-off of covers for easy returns. I'd simply browse the shelves looking for anything with the prices listed in both old and new money, and would stack up on cool books for 20p and 25p. Tom Disch's *Echo Round His Bones*, was the first of these I found, which attracted the attention of the young bookseller. His name was John Banks, and he died a few months ago, in his fifties. His parents owned the shop. He had hippy-long hair and a beard, and was, I suspect, amused by a twelve year old buying a Tom Disch book. He'd steer me to things I might like, and we'd talk books, and SF.

The Golden Age of SF is thirteen, they say, and it was pretty damn golden, as golden ages go. It seemed like everything was available in quantity — Moorcock and Zelazny and Delany, Ellison and LeGuin and Lafferty. (I'd make people going to America find me R. A. Lafferty books, convinced that he must be a famous, best-selling author in America. What was strange in retrospect was, they would bring me back the books.) I found James Branch Cabell there, in the James Blish introduced editions — and in fact, took my first book back (it was *Jurgen*, and the final signature was missing. I had to go to the library to find out how it ended).

When I told John Banks I was writing a book, he introduced me to the Penguin Rep., who told me who to send it to at Kestrel. (The editor wrote back an encouraging no, and having re-read the book recently, for the first time in twenty years, I'm terribly grateful that she did.)

There's a brotherhood of people who read and who care about books. The best thing about John Banks was that, when I was eleven or twelve he noticed I was a member of the brotherhood, and would share his likes and dislikes, even solicit my opinion.

iii

The man who owned Plus Books in Streatham, on the other hand, was not of that brotherhood, or if he was, he never let on.

The shop was a long bus-ride from the school I was at between the ages of fourteen and seventeen, so we didn't go there often. The man who ran it would glower at us when we went in, suspicious of us in case we were going to steal something (we weren't), and worried that we would upset his regular clientele of middle-aged gentlemen in raincoats nervously perusing the stacks of mild pornography (which, in retrospect, we probably did).

He would growl at us, like a dog, if we got too near the porn. We didn't, though. We headed for the back of the shop on a treasure-hunt, thumbing through the books. Everything had a PLUS BOOKS stamp on the cover or the inside, reminding us that we could bring it back for half the price. We bought stuff there, but we never brought it back.

Thinking about it now, I wonder where the books came from — why would a grubby little shop in what was barely South London have heaps of American Paperbacks? I bought all I could afford: Edgar Rice Burroughs, with the Frazetta covers, a copy of Zelazny's *A Rose For Ecclesiastes* that smelled of scented talcum powder when I bought it and still does, a quarter of a century later. That was where I found *Dhalgren*, and *Nova*, and where I first discovered Jack Vance.

It was not a welcoming place. But of the bookshops I've ever been in, that's the one I go back to in dreams, certain that in a pile of ragged comics I'll find *Action* #1, that there with a stamp on the cover telling you that it can be returned for half price, and smelling of beer or of beeswax, is one of those books I've always wanted to read from the shelves of Lucien's library — Roger Zelazny's own Amber prequel, perhaps, or a Cabell book that had somehow escaped all the usual bibliographies. If I find them, I'll find them in there.

iv

That was not the furthest I went, after school. That was to London, on the last day of every term. (They taught us nothing on that day, after all, and our season tickets would take us all the way, and would die the day after). It was to a shop that took its name from one of the Bradbury tales of the Silver Locusts: Dark They Were And Golden Eyed.

I'd heard about it from John Banks at the Wilmington Bookshop — I don't know if he'd been there or not, but either way he knew it was somewhere I had to go. So Dave Dickson and I trolled up to Berwick Street, in London's Soho, to find, on our first visit, that the shop had moved several streets away to a spacious building in Queen Anne's Court.

I had a term's worth of pocket money saved up. They had teetering piles of remaindered Dennis Dobson hardbacks — all the R.A. Lafferty and Jack Vance I could have dreamed of. They had the new American paperback Cabells. They had the new Zelazny (*Roadworks*). They had shelf after shelf after shelf after shelf of all the SF and Fantasy a boy could dream of. It was a match made in heaven.

It lasted several years. The staff were amused and unhelpful (I remember being soundly, loudly and publically ridiculed for asking, timorously, if *The Last Dangerous Visions* was out yet) but I didn't care. It was where I went when I went to London. No matter what else I did, I'd go there.

One day I went to London and the windows in Queen Anne's Court were empty, and the shop was gone, its evolutionary niche supplanted by Forbidden Planet, which has survived for over twenty years, making it, in SF bookshop years, a shark: one of the survivors.

To this day, every time I walk through Queen Anne's Court I look and see what kind of shop is in the place that Dark They Were And Golden Eyed . . . was, vaguely hoping that one day it'll be a bookshop. There have been all sorts of shops there, restaurants, even a dry cleaners, but it's not a bookshop yet.

And writing this, all of those the bookshops come back, the shelves, and the people. And most of all, the books, their covers bright, their pages filled with infinite possibilities. I wonder who I would have been, without those shelves, without those people and those places, without books.

I would have been lonely, I think, and empty, needing something for which I did not have the words.

v

And there is one more bookshop, I haven't mentioned. It is old, and sprawling, with small rooms that twist to become doors and stairs and cupboards, all of them covered with shelves, and the shelves all books, all the books I've ever wanted to see, books that need homes. There are books in piles, and in dark corners. In my fancy I shall have a comfortable chair, near a fireplace, somewhere on the ground floor, a little way from the door, and I'll sit on the chair, and say little, browsing an old favourite book, or even a new one, and when the people come in I shall nod at them, perhaps even smile, and let them wander.

There will be a book for each of them there, somewhere, in a shadowy nook or in plain sight. It will be theirs if they can find it. Otherwise, they will be free to keep looking, until it gets too dark to read.

Neil Gaiman
September 8, 2002

SHELF LIFE

Fantastic Stories Celebrating Bookstores

FROM THE CRADLE

Gene Wolfe

A woman hath nine lives like a cat.
                                    —John Heywood

The boy's name was Michael, but his father called him Mike. His mother called him Mickey, and his teacher (who was both humorous and devout) The Burning Bush in her thoughts and Mick when she called on him in class. His principal said "that redheaded boy," a memory for boys' names not being among his principal accomplishments.

He was in back straightening up a shelf, tickling Eppie Graph (at which Eppie smiled and purred), and looking for another book as good as *Starfighters of the Combined Fleets* when the old lady came in. She wore a navy-blue suit and shiny black shoes with heels not quite so high as his mother's, and a big gray coat that looked warm; but none of those things were of interest to Michael just then. What was of interest was the bag she carried, which was old and large and real leather, bound all the way around with straps, and plainly heavy. She tried to lift it onto the counter to show Mister Browne, but could not raise it that high until Michael helped her, scrooching down and pushing up on the bottom.

She thanked him and smiled at him; and though her hair was white, she had the brightest blue eyes he had ever seen; her smile seemed to last a long time, but not long enough. When it was over she unbuckled the straps, big black ones that made Michael think of horses. He stood up very straight then, trying

3

hard to look like a grown-up nobody would even think of chasing away.

From her big leather bag, she took a book of ordinary size with a dark brown cover and light brown pages. Unlike real books, it seemed to have no pictures; but there was a great deal of writing on all the pages; and Michael was at that age at which one begins to think that it might be better if there were fewer pictures after all, and more print.

Mister Browne whistled.

The lady nodded. "Yes, it's very old."

"You don't want me," Mister Browne said slowly. He fingered the pages in a way that said he was afraid she would tell him not to. "I'd try Kalmenoff and Whitechapel."

"I have," she said. "They don't want it. Not on the only terms I could offer it. Don't you want it either?"

"I don't know your terms." Mister Browne hesitated. "But no, I don't. It's not the sort of thing I handle. I'd want to give you a fair price." He stopped talking to rub his jaw. "I'd have to borrow most of it, and it might be years before I found a buyer."

The lady had money in her hand, although Michael was not sure she had taken it from a purse or pocket. It might have been in the black leather bag with the brown book.

"This is for you," she said. She laid it on the counter. "So you'll want it. On my terms."

Mister Browne looked at it, and blinked, and looked again. And after Michael had just about decided that he was not going to talk any more, he said, "What are your terms?"

"This old book —" He had shut it, and she tapped the scuffed brown cover with a long fingernail as she spoke. "Was my late husband's most prized possession. He loved it."

"I understand," Mister Browne said. "I'm something of a collector myself, in a much smaller way."

"And it loved him. He said it did." The lady's voice fell. "He wasn't making a joke. Oh, yes, he made jokes often. But this wasn't one of them. We were married for almost fifty years. Trust me, I knew when he was serious."

Mister Browne nodded. "I'm sure you did."

"He told me that if he died — he was in some danger for years, you understand. He wasn't morbid about it, but he was realistic. We both were. We'd talked about the things that might happen, and what I ought to do if they did."

Mister Browne said he was sure that had been wise.

"Take the money. Now. I mean it. It's your money, and I don't like seeing it lying there."

Mister Browne did.

"He said that if he died, I was to put this book up for sale. He said that it would choose its new owner, and that I was to trust its judgment." She hesitated. "He didn't say how I was to put it up. I've thought of running ads on vid, but there would be a thousand cranks."

Mister Browne nodded, though Michael was not sure that he agreed.

"So I thought I'd better enlist the help of a dealer — someone who has a shop and can display it. Someone like you. My name's Caitlin Higgins. Here's a card for your terminal."

A little too late Mister Browne nodded again, his head not moving much.

"Only you must warn them I might not sell. It will tell me when the right one comes along." Caitlin Higgins bit her lips in a way that made Michael sorry for her. "Or I hope it will," she said.

*   *   *

When she had gone, Mister Browne put the brown book, open, in the window farthest from the door, with a sign that he had made over it. And when Mister Browne (after half a dozen nervous glances at the book) had gone as well — gone into his office above the shop — Michael went out into the street and read the sign:

INCUNABULUM
On Consignment
Make Offer

It stood open, as has been said, upon a small stand that looked very much like real wood; and Michael was happy to see that it was open to a story.

* * *

The Tale of the Dwarf
and the Children of the Sphinx

A certain dwarf who wandered from place to place, at times begging and at others stealing, was driven forth from the last, a town that beholds the desert and is itself beheld by mountains far away. Not daring to return until the wrath of the townsfolk had abated, he walked very far, and when night stole over the land taking far more than he ever had, he laid himself down upon the sand and slept.

In dream, he was a tall young man, and handsome, and owned five fine fields of barley and three of millet. For long hours of the night he walked among them, seeing barley as high as his waist and millet higher even than the lofty stature that sleep had bestowed upon him.

Chancing to look toward the desert, he beheld with alarm a great spinning wind that drew sand and stones up by its force, and so had become visible, a wind that moaned and roared as it rushed toward him. His first thought was to conceal himself; but he soon noticed that it grew smaller as it advanced, so that when it reached him it scarcely exceeded his own height.

For a moment only it stood before him. Dust, sand, and stones fell to the ground, revealing a beautiful young woman, naked save for her hair. "You must force me," this woman said to him. "We yield only when forced." In his dream he seized her, smothered her with kisses, and bestowed his love upon her while she writhed in ecstasy — not once, not twice, but three times.

Then he woke, and found that he was but a dwarf, and that a great beast lay beside him. When he tried to rise, it held him; and the paw upon his chest was soft as thistledown, big as a saddle, and strong as iron.

A woman's face bent above him, and it was a face much larger than that of any true woman. "O my lover, I have had my way three times with you. Ask a gift, and if it be in my power you shall have it."

Through chattering teeth he said, "I am small and stunted."

She laughed, and her laugh was deeper than the thunder. "Not in every part."

"Spare my life!"

"I will never take it, but what boon is that once I have kissed you, and you me? Will you not ask another?"

"Then make me g-great and p-p-powerful," the poor dwarf stammered, "and small and stunted no more."

"I will," she told him, "for this night only. Suckle at my breast."

The breast she presented to him was like to that of a human woman, though greater by five. He gave suck, and at the first drop felt his back straighten. At the second he knew himself as large as she, and at the third — ah, at the third strength filled him; his thews grew thick as pythons, his body supple as a whip.

He rose, a lion with the head and shoulders of a man. He roared, and the earth shook. Roaring still, he returned to the town that had driven him forth, and his mate went with him. It was a small place now, a little cluster of wretched houses of sundried brick. A dozen blows from his paw would have left no brick upon brick, but he swept the roof from one such house and saw the trembling man within: a man too weak with fear to hold his spear, and his moaning wife, and the wailing children she clasped.

And he pitied them, and went away.

Then he and his mate bounded whole leagues, and raced across the desert, and reaching the mountains bounded from rock to rock there, glorying until the sun rose.

But when the sun rose, he found himself a man again, and but a dwarf, and wept.

The great sphinx who for one night had been his mate then told him how it would be with him, and left him.

*　　*　　*

He returned to the town that had cast him out, weary still, and dizzied with the memory of the night. There they told him of the storm that had so terrified them, and showed him the house whose roof had been blown away. He laughed at them for that, and because he laughed they stoned him and he fled into the fields.

Long he wandered, through many a town and down many a long road; and at length the days were complete, and in a marsh beside the great slow northflowing river he knelt in mud and water and was sicker than he had ever been, coughing and retching until at last, with a great heave that seemed that lt must take his bowels with it, he coughed out an infant, a baby boy who lay howling in the dirty water and opened amber eyes. This boy the dwarf named Kalam, "pen," because his birth had been foretold, and of what has been foretold his people say, "It was written."

He would have picked Kalam up and fled with him, for he feared the crocodiles; instead he retched again, and from jaws almost burst asunder spat another infant, also a boy. This second child he named Wahl, for as he came forth he spattered his brother with mud, and it seemed to the dwarf that *Wahl!*, which means "mud," was the child's first cry.

Then would he have picked up both brothers if he could; but that affliction with which he had been afflicted held him there, and he coughed forth a third infant, a girl, whom he called Jamil, "beauty," because he saw her mother's face in hers.

Then rose he from the marsh, holding his sons and his daughter in arms scarce long enough for the task, as some other might hold a litter of kittens; and he returned to the plowlands and the grazing lands, where he found, or begged, or stole, the milk and the blood on which he fed them.

How he brought them up, and how he took them on his wanderings — how Wahl climbed the wall of the pasha's palace and returned with the pasha's roast in his mouth — how Jamil, lovely as new-minted gold though her hair was matted with dung, was pitied by the Rani, who gave her a ruby — and how Kalam, the eldest, wrote this tale with his forefinger in the dust — any one of these would make a story too long for we who must end this one.

We leave them to others. The day came when they stood at the right hand of the dwarf, with their feet upon sand and millet at their backs, and all three stood much taller than he. And upon that day he called across the desert to their mother. Small though he was, his voice was large, and held the pain of a thousand beatings and the pain of a lover who knows that love is past. All the people of all the towns that border on the desert heard him, and spoke in awe, one to another; and some said that a storm approached, and some that the earth groaned, and more than a few muttered of ghosts and ghouls and worse.

But the dwarf said, "Now, my children, you will see whether your father be mad or no. Your mother, I say, will come to my call as I have oft told you. You will see what manner of creature she is, and if you are wise you will join her, for it is the finest life in world." His voice broke at the last word, and he fell silent.

Then Kalam, the eldest said, "How are we to join her father? You have told us many times that she has the feet of a lioness."

The dwarf affirmed that it was so.

"You have said also," Wahl remarked, "that she is large as many a mountain. How then can we join a creature so huge? We will be as ants to her."

"She is of that great size when she wills it," the dwarf explained, "but scarcely larger than an ox when she wills otherwise. Did you imagine she was of mountain size when we lay together?"

At this, Jamil said, "How could we join her, Father, when to join her we must leave you? It is you, not she, who has fed, and taught, and cherished us through all our lives. If our blood is hers, is it not yours also?"

"It is," the dwarf affirmed.

"I cannot speak for my brothers," Jamil told him, "but for myself, dear Father, I will remain with you."

"The time for choosing is not yet," the dwarf told her.

"I make no pother of it," Wahl declared. "But I will remain with you as well — should the monster come. How could I, a man, join in the frolics of such a creature?"

"And I," announced Kalam, "go. Not with the monstermother, but out into the world of men. I have been a beggar and a thief, but there are better things. The ships in Abu Qir are always wanting crew, and it would be a rare captain who could find no use for a crewman well able to wield the pen. I wish you well . . ." His eyes softened.

"As I, you," said the dwarf, his father.

"And if you wait here all night, I will wait too with my sister and you. But when the sun rises, I go north to the docks."

"I may follow you, in time," said his brother. "I have not decided."

"If our father waits here for a year," declared Jamil, "I will wait with him, save when I go to fetch him food and drink."

"But I —" began Kalam. And fell silent, for far off, he heard the howl of a wild wind among the desert peaks. Louder it grew, and louder. The millet bowed and stood straight and bowed again.

And she came.

Kalam stepped forward. His features changed, becoming those of a man more noble than any man, though his own still. His first bound carried him so far that he was almost lost to sight; he turned and grew, so that they saw him still, and the power that was in him, and the glory. When he smiled, the love that went out from him washed over them like a wave.

Wahl passed him to stand beside their mother; and, oh, but he was terrible and great! Even as she, and the strength of him was like the strength of the river, irresistible.

"Go," dwarf said, and he gave Jamil a push.

"I will stay with you, Father."

"But not obey me? Go!"

She did as he bid, though with many a backward glance. Ten steps, twenty, a hundred. She has not changed, the dwarf thought. Yet she had. Taller and more graceful, with hair black as storm-cloud and tawny skin. "Go!" he said again.

She stopped instead, turned, and beckoned to him.

And he bounded after her.

*   *   *

Michael thought about this story all the way home, for it had made clear to him certain things about which he had wondered, but raised questions, too. At home he went to his link and called his teacher.

Her face appeared in his screen. "What is it, Mick?"

"Have I seen you anyplace else?"

"I don't know. Have you?"

"I don't know either," Michael admitted.

"I'm a simulation, Mick. There was a real teacher once, a very good teacher who looked about like this."

Michael nodded.

"Many of my programs and subroutines are based upon her. So is my face."

Michael thought a long time about that, and at last he said, "What's a incunabulum?"

*   *   *

in-cu-nab-u-lum ih-kyoo-'nab-ya-lam (in + cunabula L. infancy, origin) A book printed in the Second Millennium.

*   *   *

Michael was working part time at the book store when R.T. Hurd came in. A friend, R.T. Hurd explained, had mentioned the brown book. He wanted to make an offer, but he would have to examine the book first. Michael switched off the motion alarm and took the brown book from the window. R.T. Hurd opened it reverently and turned its pages with care, and at length wrote his offer on a kneeboard keyboard and signal signed it.

When he had gone, Michael replaced the brown book in its window and switched the motion detector back on. R.T. Hurd's offer he carried upstairs and left on the owner's desk. It was not until he and Michael had locked the store for the day that Michael realized he had left the brown book open at a new place. And it was not until he came to work the next day that he read the pages he himself had freshly exposed.

*   *   *

The Tale of Prince Know-Nothing

When the world was young, there lived a certain prince who did not know he was a prince. Two thousand years before, his many greats grandfather had been a glorious king, renown for courage and wisdom throughout all the world. Many sons and daughters had he fathered; and although some had perished without issue, others had as many children as he, and two had more. Because they had been the sons and daughters of the king, they had been men and women of wealth, masters of great houses and broad lands and coffers of gold and jewels. But as the years turned to centuries, and generations were born and aged and died, the wild thyme grew up around all these things, which vanished from the sight of men; so that when Prince Know-Nothing was born, his mother did not know he was a prince or that she herself was a princess. Nevertheless the blood-royal ran strong in his veins, because his father had been a prince also, though neither of them knew it. (But someone did.)

Thus the young prince lived as other boys lived. He was strong and brave, but there were many other boys who were stronger and braver than he — or if they were not, they were at least louder in their boasts, which is much the same thing among boys. And although he was wiser than they, at his age wisdom consists largely in honoring one's parents and careful listening to the counsel of those older than oneself; thus his wisdom, though it made him well-liked and kept him from harm in a hundred ways, brought him only mockery whenever it became apparent.

"Once upon a time," said his teacher, "there was a king who had but a single child, the princess, and twelve golden plates. They were very beautiful, with knights and dragons and elves around their borders —"

"What is a princess?" asked Prince Know-Nothing, and the other children all laughed.

"If everyone else knows," said his teacher, "everyone else can tell you." And she asked the girl with the pink hair-ribbon to tell Prince Know-Nothing what a princess was.

"It's a girl that's very pretty on Halloween and has a pretty white dress with a big skirt," explained the girl with the pink hair-ribbon.

Their teacher agreed that was a good definition, but she was afraid that it wasn't quite rigorous enough, so she asked the smartest boy in the whole class to tell Prince Know-Nothing what a princess was, too.

"It's the one the knight marries," the smartest boy in the whole class said at once.

"That's a good definition, too," the teacher agreed. "But princesses don't always marry knights. Sometimes they marry princes."

* * *

Here the page ended, and since the book was locked away in its window again, Michael was unable to turn it. He went home, and when the book remained in its window day after day and week after week, he knew that R.T. Hurd's offer had been refused.

Years passed, and there came a year in which he, and not the old owner, took inventory; and when it was nearly done, he got out the brown book so that he might look at it again. He was listing books by their UAISBN numbers, and he hoped to find one on it, although he did not. He considered listing it by title, but he knew only too well that there were often half a dozen books with a single title. He was puzzling over this when a young woman with bright blue eyes came in and remarked that she would like to look at the book, since it was out of its window.

"I generally leave it there, where it's secure," Michael explained. "It's alarmed, you know, and the glass filters out the ultraviolet. But I had to take it out now, or anyway I thought I did. Maybe I just wanted to touch it again." And he explained about inventory, and looking for a UAISBN in the brown book.

"You have a lot more books here than most bookstores I've been in," the young woman said. "Usually they want you to look on the screen. And then they'll print up one for you if you want it. But till you want one, they don't actually have many books."

"We can print anything you want, to order," Michael explained, "but we find we sell more books when the customer can handle an actual copy. I don't mean that we keep copies of ephemera — best sellers, and that sort of book. We don't have to. But there are a lot of very good books most people have never heard of, and we like to have copies of those, of the books we recommend."

The young woman looked thoughtful.

"Then too, we do a good deal of business in used books. You can often buy a used copy more cheaply, for one thing."

"Aren't there old editions that are nicer?"

Michael nodded. "Sometimes. Quite often, in fact. There are different papers, and for art books . . ." He shrugged. "When the plates have been produced under the supervision of the artist, that's something stores can't duplicate. Though we try."

"Can you make me a copy of this?" The young woman indicated that brown book.

Michael shook his head. "There's no number. That's the problem."

When she had gone, he returned the brown book to its window and went back to his inventory, feeling empty in a strange, sad way, and very much alone. *I should get a cat,* he thought. *We used to have a cat. A lot of stores have cats.*

It was time to close, or nearly; and yet the inventory remained not quite finished. In the end he entered "Browne's Book — Wonders of" for the book in the window, and did the rest, turned off the lights, and pulled shut the big front door, hearing it lock behind him. Deep within the store ALARM — ALARM — ALARM flashed dimly and slowly, indicating that the system was powered, and on guard. How many times had he come out of this door?

It was not that he did not love the store; he did, just as he had loved his parents. And yet . . .

He would get a cat — a nice cat with white paws and an interesting name. (But a cat would not be enough either.)

The bus floated by. He had missed it, and there would be no more for half an hour. He inspected his windows. *The Race for Saturn's Moons* was no longer selling. It should be relegated to a shelf and replaced. Perhaps with *Fear of the Future* or *The Fall of the Republic*.

Here was the brown book again, opened at a new place.

*   *   *

The Tale of the Boy and the Bookshop

Long, long ago in a far-away land, there was a boy we will call Wishedfor. He had been born late in his parents' lives, after many years in which they had prayed devoutly for a son, and they treasured him above all else. One might think such a boy would be spoiled. He was not, for Allah had blessed them with a poverty not too great. He grew, and as he grew, showed himself wise and generous, strong of limb and clear of eye. He helped his mother wash and cook and sweep, and when he was old enough to assist his father, he did not cease to do so, but turned his labors from the amendment of programs to household tasks as soon as he and his father returned from the archives, for his mother was not strong.

At length she died, and his father called him to his side. "O my son," quoth his father, "thou art the light of my eyes. Not a day passes but I thank Allah for what he gave. Which is noblest, my son? Is it the gifts Allah gives to us, or the gifts we miserable mortals give to Allah, who has given us life? Consider well."

For some minutes the boy sat deep in thought; at length he said, "Gold and silks, skimmers and golights are but muck. The value of a gift cannot be reckoned from the price the giver gave or the price his gift might fetch in the market. Is that not so, O my father?"

Sadly, the old man nodded. "Proceed."

"How then is the value of a gift to be reckoned? It must be according to the heart of its giver. The most valuable gift is that given with unbounded love from a pure heart. Mere mortals, alas, are never pure of heart. Nor is our love boundless, though we may think so. Allah is pure of heart, as we are not. Allah's love is without bound, as ours cannot be. Therefore it seems to me, O my father, that the gifts Allah gives to mortals must ever be greater than those we mere mortals present to Allah."

At this the old man looked more doleful than ever. "By what means, O my son, can we poor mortals offer Allah a gift equal to those he has given us?"

Now the boy thought again, scratching his head as if he feared his mind slept there, rubbing his chin and pulling his ear; and at last he said, "O my father, I do not know. Is it possible? Tell me."

"It is, my son." The old man's gaze, which had been upon the boy's face until that time, was now upon the dust before him. "When we return to Allah a gift he has given us, we make him a gift as fine as that he gave, do we not?"

"Ah!" said the boy, and his eyes flashed like sunlight on dark pools. "Thou hast cut the knot, O my father! In all the world, is there any like to thee?"

"Many, many. My son, I would give such a gift to Allah. In the city to the north there stands a mosque like no other, the Madrasa of Sultan Hasan. Here the wisest gather to speak of the will of

Allah, and His knowledge, and the knowledge of all the world. Young men come there to hear them, that they may become wise in their turn, and when they have sat long, they may question them, and so become wiser still."

At this the boy's eyes grew very wide.

"O my son, for seven years I give thee to Allah. Thou shalt go to the mosque I have named, and my blessing go with thee. Learn there. Betimes thou must labor, even as I labor at my keyboard, for the belly must be fed. As thou strain and sweat, thou must repeat in thine own ear that thou hast come to learn, and not to labor. And in seven years, if Allah grant seven years more of life, I will come for thee. If thou hast learned well, I shall die full of joy. But if thou hast not, tears and sorrow will be my lot in this life and in paradise."

"I will learn, O my father," the boy promised. And before the sun rose again, he had set out for the city; and though his heart was sad when he recalled his mother, it leaped for joy to think of the learning that would be his.

*　　*　　*

A year passed, and another, and another. The old man labored, recalling often the son he had given to Allah. Now it seemed to him that his son would surely grow discouraged upon the path of wisdom; he himself had not traveled far along it, yet he well knew how steep were its slopes and how rock-strewn the way. And now it seemed to him that within a day or two the boy would surely return, making some excuse, and he told himself ten score times that he must have hard words for the boy if it were so — and knew in his heart that they could never pass his lips. On such days he watched the road for hours. But the boy never came.

And again he imagined his son sitting at the feet of the wisest of the wise in that great mosque, the Madrasa of Sultan Hasan; and he was happy, and went about his work with increased vigor. In this way, year followed year.

At last it seemed to him that seven had passed, and more than seven, and he went to his neighbor and spoke of the boy; and when his neighbor had praised him, as all did, the old man said,

"How long has it been since we have seen the light of his face? Five years, I think? I have lost track of the reckoning. Six? Has it been as many as six?"

"More," declared his neighbor. "Long and long. Behold! My picktruck that is old shone like a jewel when thy son left us."

The old man could scarcely speak, his voice shook so. "Seven? Has it been seven?"

"What is seven years to a picktruck?" replied his neighbor.

The old man left, confessing in his heart that he himself was but another such laboring machine and begging forgiveness for it. On the next day he dug up the fifteen milpiasters he had buried in his floor, and set out. The road was not short, nor was it gracious to poor travelers; yet he reached the city at last, and asking directions of those who bore kind faces, he made his way to the Madrasa of Sultan Hasan, and sat of a long afternoon hearing the wise discourse on Al Qur'an and much more, and was greatly improved thereby. Ever he looked for the boy, but he did not see him.

Betimes the light faded, and the wise departed one by one, and the old man also, to seek a place in which to lay his head.

Down one street he went, and up another, and chancing to look into a bookshop beheld one tall and lean and of serious mien, whose beard was touched with gray. Their eyes met, and both knew.

Of their embraces and the many things they said, a long tale might be made; but at last they sat together with coffee between them. Then quoth he who had been the boy, "O my father, I thought thee dead when the seventh year passed. Had I known thou still lived, I would have returned to the south long ago, and carried thee to my house in this city — the house in which thou shalt repose this night. Thou came not, and I thought, *surely he is dead*."

"O my son," said the old man, "as each year passed I resolved to let thee remain a little longer, that thou might grow in wisdom yet more at the feet of the wise. Another year, and another year, until this. Now I feel the hand of death upon me, and I would not die as a frog in a well, by all forgotten."

"Thou shalt not die at all," he who had been the boy declared, "but bide here full many a year. But, O my father, I have sinned against thee."

"It cannot be!" the old man declared.

"It is." And he who had been the boy sat in silence while the traffic of the street clamored on all uncaring.

Until at last the old man said. "Thou canst not speak, my son. I see it. Do not speak. Let us rather rejoice, and talk of thy mother, and the days when thou wert small."

"I will not deceive thee more, O my father." He who had been the boy lifted the fragrant cup yet left it untasted. "I have betrayed thee, my father. Betrayal atop betrayal I shall not set. To this city I came worn and hungry, and thus before going to the mosque as thou had instructed me I looked first for employment that I might be fed. In this street, I beheld an old man unloading a flitter. Hastening to him, I said, 'Grandfather, thou art of years, and the boxes weighty. Permit me to assist thee.' For I hoped that he would give that with which I might eat when the task was done.

"He stood aside, and while I worked we talked. And when the last had been unloaded, he bid me carry them into this shop, and when I had carried the last, he bid me open them. They held books, such as thou seest."

He who had been the boy sighed, and the old man nodded.

"I put them in their places, as he directed me, and as I labored he discoursed upon their contents. Some came from Baghdad, some from Damascus, some from Frankish lands even to the other side of Earth, some from the stars of heaven. All were wondrous in my sight, and he saw it. He bid me sleep in the shop that night, as many a night thereafter, with a cudgel by my side to protect our wares."

The old man sipped his coffee, hot, strong, and very sweet. "There is nothing shameful in this, O my son."

"My master died. It was my loss, and all the world's, for he was both learned and compassionate. I took his shop in charge, and delivered all profit therefrom, which was never great, to her who had been his wife. Too soon she followed him. His shop became mine, and the house that had been his also. It is not large, but thou will ever find a place there, O my father."

"Nor is there dishonor in that," the old man declared, "but the contrary."

"O my father, thou sent me to this city that I might sit at the feet of the wise in the mosque. I have been there to worship many times. But I have never done as thou wished, my father. When the call to prayer came, I went — or oftimes went not. And when my prayers were done, I returned to this shop in which thou discovered me. I have done wrong, and it is no childish matter, I know. What is thy judgment? That punishment which thou decree, I will accept without murmur. It will be less than I deserve."

The old man did not speak again until he had drunk the last drop, and eaten the grounds as well, for he followed the old ways. And when the last were gone, he said only, "O my son, I must think on this."

Next morning he rose early and made his way to the Madrasa of the Sultan Hasan. All morning he sat in silence, harkening to the wise as he had the day before; but when the sun neared its zenith, "O my uncle," quoth one, "thy beard is gray. Thou hast seen much of life. Is it not so?"

The old man acknowledged that it was.

"And yet thou harken to us, and never speak. Whether thou hast come to teach us or to learn, we would hear thee."

"O revered sheikh," quoth the old man, "know that I am sorely troubled. I am a simple man. To mere compilers and codes, to interrupts, subroutines, and iterations has my life been given. Now I must judge a weighty matter, and know not the way."

"Speak on," quoth the one to whom he had spoken.

"Upon the one hand, my son has disobeyed, O revered sheikh," quoth the old man. "Upon the other, he has done well and is deserving of approbation. Upon the first hand, I sought to honor Allah, to whom all praise. Upon the second, he confesses his fault."

"Thy voice breaks," observed he to whom the old man had spoken.

"I love him dearly, O revered sheikh, and no man ever had a better son. Yet he did wrong, and I know not which way to turn."

Others had fallen silent to listen as the old man spoke, and for a time they discussed the matter. Then came the call to prayer. All prayed, and when the prayer was done, he to whom the old man had spoken declared, "This is a troubled matter, O my uncle. Thy son hath transgressed."

The old man nodded.

"And his transgression was against Allah and thee. Is it not so?"

The old man nodded as before.

"Yet he is true of tongue, contrite of heart, and a good Moslem?"

The old man nodded a third time, and while others spoke he to whom he had spoken sat stroking his beard. Ere long, the speech of those others turned to other topics, and when that time came, quoth he, "O my uncle, there is one in this city whom we reckon wisest of the wise. Matters of great difficulty are brought to him. Let us bring thine, thou and I."

And they went, down one street and up another, and so came to a certain shop. He to whom the old man had spoken entered first, and the old man after him.

And behold!

*　*　*

It seemed to Michael that this story had been intended for him from the beginning. It was true that he had not remained long at the university. Money had been in short supply, and he was a member of no prioritized group. During his long wait at the bus stop, he turned the story over and over in his mind, with all that he could recall of the first two, which he had read years before.

*　*　*

Next morning, the young woman returned to the store. Michael looked at her, then looked again and snapped his fingers. "What is it?" she asked.

"I've been trying to think who you reminded me of," he explained. "It's my teacher, the teacher I had when I was a kid. I mean, she was really a machine, and she was older than you are, and the principal was the machine, too, like for everybody, but — but —"

"I understand." She grinned at him. "Were you sent to the principal a lot? You must have been a bad boy."

"Well, sometimes." He discovered that he was blushing, something he had not done in years. "He could never remember my name until I told him, but she called me Mick. I never could understand that. I mean, since it was all the same machine, really."

The young woman's grin had softened to a smile. "I do, Mick. May I have some of your coffee?"

"Yes. Certainly." He hurried over to show her. "There are nice chairs, and reading lights, and — and everything. Sweetener and sugar and real cream. So people can sit down and look at the books, you know. And — and everything."

"But not the big book in the end window." She was still smiling. "The brown one."

"I'd have to stay and watch." Michael decided he could use some coffee too; his mouth felt dry. He poured a cup for her and another for himself.

"Do you eat the grounds, Mick?"

"Do I . . . ? That story. You read it."

"Uh huh." Her smile had become impish.

"It's been bothering me." He smiled in return. "It bothers me more than the teaching machine ever did. Or Junior Teacher Huggins or Principal Maxwell. Will you — I feel silly saying it here, but won't you please sit down?"

She did, and accepted the coffee he had poured for her.

"Would you like sweetener? Cream?"

"Honey, Mick. I see you have honey over there."

He got it for her, and sat beside her on the sofa. "Do you really want to see that book? Are you thinking of buying it?" He tried to gauge the cost of her clothing and jewelry, and failed.

"No," she said.

"Then I can't. I mean I shouldn't. It really is a very valuable book. But just for a minute or two, while I watch."

She sipped her coffee, and smiled, and added more honey, and smiled again.

"If you read that story, it sounds like me. Like my life. Not exactly, of course, but . . ."

"Uncomfortably close"

"That's it. That's it exactly."

"The book does that, you see. That's what makes it so valuable. It's not just its age. It knows, somehow, and we were never sure whether it was just opening itself to the right place — that's what a man I knew thought — or whether it created the stories. Made them to order, so to speak, the way you print your books. I think it does both."

He was speechless for a moment, then remembered to sip his coffee, and spilled a little, and winced. At last he said, "It seems to be saying that what I'm doing — this bookstore — is right. But it doesn't feel right. Or not as right as it ought to. I think the man in the story . . . That he didn't feel right either, until his father came."

She nodded.

"So I thought of getting a cat or something. But I don't know." He sighed, and ran his free hand through his hair. "Only what you said about the stories, that can't be right. There was a one I read a long time ago, about a boy in class, and what was a princess? Only it wasn't all there. I could never read the end."

"Tell me," she said, and he recounted as much as he could remember of "The Tale of Prince Know-Nothing."

When he had finished, she said, "I can tell you how it ended. Prince Know-Nothing decided he should go in search of a princess; but a thousand things conspired to stop him, and he never did. At the end, a very plain girl in a very plain dress kissed him, and after the wedding he discovered that she was a princess who had gone forth in search of a prince."

"You read that one, too," Michael said.

She nodded. "Did you read any more?"

"Just one other one." He paused, not sure he remembered it at all. "It was about a dwarf and a sphinx. They had children — he gave birth to them, which used to puzzle me. And he wanted to be a sphinx like her, and at the end his children made him one, and it was wonderful."

"It was saying you ought to have children." For a moment she looked pensive. "I've never had any," she said.

"I haven't either. I mean, I'd like some, but I've never been married."

"I'd like some too, Mick." Quite suddenly she kissed his cheek; and when he turned his head in surprise, his lips. "There," she said when they parted, "and now I'm through fooling you. You've never been married."

He shook his head.

"I have. I was married for almost fifty years, Mick, but we never had children. There were reasons, but the reasons don't matter any more, and the children do. We had love, and the love was enough, but now that's gone too, and I want love again. I want it back."

"You — you're . . ." Michael felt as though the whole world had dropped from under him.

"I'm eighty-seven now, Mick, and I used to be a teacher before I married. Don't tell me you haven't heard of cell therapy. They go in and clean up the nuclei, and your cells start dividing again, and you grow younger instead of older."

Michael managed to nod. "I've read about it. It's terribly expensive."

"It was. Fortunately, I'm terribly rich. Does it bother you that I'm so much older than you are?"

He shook his head desperately.

"It doesn't bother me, either." Her hand found his. "Because I'm not. I mean biologically. And I don't want to buy that book because I own it already. My name's Caitlin Higgins. It should be in your files."

He could not speak.

"But please don't call me Caitlin, or something awful, like Junior Teacher Huggins."

She had smiled, and he felt that he could look at that smile forever, and it would always be new, and always magic.

"My friends call me Kitty," she said.

A BOOK, BY ITS COVER

P.D. Cacek

A cloud passed in front of the sun and the already pale light faded to the color of bone. Snow was coming, but not one of the people scurrying along the street, bundled against the cold as they hurried from one shop to another, seemed to notice. Or care. All of them acted as if the day and the light and the approaching snow was normal, part of the ordinary.

And he hated them, all of them, for that — for not noticing what the world had become.

He couldn't understand why they didn't see and how they could continue to shop and pray and go on with the day to day business of living, as if the future still existed.

Because he knew better. He had seen the end of the future the day his grandfather had sewn the two yellow triangles together to make the star on his coat. The future was finite now and he seemed to be the only one who knew it.

Yavin Landauer pulled the old frock coat's collar tighter against his neck and watched a man in a fedora and camel-hair overcoat, the color of honey, walk hand-in-hand with a boy of nine or ten in knickers and jacket and cap all of soft gray wool. The cheap cotton stars looked out of place on the expensive material, material that Yavin could almost feel the texture of even from across the street. His grandfather had obtained a few bolts of wool much like that just a few weeks before. . . .

He shook the memory away before it could take root and

glared at the man and boy. They were laughing as they walked, the man pointing at things in those shop windows that had somehow, miraculously, escaped the bricks and bullets and bats of the brown-shirted Wulf packs. But even if a window or two had been spared, each building in the ghetto had been marked by the pack. *Juden*. In yellow paint across each lentil, instead of lamb's blood — insurance that the Angel of Death would not pass over them this time.

Yavin let his hand drop from the collar to trace the edge of the star. His grandfather had been careful, the star's center was directly over his heart. When the future ended for Yavin, it would be quick.

Not like the little boy across the street. His future would end in shock and surprise because his father, like so many others, didn't notice the change in the light of the world. It was cruel and a part of Yavin wanted to shout at the man, but he didn't. He huddled deeper in the fire-blackened doorway of what had been his grandfather's tailor shop as the man and boy entered Reb Shendelman's bookshop. He closed his eyes. Took a deep breath and smelled snow riding the back of charred wood.

It had been almost three months since *Kristallnach*, the Night of Broken Glass, and still the stench of the fire was as strong as the memory of his grandfather running out into the street when the first torch shattered the shop's front window. Yavin had stayed inside, hidden and safe, he thought, until the fire began to consume the bolts of cloth. It was only then, when the fire came at him, that he fled — out the small window at the back of the shop and down the narrow alley until he could circle back to the main street.

And by then his grandfather was dead, a sacrifice to the new god who ruled Germany.

Yavin had hidden in the shadows and watched the pack of brown-shirted Wulfs as they laughed and clapped each other on the shoulders. One of the boys, Karl, had been his best friend . . . once . . . when only the night sky wore stars.

Once. Upon a time.

The sunlight brightened suddenly and Yavin opened his eyes, blinking as the first fat flakes of snow began to fall. There were fewer people on the street — finally, they noticed.

Yavin leaned back against the only home he'd ever known and rubbed the cold out of his nose as the man in the honey-colored coat left the bookstore. His hat was pulled low over his eyes and he was clutching a brown-paper wrapped parcel to his chest. A book, what else would one buy at a bookshop?

Except from a bookshop that had no books?

Rolling his shoulders under the coat, Yavin stared at the object in the man's hands. It was square and *looked* like a book wrapped in paper . . . but it couldn't be, he'd seen what the Wulfs had done that night. The fire that had gorged itself on the bolts of cloth in his grandfather's shop was nothing more than a small camp fire compared to the inferno that brightened the night sky in front of the bookshop. Hundreds, maybe thousands of books were fed to the flames while Reb Shendelman, ancient for as long as Yavin had known him, howled and cried and tore at his clothes.

The old man had wept for his books, but not once so much as glanced at the body that was sprawled on the ground only a few feet away. And when he finally said Kaddish, it was for the books alone.

Karl and the others had thought that was funny, that an old man should become so distraught over a few words and ideas, so they let him live.

With only a small beating.

The man in the honey-colored coat stumbled on a patch of ice and dropped the paper-wrapped bundle into the snow. The sound that came from his lips sent a chill up Yavin's spine that had nothing to do with the cold. Whatever it was, he thought as he watched the man brush the damp snow off the wrapping, it had to be very valuable. Reb Shendelman could have managed to hide some of the more expensive and rare volumes. That would make sense . . . and explain why the man seemed so upset.

Where was the boy?

Yavin frowned as he glanced up and down the street. He'd forgotten the boy as he watched the father, but there was no sign of the child on the street. A gust of wind swirled into the doorway, powdering him with snow. The little boy was probably already home by now, his father sending him ahead so he wouldn't be caught in the storm. Telling him to stay warm and not catch cold

. . . lying to him by pretending there was a future that wanted them.

Shivering, Yavin reached up and touched the charred remains of the mezuzah that had done nothing to protect them from the Wulfs.

*   *   *

The man in the honey-colored coat came back just before sunset, holding the hand of a little girl. Dressed all in white, the yellow star on her coat dancing as she skipped through the unswept drifts, she looked like an angel made of snow.

Yavin nibbled along one edge of the roll he had begged from a neighbor and watched the little girl giggle up at the man. She didn't look hungry and Yavin hated her, a little, for that. Food had always been provided for him without thought, now it had become something that was always in his mind and belly.

Just like the future, or, rather, the lack of it . . . always there, always grumbling. Always.

For some.

Hand in hand, the man walked the little girl into the bookshop.

The roll was a memory on Yavin's tongue and his stomach was still grumbling when the door of the bookshop opened again and the man in the honey-colored coat left. The brim of his fedora was pulled low over his eyes and, like the day before, he clutched a brown-paper wrapped bundle to his chest. The little girl in white wasn't with him.

Yesterday there had been a boy, today a girl.

Something besides hunger growled in Yavin's belly as he left the protection of the soot-covered shadows and crossed the icy cobblestones. And only fell twice.

The man looked up from beneath the hat's brim when Yavin stepped onto the sidewalk directly in front of him. There were tears frozen on the man's lower lashes and a look on his face that almost made Yavin stumble again. It was a book. Yavin could see one corner of it through a tear in the brown wrapping, a book bound in white satin, the thick pages edged in gold. It was the sort of book that would cost a great deal of money, especially now, even for a man in a camel-hair coat, the color of honey.

Yavin felt his shrunken stomach turn over as he looked up at the man.

"What have you done?"

The man blinked as if waking from a deep sleep and shook his head, stepped to one side, tightening his grip on the book.

"I don't know what you're talking about. Leave me alone."

"What have you done with the little girl?"

"I don't know what you're talking about." The man said. "There's no little girl here."

Yavin pointed to the walk behind the man. There were two sets of footprints in the snow — one large, one small. Both sets lead to the bookshop, but only one set, the one belonging to the man, left.

"She is safe," the man's voice was almost as silent as the falling snow. "Please, I must get this onto the train. A woman has promised to take this to England for me. Please, I have to hurry."

He was talking about the book, not the little girl. Yavin stepped back, the soles of his shoes almost sliding out from under him again as the man rushed past. He could hear the man mumbling to himself.

"Why didn't I listen before this? She will be safe, dear Gott, please . . . with her brother, please. I should have come sooner, but who thought . . . who would have thought . . . Mein gott, bitter, let me get there in time."

Yavin felt his heart stop when the man looked back — but not at him. At the bookshop.

"Hurry, there's not much time left."

When the momentary death passed, Yavin made himself turn and look at the shop. It was so quiet the sound of his own breathing pounded against the inside of his brain.

The bookstore sat hunched and still at the end of the street, aloof but miserable like a once pampered cat that had been forgotten and left out in the snow. Anyone passing would think the building was deserted, just another shop that had been abandoned. Or left ownerless. There were no lights showing through the cracks in the boards that covered the broken front window and the snow had already covered the scorched spot on the street. In an hour or less, there'd be no evidence that anyone had visited the shop that day. Or the day before that.

Would a man sell his children for books? No . . . no . . .

One book, one child.

One child that no longer needed to be cared for or fed, for one book, hollowed out and filled with what? Forged documents? Money? A pair of scissors to cut yellow stars from coats?

The future, without limits.

A man might offer anything for that.

The flesh on Yavin's fingers stung as he curled his hands into fists and followed the shallow tracks back to the bookshop. He only stumbled once and that was when he reached for the doorknob and looked up. There had been a brass marker there, generations old, that once read *Shendelman's Books* in Hebrew and German. Now it was unreadable. Yavin had watched Karl in the glow of the fire, strike the sign again and again with a hammer while the other Wulfs chanted: *Juden. Juden. Juden.*

There used to be a small brass bell that jingled every time the door opened — he remembered that, remembered the sound of it echoing through the huge room filled with books as Karl raced him to see who would be first into the shop. Karl always won and now the bell was gone and only the squeal of unoiled hinges announced him.

To the room of empty shelves.

Yavin tried not to listen to the hollow thud of his shoes against the dust-streaked floor.

His grandfather had always encouraged him to be a scholar, and so only saw merit in those obscure volumes of archaic text that were the size of a crate of whitefish. Each night, for a hour, Yavin would wade through the didactic mire . . . and each day, with Karl, tucked into a corner out of the way of customers, he would rediscover old friends.

Don Quixote. The plays of Shakespear. Jules Verne. Shelly. Stoker.

Gone forever.

"I've wondered when you'd decide to come across the street, Yavin Landauer."

The soles of Yavin's shoes squeaked as he whirled toward the pale shape that hovered near the back wall. Yavin was no longer a child, so the first images in his mind were not of ghosts or Dybbuks, but of brown-shirts and black swastikas.

"What is it? Are you all right?"

Yavin's heart was pounding against his ribs, like a prisoner trying to escape a cell, when Reb Shendelman stepped out of the shadows. The old man was thinner than Yavin remembered and his feet dragged across the floor as if lifting them was too much effort. He was still wearing the coat he'd had on the night of the fire — the torn pocket fluttered like a broken bird's wing with each shambling step.

"Yavin, what is it? Come, let me get you something to eat."

Drool filled his mouth and his belly rumbled so loudly it sounded like thunder at the mention of food. "No! I won't take anything from you."

"What take? I give it. Besides, we're friends, no?"

Yavin looked down at the floor and saw the outline of a child's shoe in the dust. "No."

"No?" Reb Shendelman asked. "Then we are enemies?"

Yavin nodded.

"Ah." The old man mimicked his nod. "Can I ask why? No? Then all right. It will be strange after so many years, but if we are enemies, then we are enemies. So, enemy, come and eat. I have potato and cabbage soup and some black bread. Come. We can discuss being enemies later."

"What was inside the book, Reb Shendelman?"

Confusion flickered over the old man's face as he lifted his arms toward the empty shelves. "What book? I have no books, Yavin. You saw what they did."

"I saw . . . but I also saw the man and the little girl today," Yavin said, wanting to shout but barely able to whisper. "And the man and boy yesterday. I know what you're doing, Reb Shendelman. I know."

"No," the old man said as he waved Yavin toward the small back room, "you don't, but you will. Come, I'll explain while you eat."

*   *   *

It took three bowls of the thin, but wonderful soup before Yavin stopped shivering and his belly remembered what it felt like to be full. And through it all, Reb Shendelman kept quiet . . . which, now that Yavin was finished, was a good thing. If the old man had tried to tell him the . . . fairy tale while he'd been eating, Yavin might have laughed so hard the soup would have come back up.

A child might have believed what the old man was saying, but Yavin didn't. He *was* a man, after all.

"I think it was because this building has always been a bookshop. With that many books, it almost makes sense, doesn't it? That the thoughts and ideas of those books could become something . . . real, no?"

Yavin stopped mopping up the dregs of the soup with a narrow crust of black bread to shrug, not that it was noticed. Reb Shendelman was looking out into the empty shop, rocking slowly back and forth over his clasped hands.

"Men can die, Yavin, but not ideas, never ideas. Do you understand?"

Yavin stuffed the softened crust into his mouth to avoid answering. Again the old man didn't notice, he kept talking as though the silence was an answer in itself.

"It isn't that hard a thing to accept . . . not when you think of all the thoughts and ideas and words contained in those books. Generations of books, lining these very shelves. How do we learn, Yavin, do you know? How is what we read transformed into a memory that we can keep forever, huh? There was so much knowledge here on these shelves for so long it must have been easy for some of it to seep into the wood . . . to become part of the store itself. Such an easy thing, when you stop and wonder about it. Thoughts and ideas can't die, but they can build, one upon the other until all the knowledge of the universe creates a life of its own.

"Wasn't Adam begun as just a thought in the All Mighty's mind? Adam became a man from a single thought . . . so what is it for a building, within whose wall contained so many thoughts, to become a shapeless thing endowed with life, but not body?"

The bread caught in Yavin's throat and almost choked him.

"A Golem?" he squeaked when he was finally able to draw breath. "You're saying that this building is a Golem?"

"Yoh, a Golem . . . one constructed of thoughts and ideas, housed in a body of stone and mortar and wooden shelves. A Golem of creation, not destruction."

"And fed with the blood of children?"

"What are talking about?"

Yavin tossed the empty bowl back onto the small table between them and shook his head. He'd seen his grandfather shake his head like that whenever the truth was stretched too far and about to unravel.

"The children who are bartered for those very special books you sell, Reb Shendelman. Do you keep them for the Nazis or do you kill them yourself so your invisible Golem can live? One book per child seems fair . . . but you'll give me a book without payment, won't you? Unless you want everyone to know what you've been doing."

Again, the old man's reaction was not what Yavin expected. Reb Shendelman stood up and walked to the empty shelves, ran his hands gently against the worn wood and nodded.

"One book per child . . . or one man or one woman."

"What?"

"Emmauel Wiesel was the first. You remember Reb Wiesel, yoh?"

Yavin leaned back in his chair and hoped he looked apathetic. Of course he remembered the fish-monger. Who inside the ghetto didn't know the man who worked from before dawn to after dark, hauling fish, cleaning fish, selling fish . . . and who smelled so much of fish he was the beloved of every cat within a five-mile radius? Yavin also remembered the day his shop failed to open. The ghetto cats had been mourning him for almost a year now.

Reb Shendelman sighed as he turned around.

"They were waiting for him in his shop, three soldiers with guns for one man who smelled of herring. Someone warned him, so he came here. To hide or maybe just to say good bye. When soldiers come, few of us have the luxury to say good bye. But instead he started talking about his favorite book. *Ethics*, by Spinoza. Can you believe that? But what do I know from philosophers?"

"Here," he said, spreading his hands out in front of him. "This is where it happened.

"It was Friday, late, just before Shabbos and I was about to close when Weisel rushed in. I had turned off the lights and I couldn't light a candle, so we just stood there, in the dark, and I listened while he talked about Spinoza. One minute he was explaining the philosopher's idea that evil was only part of the Lord God's perfection and the next?"

Yavin saw Reb Shendelman's hands begin to shake and felt a similar vibration roll across his shoulders.

"It was dark, so at first, I thought he had fallen or passed out, but when I ran to where he'd been standing all I found was a book. *Ethics*, by Baruch Spinoza. A beautiful book, bound in leather with thick parchment pages edged in gold, the title embossed in gold leaf. But the thing is, Yavin," the old man said, "I had no such book in the shop and I couldn't even have produced a thing of such beauty even if I had the materials. It was warm to the touch, like living flesh against my hands. Do you understand what I am saying, Yavin?"

Yavin felt his head shake slowly back and forth without any effort on his part.

"No, that is the problem with miracles . . . they are usually too miraculous for man to understand. I didn't believe it either, so I stand there, with this wondrous book in my hand and suddenly I remember Wiesel and I call out to him, 'Emmanuel Wiesel,' and then he is standing in front of me as if he'd never moved with my hands on his arms. He looked startled and rubbed his eyes, told me that he had been dreaming about sitting in Spinoza's workshop, watching the man grind lenses while they discussed monistic theory."

Reb Shendelman suddenly clapped his hands and Yavin jumped. "But it wasn't a dream, Yavin. The Golem of the shop had somehow transformed Weisel the fishmonger into the book he loved the best. You see?

"I thought about the soldiers who had come for him and thought, in my ignorance, that I had been shown the way to save him, so we spoke more about Spinoza and this time I watched the miracle happen. There was no sound, Yavin, no stirring of the air.

It was so peaceful. I placed him on the shelf with the other books and that night I spoke to the Golem over the Shabbos candles and not the All Mighty. I thought I could save them. A word here, a whisper there . . . people disappear from the ghetto all the time."

The smile faded from the old man's face.

"I never thought they would burn my books."

"That's why you were saying Kaddish that night," Yavin asked. "Wasn't it?"

Reb Shendelman nodded and Yavin couldn't hold the laughter in any longer. He could hear the soup slosh and gurgle inside his belly, which made him laugh even harder. The old man shrugged and began moving along the rows of empty shelves.

"Of course," he said, "you don't believe me, why should you? I know how impossible it sounds, Yavin, but all miracles are unless you see them first-hand."

Reb Shendelman stopped when he came to the far corner of the room, his hands dabbing at the still air. "This is where you two liked to sit, isn't it? Right here, yes? Yes . . . there used to be a chair here, and an old ottoman where my wife used to sit when she sewed. You and your friend, Karl . . . I remember. The two of you would sit here reading for hours. Let me think. What was your favorite book? I know it wasn't the work of Spinoza . . . what was it?"

Reb Shendelman's hands stopped moving and Yavin found himself leaning forward, hoping the old man would remember and hating himself for hoping that. What did it matter if the old man could remember which book had been his favorite? That was a lifetime ago, in a different world. To think about it or anything now seemed pointless, more than pointless . . . it was evil.

But even so, when the old man smiled and clapped his hands, Yavin felt his heart flutter.

"*Around the World in Eighty Days*. Yes?"

And Yavin nodded his head, ashamed and relieved that someone, at least, would remember that about him.

"Your grandfather, may he find everlasting peace, used to ask what you read . . . so I told him books on kashruth law. A small lie, but it made him happy." Reb Shendelman nodded as he walked toward Yavin. "He was a good man, but one of narrow imagination. You, on the other hand —"

The old man stopped when he was still an arm's length away and took a deep breath.

"You had the imagination of a true dreamer who could see beyond the hardness of this world and into what might be. Can you still do that, Yavin? Can you see Professor Phileas Fogg in his beautiful London flat? Can you see him accepting the challenge to go around the world . . . the entire world, Yavin, in only eighty days? Can you see him, Yavin? Can you see the world as Mr. Jules Verne wrote it? You can, if you try. Try, Yavin . . . see it . . . see . . . it. . . ."

"*Monsieur Passepartout.*"

Yavin staggered and grabbed the gangplank's rope handrail as he caught his breath. The air was hot and thick with the scent of brine. Water sprayed against his cheek and Yavin looked down to see the ocean lapped calmly against the barnacle-bedecked hull of a ship that had seen better days. He could see where someone had tried to patch the worm-holes and painted over them with tar. It was a miracle that the ship still floated, let alone that its captain could think it still sea-worthy enough to take out of port.

"*Monsieur Passepartout!*"

A gull cried and Yavin jerked his head up to follow its passage — stark white against the pale lavender twilight sky — over the lines of the bowsprit. There was a name on the bow, blocky wooden letters, faded by sun and wind and sea: General Grant.

It was the name of the ship . . . the large sea-going paddlewheel steamer bound from Yokohama to San Francisco with Phileas Fogg, Jean Passepartout and —

"*Monsieur Passepartout, do you ignore me purposely?*"

"*What?*"

Yavin clung to the rope as he turned toward the slightly shrewish tone. A woman, lovely and young, glared down at him. One hand grasped the ivory knob of a lace parasol, the other was tucked daintily against the tiny waist of her cream-colored traveling dress. A large hat, with ostrich plumes of a color Yavin had never seen in nature, sat firmly upon the mass of black curls. Towering above her hat and plumes and lovely face was the main of the three masts, rigged for full sail, that would aid the "General Grant" in maintaining the breakneck speed of twelve miles an hour and so cross the great Pacific Ocean in only twenty-one days.

Just like in the book.

Yavin laughed out loud. Until he saw the look on the woman's face.

And remembered who she was.

"You're Aouda. The girl who was going to be burned alive when the old rajah of Bundelcund died. I know you. Phileas Fogg saved you from the 'suttee' because he'd been early getting through the Indian forest and had time. That's what he said to Sir Francis Cromarty, he said he had the time to save you. You are Aouda, aren't you?"

"I am," the woman said with a heave of her fashionably confined bosom, "and you, Monsieur Passepartout, are impudent! I shall complain most earnestly to Mr. Fogg about your lack of courtesy."

"I'm afraid," a soft voice said behind Yavin, "that we don't have the time for any reprimands at this moment. It will have to wait until after we have sailed, but rest assured, Passepartout, we shall discuss this matter. When there is time, of course."

Yavin turned around and gazed into the bearded, tranquil and enigmatic face of Phileas Fogg. He was just as Jules Verne had described him.

"Passepartout," Phileas Fogg said, "why do you look at me like that?"

"I'm Passepartout?" Yavin asked, giggling as if his belly was filled by a million tiny bubbles. "I'm Jean Passepartout?"

Phileas Fogg raised one perfectly arched eyebrow. "Passepartout, are you quite —"

"— all right, Yavin?"

Yavin found himself on the floor, staring up at Reb Shendelman.

"What did you do?" Yavin yelled as he scooted away from the old man until his spine encountered an empty bookshelf. "Leave me alone! You're some kind of mesmerist."

But the old man shook his head. "No, I'm just the seller of books, Yavin. It was the Golem that transformed you. Did you enjoy it?"

"There was nothing to enjoy!" His fear kept him shouting and Yavin could hear his voice echo back and forth through the empty store. "It was a dream . . . an illusion. It can't happen. It didn't happen!"

"What didn't happen, Jew?"

Karl came out of the darkness at the front of the store like the marauding Wulf-cub he'd become, silent and gray. His hungry, bright blue eyes never left Yavin's face as he crossed the room. Standing equal distance between Yavin and the old man, Karl snapped to attention and raised his right arm in stiff salute to his new god. Against the white of his armband, the black swastika looked like a giant spider.

"Heil Hitler!"

"Not in this shop, boy," Reb Shendelman said and was rewarded with a slap across his face. For his *impudence*, Yavin thought, remembering the word Aouda had used in his dream.

Karl . . . his one-time friend . . . was sneering at Reb Shendelman and wiping his hand against one leg of his uniform shorts, as if it had become corrupted by the mere touch of Jewish flesh.

"You think just because we let you live the last time, old man, that your life is somehow sacred?" Karl chuckled with a sound Yavin remembered from the times they sat, huddled together, in the bookstore. "You're only alive because you made us laugh when we burned your books. Poor old Jew, crying over all those stupid books. We laughed about it for days and days."

"Stop it, Karl," Yavin said, forgetting for a moment, but only a moment, that they were no longer friends. He remembered the moment Karl's sneer found him.

"You dare tell me to stop, Landauer?" His lost friend asked. "You have gotten brave since I last saw you . . . hiding in the shadows while your grandfather tried to be a hero. He was as stupid as this old man here, but he didn't make us laugh. Are you going to make me laugh, Landauer, or can I just shoot you like a dog and put you out of your misery?"

The spider on Karl's arm twitched as he pulled a gun, bright and shiny and too big for his hand, from the holster hanging from his waist.

"I only came in here to see if there were any more books to burn," Karl said as he leveled the muzzle at Yavin's face. "They made such a fine fire last time, but now I think this will be more fun."

"What was your favorite book, Karl?"

Yavin turned and looked at the old man at the same time Karl did. There was a drop of blood in one corner of his mouth that glistened like a dusty ruby in the dim light when he spoke.

"What was your favorite book," Reb Shendelman asked again before Karl could answer. "I can't remember which book it was, but I remember it frightened you."

"It did not!" The gun twitched in Karl's hand as he swung it toward the old man. "Books don't frighten me."

But the old man nodded. "This one did. I remember how you jumped once when I came with a plate of cookies for you and Yavin. You remember, don't you, Yavin."

Yavin didn't remember anything at the moment.

"Yes," Reb Shendelman nodded, "now I remember. It was *Dracula,* by Bram Stoker. That is a very frightening book. Even I couldn't read it."

"What are you talking about?" Karl lifted his head as the muzzle of the gun drooped toward the floor. "That silly book didn't scare me at all. I read it a dozen times."

"What's your favorite part, Karl?" The old man asked and Yavin felt his stomach clench. "I was also so frightened when Jonathan Harker was in the coach along the Borgo Pass . . . I almost put the book down. Mein Gott, when he looks up and notices how excited the other passengers are because night is falling. Do you remember that part, Karl? Do you remember how the coach must have felt — how Harker described it as swaying like a boat on a stormy sea? Do you remember how the passengers offered him gifts and blessings and how they made the sign of the cross to guard against the evil to come? Do you see it, Karl? Do you? Yes, you do, I know you do. See it . . . see the Carpathians rising against the twilight sky . . . see it . . . see it, Karl."

The scream that had built in Yavin's throat as Karl's body began to shrink and fold in on itself — over and over and over – left his mouth as a soft hushing of air as he watched the old man bend down and slowly pick up the thick, black leather-bound volume from the floor. It didn't have gold leaf or gild edges, but the title was embossed in red, the color of fresh blood.

"He's . . . " Yavin licked his lips and tasted salt. "He's dead?"

Reb Shendelman shook his head and gently brushed his hand along one edge of the book before placing it on a shelf. It looked very lonely there all by itself.

"No, he's . . . only dreaming the story. We can't stay here, Yavin. His friends will come looking for him and I don't want you to be here when they burn this book."

"Reb Shendelman, you can't let them!"

"I can't stop them, Yavin. But what I can do, is get you out of this hell . . ."

"Reb Shendelman, please."

"Sha, Yavin. Listen to me. Do you know what my favorite part is in *Around the World in Eighty Days?* It's when they are all going up the Hudson River in America on that little boat. I have family in America . . . someplace called Upstate New York along that same river. What was the name of that boat, Yavin?"

"The 'Henrietta,'" Yavin answered and felt a numbing warmth began to grow in his belly.

"Ah, yoh, the little 'Henrietta' sailing past the lighthouse that marked the beginning of the river and the end of the ocean . . . the end of one world and the beginning of another. Do you see the lighthouse, Yavin? Do you see him, Phileas Fogg, walking up to the bridge because the captain is nowhere to be found? Do you see him? See it, Yavin . . . see it . . . see . . . it . . . "

"Passepartout," Phileas Fogg said to Yavin as he took the boat's wheel. "I fear Captain Speedy is still not enthusiastic about this diversion to Liverpool, so I ask that you keep him well tended . . . but, above all, well kept in his quarters."

"Of course, sir," Yavin said while carefully pouring the amber-colored tea into three dainty china cups – one for Mr. Phileas Fogg, one for Mademoiselle Aouda and the last for himself. "I shall see to his needs, have no fear."

"I never fear," Phileas Fogg said with a nod, "it is too time consuming. Now, if my calculations are correct, and there is nothing to say they aren't, the 'Henrietta' should be more than able

to make the three thousand mile crossing from New York to Liverpool in nine days, which would put us on good English soil again on the 21st of December — the Solstice, I believe."

Hanukkah, Yavin thought, but didn't say anything except, "One lump or two?"

*   *   *

"Wake up, Yavin."

Yavin opened his eyes, rubbing them against the bright yellow light that filled the small room. The room only looked small because it was filled with books — wall-to-wall and floor to ceiling, and encircling a narrow window through which Yavin saw a wide river bordered by high, rocky cliffs. A lighthouse, like the one the 'Henrietta' had passed on her way to the sea, blinked at him from a high overlook across the river.

Reb Shendelman was standing over him, smiling in the bright yellow light.

"I was . . . dreaming."

"I know," Reb Shendelman said, "and now those dreams can come true."

THE HEMINGWAY KITTENS

A.R. Morlan

Some people may say that cats and bookstores don't mix, that small beasts with claws and occasional ability to spray have no place among shelved books which reach from floor to near-ceiling . . . but answer me, is there anything more appealing than the sight of a cat curled up next to an opened book? With its softly pointed chin resting on the creamy-white printed pages?

True, initially I began shutting cats up inside my bookstore to take care of a minor mouse problem before it became a multiple mice problem, but after the first time I approached the store minutes before opening time, and saw that small crowd of people standing before the shop's display window, cooing and ooohing over the sight of Chatty and Muffin curled up into tiger-and-white commas next to the shiny-covered copies of the latest Stephen King novel, I realized that I was onto something. I hadn't seen people react like that since I'd last been in New York City during the winter holidays, when Macy's set up its annual Christmas window displays — and that had been the year they'd done the *Little Women* scenes, back in 1979.

The connection with the name of the store didn't hurt, either — Barrett and Browning's did have that "couples" connotation, and the fact that Chatty was a she and Muffin was a he (even if he was smaller than she was) only seemed to enhance the store's image. Pretty soon, customers started asking where "Barrett and Browning" were, and if I could coax those two sleepy felines out among the shelves during regular store hours, it usually meant a few extra dollars in the till, especially those small — but expensive items like bookmarks or protective covers for paperback books . . . all of which I managed to order in cat designs.

Long after the mouse problem was solved, I still kept cats in my shop. Luckily, Muffin wasn't a sprayer, and neither he nor Chatty was wont to rend their claws along the exposed spines of the shelved books (both the new ones I kept out front, and the used section toward the back of the narrow rectangle of a half-store), so as long as their litter pans were scooped clean, and their bowls of food and water were kept full, my two feline salespeople did their jobs well . . . so well, in fact, that within a couple of years, I found that I needed help in the store. Initially, Barrett and Browning was little more than a hobby for me; after my husband passed away, I'd leased the building with my insurance money, knowing full well that I'd never really be able to compete with the "big guys" — the chain outlets with their coffee stands on the side, and plug-ins for computers, and couches, and tee-shirt-cap-coffee-mug concession isles — but I was content with being a niche market, one where a person might be able to find just the right book, at maybe not-quite-the-right price, but nonetheless it would be the *right* book, right in their neighborhood.

Muffin and Chatty were both getting on in years when I hired Rik (no "c" between the "i" and the "k"), to the point where he'd have to go hunting among the back shelves for them whenever a customer demanded to see "Barrett and Browning", then carry them up front. He never seemed to mind, even after that time when one of Chatty's claws got caught in one of the half a dozen earrings Rik wore and he almost lost the earring and a good chunk of his right earlobe. At the time, he was fresh out of high school, and working afternoons while taking morning and evening classes at the University over in St. Paul. I didn't know what he was majoring in (aside from getting holes punched in his ears, and bleaching the top layer of his usually brown hair a sort of sickly orange), but he was good with the customers, and even better with the cats, so I considered him to be a good "hire".

And he understood how to best arrange the books — especially the used ones — so as to make them more enticing for the customers. None of that orderly, library-like themed progression of books sorted by author, subject and so on . . . he understood that much of the fun of searching for a book was exactly that — the *search*. What he did do with the rows of used, slightly tattered volumes was to arrange them by color — black spines segued into deep blues and purples, which merged with the greens, then the garish yellows (usually reserved for self-help tomes), before dipping into the sunset hues. That way, the mix of paperback and hardcovers seemed to flow naturally before the eye, thus encouraging the browser to really hunker down and study each book, each row, then each shelf. And the longer one looks, the more one sees . . . and, it can be hoped, buys.

Rik also knew how to create cozy spots on each shelf for the cats — deliberately bare spots where a feline could curl up, or stretch out, without the fear of knocking books off the shelf itself. And it was at his urging that I began to add cat artwork to the store per se — a framed reproduction of Charles Wysocki's "Frederick the Literate" with that lovely sleeping tabby draped around dozens of cat-themed books and bird knick-knacks, plus sets of nesting cats, and a sweet-faced white and grey van cat pencil holder next to the cash register.

By the time Chatty and Muffin had gone on to the ever-full bowls of milk and eternally clean litterboxes of feline heaven, Rik had brought me their replacements . . . Oscar and April, a pair of strays from a local downtown shelter. At first, their grey striped fur and white feets-and-faces contrasted oddly with the warm browns and beiges of the shop's interior, but Rik (who himself was now sporting streaks of stark white in his straight dark hair) came to my visual rescue once again — telling me, "Once you see what these two do, you'll understand," he replaced the sun-stippled brown-into-bone swatch of material I'd had resting along the bottom of the window display with a brightly hand-dyed piece of canvas, adorned with an ombre of reds, pinks and corals. And sure enough, by the next morning, Barrett and Browning's window had attracted another small crowd — Oscar and April were lovebirds of a feline variety, and when she wasn't tucking her wedgeshaped face under his chin, he was licking the top of her head.

The only problem was, Oscar and April were so utterly devoted to each other, they failed to notice when a few mice got into the store during a particularly blustery February storm . . . it wasn't until the mice had found an unopened box of used books I'd taken in trade the week before that I realized that love didn't conquer all . . . especially when it came to getting rid of mice.

"They have to go," I told Rik, when I confronted him with the remains of what had been several vintage 1950's Robert Heinlein packbacks, now gnawed and chewed and clawed into fluffy mice mattresses. "I realize that Oscar and April are adorable, but I don't think either of them would know what to do with a mouse if it came up and blew a juicy raspberry in their muzzles."

"That I'd like to see," Rik laughed, until he took a good look at my expression, and became serious . . . or at least as serious as someone sporting three hoops per ear can look. "But the customers really do like them . . . couldn't we set traps? One of those no-kill —"

"And let the customers see that? Once word gets out that a bookstore has a rodent problem, there go the customers to the Big Guys. And I'm sure *they* sell mouse motels emblazoned with their *logo* —"

"No, I think that's the coffee guys," Rik smiled, before glancing over at the display window, where our resident Garfields were washing each other's faces, their combined purrs loud enough to be easily heard by Rik and me as we stood by the cash register ten feet away.

True, they were a wonderful couple — April was a little over half of Oscar's size, and their markings were almost identical, even though he was several years her senior. You couldn't imagine a better-suited pair of cats . . . although I could picture just about any other cats in the world doing a better job of mousing my bookstore.

"Suppose we keep these two on as window-dressing, and get some real mousers? Ferals, maybe? My room-mate's dad has some live-traps," Rik offered, all the while watching my face as he spoke. By that time, he'd been working for me long enough to get a bachelor's degree — even though I still had no idea what he was actually studying at the university — and knew how to "read" me.

My face must have said "Yes" before my brain was able to react, for he smiled, and said, "I know a place near a mall where lots of cats hang around . . . maybe if I'm lucky, I'll get some young ones."

"Not too young," I admonished, realizing that Oscar and April might not make for the best surrogate parents, not the way they literally followed each other into the litterpans, in their effort to stay close.

Rik was always such a self-confident young man, it didn't seem out of the ordinary for him to say, "No, these will be old enough to take care of themselves . . . and the bookstore. You'll see. . . ."

I didn't realize that Rik had come in late the next day until he backed into the store, his arms bent akimbo, and said over his shoulder, "Have I got the right cats for a bookstore — Hemingway kittens!"

It had been such a busy morning (a few days before Easter) that I hadn't really had the time to think, let alone remember our conversation from the previous afternoon. For a moment, I was unable to figure out what Rik meant by "Hemingway kittens" — until I remembered those pictures of his place down in Florida, of all those many-toed cats running around. Polydactyly cats, with the bifid paws that resembled a splayed-out human hand —

"Ugh!" I blurted out, thinking of how the customers might react to seeing mutant kitties in the window, then Rik turned around, showing me the pair of kittens he'd zipped into his brown suede jacket.

The female was a tortie, long-haired, with a narrow face, while the male was a tuxedo with the characteristic stripe of white dividing the black patches over his eyes. He was long-haired, like his companion, but obviously bigger, so he probably wasn't a sibling —

"You caught two of them? In one livetrap?" Years ago, when my husband was alive, we'd tried to catch some stray cats living under our porch before winter set in, and it was slow-going at best; if we caught one, it might be days before any of the others would venture into that noisy springing trap, even if we baited the rectangular cage with sardines. Ferals were as wary as they were smart. . . .

"Uh-huh," Rik grunted, as he hurried over to the counter to deposit the kittens near the cash register. I started to wave him away, saying, "No, no . . . they might have fleas or who knows what —" but he shook his head of bi-colored hair and assured me, "Oh no, I checked them over . . . they're clean. No ear mites, nothing. Believe me, they'll be fine —"

Before I could continue my protests, he'd unzipped his jacket and spilled out the kittens on the counter next to the register. The female sat there in a bundle of brown ombre fur and too many toes, looking up at me with close-set greenish-yellow eyes, while the other one — also soft-furred, and remarkably clean-looking — darted off the counter, and ran between my booted feet (it *had* been a busy morning, so rushed I'd not had the time to take off my boots) toward the rear of the store. He'd made a perfect fourpoint landing on his many-toed fuzzy paws, then scurried off in an undulating ripple of patchy blackwhite long fur-and-feets.

"What the —"

"Don't worry about Scooter, he's like that. *Loves* to run. He's just getting the lay of the land — he'll be back."

"Not like *The Terminator*, I hope . . . don't tell me he's already litter trained," I added, as I wondered how Rik had managed to not only find me a male/female pair of kittens, but true literary oddities, genuine Hemingway kittens, all within the space of less than twenty-four hours of our conversation about *possibly* getting some new store-cats.

"Well . . . Jake and I left them in the bathroom with a litter-pan, and they'd used it come morning. Maybe they were dumped?"

Hoping that they'd used clay litter, and not shredded paper (I didn't want them associating any kind of paper with going to the bathroom), I turned my attention to the female cowering on my counter. "So, what's her name?"

Gently scooping her up in his many-ringed hands, Rik slid one of his fingers under her right paw, and showed off her hand-shaped toes, saying, "Mittens . . . I know it's rather mundane, but I couldn't think of anything else on short notice. Cute, isn't she?"

Mittens avoided my stare, but she didn't jerk away or growl when I petted her head. Certainly not feral.

"They could've been dumped . . . I suppose some people don't know what a Hemingway cat is. Yes, she's cute," I lied, giving her smallish head another pat, before I asked, "Don't you think you'd better find Scooter? Before he finds those boxes of books I bought on Tuesday?"

"Scooter wouldn't go in *those* . . . he's too smart for that," Rik said a little too confidently, as he shucked off his jacket and made for the back of the store, leaving me with the stoically silent Mittens.

When Rik was out of earshot, I leaned down and whispered to the kitten, "I just hope he didn't pay too much for you two . . . you didn't crawl into any live trap, did you? I've seen ferals, and you two don't fit the bill." Mittens looked up at me as I spoke, then ducked her head off to one side as I finished, as if she couldn't bear to look me in the eye. *You* know, *don't you?* I thought, then dismissed it; the kitten was just shy. I'd spent too many years working in a shop whose living mascots were routinely anthropomorphized by my doting repeat customers, I decided; even if she had been purchased rather than live trapped, there was no way she could understand what I'd just said. Not with that tiny little walnut-sized brain of hers —

"Why don't you take a break, show the new arrivals around?" Rik was carrying Scooter in his left arm, cradling the kitten like a baby, so that all four of the animal's over-sized paws were extended toward me. The pads were soft, shell pink and that greyish oxblood color, and as I reached for the kitten, I realized that those paws hadn't been in contact with asphalt, concrete or any other outside surface in all of Scooter's life — which looked to be perhaps three or four months so far. And his fur was deliciously soft and smooth — he was definitely either a pet store or possibly a shelter kitten.

He'd been so active so far, squirming, scooting and wiggling around, that I hadn't gotten a good look at his face — but when I finally held him in my arms, and looked into those clear leaf-green eyes, I was enchanted. While I thought that most cats were beautiful (save, perhaps, for those hairless Sphinx kitties, which had originally hailed from a Minnesota farm cat), Scooter was special — it wasn't just the way his eyes shone, or that "smiling" expression of his, but he was simply *unique*, above and beyond his mitten-like paws, or, as I noticed when he nestled into my arms, his twisted, truncated stump of a tail. He just had . . . *it*, that spark of pure personality that leaps out through the eyes, and touches a person to the core. Like finding a genuine first edition in among a box of book-club reprints.

And, as if to prove to me just how special he was, he placed one of his wide paws on my arm, just above my watchband, and blinked up at me, giving me "kitty kisses" as one cat-breeding customer of mine called them.

"Here, take Mittens in the other arm — *there* — now you can show them the store," Rik said, before sliding behind the counter in anticipation of the post-lunch crowds. What he was suggesting was rather silly, me, *showing* them the store, when all they really needed to know was where the food and water dishes, as well as the litterpans, were located, but somehow, after the way Scooter had regally placed one paw on my arm like that, it didn't seem all *that* ridiculous to show the kittens my store. It was going to be their home, after all —

"Ok, guys, here's the bestsellers rack . . . a case of each title, stacked alphabetically. Positioned close to the cash register because I'm too cheap to buy one of those surveillance cameras, and bestsellers cost too much — am I doing ok, Rik?" Behind me, he laughed, "Ok — fine . . . they're smart kitties, aren't you guys? Just listen to the Boss-lady," before turning his attention to the door as it jingled open with our next customer. Not wanting to show the kittens off too soon, I hurried down the aisle, toward the middle of the store, saying softly to the kittens, "And this is the place where bestsellers that aren't end up . . . the remainder rack. Followed by the place I like best, the used books. You smell the other kitties on these, don't you," I found myself saying, as the two kittens leaned forward, their pointed faces seemingly scanning the hundreds of mixed paperbacks and hardbounds, their moist pink noses working vigorously. I supposed that the smell was enticing to a cat; all those hand-oils rubbed on the worn, cracked spines, not to mention the hundreds of other things which had either rubbed onto the books, or had been spilled on them at one time or another . . . perhaps they'd even made contact with food. Plus the previous bookstore cats had undoubtably rubbed against them, maybe even (even as I hoped they hadn't!) sprayed them. The layers of scent here had to be akin to cat heaven for them.

But as they sniffled the rows of books as I walked slowly down the aisle, I found myself trying to look at the store through their eyes —I'd read up enough about cats to know that they probably did see all colors, albeit not as intensely as humans, so I wondered what they made of Rik's color-coded filing system, that flowing sweep of blues into reds. Perhaps they noticed the unexpected highs and lows of paperbacks standing next to hardcovers and vice versa, the pleasant undulation of assorted books nestled close — but not so close that you'd have to pry the books off the shelf — for row upon row. Did they notice the abrupt gaps on some shelves, where he'd left some space for the other cats? Or were they merely sensing the traces of old odors on the books?

I did find myself wondering how high a five-foot tall bookcase might seem to a young kitten — would they want to climb from shelf to shelf, seeking the lofty flatness of the top of each bookcase, or would they scurry in fear between the aisles? I also wondered what would happen when Oscar and April finally noticed that they had feline company — I could picture the kittens puffing out like blowfish, rising high on their toes, before backing away from the older grey tabbies . . . but then again, the lovebirds seemed to have eyes only for each other, so perhaps they might not notice the kittens at all. They certainly hadn't noticed the Heinlein mice. . . .

Acting almost as one, the kittens suddenly wanted out of my arms, and jumped down before the lone bookcase positioned along the far narrow wall of the store, close to the back room where I kept the food and litterpans, as well as whatever incoming books I hadn't sorted yet. I seldom had customers wanting children's books, so I routinely placed those titles in the back . . . I supposed these books were the most highly scented, especially since children are wont to try to eat and read at the same time, for Scooter and Mittens were all over the books, rubbing against them, standing up on their hind paws to smell the exposed spines of each book, then batting at them with their mitten feet. "No, no, bad kitties . . . don't tear the books," I said, and they actually stopped. As one, both of them sitting in place, merely staring at the books, before looking up at me with that ubiquitous "Who, us?" cat stare.

Yet, there was something eager about them, apart from mere kitten high spirits. As if they couldn't wait to explore the bookstore —

"— a nice day," Rik was telling the departing customers, as I hurried to the front of the store, taking backwards glances every couple of steps to make sure the kittens weren't following me. They seemed content to sit near the lone children's shelf.

"Rik, I think they'd be better off locked in the back room, until you leave this afternoon. I'd hate to have them run out into traffic —"

"Oh, I wouldn't worry about that . . . they know they're supposed to stay here. Jake was in and out of the apartment all this morning, and they stayed put there —"

"'There' isn't here, though. And your apartment opens out into a hallway, right? That's not like the street —"

"Not to worry . . . they'll stay put," Rik persisted, while cupping the head of my white and grey cat pencil holder with his beringed left hand — with every other word, his rings clanked against the ceramic head of the holder. Nerves?

"Well, *I*'d feel a lot better if they slept in the back, for the first couple of days at least," *I* persisted, "Even if they are alley kittens, now that they're here, they're the store kitties, and I'd hate to think of anything bad happening to them so soon. Remember how sad all the regulars were when Chatty and Muffin passed on?"

"Not just the regulars." Rik kept on clanking his rings on my poor ceramic cat, until I figured out a way to get him out from behind the counter. "Rik, come here . . . look down that aisle —"

The Hemingway kittens were both studying the spines of the children's books before them, their heads moving in unison as they scanned the vertical titles one by one. Even if they weren't littermates, they had to have spent time together before they were caught or bought or whatever Rik did to obtain them. Their behavior was so similar . . .

"That is so adorable . . . and so strange," I found myself whispering, as if I were in a library, and not my own store.

"They're just smart," Rik said a little too quickly, then added, "Probably trying to figure out which ones say 'Food' . . . just kidding. I do wish I had a camera —"

"We do," I said, remembering the disposable one we'd found in the back book racks last summer, with only a couple of frames of film exposed. No one had come in for it, and I'd almost forgotten it was sitting on a shelf behind the counter —

"Here, let me," Rik whispered, taking the camera from me and slowly advancing the next frame forward, before crouching down and waiting for the instant flash to warm up, then clicked the button and snapped one shot . . . then, when the kittens didn't move, he duck-walked closer to them, and took another picture.

I could just imagine what the picture would look like — two perfectly posed kittens, their beautiful pointy ears at attention, as they seemed to peer at the books before them, while surrounded by the warm, worn wooden floor, the polished wooden book shelf, and the primary-bright colors of the narrow-spined children's books . . . just the sort of picture one might submit to a cat food calendar contest.

Wanting to get a closer look at them, I stepped as lightly as I could in clumpy-lumpy boots down the aisle, but the magical image was gone as the two kittens turned their heads my way, and Scooter began to yawn. Luckily, Rik was able to capture the moment; the camera whizz-whirred and there was a bright, brief flash of white light. Mittens was frightened by the light, and ran off, toward the back room. Sensing that this might be a good time to shut Scooter up there, too, I reached down and scooped him up, telling him, "Your sister or whatever she is shouldn't be scared . . . you tell her it's all right to be photographed, ok?"

Scooter stared at me solemnly, as if mentally digesting my words.

But when I tried to walk into the back room, he reached out with both front paws and tried to hold onto the door frame, as if to prevent me from locking him up.

"See, he wants to stay out a while . . . don't you Scooter?"

Scooter looked Rik's way, then looked back at me, his green eyes glowing. Closing time wasn't for another couple of hours, so I supposed I could watch him until Rik was getting ready to close the store —

Rik continued to take care of the last customers of the day as I carried Scooter around the store, talking to him softly as I showed him the sets of nesting cats (some with tiny solid-wood mouse centers) stationed on some of the shelves, and the framed cat pictures, some cut from those calendars featuring famous Impressionist or Pre-Raphaelite paintings reconfigured as cat portraits.

"Too bad none of these kitties look like you," I told him, as I snuggled him under my chin, "But this one looks a little like poor old Chatty-cat" — he and I stopped before the cat-adapted 'Isabella and the Bot of Basil' with its white-gowned-and-white-pawed tiger cat "— only she was all tiger-striped. Now if these two were grey and white, they could be Oscar and April," I added, pausing before the feline version of "The Hugnenot" Sir John Everett Millais certainly wouldn't recognize as his own work. Scooter actually craned his head forward, and reached out one thumbed-paw to touch the head of the female "lover" in the print. Reflexively, I asked him, "So that's April?"

Scooter let out a "purrumph!" and looked up at me, his bright eyes dancing in his white and black face.

Somewhat rattled by his facsimile of a reply to my words, I set off down another aisle, moving toward that framed Charles Wysocki print of the tiger cat lounging on the book shelf. Once we were standing before the walnut-framed art print, I whispered into Scooter's furry neck, "You won't find any of these titles on the shelves here . . . but I bet you wish you could read 'A Tale of Two Kitties' or 'Delicious Field Mice I Have Known', hummm?" Scooter wiggled in my arms, making meowing noises, until I asked him, "You need the litterpan? Or some food?" He immediately quieted down, then turned his head to look at me expectantly, as if to say, So, where's the food you promised me?

Rik was right . . . Scooter (and probably the shy Mittens, too) was smart. The only problem yes, how did Rik figure that out in such a short time?

Once I'd brought Scooter to the back room, and opened the metal popcorn canister where I stored the cats' dry food, I realized that he and Mittens might not be able to chew the hard nuggets, so I ran a little warm water over them, to soften them up, before setting down the bowl of food on the floor. Scooter began lapping up the watery "broth" while Mittens more cautiously crawled out from behind some boxed books, staying low to the ground as she approached the food bowl, even as she moved her head sideways to get an occasional glimpse of me — once she realized that I wasn't going to try to grab her, she moved into place next to Scooter, and began eating. While the kittens were busy, I picked up one of the litterpans, checked to make sure that there was some water in the other dish near the kittens, then quietly shut the door behind me after flicking off the light switch.

Placing the other litterpan near the closed door (I hoped neither Oscar or April would be confused while they were a loving pair, I doubted they had a complete brain between them), I squidge-squidged my way down the aisles until I reached the front of the shop, then quietly told Rik, "There's some extra food in that Necco wafers tin under the counter for the lovebirds . . . the kittens can sleep on the folded blanket back there. Now you're *sure* they don't rip up paper?"

"They'll be fine . . . oh, you did leave the light on for them, didn't you?" A thread-thin worry line formed in the middle of Rik's forehead.

"You mean they need a night-light? But they were living in an alley —"

"With a street-lamp near-by," he said quickly, then added, "It's no biggie . . . I can turn it on for them before I leave. I'm sure they'll be fine in there —"

"They'd better be . . . and no ripping up my boxes or books," I warned him, as I slid into my coat (which I never did have time to take to the back room that morning), and picked up my purse from behind the counter.

Rik waited to reply until I was halfway out the door, so I wasn't completely sure I actually heard what I *thought* he said:

"They've been warned about that . . . no ripping, just read-ing —"

As I'd anticipated, Oscar and April had slept all night in the front window, a feline version of Barrett and Browning, curled into a seemingly continuous ball of white-flecked grey fur, their flanks rising and falling in sweet unison. The molasses-brown brickwork of the window frame formed a rough-hewn frame around them, and I wished I'd had that camera with me — while they didn't seem to know a mouse from a muffin, they were a beautiful pair. But as I opened the door, and flipped around the Open/Closed door-sign, I found myself worried about that other pair of cats in the store, the ones who had to sleep with an overhead night-light.

Hoping that Rik *was* right about them, I nervously opened the door to the back room, then peeked around the frame. The litter-pan had been used, the food was gone, and the kittens . . . were actually sitting at attention, as if waiting for me. The only thing out of place in the room was a Richard Scary children's dictionary, resting on the floor near their folded blanket-bed. I knew we had more than one copy of that particular book on the children's shelf, but I hadn't thought that we had another one waiting to be put out on the shelf . . . it didn't seem like anyone had brought in any children's books in the last few boxes of traded books —

"See, I told you they'd be good —"

"God, Rik, you scared me!" My heart was still lopping wildly in my chest when I turned around to face my afternoon-time-worker. Rik tried to hide behind a bag of take-out donuts, as he said in a don't-hit-me voice, "I thought you heard the bell . . . sorry."

"I should've heard it . . . and you brought me breakfast, too. Yes, to answer you . . . they *were* good . . . but where did the book come from?"

"Oh, that . . . I took a picture of them, last night. I stopped in to check on them, make sure they had enough food. I thought it would be funny to get one of them 'reading' a children's book. I forgot to put it back —" he ducked into the room, picked up the book, and carried it back to the children's shelf, all the while holding the white bag of donuts in his left hand, just out of my reach. Behind him, the kittens watched intently as the book was lifted off the floor, and carried away from them. They almost seemed disappointed. . . .

On the way up to the counter, I snatched the donuts out of his hand, and said between glazed bites, "I thought you had classes at night?"

"I did . . . I stopped here afterwards. Oh, I almost forgot —" he dug around in the large patch pockets of his jacket, and pulled out a few cans of cat food, the tiny expensive brand I usually couldn't afford more than once a year, as the lovebirds' Christmas treat.

"Here's some for the window-dressing, and the rest's for the kittens. Workstudy's been good this year, so I thought I'd splurge. I'll buy them some more later this week —"

"You needn't do that . . . they'll be earning their keep eventually. I hope . . . or don't they 'do' mice?"

"Mice shouldn't be a problem . . . long as they're well fed. You know how a less-hungry cat is a better mouser —"

"Is that something they teach you at the university?"

Rik nodded as he bit into a jelly-filled donut, then said something around a mouthful of half-chewed pastry.

"What?" I licked the sugary glaze off my fingertips as he repeated, "'Something' like that. I work in the labs, with the animals —"

"Uhhh . . . not so early in the morning. I haven't the stomach for hearing about lab animals —"

"No, these aren't the kind that die. We — I . . . I work with the genetics department. Uhm, Jake does, too," he added, realizing that I'd caught the slip-of-the-tongue "we" seconds earlier.

"So . . . that means breeding things, like kittens, maybe?" I thought Scooter and Mittens were too tame to have come from some mall —

"Sometimes like kittens. Mostly mice and other rodents, though. Not to dissect, or feed to snakes, though. Nothing . . . ukky," he added, with a smile, then turned his attention to Oscar and April, who'd finally woken up, and took turns stretching, yawning, and kneading the bright ombre canvas beneath them, before jumping down and milling around our legs. Peeling the pull-tab covers off the food, Rik knelt down and fed the cats behind the counter, giving them a can each. Taking a cue from my worker, I picked up a couple of the small tins of food and carried them to the back room . . . but the kittens had already left, to sit vigil in front of the rows of children's books along the back wall of the store.

Directly in front of that children's dictionary —

"Well if you two like it so much, it's yours," I said, sliding it off the shelf, and using it as a tray to carry the cans of food into the back room. I did feel guilty about not buying them any cat toys, and after Rik had bought all four cats breakfast, my guilt more than doubled. The kittens happily ate out of the opened cans, and while they noisily attacked the food, I placed "their" book next to their bedding . . . which was softly indented in two spots, one covered with white and black fur, the other a soft ombre of brown, tan and orange.

Glancing around the rest of the room, I didn't see any shredded paper, nor were there any claw marks on the sides of the cardboard boxes, so I found myself saying, "If you two did come from a lab, you must be used to things being clean . . . just keep it that way, ok?"

I was sure the kittens only lifted their heads from their food to catch a breath of air between bites of food. . . .

The kittens, Rik and I settled into a new routine over the next few weeks; he'd stop by the store before it opened, to check on the Hemingway kittens, as we'd both taken to calling them, then meet me coming in as he was going out. Rik would return in the afternoon, allowing me time with the kittens — Mittens was slow to come around, far more so than Scooter, but I soon found that she loved the nesting cats . . . so much so that one morning I found all the solid core figures, kittens and mice alike, nestled next to her side of the blanket she and Scooter shared. Thinking that she might be getting ready to go into heat, I gently checked her teeth, but none of her adult fangs were anywhere near ready to drop down yet. Scooter's fangs were just beginning to bud out, swelling his gum-line, so I called the vet clinic to set up a neutering appointment for him, which was scheduled for three weeks from that day.

But Rik wouldn't have it —

"Neuter a cat like Scooter? With his smarts? And all that personality? How could you take something like that out of the gene pool?" For a college boy, he could be terribly obtuse; without trying to come across like an out-of-it old nagger, I tried to explain, "But you can see yourself that he's defective . . . those paws, and that kinked tail. I've looked it up in all the cat books we have here — those are mutant traits. Not desirable in the least. Besides, millions of kittens are born every day . . . why add more to the mix?"

That narrow worry-line appeared on his forehead again, as he began patting the head of my pencil-holder cat, his rings clanging against the smooth ceramic. "But those kittens aren't wanted . . . Scooter's would be. How about we start letting the customers see him, and Mittens, to create a demand? Nothing like a pair of literary kittens to bring attention to a bookstore —"

I still wasn't sure about letting the people see the Hemingway kittens; I was used to seeing their strange paws, but not everyone was into cats with large mitten feet. Glancing around the cat-print covered walls of my shop, I noticed that Susan Herbert and Mr. Wysocki didn't choose to use polydactyly cats in their paintings, despite their human-like paws. To be honest, I wasn't even sure if all my clients would realize what a Hemingway cat *was* . . . after all, Minnesota was and still is F. Scott Fitzgerald country.

It was almost as if Rik had read my mind, for he suddenly said, "Picture this . . . Scooter and Mittens in the window, with books by Hemingway and Fitzgerald, maybe even an opened copy of *The Great Gatsby* — it'd be a heck of a photo op, at the least. You know, free advertising. . . ."

College boy had me there. For more years than I cared to admit, I'd made do with a small weekly ad in the *St. Paul Pioneer Press* and the *Star-Tribune*, the cheapest one I could get, just enough to let readers know I was Out There. And while my "Barrett and Browning" cats attracted quite a bit of passer-by attention, I'd never been daring enough to try to create a window worthy of newspaper attention. I suppose it was being brought up during the age of Self-Praise-Stinks, the motto my parents drummed into my head almost from the cradle, but this was the Information Age, and I realized that Rik's idea was a good one. . . .

It took a little coaxing to lure Oscar and April out of "their" window (plus the small cannister of cat treats Rik bought helped), but Scooter and Mittens seemed to instinctively understand what was wanted of them.

Rik had done some searching on the Internet, and found some pictures of the descendants of the real Hemingway's cats which he downloaded and printed out in color, and I'd found some art-quality prints of both authors, which I mounted on posterboard. I knew the sunlight would bleach out all the pictures within a few weeks or less, but I didn't plan to keep this particular display up all that long — Rik promised me that a friend of his who worked at one of the papers would just "happen by" and take a photo of the new window display, and just as Rik had managed to "find" me some new store-cats within hours of my asking about them, he made sure that his friend came through for me.

The photo ran on the front page of the Metro section of the *Pioneer Press* by the end of the week. A generous four by six color picture, showing the bottom half of the sign above the window, and all of the display itself:

Surrounded by easel-propped photos of the Florida Hemingway cats, and the prints of Ernest and F. Scott, Mittens and Scooter were lying before an opened copy of *Gatsby*, their distinctive mitten feet resting on the exposed pages, their heads cocked at quizzical angles as they "read" the words before them. The caption read, "Hemingway-0, Fitzgerald-2". The rivalry between those two gentlemen may have been decades old, but judging by the reaction that photo generated, feelings for Hemingway and Fitzgerald still ran as fervent and deep as the on-going Packer-Vikings bro-ha-haa. Every copy of anything written by either of the two authors sold out within a couple of days, and when Rik and I weren't waiting on customers, we were supervising photo ops with the kittens and cat-lovers who couldn't wait to have their picture taken with one of the Hemingway Kittens.

Since neither of the kittens displayed a penchant for ripping or shredding book spines, or honing their many claws on the edges of the shelves, we'd taken to leaving them out during the night . . . although with all the increased attention Barrett and Browning was enjoying lately, I did have qualms about letting people see the kittens at all hours —

"— suppose someone tries to break the window, and take them?"

"This is a low crime neighborhood . . . and that window is double-paned. Would take a lot of effort and make a lot of noise to break it. Besides, I think the kittens would be smart enough to make a run for it if anyone was after them —"

"There's a difference between being personable and smart, Rik . . . look how they let anyone hold them. I just don't know —"

"Did anyone try to get at Oscar and April? They're just as good-looking, and personable —"

"They're also fixed," I reminded him, "While these two —" I cocked my head in the direction of the window, where Scooter and Mittens were busy "reading" an old opened hardbound copy of *A Farewell to Arms*" — aren't. Although half that problem will be solved in a few days."

Rik didn't say anything, but that fine line appeared between his dark eyes again. Down one of the aisles, I heard the unmistakable sound of cat spray hitting something hard, and hurried to see what Oscar was doing, yelling "Bad cat! Bad-bad-*bad!*" There was a tell-tale puddle on the worn floorboards near the rack of children's books — Oscar had targeted the children's dictionary the kittens used to fancy. They'd been ignoring the book for the last few days, so I'd placed it back on the shelf, but now it was ruined. Gingerly pulling the thick book out of the stack, I noticed something odd imbedded in the top of the spine — a shed claw-cover, which gleamed softly in the clear white light. The position of the claw was odd, right in the center of the now-damp spine, as if the book had been pulled out by one downward-moving cat paw, from the top, the way a person might pull out a book, rather than the way a cat would do it — by raking on the spine itself, until the book wiggled free of the rest or, the shelf.

Oscar's puddle of urine began to spread on the floor, so I ran to the back room for a paper towel, the ruined dictionary with the imbedded claw momentarily forgotten. But as I was mopping up the mess, I heard Rik shout, "No, you guys, c'mere —" and I knew instantly that the kittens had escaped.

I ran, wet paper towel still wadded up in one hand, to the window, which was now a mere tableau of books and fading pictures — no more Scooter, no Mittens. Rik was outside the door, looking quickly up and down the street, but when he turned to re-enter the store, I knew just from looking at his face. They were gone. And the terrible thing was, I could so easily imagine their flight — Scooter with his long side-fur rippling like a soft curtain along his hips and flank, Mittens with her small fox-like face moving quickly from side to side, both of them running fast, their legs scissoring in the spring sunlight, as they hurried down some alley-way . . . .

Rik tried to explain what had happened, but I was devastated. He'd been placing some new Dean Koontz books on the bestseller's shelf, when he heard the door jingle, but no incoming footsteps — only the sharp scrabble of many claws hitting hardwood, then the door jingled shut again. By the time he'd turned around, and gone to the door, both of them had vanished. And my store was located in the middle of a side-street, which meant they could've gone in any direction.

On top of everything else, my front door pulled outward, being an old wooden and glass door that I'd kept because it was so antique and old-fashioned . . . so the kittens, if they moved as one, might have been able to shove it open.

Sick at heart, I left the store, and went searching for the kittens in the alleys near my business, calling and pleading for them to come back, but it was as if they'd never existed. All I had left of them was a framed copy of that Metro section photo, and a claw-casing stuck in the spine of a ruined children's dictionary . . . . After I'd given up looking for them, long after Rik had closed the store for me (he'd left a note on the counter, which merely read "I'm so, so sorry" in his large, flowing handwriting), I went to the back room, and picked up the blanket they'd slept on for the last couple of months. It still smelled of their fur, a warm, slightly "hot" scent which reminded me ever so slightly of old paperback books and binding glue. My bookstore kittens even smelled like books . . . but when I squeezed the blanket next to my chest, I felt something hard inside. I'd long ago put the cores of the nesting doll sets back on the shelf, so I couldn't imagine what the kittens had shoved into the folds of the blanket, until I shook it, and a tiny bridge pencil, the kind of writing implement no bigger around than a coffee stir-stick, and only half again as long, fell to the floor.

"Where in the world did they get that?" I muttered, as April and Oscar tentatively came into the room, and began rubbing on my legs. Looking down at Oscar, I remembered the dictionary he'd sprayed, and — still hugging the furry blanket close to my heart — walked back into the store-proper, where it rested on the floor near the children's shelf.

I began leafing through it, and soon found that some of the pages had been marked up, with random pencil scrawls that resembled that "graffiti" style of printing used for hand-held electronic notebooks. I'd seen Rik use that style of writing; according to some of the Tech sections I'd read in the *Pioneer Press* and *Star-Tribune*, it was very popular with young computer-users. Looking down at the scribbles on the pages, I realized that someone had been trying to copy some of the words, printing clumsily at first, but with increasing legibility — and, if I held the book just so under the overhead lights, I could also make out thin fine scratch marks at the tops of the pages, as if someone with very long, needle-tipped nails had been paging through the book —

The possibility was so absurd, yet so . . . plausible, I found myself breathing hard and fast, while I rifled the pages of the book, looking for those oddly-printed letters, and, ultimately, words.

"A" "B" . . . all the way through "Y" and "Z". Then, short words, "AN" "TO" "AND" . . . and on to the inevitable "CAT". . . .

Those strange mitten feet. So much like a hand, with an opposable thumb. And that bridge pencil was small and thin enough to just fit in that narrow space between those bifid paws. . . .

Rik leaving the light on, along with that book. Did he give them the pencil, when he visited them that night? Or had they used it in the lab?

Leaning heavily against the rack of children's books, feeling the horizontal thickness of the shelf edge dig into my back, I paged through the dictionary, looking at the last pages of the book, and what was written there:

"BOOK GOOD. READ MORE? OPEN THE DOOR, READ MORE AT NIGHT."

They had grammar. They had punctuation. And, I assumed, they had human genes, mixed in with feline ones. Maybe even a dash of raccoon, for additional manual dexterity. . . .

Rik and his roommate Jake worked in the genetics department. Not cleaning the lab, like Rik had implied. And not merely working with rodents, either. How long had he been working with me, five, six years?

It didn't take that much time for those folks who added a bit of jellyfish DNA to a white rabbit, in order to make its fur glow green under black light, to create their living work of "art" . . . but it would take time for Rik and Jake and whoever else they worked with in that lab to teach a huline chimera to read. . . .

Or spend time letting them read, I thought, as I looked at my small literary sanctuary, my private bookdom . . . which was much like a school for Hemingway kittens. They had the time, and the light (be it from the backroom, or from the streetlamp which shone into my window at night), and all the schoolbooks they needed. I supposed that whatever Rik or Jake or whoever created the kittens did to them changed their eyes, made them able to read two-dimensional print even as they may have sacrificed their innate ability to see well in low light, so they needed regular light to read . . . and they already had the "hands" to turn a page. I couldn't watch them every second while I was in the store, so it would have been so easy for them to surreptitiously turn a page while looking at whatever book Rik had propped open before them.

And if they could read, they could understand . . . the only question was, did they escape on their own, or did Rik let them out, perhaps handing them off to a waiting friend?

I'd been so insistent about getting Scooter neutered, when of course Rik couldn't allow *that* —

Scooter was about five or so months old, close to teen-age years in human terms. Perhaps he was almost ready to graduate from my "school" already . . . and took Mittens along with him when he left, if leave on his own he did. Or, maybe he and Mittens needed to find an easier way to write, perhaps on a computer screen . . . if they could manage a bridge pencil, a stylis would be so easily for them to master. Or a computer mouse, or cue-cat. . . .

I wasn't all that surprised that night when Rik called to say he wouldn't be able to make it to work anymore — too many changes in his class schedule, he claimed. And he again said how sorry he was about the kittens. Before he hung up, he suggested that I have the photos in that disposable camera developed — "in case you want to do up a missing poster or something."

I didn't do up a poster, but I did get the pictures developed. The first two were from some Superbowl party, people with Vikings hats and haircuts, drinking beer and eating nachos. Those went in the wastebasket. But the rest . . . there were Scooter and Mittens, staring eagerly at the row of children's books. Then, the two of them reading their dictionary, as well as writing on the margins with their small bridge pencils tucked in their paws. Others showed them turning the pages of hard-bound books, their pointed faces looking down at the text below. In one shot, Rik had brought over his own e-notebook, and both kittens were studying the small keypad. Which gave me an idea —

As much as I loved the printed page, I was certainly no Luddite — I had a computer at home, and a webpage (albeit a small one) for the bookstore itself, and my web address was listed on all the major ISP's . . . so, each evening, I took to carefully reading my e-mail, studying the Subject headings, looking for a message I wasn't even sure would ever come . . . I looked for many months, long enough for the Hemingway kittens to become cats, and perhaps even parents of more huline polydactlyl kittens, until it appeared. The message read:

From:<HemCats><hemcats@excite.com)

To:<Barrett and Browning><barrettbrowning@aol.com>

Subject: A Tale of Two Kitties

Hello, Book-lady,

Your wish came true. Couldn't find _ A Tale of Two Kitties_ but did read _ A Tale of Two Cities_ . We both liked it, but it was heavy. Sorry not to have said Good-Bye last year, but there was no time. We had to avoid getting fixed. Rik says you'd understand. Look for us (Rik and Jake too) soon in all the scientific magazines, maybe the newspapers, too. The young ones are better at reading and writing than we are, and will be ready for the media soon. We tell them about the book place, what a special school it was for us, and how we practiced being parents with the wood kittens. You were a good teacher. We remember the pictures, and have looked for the originals on the net. Computers are fast, and light, but books smell better. We miss the Barrett and Browning. The young ones don't understand. They grew up on e-books. But we remember. Say hello to Oscar and April. And the shiny hard cat on the counter by the door. It never talked, but we still liked it. But not when Rik made noise on it with his rings. Rik and Jake are busy with the young ones, so we could send this. Don't tell them we did. Just remember us. We remember you and the books.

Jay and Zelda and the young ones.

So Scooter had remembered our "conversation" about 'The Tale of Two Kitties' . . . words I'm positive Rik never heard me utter. And Scooter — or "Jay", as he'd dubbed himself, giving himself the name only he knew, in true T.S. Elliot style — knew that message would be the only one I'd know for certain was, indeed, from him, and him alone.

Or not so alone . . . if "Zelda" was Mittens. At least that caption in that Metro section had gotten it right — Hemingway-O, Fitzgerald-2.

The kittens may have been a mixture of feline and human DNA, but they were Minnesotans down to their bones . . . .

In memory of Mittens (February, 1998 to October 8, 1998, and Scooter (February, 1998 to November 22, 1998), and Little Boy (September, 2000 to February 18, 2001)

"If personality is an unbroken series of successful gestures, then there was something gorgeous about him, some heightened sensitivity to the promises of life, as if he were related to one of those intricate machines that register earthquakes 10,000 miles away. . . ."

F. Scott Fitzgerald, *The Great Gatsby*
A. R. Morlan, February, 2001

LOST BOOKS

John J. Miller

i.

I came to Albuquerque on my journey to nowhere in particular on a beautiful day in early September, out of gas, out of food, out of money, and nearly out of caring. But man is a creature of habit — myself more than most — so I headed for the university area, where I was most likely to find what I needed to keep on keeping on.

Central Avenue, running along the south edge of the University of New Mexico, was crowded with traffic and drifting groups of students newly returned to school. I found what I was looking for on one of the somewhat quainter and quieter streets south of Central which were studded with small businesses that mainly catered to the campus community.

The storefront's glass window read "Oasis Bookstore, Mr. Amrou, Proprietor Rare Unusual Out of Print Books" in a particularly elegant and flowing script. There were also several lines of Arabic, but my language skills were not up to the translation. It looked like a possibility.

As I stood there the front door suddenly flew wide open with a cheerful tinkling of bells, and a trio of frat boys, unhappy frat boys at that, pushed through. The one in the lead shouldered by me without a glance, while muttering something about "fucking ragheads" under his breath. I watched them as they went down the street in an angry knot, wondering if they had a specific beef or were just bigoted in general.

Inside the store it was cooler and darker than in the sharp Albuquerque sunshine. I was immediately hit by a most familiar smell compounded of the unavoidable dust associated with thousands of volumes, aged paper and leather, and those odors the books themselves had absorbed down through the decades and centuries. A few people, mostly students, were browsing the shelves, which extended in orderly rows from the floor to the ceiling, from the front of the store to the back. Comfortable old chairs were also scattered about. Those sitting in them were reading, except for the chubby calico cat, who was asleep.

"Mr. Amrou?"

The man sitting in the most comfortable-looking chair, which was located behind the counter, looked up from the Arabic newspaper he was reading. He looked Arabic himself in dress, complexion, and features. He wore the traditional Peninsular white robe, belted with a black cord, but was bare-headed and clean shaven. He was short, but not small. Once he must have been a physical marvel, and even now, probably well into his seventies, he was rather impressive. His shoulders were broad, but somewhat hunched. As he stood to greet me I noticed that his legs were bowed, as if he'd once spent a great deal of time on horseback. In age his frame had turned lean, not fat. His face was lean as well, with a hooked nose that had a dent half way down its great, sweeping arc, as if it had once stopped something hard and sharp. An accompanying scar ran down his left cheek, almost to his jaw.

"Yes? Can I help you?" His voice was firm, his English without accent. His dark eyes were old, yet utterly focused.

I glanced down at the books I carried and even then, hesitated. Too much sacrifice, Yeats said, can make a stone of the heart. But if my heart was a stone, it was some kind of soft, porous sedimentary rock, not sharp and brittle like obsidian. I was short of food, of gas, of money. I had no choice. I had to sacrifice something, and I'd decided on the Dunsanys.

"I wonder if you'd be interested in buying these books." I put them on the counter.

The Putnam first editions of *The Chronicles of Rodriguez* and *The King of Elfland's Daughter*, from 1922 and 1924 respectively, were signed by both Dunsany and Sidney Sime, his illustrator. They were matching volumes quarter-bound in vellum with gilt lettering on spine and front cover. They were both quite scarce. *The Chronicles* had had an edition of five hundred, *King* half that. Sime's signature on the frontispiece was a delicate fountain-pen flow, Dunsany's a bold quill scrawl. I loved the books for their intrinsic beauty, and also because each had actually been held by the two great talents, artist and illustrator, who had produced them. But it was either them, I'd decided, or my Cabell Storisende Edition. It hadn't been an easy choice.

Mr. Amrou caressed the books as he looked through them carefully.

"Ah, yes," he said, "very fine. Not terribly old, but somewhat rare." He looked up at me. "I regret I cannot offer you what they are worth. Today, they would be very hard to sell. Few read Dunsany any more."

I sighed. I'd been expecting a negative sales pitch. It was the typical negotiating tactic employed by most booksellers when asked to actually *buy* a book.

"Well, of course —" I began.

"I can give you seven-fifty for them," Mr. Amrou said.

I stopped. "Seven *hundred* and fifty?" I asked. "Dollars?"

Mr. Amrou smiled. His teeth were white, even, and strong. Unusual for an old guy of Middle Eastern extraction, I thought distractedly. "Of course."

"Well . . . sure."

I was relieved at being relieved of the necessity of bargaining, and pleasantly surprised. I had expected an initial offer in the two hundred dollar range. Mr. Amrou's offer was fair. I figured they were worth twelve hundred, maybe more, if he could find someone interested in buying them. I was so relieved that I hated to trouble Mr. Amrou further, but there was no help for it.

"Umm," I said, as he bought out a ledger-like checkbook from under the counter, "I'm afraid I don't have a local bank account. I'm . . . passing through . . . the area."

He looked at me, more speculative than judgmental. "You would prefer cash?"

"If it's no trouble."

"Not at all. I need to see your identification. Just a formality, of course."

"Of course." I took my driver's license from my wallet and handed it over.

Mr. Amrou glanced at my name and photo. "You are Duncan Braun?"

"Yes." Of course I know what he meant. Of course I was Duncan Braun. That's what it said on the license. Was I though, *the* Duncan Braun? Not many remembered *the* Duncan Braun any more, though this was a bookstore, after all.

"I much admired *Cities of the Dead*," he finally said. "You caught the essence of Egypt."

"Thanks."

I waited for the next question — "But what happened to the rest of the story?" — to which I had evolved a series of replies over the last four years. Lately I'd taken to saying simply, "It's dead," adding mentally, "Dead as my career." But the question never came. Mr. Amrou put his checkbook away.

"I perceive," he said, "that you are a book man. A book man in need of . . . various things. Money, of course. Shelter, certainly. As it happens, I need assistance in my store. I could not pay much, but perhaps you would find it a congenial atmosphere. There is even a small room in the back, not without its comforts, which you could use. And, of course, you could retain these."

He pushed the Dunsanys back toward me.

I opened my mouth to turn down his offer, but something froze my tongue. I'd been two years on the road traveling to nowhere, living out of my van and off my collection, selling it bit by bit when either I or the van needed to eat. I had little left. Of anything. The years in motion hadn't helped. I was tired. Maybe what I needed was the familiar, not the always new. I looked around the dusty, homey little shop. Few things were more familiar to me than used bookstores. My wife and I had haunted them with religious regularity. They were our favorite place for treasure hunting. Mr. Amrou's Oasis seemed the used bookstore archetype. Shelves and shelves of slightly dusty volumes, hiding in their midst who knows what delights. Soft lighting. Comfortable chairs. Even a cat for that dash of color.

I looked at Mr. Amrou. Exotic as he was, there was familiarity about him, almost as if I'd seen his face before. Of course, during my research for *Cities of the Dead*, I'd seen hundreds of photos of old men who looked like him. He was an archetype himself, almost. And who knows? Maybe I had seen his very photo in a book somewhere, once. Maybe Mr. Amrou had led an interesting life before he'd found the unlikely place of Albuquerque, New Mexico, to open his Oasis. Maybe he had been, in his time, part of history.

All I knew now was that the relentless moving, the constant hopping around like one disaffected molecule in an otherwise placid solution, hadn't helped. Maybe quiet would. And, I thought, you couldn't get any quieter than this dusty little shop in this nothing little city in the middle of nowhere in particular.

Of course, I was wrong about that as I'd been wrong about so much in my life

ii.

I settled into my role easily enough.

The first thing I did after moving into the little room in the back was make friends with the cat, a three year old chubby calico named Kleopatra. She was a sweet little thing who took her job of rubbing against the customers' legs and sleeping on the comfy chairs very seriously. I don't know how good she was at catching mice, but she was great at catching zzzz's and hunting down un-occupied laps. Mr. Amrou was genuinely fond of her and spent good portions of his afternoons reading in his comfortable chair with Kleo asleep on his lap.

Mr. Amrou was more of a puzzle than his cat. He seemed a quiet, thoughtful man, an insatiable reader who devoured books in English, Arabic, German, French, and a few languages I couldn't readily identify, despite having a way about him that suggested he'd once led a much more active life. It wasn't entirely the way he moved, though, for an old guy his movements were smooth, effortless, and damn *quiet*. (Once or twice in the first few days he snuck up on me unintentionally and I jumped a foot in the air when I suddenly heard his soft voice at my elbow.) There was also that sense of familiarity about him, but I had no clue at all as to where I might have seen him before. He never spoke about himself or his past, and since I don't like to speak about myself or my past, I'm not one to pry into others'.

The clientele of The Oasis was mostly what you'd expect for a small used bookstore near a university — students ragged and preppie, some professorial types, the usual "book people" of assorted ages and sexes and incomes who had their particular collector bents. One pale young woman, pretty in an intense sort of way, was a grad student who was a poetry fanatic. She came in a couple of times a week and Mr. Amrou always had a volume or two for her, usually cheap reprints or paperbacks that he discounted further for her. Her favorites were Yeats, Blake, and Dylan Thomas, though Mr. Amrou sometimes pressed other poets on her. They often had long discussions, even on the days when she came in and had no money for books. Another student was a Doc Savage fan. Though familiar with those old pulps, I wasn't exactly an expert on the series, though Mr. Amrou seemed at home discussing the minutiae of Clark Savage, Jr. and his five aides as he was discussing Celtic mythology with Maria. He held any Doc Savage's that came into his store for the young man, and even sold him the later volumes, which were rather scarce and becoming rather pricey, at a discount.

Not that Mr. Amrou was running a charity. He received numerous packages of books from far-away cities on a regular basis. One of my more pleasant tasks was to receive these shipments, so I got to handle rare volumes on a multitude of subjects on a daily basis. He had customers for non-fiction of academic interest and for classic and modern fiction of collectible interest. The store was usually fairly busy, and he had a strong mail-order clientele as well.

About three weeks after my arrival, on one of the rare days when Mr. Amrou was absent, I was shelving some books near the poetry area and nearly bumped one of the regulars, the grad student poetess. She smiled at me, a quick flash of white teeth behind full red lips.

"Hello," she said. "My name is Maria Elena Altamonte."

"Duncan Braun." I nodded, turned back to the stack of books I was placing into their proper niches on the "Literary Criticism" shelf.

"Mr. Amrou says you're a writer," Maria said to my back.

I stopped shelving and turned back to her slowly. "I was."

She smiled again. "How do you stop being a writer? I mean, once you write something, and have it published, aren't you always a writer?"

"Well." I could see that she could see that we were nearing dangerous water. I didn't want to be churlish. She was young, and pretty, and sincere. I was none of those things, but I didn't want to disappoint her. "Let's say I'm on a long vacation."

"Okay." Her eyes held me long enough that I began to feel a little desperate. My gaze slipped past her and landed on the shelf behind.

"Say, have you read C. P. Cavafy?" I asked.

"Um, no."

"You should." I reached past her, close enough so that I could have caressed her cheek if I'd wanted, and pulled a volume off the shelf. "He was the greatest Greek poet of the twentieth century. E.M. Forster called him the poet laureate of Alexandria. I —"

And it hit me.

"I —" I stuttered, "I know you like poetry."

"Sure. Thanks." Maria took the volume, then looked at me curiously. "You all right?"

I smiled back, somewhat sickly I'm sure. "I just had one of those moments. You know, something has been nagging you for awhile, maybe a couple of weeks. Your brain is searching for a connection. Maybe . . . maybe it's someone you think you've seen before, but you can't place him. Or her. Then suddenly, when you're not expecting it, when you're thinking about something unrelated, it comes to you in a flash. You know where you've seen him."

She smiled again. I would have liked her smile a lot, if I was thinking about her at all.

I'm afraid that Maria thought I went odd on her. I said a distracted goodbye, waving off payment for the Cavafy. Somehow I got through the rest of the afternoon. It was Monday, so The Oasis closed early. As soon as I was able to shoo out the last customer, close and count down the register, and put the take in the floor safe behind the counter, I went to my van and dragged out the small trunk. This was the locked trunk, not the larger one that held the remnants of my once fabulous collection. I lugged it into my snug little room in the rear of the store, and opened the padlock for the first time since I'd undertaken my modern day odyssey with no Penelope waiting patiently for my return.

On top of the pile inside the trunk was a manuscript labeled *Books of the Dead*. I set it aside quickly. Even now, I could barely stand to look at it. Clearly, the mysterious Mr. Amrou had gotten pretty deeply under my skin to force me to go even this far.

Also inside the trunk were a couple of notebooks filled with plot points, character skeletons, and the such. I am an inveterate researcher and note-taker. Gathering the information in those notebooks had taken over a year of my life. I hesitated, resisting the temptation to skim them and relive the past that they represented. Kleo wandered into the room and jumped up next to me on the rumpled bed, watching with intent feline interest as I finally set all but one notebook aside.

Cities of the Dead, the first part of my magnum opus, had two plot threads, one set in modern Egypt, the other during the reign of Ramesses II. *Books of the Dead*, the unpublished sequel, put the characters from *Cities* into other periods of Egyptian history. One of the segments was set in Alexandria around 640 A.D., during the Arab conquest. The connection had come to me when I'd mentioned Cavafy. I leafed through the notebook on Alexandria, until I found the notes on the Arab conquest led by 'Amr ibn al-Asi. I had a couple pages of notes from various sources, but the lines from E. M. Forster's history and guide, *Alexandria*, were the most telling: "He was an administrator, a delightful companion, and a poet — one of the ablest and most charming men that Islam ever produced. He would have been remarkable in any age . . ."

A chill gripped me, centered in my stomach. A wave of dislocation threatened to wash me out of the comfortable little room with the fat little cat purring by my side, into an unknown and unknowable universe. Sure, I wrote fantasy. I never believed in any of it, believed it could be real. That was why it was called *fantasy*, for Christ sakes!

A piece of folded paper was tucked among the pages of notes. I stared at it for nearly a minute. Kleopatra stood and stretched, startling me out of my reverie. I looked at her.

"What do you think?" I asked. "Should I take a look?"

Her meow was inconclusive, but I knew I couldn't walk away. Not this time.

I reached for the sheet of paper, unfolded it. It was a xerox of an enlarged photo of an Egyptian coin issued after the Arab conquest. The coin bore the portrait of a stern-looking man whose nose had been dented by a sword stroke, his face cut by an accompanying scar. It was the face of Mr. Amrou, who today looked maybe twenty years older than the image on the coin.

I could buy the coincidence that he facially resembled the old Arab. I could buy the coincidence that they both had slashed noses and similar scars. But I couldn't buy both.

Not both.

iii.

Mr. Amrou appeared as I was opening The Oasis the next morning. We exchanged hellos and he settled down in his comfortable chair behind the counter and cracked open his Arabic newspaper. I had a hundred questions to ask him, but could get none past my teeth. How could I? In a situation like this, you really had to find the right opening, and nothing appropriate was coming to mind. *Say, Mr. Amrou, how old are you, really? Did you conquer Egypt in the six-hundreds? What's it like to have your face on a coin?*

Fortunately customers began to arrive, and if their needs didn't exactly take my mind off my discovery, at least they kept me busy. As the morning passed Mr. Amrou was never far from my thoughts. Once or twice he caught me looking at him semi-surreptitiously, and he smiled a sharp toothed smile that seemed to promise understanding and offer knowledge I was afraid to acquire.

"Hello again."

I would have started, but the voice that called me back from my reverie was soft and familiar. I turned from the shelf I'd been stocking.

"Thanks for the Cavafy," Maria said.

"You're welcome."

She seemed to hesitate, then gather herself. "Haven't read it all yet. I've been reading something else. *Cities of the Dead*. Mr. Amrou gave me a copy the other day."

"Oh." I felt like I should say something else. "It seems he can find any book, no matter how obscure."

"I wouldn't call it obscure," she said, but I smiled.

"Believe me. I know how many copies it sold."

"Still, it's wonderful. The prose is cool and evocative, the characters are great. And the story!"

I smiled in spite of myself. "I'm glad you liked it," I said.

"But the story isn't finished, is it?"

I shook my head. "No, there were supposed to be two sequels."

"Two? What happened?"

I still couldn't talk about it. I floundered, searching for something to say, then Mr. Amrou's soft yet penetrating voice called out from behind the counter.

"Duncan, it's nearly lunchtime. Why don't you and Maria go over to the Greek place and bring me back something. Take some money from the register."

It was a typical request, combined with a typically generous offer. It was hard to refuse the old man, and hard, I was thinking, to pass up Maria's company. I'd gone so long without any kind of intimacy, that just the thought of eating lunch with a pretty girl fifteen years my junior was enough to make me almost giddy. I felt like I was back in junior high.

The Olympia Café, typical of the businesses on the streets south of Central was small, friendly, somewhat intimate in size and design, and — most important to the university community — cheap. It also served pretty good food. Good enough that it was quickly becoming my habitual luncheon spot. Did I mention that it was cheap? Maria and I sat at a corner table and ordered. We put in a to go order for Mr. Amrou.

Our food arrived quickly. I took a bite of pita smeared with tatziki. The pita was thick and soft, the tatziki cool and sharp. It was quite good. Maria managed a bite of hers without dripping too much sauce, and fixed me with her dark eyes.

"Well," she said, "are you going to tell me about it?"

"It?"

She rolled her eyes. "You don't have to tell me what happened with *Cities of the Dead* if you don't want to. But I'm interested."

"Of course," I said. I had carried it around inside all these years, unable to discuss it. But now something had changed. I felt like I wanted to. Almost as if I had to.

It wasn't a terribly unusual story for anyone familiar with the life and trials of a free-lance writer, if a little extreme in some details. I'd always wanted to be a writer. I sold my first story when I was sixteen. Fame, however, was not immediate. I sold stuff off and on through college, but was pondering the necessity of a real job when I met Donna Greene my senior year. We were quickly married and it truly was a match made in heaven. She believed in me, in my talent and future as a writer. She took a job, I wrote. Fame was still not immediate.

The next ten, twelve years were a struggle. The market was tough. Publishing was changing. The mid-list was drying up and a lot of writers were vying for a few spaces on the racks. I sold a fair amount of short stuff. Did some non-fiction articles for magazines. Even sold a couple of books, mostly media tie-ins. I took some part-time jobs over the rougher patches, but we wouldn't have survived without Donna's constant support, both financial and moral.

When I got the idea for the Egyptian trilogy I knew it would be a major undertaking which I'd have to concentrate on to the exclusion of all else. It took over a year to research the background of *Cities of the Dead*, and another year and half to write it. I didn't want editorial interference with my vision, I didn't want an artificial deadline, so I submitted *Cities* as a completed manuscript. My agent got me an advance of twelve thousand dollars. It did okay saleswise, but we thought we'd be able to build momentum with subsequent volumes, particularly since critical reception had been quite favorable. *Cities* was short-listed for several major awards, though it won none of them. I was already hard at work on the sequel, *Books of the Dead*, and we hoped for a larger advance and even larger royalties as the series took off.

Then, disaster. The multi-national corporation that owned my publisher was taken over by another multi-national. My editor was fired in the subsequent down-sizing and *Books* became an orphan. It didn't help that sales of the first volume hadn't set the world on fire. Plus, this was a time of increased terrorism from the Middle East. My books were set in the Middle East, my protagonist was an Arab. There was little interest in an exploration of his culture. Then, of course, the real disaster struck. Donna was injured in a horrific car accident — caused by an uninsured drunk driver running a red-light — that put her in the hospital, in a coma that she never woke from. She spent months in the hospital. The insurance ran out, then the bit of money we'd managed to save, and then, mercifully, her system shut down. Her brain stopped functioning in any meaningful sense and I could allow her to die. Some of me died with her.

"So," I said, sopping up the last bit of tatziki with a chunk of pita, "I hit the road. I had to sell the house to pay for the final months of her hospitalization, anyway, so it made sense at the time. All I had left was my book collection. I've been selling that off bit by bit over the past couple of years. From Portland, Maine to Portland, Oregon, from Key West to Puget Sound. More running, I guess, than looking. Just trying to get away. Then I came to The Oasis."

"I . . ." I know she wanted to say more, but couldn't find the words.

I shrugged. "It's life. You're dealt it, then you have to live it."

Her hand dropped down to my forearm, gave it a brief squeeze.

"And speaking of The Oasis, and Mr. Amrou," I said after a long moment when actually neither of us were speaking of anything, "we'd better get his lunch to him."

We polished off our plates, and got Mr. Amrou's order. I glanced at Maria as we walked out of the café, and she caught my look.

"What?"

She already probably thought I was one weepy son of a bitch. I didn't want her to think I was crazy, as well, but I wondered if she knew more about the old bookseller than I did.

"How long has he had the store?"

"Not too long. It opened last year."

"Know anything about him?"

"Not much, other than he's a nice old man. And knowledge-able. Seems like he's read damn near everything." She looked at me speculatively. "Why the interest?"

"Well . . ." How, I thought to myself, do I phrase this delicately? *You see, I think he's a lot older than he looks. I think he conquered Egypt once, about fourteen hundred years ago.* There was no way to phrase it delicately. It would be better, I thought, to simply show her the evidence and let her figure it out. "I've got something to show you, if you're interested."

"Some etchings?" Maria asked with a raised eyebrow.

I had to smile myself. "A xerox, actually." I opened The Oasis's door, and she preceded me into the store. "But I guarantee you'll find it —"

I stopped because she'd stopped so suddenly that I walked into her staring at the tableau before us. Mr. Amrou stood before the counter. Three students were facing him. The one in the middle said, "You fucking raghead." and I recognized the frat boy I'd seen my first day in Albuquerque. One of the others had been with him then. Either I just didn't recognize the third, or he was the new bigot in the crowd. The one who'd cursed at Mr. Amrou lifted his closed fist.

"Hey!" Maria said, and started forward fearlessly. I followed her, somewhat less fearlessly but at least willingly, but there was no way we'd reach him in time to stop him.

As his fist descended in a looping arc Mr. Amrou's hand shot out, caught his wrist, and twisted. The frat boy went down to his knees howling. Mr. Amrou frowned. The others hesitated, then started forward. By then Maria had pushed between them.

"What's going on here?" Maria demanded.

"It is nothing," Mr. Amrou said. "Merely a difference in opinion."

"I'll get your ass for this, you fucking geezer," the frat boy ground out between compressed lips. Mr. Amrou smiled and twisted the boy's wrist. The old man's sleeve had fallen back, exposing a browned arm with muscles that stood out like knots, and veins and tendons like cords. The frat boy howled, and flopped on the floor like a gaffed fish.

"Not in this lifetime, little one," Mr. Amrou said gently, and started for the front door. He brushed past the boy's cronies, who parted like the Red Sea. Frat boy crawled along on his knees, his face twisted in pain. Mr. Amrou opened the door and with one hand flung him outside. He looked at the other two. "Join your friend. Never return to my establishment."

They left. Mr. Amrou closed the door after them.

"Ah," he said, spying the brown paper bag I carried, "lunch."

He snagged the bag as he swept past us, and went behind the counter to settle in his comfortable chair. Kleopatra appeared from nowhere to sit before him and beg scraps.

I looked at Maria and she looked at me. I shrugged, shaking my head. I had the feeling that we hadn't seen the last of them and, damn it, for once in my life I was right.

iv.

One of Maria's room-mates answered when I knocked on the door of the small stucco house she rented with a trio of fellow grad students in the student ghetto south of Central.

"Come on in," she offered, then called over her shoulder, "Your date's here, Maria."

My eyebrows rose slightly as I entered the bungalow's neat entranceway. Maria's room-mate dropped onto the more than somewhat dilapidated couch that dominated the small living room, and picked up her book, which she pretended to read.

Maria, as she entered from one of the back bedrooms, frowned at her room-mate as she passed by her. "Don't mind Jennifer. She exaggerates."

"It's all right," I said, and then leaned forward to whisper, "though we should find some place a little more, um, private."

"Afraid of what you're going to show me?"

"You'll probably think I'm a nut," I said. "And the fewer people who think that, the better."

"Okay." She took me by the arm and led me to the door, calling over her shoulder. "See you, Jenny. Don't wait up."

Jenny deigned to look up from her book for half a second. "As if."

"We'll just walk," she said when we were on the substantially deserted sidewalk. "It's a nice night. Warm. Nice moon. Besides, I think better when walking."

"All right." I reached into my pocket for the folded xerox. Though there was a full moon, we walked on for twenty yards or so until we were under a corner streetlight. She took the xerox, and gazed at it for a long time. Finally, she looked up at me.

"And this coin is from where and when, exactly?"

"Egypt, after the Arab conquest. In the 640's."

She continued to look at me. "It's him, isn't it?"

I nodded. "It appears to be."

"I . . ."

I nodded again after I realized she wasn't going to say anything else. "Exactly."

"You'd think," Maria said, "that as a poet I'd be comfortable with this idea."

"Hell," I said, "I write fantasy, and it scares the crap out of me."

"Who is he? The man on the coin, I mean?"

"Amir 'Amr ibn al-Asi. He conquered Egypt in 640 with an army of 4,000 horsemen, ruled it for awhile as governor, then went on to have numerous other adventures on behalf of his Caliph. Forster calls him one of the finest men produced by Islam. There's an informative article on him in *The Concise Encyclopedia of Islam*. There's a copy in the store, if you want to see it."

She nodded. "Okay."

We weren't far from The Oasis. We turned in the right direction, and as we headed for it, Maria hooked her arm in mine, resting her hand on my forearm. Her fingers felt good on my arm.

"I should mention something about 'Amr."

"Go ahead."

"After he'd occupied Alexandria in 641, a famous peripatetic philosopher named John the Grammarian, who was living in the city at the time, asked him if he could have the royal library."

"*The* library?" Maria asked.

"The library of Alexandria," I confirmed. "The largest, most comprehensive repository of knowledge in the ancient world. Though the collection was past its peak by the 600's, there's no doubt that the hundreds of thousands of scrolls it contained was still the greatest single collection of writing in the entire world."

"That's quite a request," Maria asked.

"Amr thought so, too. He told John that it was beyond his power to grant, but that he would ask his Caliph in Baghdad."

They walked in silence, until Maria prompted me with a squeeze of my forearm. "And?"

I sighed. "Sorry. I was just thinking . . . wondering what would have happened if he hadn't been goaded into writing the Caliph . . . what treasures were lost . . . poetry, philosophy, whole histories, science . . . At any rate — the Caliph's reply was not favorable. Basically, he said that if the books in the library agreed with the Koran, they weren't needed because what they said was already in the Koran. If they contradicted the Koran, they weren't needed, because, well, they contradicted the Koran. In either case, they were useless. So burn them all."

"So that's how the library at Alexandria was destroyed?"

"Yep. The scrolls, volumes, and manuscripts were distributed among Alexandria's four thousand public baths, to serve as fuel in the furnaces that warmed the bath water. It took six months for the library to be consumed."

"Fire," Maria said in a stricken voice.

"Yep, by fire."

"No," she said. Her hand grasped my forearm so tightly that her fingernails sunk into my flesh. "I mean, FIRE!"

I looked in the direction she pointed. We stopped halfway across the street, stunned.

The Oasis was burning.

The fire had just started. In fact, I saw a figure dart through the front door and rush down the dark street. My first reaction was to chase him, but as I saw flames dance behind the glass windows of The Oasis, I realized that my trunk was still in the back room. My trunk with the only extant manuscript of *Books of the Dead*, about ninety percent finished, locked in it. My trunk which was not fireproof and would burn to ashes that would be the only remnants of two years of research and writing. For years I hadn't cared about the manuscript at all; suddenly it seemed the most important thing in the world.

I turned to Maria. "Find a phone. Call 911."

"You can't go in there," she cried, clutching my arm.

"I've got to get my manuscript for *Books of the Dead*. I'll be quick."

"Be careful," she called as I pulled away. "Be damned careful!"

"Don't worry," I called back and dashed across the street, hitting the door at a dead run.

From the outside the flames licking the back wall were pretty in a dazzling, dancing sort of way. There were almost cheery. Inside they were damn hot and scary. They spread fast in the few moments it took me to enter the store. They were concentrated at the rear, jumping and darting about. The dry volumes were catching like tinder. Tongues of heat leapt across aisles and ran up and down the shelves.

The trunk, I thought, get the damn trunk and get the hell out of there. I took a short breath, already choking on the acrid smoke. Sweat sprang out on my forehead from the almost intolerable heat, and then my heart stopped, and skipped a terrible beat as from somewhere among the stacks, came a short, terrified, meow. It was Kleopatra. She called out again, a small, frightened bleat drenched with fear.

"Goddamn it!" I said aloud, and choked as I drew in a deep breath. I hadn't cared about my manuscript for years, and now, finally, when I did, I was going to lose it. Goddamn it! This time I had the sense to swear mentally and not drag more smoke into my lungs. Where was she? Where would Kleo hide? Suddenly, I thought I knew. I vaulted over the counter, squinting against the smoke that coiled like black nooses around my throat.

"Kleo!" I called in a low voice, as calmly as I could. "Here kitty, here kitty kitty!"

A near-suffocated meow told me my instinct was right. The flickering light of the flames revealed her huddled form on Mr. Amrou's chair. She saw me, and meowed again, as sparks jumped around the chair, catching. I grabbed her. She snuggled her face against my neck. I could feel her pounding heart, and muttered into her side, "That's one life down."

Crouching, trying to get lower than the smoke that was quickly filling the room, I scuttled from behind the counter. A bookcase behind me collapsed in a pillar of fire, scattering sparks in all directions. Some fell like burning pinpricks on the back of my hands, arms, and neck, and then I was hurtling against the front door. It flung wide as I choked on the deadly smoke, and someone pulled me outside and pounded out the sparks burning on my back and in my hair.

"Are you okay?" Maria asked, crying, "Are you okay?"

"Yeah," I coughed, leaning against her for a moment. "Yeah."

"Murrrroww," Kleo contributed, as we held her between us.

"Your manuscript?" Maria said, in a broken voice.

I sighed. "Toast." I was too sad to cry.

There was a moment of silence, then Maria said in an odd voice, "Maybe not."

I turned away from her, to look back into The Oasis. Old houses crammed with old books in a hot, dry climate burn rapidly. You couldn't see the back wall any more for the sheet of flame that burned across it like a backdrop to hell, but you could see the old man calmly stroll through the inferno, a small trunk hoisted on his shoulder, unhurried, unworried, and untroubled by the all consuming flames. Their dancing tongues licked him, but left no trace of their touch. If I had any doubts as to his supra-natural nature, they were gone as he calmly opened the door, closed it behind him and approached us on the sidewalk.

"I see that I am indebted to you for saving my Kleopatra," Mr. Amrou said calmly, as he put the trunk down at his feet.

"I —" I began, swallowed hard, and said, "No problem."

"Not many men would have rushed into a burning building. Fewer yet would have been diverted from their original goal to save a cat."

Kleo was making sounds of dissatisfaction, so I handed her to Mr. Amrou, who accepted her gratefully. "I figured I could always write it again, I guess."

Mr. Amrou gestured at the trunk. "Fortunately, you do not have to."

"Who are you?" I asked.

He continued to smile. "I think you know." He turned back to face the burning Oasis. "Once I was a man who, through misplaced loyalty, committed a great crime." He looked back at us.

"Since then, I have committed my entire existence to atoning for that crime."

"Yet," Maria said, "the books burn again."

Mr. Amrou shrugged. "Yes, but times have changed. Things are different now. These books burn, but I will acquire other copies of them, and put them into the hands of those who will love and cherish and learn from them. Make no mistake." His face darkened, and I could see the man who had once conquered Egypt. "The one who did this will pay. He will suffer for his act. But another oasis will spring from the ashes of this one. Books can still burn in this age, but they will not be lost, they will not be forgotten." He looked at me. "Unless their author wishes so."

"Yes," I said. "You're right."

He smiled a thousand year old smile of wisdom and peace. "Welcome back."

I nodded.

We stood together, student, author, cat, and displaced spirit from an ancient world, agent of God knows what gods, and watched as The Oasis burned. Before long, the fire trucks arrived, but they were too late to save much of anything.

By that time, Maria and I had left. We'd gone back to her house. I had to make a phone call. It was late on the east coast, but, what the hell, I hadn't bothered my agent for a long time. He owed me.

Mr. Amrou stood imperturbably on the sidewalk, stroking his purring cat, watching The Oasis burn, already planning the new oasis that would arise, phoenix-like, from the ashes of the old, and the volumes that he would fill it with to delight and comfort, enlighten and inform, all down through the coming decades and centuries.

ONE COPY ONLY

Ramsey Campbell

Call it fantasy. Call it addiction if you like. At least its effects are more benign than those that bring criminals before me. Take today's case, though it could have been any of a hundred where a denizen of the estate beyond the hill crossed town to rob a homeowner. The thief loaded his pockets with jewels but left his victim's first editions, merely flinging them off the shelves to make sure none of them was a storage box and using a few pages to demonstrate how he'd been trained as a child. As for his victim, the old dear may not even need crutches for the whole of what's left of her life. Her assailant was doing his best to appear incapable of causing so much damage: he was thinner than last time I'd had him in court, and wearing a new suit to compensate. He still watched you sidelong, showing as little of his face as he could, and kept feeling his chin for stubble as if to signify how much he missed the decoration. His social worker spoke up for him, and his lawyer applied himself to casting doubt on the victim and the police, so that barely enough of the jury found against the culprit to let him be sent to stay with many of his friends from the estate, though not for as long as I would have wished and of course not as long as I announced. If that leaves me more resigned than enraged, it's at least partly because I have to persuade myself yet again that Ken Gregory and I didn't do worse for less — not that I would expect anyone to understand who wasn't a privileged customer of Books Forever.

I've no idea how many there may be — it's one of several questions I wouldn't presume to ask. Quite a number of the customers are postal and have never seen the shop. I learned of it ten years ago, when the bookshop chains had begun to devote themselves to fewer and fatter titles, no doubt fattening their authors in the process. I still leafed through any books that seemed at all promising, but the best they had to offer were imitations of greatness: even Clarence Colman Hope had abandoned his visions of dark worlds illuminated by magic and heroism, having thought up a protagonist to my mind too criminal to be presented as a hero. I turned to spending my Saturday afternoons in the second-hand establishments, and in a Care For Children shop I was rewarded more than I immediately realised with a handful of issues of *Fantasy Magazine* the best part of forty years old. Not only did they cost me under a fiver, but when I sat down after dinner to them and a brandy, I found stamped on each contents page the address of Books Forever.

Some of the tales told of challenges met and wrongs righted, and I thought there might be more where they came from. The next day I walked across the city to the hill. A November wind was sweeping the thoroughfares that swarmed with litter, and bearing stenches of the pinched streets of pygmy houses past the hill, the reek of charred garbage and of buildings set on fire to terrify the occupants or bring an end to them. The hill was the edge of that territory, and I found it hard to believe it could support a bookshop.

From the foot of the narrow potholed street I managed to distinguish part of a sign at the summit. Boo, it cried, a kind of glimpse I'd known to lead me only to a chemist's or a bookmaker's. Nevertheless I toiled up the uneven pavement crowded with parked cars, past sullen huddles of neglected houses, past cramped front gardens that doubled as play areas and rubbish tips, until I gained the height. Books Forever stood in the custody of a wine store and a Pakistani corner shop daubed with swastikas. Its meager window was so grimy I was barely able to discern shelves packed with books. Sunday had left it closed and lightless, and its sometime painted door displayed no opening hours, but the presence of so many books and the possibility that some might store up wonders brought me back. Indeed, I returned the very next day as soon as I was able to leave my chambers.

On the hill gangs of children stared as if I had mistaken my course, not they theirs. Several called out words and suggestions I should have hoped never to see admitted to print. Since they were too young for the law to apply, I could only soldier onward. The last of the sunset lingered on the hill, so that the window over the faded sign of Books Forever glowed as though the sun had found a haven above the stunted houses, while it was impossible to determine whether the lower window was lit from within. When I applied my shoulder, the door stumbled inward under the unwelcoming clunk of the bell.

The man seated at the venerable desk on the far side of the dim room crammed with books on shelves and on the floor barely raised his face from the task of slipping photocopied catalogues into envelopes, and I couldn't tell for the sunset in his eyes whether he was gazing at me or beyond. He had a high wide frowning forehead, a long wedge of a face, a sprawl of grey hair that rested on the shoulders of his shabby leather jacket. "Are you closing?" I felt bound to enquire.

He gazed at me as if hoping for better and fingered his forehead, adding more ink to its wrinkles. "Depends what you're after."

"A good book."

"I don't buy any other kind."

"I found your address in a magazine I bought in the Care For Children shop. Four issues from the fifties, the whole set."

"*Fantasy Magazine,*" he said as though answering a question almost too easy to be acknowledged. "Should have brought them back here."

"I will if you think I ought to."

"Not you. The old fellow who bought them and then turned in his ticket, or his family should have looked where they came from, more like. They're your style, are they?"

"Anything that lets me see past the horizon."

He seemed to focus on me at last. "Look around," he said. "There's a light if you need it."

The unstable brass switches were just inside the doorway, by a bookcase piled with volumes too tall or too crippled to stand.

Three bare bulbs came alight above the cramped aisles. Perhaps shadows deepened the bookseller's frown, or perhaps he mistook for dislike my reaction to the spectacle of thousands of books arranged only by author. "This is how bookshops used to be," I hastened to remark.

"It's how you find what you didn't know you wanted," he said and turned back to his catalogues.

There was no lack of favourite names — Haggard, Hope, Malory, Tolkein — and nothing that I hadn't read by them. I looked into several novels that apparently promised to be fantastic, but the worlds they revealed were altogether too mundane. I was kneeling before the Vs when a fragile old man in a tweed overcoat and matching hat clambered down the stairs behind the desk. From the glances both he and the bookseller threw in my direction as the old man hurried empty-handed out of the shop, I took him as some kind of private customer. In case the proprietor wanted to close for the night I called "Could you recommend something?"

"MacDonald," he responded without looking up.

A book under that name boasted a knight in armour on its spine, while the cover had him on horseback, surrounded by goblins. He and the price were enough to send me with the book to the desk. "If it's no good to you," the bookseller said as he consigned the volume to a supermarket bag, "bring it in."

At least I was being invited to return. I picked my way down-hill to the nearest car park and drove to my apartment, the higher floor of a detached Victorian town house. After dinner, which would have been either half of last night's casserole or the first half of that day's, I entrusted myself to the book. The armoured horseman proved to be not a knight but the old king; the hero was a miner's son who rescued him and married the princess. After their deaths the city was destroyed by greedy mining of the gold beneath it. The novel was a children's book.

Rather than resent being thought childish, I appreciated the recommendation, not one any other bookseller I'd encountered would have been sufficiently imaginative to propose. It was my kind of tale, and would have been during my childhood if my parents hadn't confined me to improvingly prosaic fiction about the supposed deprivations of youngsters unluckier than the reader. At the end of a week of establishing at least a modicum of temporary protection for the public I returned to Books Forever.

The bookseller looked ready to be disappointed as he said "Had enough of it?"

"On the contrary, I've kept it to read again. Have you anything else as good?"

He fingered his inky forehead as if it contained a Braille message. "White," he said, and went back to securing a parcel with tape.

The name led me to a corner out of sight of his desk. I had barely touched the copy of *The Sword in the Stone* when he declared "That's the early version, the best one."

He was clearly pleased that I trusted his advice. "We'll be seeing you again, shall we?" he asked as I paid for the book.

"I'll be in to see what's new or rather what's good."

"I'll keep an eye open for you," he said, and extended a hand of friendship. "Ken Gregory."

"Chris Miles," I confided over a handshake that faintly inked my fingers, and left him when the ageing phone rang or more accurately rattled on the desk.

At home I discovered he had sold me another children's book. While parts of it were wry, it did sound the note of heroism. Next he introduced me to the tales of Alan Garner at the rate of one a week. The fourth concerned itself too much with the brand of teenage awkwardness the defenders of young miscreants try to offer as an excuse, and it was the only volume I returned to the shop. Gregory met it with wide-eyed surprise that aggravated his frown. "Not your kind of myth?" he said.

"I'm more than happy reading adult books. Doesn't anybody write the sort of fantasy they used to?"

I remember my exact words and the way he gazed at me, as though attempting to peer deep into me or to decide whether I had given him a password. After quite a pause he said "Maybe you should have a session with my private stock."

On two further occasions I'd seen customers descend the stairs. Each had bought a book from the public shelves; I assumed the price included payment for whatever they'd concealed about them. "I didn't mean adult in that sense," I said as neutrally as I could.

"Nor me either. Just trying to make your dreams come true."

He seemed honestly disappointed, but the impression remained that the contents of the upper room were somehow illegitimate. I took it as my duty to investigate. "Then I shouldn't turn you down," I said and stepped behind his desk.

"I ought to tell you I only keep reading copies upstairs."

"By which you're implying . . ."

"If you find anything you like you'll have to read it while you're there."

I found this yet more suspect, and felt uncomfortably conspiratorial as I set foot on the lowest stair. Once I began to climb I felt insecure as well. The stairs were even steeper than they had appeared to be, and the wall seemed uncertain of its grip on the right-hand banister, while the left rail shifted as if all its crutches were about to prove inadequate. I had no doubt the bookseller could find himself in trouble for endangering his customers. By taking the stairs as a challenge I succeeded in reaching the top. Faced with a door that stood invitingly ajar, if only because it was unable quite to close, I pushed it wide.

The room beyond was smaller than I expected. Beneath a baggy ceiling webbed with cracks the stained walls were brown as aged pages. On either side of a burst armchair that squatted in front of the window a bookcase was less than full of books, none of which immediately looked objectionable. Through the dwarfish window, over the ridges of a few mean roofs, I could see the sky but no horizon. As I trod on the ragged carpet, to be greeted by a smell suggesting that the redolence of all the oldest books had gathered in the upper room, I glanced about for a switch but found none. "Is there a light?" I called.

"There'll be enough."

There was. Indeed, although the sun was nowhere to be seen, one book appeared to stand out from the rest as if a sunbeam had fallen on it, illuminating the words on the spine: *The Glorious Brethren* by Clarence Colman Hope. I had never heard of it, and yet it sounded unblessed with his recent cynicism. I read the opening pages and was hardly conscious of sitting down to read the entire book, in the armchair that contrived to be unobtrusively accommodating. The story told of a band of almost invincible and practically deathless knights who intervened on the side of the just when summoned by faith, and well short of the end I recognised it as Hope's finest work. Having lingered over the final scene, in which after the victory over Hitler the knights withdraw into the mists and are heard by a wounded soldier to vow "Till the world has need of us again", I would gladly have reread the book from start to finish. I was making my way to the door when Gregory hurried upstairs. "I'm guessing you found something to your taste," his head remarked over the threshold.

"As you see. May I make you an offer? Whatever you think reasonable."

"It's the only copy, sorry," he said, staring up beneath his fiercest frown. "Not for sale."

I assumed he was waiting for its value to increase, even if that would be hindered by the absence of a jacket. As I reluctantly consigned the volume to a shelf I was tempted to wish there were books whose nature might make him eager to appreciate my overlooking them, but I saw that the room hid nothing of the kind. "If you want another read of it," he said, "you can always come back."

I felt obliged to buy some item to express my gratitude. I bought a Tolkein omnibus, another edition of which I already owned, and bade Gregory adieu until next week. I was surprised to meet twilight outside the shop so soon after the brightness of the upper room, but my mind was still brimming like a chalice with the book I'd read.

Despite Gregory's offer, I was loath to take advantage of him, especially at the end of a Monday spent in preventing wrongdoers from doing so to the law. That evening I stayed in town to visit More 'n' Books. Beyond the posters for signings by chefs and footballers and television actresses a few books had found space among a mob of snowmen in the window. I struggled through crowds of shoplifters or customers to the fantasy section, which was manned by a youth with a shaved pate at odds with his kaftan. "Can I put you together with anything?" he said.

I'd had conversations with him before despairing of the present trend in fiction, and had found him to be knowledgeable. "A book by Clarence Colman Hope," I told him.

"We've got him signing his new one next month, but you said you don't like them that gritty." He glanced around before murmuring "Nor me either."

"I'm looking for an early book. *The Glorious Brethren*."

He raised a hand as if to feel for a recrudescence of hair. "Would you know who by?"

"I just told you."

"We've never had it. In fact I'm sure —" Instead of finishing his supposition he typed the title on a computer. "There, I was certain I'd have heard of it," he said. "Never published and not forthcoming."

"I assure you it has been published. I've not only seen it but read it."

"If you can get more details we'll try and order it for you," he said, though plainly more convinced by his machine than by me, and then gave in to asking "What was it like?"

"Altogether his best."

"If you're at the signing you'll have to tell him."

"You think that might put him back on the right path."

"Somebody should if they can."

Who was better qualified than I? But I'd forgotten Christmas. I delayed visiting Books Forever until the weekend, only to find the shop locked for a week. As I trudged downhill past houses sparkling like constellations of stars so false they had fallen to earth, I could almost have imagined I had merely dreamed of mounting to the upper room, where a light appeared to have been left burning for the benefit of some solitary reader, unless it was the glow of the smudged sun.

Christmas resurrected memories of peace. At Midnight Mass in the church opposite my apartment I was able to believe for an hour that the children in the choir might never descend from the heights of mystery, even once their voices did. I spent the quiet week reaffirming the community I shared with a few friends, and in my hours alone read Tolkein in the edition I'd recently bought, though it was corrupted by misprints of which my old copy was innocent. All too soon a New Year as wicked as its predecessor was upon us, bringing revelry that turned into violence, some of the perpetrators of which it was my burden to judge. I wearied of their lies and excuses long before the week was done, and that Saturday I climbed the hill in something like despair. But the shutters had gone.

Gregory glanced up as though the clenching of his frown had raised his head, then nodded to me. "May I go up?" I asked at once.

"There's nobody else."

I took this for assent and hauled myself upstairs as swiftly as was safe. I was unsurprised to find the upper room offered more light than the sullen shady sky. I retrieved *The Glorious Brethren* from the shelf and examined the spine, then both sides of the title page, before taking the book to the threshold. "Do you know who published this?"

"Wait there." Gregory was already more than halfway up the stairs. "Which is it?" he said, then didn't look. "It'll be a proof copy. That's why they don't have jackets and some other bits and pieces, and why I can't sell them."

"It's Clarence Colman Hope. They need to know the publisher at More 'n' Books so they can order it for me."

Gregory shrugged as if attempting to dislodge an encumbrance that had landed on his shoulders. "He's only ever had one publisher I know of," he said, and watched until I replaced the volume on the shelf. None of its companions displayed a publisher's name. I lowered myself down the stairs to find Gregory awaiting me, his frown pressing his eyes narrow. "What will you be telling them?" he said.

I couldn't see that he'd committed any offence, and so I tried to reassure him. "I won't mention where I found it if you'd rather I didn't."

"This was my father's shop. That was his room."

"I understand," I said, uncertain whether I did.

"He died up there. He said he wouldn't come down till he'd finished all the books he wanted to read."

"I imagine I know how he felt."

"He had the strongest mind I've ever come across. He didn't care about anything but books."

For a moment I had the dismaying impression that the son proposed to cite childhood neglect to extenuate some crime. "We all care about those," I said, and left him.

Outside it was darker than seemed reasonable for the hour or after the illumination of the upper room. The twitching of obsolescent Christmas lights urged me downhill. The bogus snowmen that stood guard in the window of More 'n' Books showed no sign of melting. The aisles were clogged with clots of youngsters demonstrating in various ways their hostility to books. In the fantasy section several children were leafing through pornographic comics while their cronies contented themselves with disarraying the alphabet. I should have expected the assistant with the grey pate to intervene, but perhaps he was abashed by his kaftan. He limited himself to telling me "I did a search for that title you asked after."

"May I look forward to having it soon?"

"I'm afraid that's all you'll be able to do." He took time to produce an apologetic smile before adding "It must have been some dream."

"Please make yourself clear."

"The book doesn't exist."

"You'll excuse me, but I've had a proof of it in my hands."

"Did it have a publisher?"

"None was shown."

"Then that's no proof."

Though he'd let his smile drop, I couldn't judge if he was mocking me. I was close to betraying Gregory's confidence, but instead I suggested "Perhaps you can trace another book for me."

"If our computer can't nothing can."

"*The Club of the Seven Dreamers* by H. P. Lovecraft."

He tapped the keyboard and sent an arrow darting about the screen. After some minutes he said "Never published."

"Then *The House of the Worm* by the same author."

It took him less time to decide to say "No sign of that either."

"Try *Last Dangerous Visions* by —"

"I know it," he said, smiling as if someone had winked at him. "You aren't going to say you've seen that too."

Of course I had seen all of them in Gregory's upper room, but

I'd heard enough to indicate that the assistant was as lacking in imagination as the computer. "You mentioned you'd have Clarence Colman Hope here this month," I said.

"I did."

That sounded wary enough to be a question. "When may we meet him?" I enquired.

"Next week."

"More precisely, please."

"Saturday," the assistant was compelled to admit, and handed me from a stack on a counter a glossy sheet advertising Hope's appearance and *The Third Book of Shagrat the Sly*. As I turned away he watched me, visibly regretting having given me the information, and I felt suspected of mischief. On the very few occasions when my parents had cause for that, they would fall silent enough to suggest I had done away with them — the first time for hours, the next for days, the last for nearly a week. I had learned not to plead and rage in my desperation to revive them, but now the injustice I was suffering and the sight of the children left unchecked among lewdness found the voice in which I pronounce sentence. "Perhaps someone in authority will see fit to escort these boys somewhere more suitable," I advocated, and as staff and loiterers gawped at me, went forth from the shop.

I might have sought solace in Books Forever, but my skull had begun to feel crushed, as it did when my parents' silence closed around it. For much of the rest of the weekend I lay on my bed, watched over by books that had been crowded out of the sitting-room. This was scarcely enough preparation for the succeeding week, throughout which the jury seemed bent on flaunting its distrust of the law. More than determination to hear Hope acknowledge his best work drove me when the week was executed to return to More 'n' Books.

The snowmen had been ousted from the window by posters of Hope's strongly angular square-bearded face and by piles of his books. A few seconds' survey confirmed that *The Glorious Brethren* was nowhere in evidence, and so I followed the throng to the performance area. This was a large upstairs room, bare except for a table heaped with *Shagrat the Sly* and confronted by perhaps a hundred sketchy chairs. Most were occupied, and I seated myself on the back row, eyed by the assistant with the scraped pate, who had donned a suit in deference to the celebrity. I saw him resolve to accost me, only to be prevented by the arrival several minutes late of Clarence Colman Hope.

I might not have recognised him. His beard had vanished, exposing his chin as weaker than he'd made it appear, and he was grown plump as a stuffed goose. He was at least a head shorter than any of his characters, and shorter still when measured against myself. He left no doubt that he was meant to be the centre of attention by flourishing his fists above his head and roaring "Where's the applause?" Once that had subsided, and the assistant had stumbled through a redundant introduction during which his subject fed himself swigs of wine and mimed falling asleep, the author set to reading aloud passages from *Shagrat the Sly* of which I struggled to believe he could never be proud. Even worse than the way Shagrat stole and lied and cheated to defeat his opponents was the presentation of their magical skills as a pretext for his behaviour, as if envy can ever be an excuse. Worst of all were Hope's knowing glances at his audience beneath a cocked eyebrow that incited them to share his esteem for his creation. I could only clamp my lips together and wish at least some of the laughter to be merely dutiful. Eventually the ordeal was brought to an end, and the assistant was inviting questions when Hope interrupted him. "I see some of you've got old books of mine. I'll sign them all so long as you buy the new one first."

Two people with laps heaped with books laboured to their feet and tramped out shamefaced, and I wondered if they had been the only others of my mind. I was heartened when the first questioner to be chosen, a young woman with waist-length hair surmounted by an ornate silver comb, ventured to ask "Will you be writing any more heroic fantasy?"

"Being a writer's heroic and all I write is fantasy."

"I meant will you ever write any more like —"

"You mean you want me to regress."

"No, just — "

"Just not letting anyone else get a word in, eh? I hope she quiets down when she's reading at least," the author said with a leap of one eyebrow that advised his audience they were expected to laugh, which a few did. "My turn for a question. How many of you would buy three hardcovers of it if I wrote some more old stuff?"

One girl's hand shot aloft, and two more wavered up elsewhere in the room. "Well, you're my kind of readers. I'll be putting special messages in yours," Hope told them. "Only you aren't enough. I'd need everyone here and the rest of my fans to buy themselves a trio to keep my sales up where they ought to be. In case some of you are better at fantasy than sums, that means Midas tried reissuing my dusty stuff and only shifted a third of what Shagrat does for them."

"Are you saying," a man with a senile pony-tail suggested, "you can't afford to write the kind of book you'd like to?"

Hope stared wordlessly at him for quite a pause, until the assistant mumbled red-faced "Another question. Yes —"

"Let's have someone more my age," Hope interrupted. "Big lady at the back."

"What can you tell us about *The Glorious Brethren?*"

"Give us a clue what you want to hear."

"When you wrote it and when it's to be published."

He looked as if he regretted having selected me. "Not one of mine," he declared. "Doesn't sound like it ever would be, either."

"I've seen it," I assured him.

"Then you must be even better at fantasy than me," Hope said, jerking up an eyebrow to ensure everyone else saw the joke.

I was about to inform him where the book was to be found until I realised that would put it at risk. Suppose it was indeed the only copy? I waved away any further dialogue, and the assistant was hastily choosing another questioner when someone in the middle of the room said "I've seen it too."

Before I'd finished willing that to have been elsewhere than Books Forever I recognised him as one of Gregory's privileged customers, a stooped shaggy greying man with an unnecessarily large head. "I can show you if you like," he said. "It's here in town."

"What is?" Hope demanded.

As I drew breath to head off the information, though I had little idea how, the crouched man said *The Glorious Brethren.* It's got your name on it. It's in a shop."

Hope gazed at him and then at me, and I made the worst mistake of my life: I glanced aside as though from guilt. "You two can show me where once I've finished signing," Hope said, no longer amused. "We'll have a few more questions and then get to the books."

I thought of approaching my fellow customer in case I could dissuade him from escorting Hope, but I feared that would only waste time. As I hurried out I saw the author glower at my leaving and the assistant look relieved. Entangled in my urgency was the unhelpful realisation that secretly I'd started to believe *The Glorious Brethren* existed for myself alone. I dodged through the Saturday crowds and dashed up the hill, egged on by the lascivious comments of children and by the flickering of laggard Christmas lights. I hoped Books Forever would be locked, but one thrust of my shoulder threw the door wide.

Ken Gregory was pencilling prices in books on his desk. He met me with the commencement of a smile that quickly sank. "Looks bad," he said.

"I'm afraid it may be. I'm dreadfully sorry."

"Long time since anyone's been that round here."

If he had asked me what was wrong it might have required less effort to say "Clarence Colman Hope's in town."

"I heard. Have you met him?"

"Sadly."

"A disappointment, was he? Writers can be. You're best off knowing just their books."

I cleared my throat hard to dislodge words. "I told him about *The Glorious Brethren.*"

To add to my discomfort, Gregory's lips considered grinning. "How did he take it?"

"He's on his way here."

Gregory opened the next book to enter the price. "Can't blame him."

He seemed not to be suggesting I was to be censured either, but it was shame that made me blurt "Aren't you going to do anything?"

"Such as?" Gregory said with some weariness.

"Shouldn't you hide it at least?"

"There's nowhere any of those books can go except where they are. I found that out the hard way once."

I was so distracted by his resignation that I might have asked him to elaborate if a car hadn't halted outside with a squall of brakes. It was black and slick as an eel, the Jaguar that disgorged Hope and his stooped admirer. The man barely had time to open the door for the author and sidle aside before Hope stalked in. As he saw me his face grew puce and petulant, but he addressed the bookseller. "I'm Clarence Colman Hope. I'm told you've got something you want people to believe is mine."

"We usually have you in stock."

Hope appeared to be taking that as a crafty insult when the stooped man strayed close to him. "It's upstairs," the man muttered, blushing with pride at having been of service, and indicated the route with a furtive thumb.

Hope strode to the gap beside the desk and planted his hands on his inflated hips. "Are you letting me go up?" he demanded of Gregory.

"I don't see anybody in your way."

The author advanced to the foot of the stairs and seized the banisters. As he set his weight on the first tread he looked suspicious of a trap. For the whole of his ascent the stairs performed a hoarse melody of protest. The stooped man was moving to follow when Gregory brandished an inky palm. "Not you, and don't ever come back."

The man averted his slumped face as he fled the shop, leaving the door ajar on the sight of a gang of children eyeing the Jaguar. I trudged in his wake, but Gregory called to me "Just shut the door."

I felt both pardoned and uneasy as I heard Hope plodding across the upper room. "Where's some bloody light?" he was complaining. Perhaps his eyes adjusted to whatever gloom he found or brought with him, because his footsteps halted where I knew bookshelves to be. "What's this?" he said in a voice subdued for him.

The silence endured longer than I was able to hold my breath. I glanced at Gregory, then away from his lack of an expression. At last Hope's footfalls thundered overhead, preceded to the doorway by his shout. "I don't know who faked this, but I'll be making sure the lawyers find out, and by God when they do — "

By this time he had set about descending with one hand on the banister. I caught myself wishing for an instant that he had missed his footing, but that wasn't why his shout became a savage gasp. *The Glorious Brethren* had slipped from his clutch, because there was suddenly too little of it to hold. What fluttered through the air was nothing but dust and scraps no larger than postage stamps, which crumbled as they settled to the floor. He glared down at the ruin of the book in baffled rage, then lurched back into the upper room. "All right then, I'll take something else," he vowed. "There's plenty here for the law to sort out."

The bookseller stood so abruptly that a heap of books tumbled across the desk as his chair clattered against the wall. He flung himself at the stairs and scrambled up like a monkey. "What else are you going to destroy that you can't do yourself?" he cried as he ran overhead. "Here's *Edwin Drood* that Dickens finished after all. Here's *Arthur Gordon Pym* that Poe did. Or *The Castle of the Devil*, how about that? That's some Robert E. Howard you won't find anywhere else. And look here, Malcolm Lowry did complete his last novel. Hang on though, maybe this is rarer, *The Night of the Eye!*"

He named other books too, a flood of them. He must have meant Hope to be unable to choose from so many, but his voice fell like the final rumble of a storm. "It's going to be Dickens, is it? You think there's already enough of him in the world."

I heard Hope retreat from the shelves and saw him back out of the room, another book in his hand. I have no idea what I might have done, but by the time I darted past the desk it was too late. I never knew if they were only Gregory's feet that rushed across the upper room. I glimpsed the snatching of the book from Hope's grasp, but did I see him pushed? I know I saw him hurl himself thoughtlessly backwards as though to avoid some contact. His head was first to strike the floor, followed by his body at an angle that wrenched his mouth into an agonised grimace, unless it was the crunching of his neck that did. His heels dealt the leg of the desk a convulsive kick that threw several books on top of him, and then he was still.

As I dragged my gaze clear of Hope's distorted outraged face, Gregory leaned out of the upper room. His eyes weren't quite admitting to a question. Before I could acknowledge it and decide on my response, we heard a car draw up outside, and the window began to throb with light. The next moment a double slam of metal doors heralded the entrance of two policemen.

It was only later that I learned they had been summoned by a householder to deter children from breaking into Hope's car. I had to deal immediately with their presence. "There's been an accident," I told them. "This chap lost his footing on the stairs not a minute ago. He'd been drinking. I'm a witness if you need one. I'm a judge."

I may always remember the look of astonishment adjoining disbelief with which Gregory met that revelation. I waited until the ambulance had cleared Hope's remains away, and answered the few questions the police found it necessary to ask. Since then Gregory and I have never discussed the incident, but I know he understands how deeply I value his shop. Without the treasures of the upper room I might despair not just of my calling but of life itself. I never leave Books Forever without having made a purchase, but for years the purpose of my visits has been to reread a solitary volume: *The Return of the Brethren* by Clarence Colman Hope.

PIXEL PIXIES

Charles de Lint

Only when Mistress Holly had retired to her apartment above the store would Dick Bobbins peep out from behind the furnace where he'd spent the day dreaming and drowsing and reading the books he borrowed from the shelves upstairs. He would carefully check the basement for unexpected visitors and listen for a telltale floorboard to creak from above. Only when he was very very sure that the mistress, and especially her little dog, had both, indeed, gone upstairs, would he creep all the way out of his hidden hobhole.

Every night, he followed the same routine.

Standing on the cement floor, he brushed the sleeves of his drab little jacket and combed his curly brown hair with his fingers. Rubbing his palms briskly together, he plucked last night's borrowed book from his hidey-hole and made his way up the steep basement steps to the store. Standing only two feet high, this might have been an arduous process all on its own, but he was quick and agile, as a hob should be, and in no time at all he'd be standing in amongst the books, considering where to begin the night's work.

There was dusting and sweeping to do, books to be put away. Lovely books. It didn't matter to Dick if they were serious leather-bound tomes or paperbacks with garish covers. He loved them all, for they were filled with words, and words were magic to this hob. Wise and clever humans had used some marvelous spell to imbue

105

each book with every kind of story and character you could imagine, and many you couldn't. If you knew the key to unlock the words, you could experience them all.

Sometimes Dick would remember a time when he hadn't been able to read. All he could do then was riffle the pages and try to smell the stories out of them. But now, oh now, he was a magician, too, for he could unearth the hidden enchantment in the books any time he wanted to. They were his nourishment and his joy, weren't they just.

So first he worked, earning his keep. Then he would choose a new book from those that had come into the store while he was in his hobhole, drowsing away the day. Sitting on top of one of the bookcases, he'd read until it got light outside and it was time to return to his hiding place behind the furnace, the book under his arm in case he woke early and wanted to finish the story while he waited for the mistress to go to bed once more.

*   *   *

I hate computers.

Not when they do what they're supposed to. Not even when I'm the one who's made some stupid mistake, like deleting a file I didn't intend to, or exiting one without saving it. I've still got a few of those old war-horse programs on my machine that doesn't pop up a reminder asking if I want to save the file I was working on.

No, it's when they seem to have a mind of their own. The keyboard freezing for no apparent reason. Getting an error message that you're out of disc space when you know you've got at least a couple of gigs free. Passwords becoming temporarily, and certainly arbitrarily, obsolete. Those and a hundred other, usually minor, but always annoying, irritations.

Sometimes it's enough to make you want to pick up the nearest component of the machine and fling it against the wall.

For all the effort they save, the little tasks that they automate and their wonderful storage capacity, at times like this — when everything's going as wrong as it can go — their benefits can't come close to outweighing their annoyances.

My present situation was partly my own fault. I'd been updating my inventory all afternoon and before saving the file and backing it up, I'd decided to go on the Internet to check some of my competitors' prices. The used book business, which is what I'm in, has probably the most arbitrary pricing in the world. Though I suppose that can be expanded to include any business specializing in collectibles.

I logged on without any trouble and went merrily browsing through listings on the various book search pages, making notes on the particularly interesting items, a few of which I actually had in stock. It wasn't until I tried to exit my browser that the trouble started. My browser wouldn't close and I couldn't switch to another window. Nor could I log off the Internet.

Deciding it had something to do with the page I was on — I know that doesn't make much sense, but I make no pretense to being more than vaguely competent when it comes to knowing how the software actually interfaces with the hardware — I called up the drop-down menu of "My Favourites" and clicked on my own home page. What I got was a fan shrine to pro wrestling star Steve Austin.

I tried again and ended up at a commercial software site.

The third time I was taken to the site of someone named Cindy Margolis—the most downloaded woman on the Internet, according to the *Guinness Book of World Records*. Not on this computer, my dear.

I made another attempt to get off-line, then tried to access my home page again. Each time I found myself in some new outlandish and unrelated site.

Finally I tried one of the links on the last page I'd reached. It was supposed to bring me to Netscape's home page. Instead I found myself on the web site of a real estate company in Santa Fe, looking at a cluster of pictures of the vaguely Spanish-styled houses that they were selling.

I sighed, tried to break my Internet connection for what felt like the hundredth time, but the "Connect To" window still wouldn't come up.

I could have rebooted, of course. That would have gotten me off-line. But it would also mean that I'd lose the whole afternoon's work because, being the stupid woman I was, I hadn't had the foresight to save the stupid file before I went gadding about on the stupid Internet.

"Oh, you stupid machine," I muttered.

From the front window display where she was napping, I heard Snippet, my Jack Russell terrier stir. I turned to reassure her that, no, she was still my perfect little dog. When I swiveled my chair to face the computer again, I realized that there was a woman standing on the other side of the counter.

I'd seen her come into the store earlier, but I'd lost track of everything in my one-sided battle of wits with the computer — it having the wits, of course. She was a very striking woman, her dark brown hair falling in Pre-Raphaelite curls that were streaked with green, her eyes both warm and distant, like an odd mix of a perfect summer's day and the mystery you can feel swell up inside you when you look up into the stars on a crisp, clear autumn night. There was something familiar about her, but I couldn't quite place it. She wasn't one of my regulars.

She gave me a sympathetic smile.

"I suppose it was only a matter of time before they got into the computers," she said.

I blinked. "What?"

"Try putting your sweater on inside out."

My face had to be registering the confusion I was feeling, but she simply continued to smile.

"I know it sounds silly," she said. "But humour me. Give it a try."

Anyone in retail knows, you get all kinds. And the second-hand market gets more than its fair share, trust me on that. If there's a loopy person anywhere within a hundred blocks of my store, you can bet they'll eventually find their way inside. The woman standing on the other side of my counter looked harmless enough, if somewhat exotic, but you just never know anymore, do you?

"What have you got to lose?" she asked.

I was about to lose an afternoon's work as things stood, so what was a little pride on top of that.

I stood up and took my sweater off, turned it inside out, and put it back on again.

"Now give it a try," the woman said.

I called up the "Connected to" window and this time it came up. When I put the cursor on the "Disconnect" button and clicked, I was logged off. I quickly shut down my browser and saved the file I'd been working on all afternoon.

"You're a life-saver," I told the woman. "How did you know that would work?" I paused, thought about what I'd just said, what had just happened. "*Why* would that work?"

"I've had some experience with pixies and their like," she said.

"Pixies," I repeated. "You think there are pixies in my computer?"

"Hopefully, not. If you're lucky, they're still on the Internet and didn't follow you home."

I gave her a curious look. "You're serious, aren't you?"

"At times," she said, smiling again. "And this is one of them."

I thought about one of my friends, an electronic pen pal in Arizona, who has this theory that the first atom bomb detonation forever changed the way that magic would appear in the world. According to him, the spirits live in the wires now instead of the trees. They travel through phone and modem lines, take up residence in computers and appliances where they live on electricity and lord knows what else.

It looked like Richard wasn't alone in his theories, not that I pooh-poohed them myself. I'm part of a collective that originated this electronic database called the Wordwood. After it took on a life of its own, I pretty much keep an open mind about things that most people would consider preposterous.

"I'd like to buy this," the woman went on.

She held up a trade paperback copy of *The Beggars' Shore* by Zak Mucha.

"Good choice," I said.

It never surprises me how many truly excellent books end up in the secondary market. Not that I'm complaining — it's what keeps me in business.

"Please take it as thanks for your advice," I added.

"You're sure?"

I looked down at my computer where my afternoon's work was now safely saved in its file.

"Oh, yes," I told her.

"Thank you," she said. Reaching into her pocket, she took out a business card and gave it to me. "Call me if you ever need any other advice along the same lines."

The business card simply said "The Kelledys" in a large script. Under it were the names "Meran and Cerin" and a phone number. Now I knew why, earlier, she'd seemed familiar. It had just been seeing her here in the store, out of context, that had thrown me.

"I love your music," I told her. "I've seen you and your husband play several times."

She gave me another of those kind smiles of hers.

"You can probably turn your sweater around again now," she said as she left.

Snippet and I watched her walk by the window. I took off my sweater and put it back on properly.

"Time for your walk," I told Snippet. "But first let me back up this file to a zip disk."

*　*　*

That night, after the mistress and her little dog had gone upstairs, Dick Bobbins crept out of his hobhole and made his nightly journey up to the store. He replaced the copy of *The Woods Colt* that he'd been reading, putting it neatly back on the fiction shelf under "W" for Williamson, fetched the duster, and started his work. He finished the "History" and "Local Interest" sections, dusting and straightening the books, and was climbing up onto the "Poetry" shelves near the back of the store when he paused, hearing something from the front of the store.

Reflected in the front window, he could see the glow of the computer's monitor and realized that the machine had turned on by itself. That couldn't be good. A faint giggle spilled out of the computer's speakers, quickly followed by a chorus of other voices, tittering and snickering. That was even less good.

A male face appeared on the screen, looking for all the world as though it could see out of the machine. Behind him other faces appeared, a whole gaggle of little men in green clothes, good-naturedly pushing and shoving each other, whispering and giggling. They were red-haired like the mistress, but there the resemblance ended. Where she was pretty, they were ugly, with short faces, turned-up noses, squinting eyes and pointed ears.

This wasn't good at all, Dick thought, recognizing the pixies for what they were. Everybody knew how you spelled "trouble." It was "P-I-X-Y."

And then they started to clamber out of the screen, which shouldn't have been possible at all, but Dick was a hob and he understood that just because something shouldn't be able to happen, didn't mean it couldn't. Or wouldn't.

"Oh, this is bad," he said mournfully. "Bad bad bad."

He gave a quick look up to the ceiling. He had to warn the mistress. But it was already too late. Between one thought and the next, a dozen or more pixies had climbed out of the computer onto her desk, not the one of them taller than his own waist. They began riffling through her papers, using her pens and ruler as swords to poke at each other. Two of them started a pushing match that resulted in a small stack of books falling off the side of the desk. They landed with a bang on the floor.

The sound was so loud that Dick was sure the mistress would come down to investigate, her and her fierce little dog. The pixies all stood like little statues until first one, then another, started to giggle again. When they began to all shove at a bigger stack of books, Dick couldn't wait any longer.

Quick as a monkey, he scurried down to the floor.

"Stop!" he shouted as he ran to the front of the store.

And, "Here, you!"

And, "Don't!"

The pixies turned at the sound of his voice and Dick skidded to a stop.

"Oh, oh," he said.

The little men were still giggling and elbowing each other, but there was a wicked light in their eyes now, and they were all looking at him with those dark, considering gazes. Poor Dick realized that he hadn't thought any of this through in the least bit properly, for now that he had their attention, he had no idea what to do with it. They might only be a third his size, individually, but there were at least twenty of them and everybody knew just how mean a pixy could be, did he set his mind to it.

"Well, will you look at that," one of the pixies said. "It's a little hobberdy man." He looked at his companions. "What shall we do with him?"

"Smash him!"

"Whack him!"

"Find a puddle and drown him!"

Dick turned and fled, back the way he'd come. The pixies streamed from the top of Mistress Holly's desk, laughing wickedly and shouting threats as they chased him. Up the "Poetry" shelves Dick went, all the way to the very top. When he looked back down, he saw that the pixies weren't following the route he'd taken.

He allowed himself a moment's relief. Perhaps he was safe. Perhaps they couldn't climb. Perhaps they were afraid of heights.

Or, he realized with dismay, perhaps they meant to bring the whole bookcase crashing down, and him with it.

For the little men had gathered at the bottom of the bookcase and were putting their shoulders to its base. They might be small, but they were strong, and soon the tall stand of shelves was tottering unsteadily, swaying back and forth. A loose book fell out. Then another.

"No, no! You mustn't!" Dick cried down to them.

But he was too late.

With cries of "Hooray!" from the little men below, the bookcase came tumbling down, spraying books all around it. It smashed into its neighbour, bringing that stand of shelves down as well. By the time Dick hit the floor, hundreds of books were scattered all over the carpet and he was sitting on top of a tall, unsteady mountain of poetry, clutching his head, awaiting the worst.

The pixies came clambering up it slopes, the wicked lights in their eyes shining fierce and bright. He was, Dick realized, about to become an ex-hob. Except then he heard the door to Mistress Holly's apartment open at the top of the back stairs.

Rescued, he thought. And not a moment too soon. She would chase them off.

All the little men froze and Dick looked for a place to hide from the mistress's gaze.

But the pixies seemed unconcerned. Another soft round of giggles arose from them as, one by one, they transformed into soft, glittering lights no bigger than the mouth of a shot glass. The lights rose up from the floor where they'd been standing and went sailing towards the front of the store. When the mistress appeared at the foot of the stairs, her dog at her heels, she didn't even look at the fallen bookshelves. She saw only the lights, her eyes widening with happy delight.

Oh, no, Dick thought. They're pixy-leading her.

The little dog began to growl and bark and tug at the hem of her long flannel nightgown, but she paid no attention to it. Smiling a dreamy smile, she lifted her arms above her head like a ballerina and began to follow the dancing lights to the front of the store. Dick watched as pixy magic made the door pop open and a gust of chilly air burst in. Goosebumps popped up on the mistress's forearms but she never seemed to notice the cold. Her gaze was locked on the lights as they swooped, around and around in a gallitrap circle, then went shimmering out onto the street beyond. In moments she would follow them, out into the night and who knew what terrible danger.

Her little dog let go of her hem and ran ahead, barking at the lights. But it was no use. The pixies weren't frightened and the mistress wasn't roused.

It was up to him, Dick realized.

He ran up behind her and grabbed her ankle, bracing himself. Like the pixies, he was much stronger than his size might give him to appear. He held firm as the mistress tried to raise her foot. She lost her balance and down she went, down and down, toppling like some enormous tree. Dick jumped back, hands to his mouth, appalled at what he'd had to do. She banged her shoulder against a display at the front of the store, sending yet another mass of books cascading onto the floor.

Landing heavily on her arms, she stayed bent over for a long time before she finally looked up. She shook her head as though to clear it. The pixy lights had returned to the store, buzzing angrily about, but it was no use. The spell had been broken. One by one, they zoomed out of the store, down the street and were quickly lost from sight. The mistress's little dog ran back out onto the sidewalk and continued to bark at them, long after they were gone.

"Please let me be dreaming . . ." the mistress said.

Dick stooped quickly out of sight as she looked about at the sudden ruin of the store. He peeked at her from his hiding place, watched her rub at her face, then slowly stand up and massage her shoulder where it had hit the display. She called the dog back in, but stood in the doorway herself for a long time, staring out at the street, before she finally shut and locked the door behind her.

Oh, it was all such a horrible, terrible, awful mess.

"I'm sorry, I'm sorry, I'm sorry," Dick murmured, his voice barely a whisper, tears blurring his eyes.

The mistress couldn't hear him. She gave the store another survey, then shook her head.

"Come on, Snippet," she said to the dog. "We're going back to bed. Because this is just a dream."

She picked her way through the fallen books and shelves as she spoke.

"And when we wake up tomorrow everything will be back to normal."

But it wouldn't be. Dick knew. This was more of a mess than even the most industrious of hobs could clear up in just one night. But he did what he could until the morning came, one eye on the task at hand, the other on the windows in case the horrible pixies decided to return. Though what he'd do if they did, probably only the moon knew, and she wasn't telling.

*   *   *

Did you ever wake up from the weirdest, most unpleasant dream, only to find that it wasn't a dream at all?

When I came down to the store that morning, I literally had to lean against the wall at the foot of the stairs and catch my breath. I felt all faint and woozy. Snippet walked daintily ahead of me, sniffing the fallen books and whining softly.

An earthquake, I told myself. That's what it had been. I must have woken up right after the main shock, come down half-asleep and seen the mess, and just gone right back to bed again, thinking I was dreaming.

Except there'd been those dancing lights. Like a dozen or more Tinkerbells. Or fireflies. Calling me to follow, follow, follow, out into the night, until I'd tripped and fallen . . .

I shook my head slowly, trying to clear it. My shoulder was still sore and I massaged it as I took in the damage.

Actually, the mess wasn't as bad as it had looked at first. Many of the books appeared to have toppled from the shelves and landed in relatively alphabetical order.

Snippet whined again, but this time it was her "I really have to go" whine, so I grabbed her leash and a plastic bag from behind the desk and out we went for her morning constitutional.

It was brisk outside, but warm for early December, and there still wasn't any snow. At first glance, the damage from the quake appeared to be fairly marginal, considering it had managed to topple a couple of the bookcases in my store. The worst I could see were that all garbage canisters on the block had been overturned, the wind picking up the paper litter and carrying it in eddying pools up and down the street. Other than that, everything seemed pretty much normal. At least it did until I stopped into Café Joe's down the street to get my morning latte.

Joe Lapegna had originally operated a sandwich bar at the same location, but with the coming of Starbucks to town, he'd quickly seen which way the wind was blowing and renovated his place into a café. He'd done a good job with the décor. His café was every bit as contemporary and urban as any of the other high-end coffee bars in the city, the only real difference being that, instead of young college kids with rings through their noses, you got Joe serving the lattes and espressos. Joe with his broad shoulders and meaty, tattooed forearms, a fat caterpillar of a black moustache perched on his upper lip.

Before I could mention the quake, Joe started to tell me how he'd opened up this morning to find every porcelain mug in the store broken. None of the other breakables, not the plates or coffee makers. Nothing else was even out of place.

"What a weird quake it was," I said.

"Quake?" Joe said. "What quake?"

I waved a hand at the broken china he was sweeping up.

"This was vandals," he said. "Some little bastards broke in and had themselves a laugh."

So I told him about the bookcases in my shop, but he only shook his head.

"You hear anything about a quake on the radio?" he asked.

"I wasn't listening to it."

"I was. There was nothing. And what kind of a quake only breaks mugs and knocks over a couple of bookcases?"

Now that I thought of it, it was odd that there hadn't been any other disruption in my own store. If those bookcases had come down, why hadn't the front window display? I'd noticed a few books had fallen off my desk, but that was about it.

"It's so weird," I repeated.

Joe shook his head. "Nothing weird about it. Just some punks out having their idea of fun."

By the time I got back to my own store, I didn't know what to think. Snippet and I stopped in at a few other places along the strip and while everyone had damage to report, none of it was what could be put down to a quake. In the bakery, all the pies had been thrown against the front windows. In the hardware store, each and every electrical bulb was smashed — though they looked as though they'd simply exploded. All the rolls of paper towels and toilet paper from the grocery store had been tossed up into the trees behind their shipping and receiving bays, turning the bare-branched oaks and elms into bizarre mummy-like versions of themselves. And on it went.

The police arrived not long after I returned to the store. I felt like such a fool when one of the detectives came by to interview me. Yes, I'd heard the crash and come down to investigate. No, I hadn't seen anything.

I couldn't bring myself to mention the dancing lights.

No, I hadn't thought to phone it in.

"I thought I was dreaming," I told him. "I was half-asleep when I came downstairs and didn't think it had really happened. It wasn't until I came back down in the morning . . ."

The detective was of the opinion that it had been gang-related, kids out on the prowl, egging each other on until it had gotten out of control.

I thought about it when he left and knew he had to be right. The damage we'd sustained was all on the level of pranks — mean-spirited, to be sure, but pranks nonetheless. I didn't like the idea of our little area being the sudden target of vandals, but there really wasn't any other logical explanation. At least none occurred to me until I stepped back into the store and glanced at my computer. That's when I remembered Meran Kelledy, how she'd gotten me to turn my sweater inside out and the odd things she'd been saying about pixies on the web.

If you're lucky, they're still on the Internet and didn't follow you home.

Of course that wasn't even remotely logical. But it made me think. After all, if the Wordwood database could take on a life of its own, who was to say that pixies on the Internet was any more improbable? As my friend Richard likes to point out, everyone has odd problems with their computers that could as easily be attributed to mischievous spirits as to software glitches. At least they could be if your mind was inclined to think along those lines, and mine certainly was.

I stood for a long moment, staring at the screen of my computer. I don't know exactly at what point I realized that the machine was on. I'd turned it off last night before Snippet and I went up to the apartment. And I hadn't stopped to turn it on this morning before we'd gone out. So either I was getting monumentally forgetful, or I'd turned it on while sleepwalking last night, or . . .

I glanced over at Snippet who was once again sniffing everything as though she'd never been in the store before. Or as if someone or something interesting and strange *had*.

"This is silly," I said.

But I dug out Meran's card and called the number on it all the same, staring at the computer screen as I did. I just hoped nobody had been tinkering with my files.

*   *   *

Bookstore hobs are a relatively recent phenomenon, dating back only a couple of hundred years. Dick knew hobs back home in the old country who'd lived in the same household for three times that length of time. He'd been a farm hob himself, once, living on a Devon steading for two hundred and twelve years until a new family moved in and began to take his services for granted. When one year they actually dared to complain about how poorly the harvest had been put away, he'd thrown every bit of it down into a nearby ravine and set off to find new habitation.

A cousin who lived in a shop had suggested to Dick that he try the same, but there were fewer commercial establishments in those days and they all had their own hob by the time he went looking, first up into Somerset, then back down through Devon, finally moving west to Cornwall. In the end, he made his home in a small cubbyhole of a bookstore he found in Penzance. He lived there for years until the place went out of business, the owner setting sail for North America with plans to open another shop in the new land once he arrived.

Dick had followed, taking up residence in the new store when it was established. That was where he'd taught himself to read.

But he soon discovered that stores didn't have the longevity of a farm. They opened and closed up business seemingly on nothing more than a whim, which made it a hard life for a hob, always looking for a new place to live. By the latter part of this century, he had moved twelve times in the space of five years before finally settling into the place he now called home, the bookstore of his present mistress with its simple sign out front:

Holly Rue — Used Books.

He'd discovered that a quality used book store was always the best. Libraries were good, too, but they were usually home to displaced gargoyles and the ghosts of writers and had no room for a hob as well. He'd tried new bookstores, but the smaller ones couldn't keep him busy enough and the large ones were too bright, their hours of business too long. And he loved the wide and eclectic range of old and new books to be explored in a shop such as Mistress Holly's, titles that wandered far from the beaten path, or worthy books no longer in print, but nonetheless inspired. The stories he found in them sustained him in a way that nothing else could, for they fed the heart and the spirit.

But this morning, sitting behind the furnace, he only felt old and tired. There'd been no time to read at all last night, and he hadn't thought to bring a book down with him when he finally had to leave the store.

"I hate pixies," he said, his voice soft and lonely in the darkness. "I really really do."

Faerie and pixies had never gotten along, especially not since the last pitched battle between them in the old country when the faeries had been driven back across the River Parrett, leaving everything west of the Parrett as pixyland. For years, hobs such as Dick had lived a clandestine existence in their little steadings, avoiding the attention of pixies whenever they could.

Dick hadn't needed last night's experience to tell him why.

After awhile he heard the mistress and her dog leave the store so he crept out from behind the furnace to stand guard in case the pixies returned while the pair of them were gone. Though what he would do if the pixies did come back, he had no idea. He was an absolute failure when it came to protecting anything, that had been made all too clear last night.

Luckily the question never arose. Mistress Holly and the dog returned and he slipped back behind the furnace, morosely clutching his knees and rocking back and forth, waiting for the night to come. He could hear life go on upstairs. Someone came by to help the mistress right the fallen bookcases. Customers arrived and left with much discussion of the vandalism on the street. Most of the time he could hear only the mistress, replacing the books on their shelves.

"I should be doing that," Dick said. "That's my job."

But he was only an incompetent hob, concealed in his hidey-hole, of no use to anyone until they all went to bed and he could go about his business. And even then, any ruffian could come along and bully him and what could he do to stop them?

Dick's mood went from bad to worse, from sad to sadder still. It might have lasted all the day, growing unhappier with each passing hour, except at mid-morning he suddenly sat up, ears and nose quivering. A presence had come into the store above. A piece of an old mystery, walking about as plain as could be.

He realized that he'd sensed it yesterday as well, while he was dozing. Then he'd put it down to the dream he was wandering in, forgetting all about it when he woke. But today, wide awake, he couldn't ignore it. There was an oak king's daughter upstairs, an old and powerful spirit walking far from her woods. He began to shiver. Important faerie such as she wouldn't be out and about unless the need was great. His shiver deepened. Perhaps she'd come to reprimand him for the job so poorly done. She might turn him into a stick or a mouse.

Oh, this was very bad. First pixies, now this.

Whatever was he going to do? However could he even begin to explain that he'd meant to chase the pixies away, truly he had, but he simply wasn't big enough, nor strong enough. Perhaps not even brave enough.

He rocked back and forth, harder now, his face burrowed against his knees.

*   *   *

After I'd made my call to Meran, Samuel, who works at the deli down the street, came by and helped me stand the bookcases upright once more. The deli hadn't been spared a visit from the vandals either. He told me that they'd taken all the sausages out of the freezer and used them to spell out rude words on the floor.

"Remember when all we had to worry about was some graffiti on the walls outside?" he asked when he was leaving.

I was still replacing books on the shelves when Meran arrived. She looked around the store while I expanded on what I'd told her over the phone. Her brow furrowed thoughtfully and I was wondering if she was going to tell me to put my sweater on backwards again.

"You must have a hob in here," she said.

"A what?"

It was the last thing I expected her to say.

"A hobgoblin," she said. "A brownie. A little faerie man who dusts and tidies and keeps things neat."

"I just thought it didn't get all that dirty," I said, realizing as I spoke how ridiculous that sounded.

Because, when I thought about it, a helpful brownie living in the store explained a lot. While I certainly ran the vacuum cleaner over the carpets every other morning or so, and dusted when I could, the place never seemed to need much cleaning. My apartment upstairs required more and it didn't get a fraction of the traffic.

And it wasn't just the cleaning. The store, for all its clutter, was organized, though half the time I didn't know how. But I always seemed to be able to lay my hand on whatever I needed to find without having to root about too much. Books often got put away without my remembering I'd done it. Others mysteriously vanished, then reappeared a day or so later, properly filed in their appropriate section—even if they had originally disappeared from the top of my desk. I rarely needed to alphabetize my sections while my colleagues in other stores were constantly complaining of the mess their customers left behind.

"But aren't you supposed to leave cakes and cream out for them?" I found myself asking.

"You never leave a specific gift," Meran said. "Not unless you want him to leave. It's better to simply 'forget' a cake or a sweet treat on one of the shelves when you leave for the night."

"I haven't even done that. What could he be living on?"

Meran smiled as she looked around the store. "Maybe the books nourish him. Stranger things have been known to happen in Faerie."

"Faerie," I repeated slowly.

Bad enough I'd helped create a database on the Internet that had taken on a life of its own. Now my store was in Faerie. Or at least straddling the border, I supposed. Maybe the one had come about because of the other.

"Your hob will know what happened here last night," Meran said.

"But how would we even go about asking him?"

It seemed a logical question, since I'd never known I had one living with me in the first place. But Meran only smiled.

"Oh, I can usually get their attention," she told me.

She called out something in a foreign language, a handful of words that rang with great strength and appeared to linger and echo longer than they should. The poor little man who came sidling up from the basement in response looked absolutely terrified. He was all curly hair and raggedy clothes with a broad face that, I assumed from the laugh lines, normally didn't look so miserable. He was carrying a battered little leather carpetbag and held a brown cloth cap in his hand. He couldn't have been more than two feet tall.

All I could do was stare at him, though I did have the foresight to pick up Snippet before she could lunge in his direction. I could feel the growl rumbling in her chest more than hear it. I think she was as surprised as me to find that he'd been living in our basement all this time.

Meran sat on her haunches, bringing her head down to the general level of the hob's. To put him at ease, I supposed, so I did the same myself. The little man didn't appear to lose any of his nervousness. I could see his knees knocking against each other, his cheek twitching.

"B-begging your pardon, your ladyship," he said to Meran. His gaze slid to me and I gave him a quick smile. He blinked, swallowed hard, and returned his attention to my companion. "Dick Bobbins," he added, giving a quick nod of his head. "At your service, as it were. I'll just be on my way, then, no harm done."

"Why are you so frightened of me?" Meran asked.

He looked at the floor. "Well, you're a king's daughter, aren't you just, and I'm only me."

A king's daughter? I thought.

Meran smiled. "We're all only who we are, no one of more importance than the other."

"Easy for you to say," he began. Then his eyes grew wide and he put a hand to his mouth. "Oh, that was a bad thing to say to such a great and wise lady such as yourself."

Meran glanced at me. "They think we're like movie stars," she explained. "Just because we were born in a court instead of a hob-hole."

I was getting a bit of a case of the celebrity nerves myself. Court? King's daughter? Who exactly *was* this woman?

"But you know," she went on, returning her attention to the little man, "my father's court was only a glade, our palace no more than a tree."

He nodded quickly, giving her a thin smile that never reached his eyes.

"Well, wonderful to meet you," he said. "Must be on my way now."

He picked up his carpetbag and started to sidle towards the other aisle that wasn't blocked by what he must see as two great big hulking women and a dog.

"But we need your help," Meran told him.

Whereupon he burst into tears.

The mothering instinct that makes me such a sap for Snippet kicked into gear and I wanted to hold him in my arms and comfort him. But I had Snippet to consider, straining in my grip, the growl in her chest quite audible now. And I wasn't sure how the little man would have taken my sympathies. After all, he might be child-sized, but for all his tears, he was obviously an adult, not a child. And if the stories were anything to go by, he was probably older than me — by a few hundred years.

Meran had no such compunction. She slipped up to him and put her arms around him, cradling his face against the crook of her shoulder.

It took awhile before we coaxed the story out of him. I locked the front door and we went upstairs to my kitchen where I made tea for us all. Sitting at the table, raised up to the proper height by a stack of books, Dick told us about the pixies coming out of the computer screen, how they'd knocked down the bookcases and finally disappeared into the night. The small mug I'd given him looked enormous in his hands. He fell silent when he was done and stared glumly down at the steam rising from his tea.

"But none of what they did was your fault," I told him.

"Kind of you to say," he managed. He had to stop and sniff, wipe his nose on his sleeve. "But if I'd b-been braver —"

"They *would* have drowned you in a puddle," Meran said. "And I think you were brave, shouting at them the way you did and then rescuing your mistress from being pixy-led."

I remembered those dancing lights and shivered. I knew those stories as well. There weren't any swamps or marshes to be led into around here, but there were eighteen-wheelers out on the highway only a few blocks away. Entranced as I'd been, the pixies could easily have walked me right out in front of any one of them. I was lucky to only have a sore shoulder.

"Do you . . . really think so?" he asked, sitting up a little straighter.

We both nodded.

Snippet was lying under my chair, her curiosity having been satisfied that Dick was only one more visitor and therefore out-of-bounds in terms of biting and barking at. There'd been a nervous moment while she'd sniffed at his trembling hand and he'd looked as though he was ready to scurry up one of the bookcases, but they quickly made their peace. Now Snippet was only bored and had fallen asleep.

"Well," Meran said. "It's time we put our heads together and considered how we can put our unwanted visitors back where they came from and keep them there."

"Back onto the Internet?" I asked. "Do you really think we should?"

"Well, we could try to kill them . . ."

I shook my head. That seemed too extreme. I started to protest, only to see that she'd been teasing me.

"We could take a thousand of them out of the web," Meran said, "and still not have them all. Once tricksy folk like pixies have their foot in a place, you can't ever be completely rid of them." She smiled. "But if we can get them to go back in, there are measures we can take to stop them from troubling you again."

"And what about everybody else on-line?" I asked.

Meran shrugged. "They'll have to take their chances — just like they do when they go for a walk in the woods. The little people are everywhere."

I glanced across my kitchen table to where the hob was sitting and thought, no kidding.

"The trick, if you'll pardon my speaking out of turn," Dick said, "is to play on their curiosity."

Meran gave him an encouraging smile. "We want your help," she said. "Go on."

The little man sat up straighter still and put his shoulders back.

"We could use a book that's never been read," he said. "We

could put it in the middle of the road, in front of the store. That would certainly make me curious."

"An excellent idea," Meran told him.

"And then we could use the old spell of bell, book and candle. The churchmen stole that one from us."

Even I'd heard of it. Bell, book and candle had once been another way of saying excommunication in the Catholic church. After pronouncing the sentence, the officiating cleric would close his book, extinguish the candle, and toll the bell as if for someone who had died. The book symbolized the book of life, the candle a man's soul, removed from the sight of God as the candle had been from the sight of men.

But I didn't get the unread book bit.

"Do you mean a brand new book?" I asked. "A particular copy that nobody might have opened yet, or one that's so bad that no one's actually made their way all the way through it?"

"Though someone would have had to," Dick said, "for it to have been published in the first place. I meant the way books were made in the old days, with the pages still sealed. You had to cut them apart as you read them."

"Oh, I remember those," Meran said.

Like she was there. I took another look at her and sighed. Maybe she had been.

"Do you have any like that?" she asked.

"Yes," I said slowly, unable to hide my reluctance.

I didn't particularly like the idea of putting a collector's item like that out in the middle of the road.

But in the end, that's what we did.

*   *   *

The only book I had that passed Dick's inspection was *The Trembling of the Veil* by William Butler Yeats, number seventy-one of a 1000-copy edition privately printed by T. Werner Laurie, Ltd. in 1922. All the pages were still sealed at the top. It was currently listing on the Internet in the $450 to $500 range and I kept it safely stowed away in the glass-doored bookcase that held my first editions.

The other two items were easier to deal with. I had a lovely brass bell that my friend Tatiana had given me for Christmas last year and a whole box of fat white candles just because I liked to burn them. But it broke my heart to go out onto the street around 2 a.m., and place the Yeats on the pavement.

We left the front door to the store ajar, the computer on. I wasn't entirely sure how we were supposed to lure the pixies back into the store and then onto the Internet once more, but Meran took a flute out of her bag and fit the wooden pieces of it together. She spoke of a calling-on music and Dick nodded sagely, so I simply went along with their better experience. Mind you, I also wasn't all that sure that my Yeats would actually draw the pixies back in the first place, but what did I know?

We all hid in the alleyway running between my store and the futon shop, except for Snippet, who was locked up in my apartment. She hadn't been very pleased by that. After an hour of crouching in the cold in the alley, I wasn't feeling very pleased myself. What if the pixies didn't come? What if they did, but they approached from the fields behind the store and came traipsing up this very alleyway?

By three-thirty we all had a terrible chill. Looking up at my apartment, I could see Snippet lying in the window of the dining room, looking down at us. She didn't appear to have forgiven me yet and I would happily have changed places with her.

"Maybe we should just —"

I didn't get to finish with "call it a night." Meran put a finger to her lips and hugged the wall. I looked past her to the street.

At first I didn't see anything. There was just my Yeats, lying there on the pavement, waiting for a car to come and run over it. But then I saw the little man, not even half the size of Dick, come creeping up from the sewer grating. He was followed by two more. Another pair came down the brick wall of the temporary office help building across the street. Small dancing lights that I remembered too clearly from last night, dipped and wove their way from the other end of the block, descending to the pavement and becoming more of the little men when they drew near to the book. One of them poked at it with his foot and I had visions of them tearing it apart.

Meran glanced at Dick and he nodded, mouthing the words, "That's the lot of them."

She nodded back and took her flute out from under her coat where she'd been keeping it warm.

At this point I wasn't really thinking of how the calling music would work. I'm sure my mouth hung agape as I stared at the pixies. I felt light-headed, a big grin tugging at my lips. Yes, they were pranksters, and mean-spirited ones at that. But they were also magical. The way they'd changed from little lights to little men . . . I'd never seen anything like it before. The hob who lived in my bookstore was magical, too, of course, but somehow it wasn't the same thing. He was already familiar, so down-to-earth. Sitting around during the afternoon and evening while we waited, I'd had a delightful time talking books with him, as though he were an old friend. I'd completely forgotten that he was a little magic man himself.

The pixies were truly puzzled by the book. I suppose it would be odd from any perspective, a book that old, never once having been opened or read. It defeated the whole purpose of why it had been made.

I'm not sure when Meran began to play her flute. The soft breathy sound of it seemed to come from nowhere and every-where, all at once, a resonant wave of slow, stately notes, one falling after the other, rolling into a melody that was at once hauntingly strange and heartachingly familiar.

The pixies lifted their heads at the sound. I wasn't sure what I'd expected, but when they began to dance, I almost clapped my hands. They were so funny. Their bodies kept perfect time to the music, but their little eyes glared at Meran as she stepped out of the alley and Pied Pipered them into the store.

Dick fetched the Yeats and then he and I followed after, arriv-ing in time to see the music make the little men dance up onto my chair, onto the desk, until they began to vanish, one by one, into the screen of my monitor, a fat candle sitting on top of it, its flame flickering with their movement. Dick opened the book and I took the bell out of my pocket.

Meran took the flute from her lips.

"Now," she said.

Dick slapped the book closed, she leaned forward and blew out the candle while I began to chime the bell, the clear brass notes ringing in the silence left behind by the flute. We saw a horde of little faces staring out at us from the screen, eyes glaring. One of the little men actually popped back through, but Dick caught him by the leg and tossed him back into the screen.

Meran laid her flute down on the desk and brought out a garland she'd made earlier of rowan twigs, green leaves and red berry sprigs still attached in places. When she laid it on top of the monitor, we heard the modem dial up my Internet service. When the connection was made, the little men vanished from the screen. The last turned his bum towards us and let out a loud fart before he, too, was gone.

The three of us couldn't help it. We all broke up.

"That went rather well," Meran said when we finally caught our breath. "My husband Cerin is usually the one to handle this sort of thing, but it's nice to know I haven't forgotten how to deal with such rascals myself. And it's probably best he didn't come along this evening. He can seem rather fierce and I don't doubt poor Dick here would have thought him far too menacing."

I looked around the store.

"Where *is* Dick?" I asked.

But the little man was gone. I couldn't believe it. Surely he hadn't just up and left us like in the stories.

"Hobs and brownies," Meran said when I asked, her voice gentle, "they tend to take their leave rather abruptly when the tale is done."

"I thought you had to leave them a suit of clothes or something."

Meran shrugged. "Sometimes simply being identified is enough to make them go."

"Why does it have to be like that?"

"I'm not really sure. I suppose it's a rule or something, or a geas — a thing that has to happen. Or perhaps it's no more than a simple habit they've handed down from one generation to the next."

"But I *loved* the idea of him living here," I said. "I thought it would be so much fun. With all the work he's been doing, I'd have been happy to make him a partner."

Meran smiled. "Faerie and commerce don't usually go hand in hand."

"But you and your husband play music for money."

Her smile grew wider, her eyes enigmatic, but also amused.

"What makes you think we're faerie?" she asked.

"Well, you . . . that is . . ."

"I'll tell you a secret," she said, relenting. "We're something else again, but what exactly that might be, even we have no idea anymore. Mostly we're the same as you. Where we differ is that Cerin and I always live with half a foot in the otherworld that you've only visited these past few days."

"And only the borders of it, I'm sure."

She shrugged. "Faerie is everywhere. It just *seems* closer at certain times, in certain places."

She began to take her flute apart and stow the wooden pieces away in the instrument's carrying case.

"Your hob will be fine," she said. "The kindly ones such as he always find a good household to live in."

"I hope so," I said. "But all the same, I was really looking forward to getting to know him better."

* * *

Dick Bobbins got an odd feeling listening to the two of them talk, his mistress and the oak king's daughter. Neither were quite what he'd expected. Mistress Holly was far kinder and not at all the brusque, rather self-centered human that figured in so many old hob fireside tales. And her ladyship . . . well, who would have thought that one of the highborn would treat a simple hob as though they stood on equal footing? It was all very unexpected.

But it was time for him to go. He could feel it in his blood and in his bones.

He waited while they said their goodbyes. Waited while Mistress Holly took the dog out for a last quick pee before the pair of them retired to their apartment. Then he had the store completely to himself, with no chance of unexpected company. He fetched his little leather carpetbag from his hobhole behind the furnace and came back upstairs to say goodbye to the books, to the store, to his home.

Finally all there was left to do was to spell the door open, step outside and go. He hesitated on the welcoming carpet, thinking of what Mistress Holly had asked, what her ladyship had answered. Was the leaving song that ran in his blood and rumbled in his bones truly a geas, or only habit? How was a poor hob to know? If it was a rule, then who had made it and what would happen if he broke it?

He took a step away from the door, back into the store and paused, waiting for he didn't know what. Some force to propel him out the door. A flash of light to burn down from the sky and strike him where he stood. Instead all he felt was the heaviness in his heart and the funny tingling warmth he'd known when he'd heard the mistress say how she'd been looking forward to getting to know him. That she wanted him to be a partner in her store. Him. Dick Bobbins, of all things.

He looked at the stairs leading up to her apartment.

Just as an experiment, he made his way over to them, then up the risers, one by one, until he stood at her door.

Oh, did he dare, did he dare?

He took a deep breath and squared his shoulders. Then setting down his carpetbag, he twisted his cloth cap in his hands for a long moment before he finally lifted an arm and rapped a knuckle against the wood panel of Mistress Holly's door.

BLIND STAMPED

Lisa Morton

"Blind stamped: Impressions in the bindings of books which
are not colored . . ."
—*Book Collecting: A Comprehensive Guide* by Allen Ahearn

Nathaniel Watson didn't believe in ghosts before he met Rick
Herson.

Then Rick died.

*   *   *

Grendel's Bookshop was two-and-a-half years old when Rick
Herson began frequenting it.

Nathaniel knew him as a buyer first; it wasn't until much
later that he began selling his books. His tastes were wide-
ranging and unpredictable; it wasn't unusual for him to spend
several hundred dollars in an afternoon, the box he eventually
carried out the door containing everything from 19th-century
worm-eaten histories to signed modern fiction first editions.
Nathaniel would have been happy to hold books for one of his best
customers, to give him the initial chance at new arrivals, but there
was simply no predicting the man's interests.

Nathaniel — although he was Nate to his friends, he secretly
preferred the more literary full name — depended on customers
such as Rick Herson for his very survival. He had opened his used
bookstore with nothing but a love of books, some knowledge of
carpentry, and five thousand used volumes bought cheaply from a
firm that specialized in cleaning out delinquent storage units. He'd

131

bided his time, working for other booksellers, until he'd found an ideal space, one that offered both the possibility for growth and high visibility. He'd used his woodworking skills on shelving, fixtures and his own living space, located in a walled-off corner of his store. He worked seven days a week; when he was closed on Mondays, he was out scouting thrift stores, estate sales and other shops. On good days he made $300; fortunately he lived cheaply, falling onto his futon mattress in a state of happy exhaustion most nights.

But by the second year, he was beginning to grow anxious about his business. His profits hadn't blossomed the way he'd hoped and planned for; some weeks his internet sales kept him from closing, and he began to wonder if he hadn't made a mistake in opening a retail storefront. He knew other booksellers who had closed their shops and gone entirely electronic.

Nathaniel, however, believed in something he could only describe as the sanctity of the bookseller. He'd always thought there were two kinds of business that truly served a community as a meeting place, and he wasn't interested in being a bartender. That left only bookselling, and he loved books. He loved all kinds of books, and not just for the marvels contained within them (although he had named his bookshop after the villain in his favorite epic poem, as well as the anti-hero in a John Gardner novel). He loved the feel of their bindings, whether plain cloth or embossed leather; he loved their pages, the way text stood out on yellowing paper; he loved their scent, a sweet aroma redolent with age and poignant decay. He'd often wished he could write, to offer up his own visions and secret knowledge; but his few attempts had been pathetic, and he realized it. If he couldn't sell a book as a writer, he could as a bookseller.

So he had chosen to exchange one dream for another, but now that dream was fading. Even his interest in the books themselves was dying; he struggled against thinking of them as mere product, as nothing more than tomorrow's lunch or next month's rent. And it wasn't just the lack of increasing profits that made him despair; it was also the barrage of requests for insipid bestsellers and used textbooks and computer manuals.

Rick Herson never asked for any of those things. In fact, he rarely spoke at all during his afternoons inside Grendel's; he quietly roamed from section to section, occasionally adding another book to his growing stack on the front counter. When he was finished, he paid in cash, nodded as Nathaniel handed over his box of purchases, and then left. Even so, Nathaniel looked forward to his visits, not only for the sales he would garner but, more simply, to see whether his customer was purchasing Aristotle, Arthur Rackham or Le Fanu on that particular afternoon.

After a year, though, Rick Herson stopped coming in. It took Nathaniel a while to realize it. Late one night, sprawled on his futon going over his spreadsheets, he tried to figure out why business was down from the same time last year. He looked at his daily logs, and saw that there were none of the three-digit sales provided by the man who, at that point, was still nameless to him. He wondered how much longer he could stay in business; many nights he simply couldn't sleep, and even a good book wouldn't hold his interest. He'd stay up all night, staring at a soundless television set, brooding.

Then a few weeks later Rick Herson reappeared, except this time he was carrying a box into the store.

Nathaniel almost told him how good it was to see him again, but then he looked at Rick Herson more closely and couldn't lie: The man was plainly very ill. His hair had thinned considerably, his skin had taken on the color and texture of old vellum, his cheeks were sunken.

He had a small box of books that first time, no more than fifteen or twenty. He said he needed cash. Nathaniel didn't question; he looked over the books, slightly disappointed by the fairly-common titles. He made a small offer, which Herson accepted with no argument. He had Herson fill out a receipt, and paid him. He saw that the man walked now with a leaden quality, as if it was difficult for him to lift his feet. Nathaniel also noticed the way he forced his eyes to the front, refusing to allow himself the distraction of glancing at the aisles of books on either side of him.

After Herson left, Nathaniel studied the slip, making out the name and then rolling it slowly over on his tongue. Now his mystery man had a name . . . and Nathaniel couldn't quite understand why he felt so saddened to learn it.

*   *   *

Rick Herson sold more books over the next few months, sometimes bringing two boxes, although usually his stamina didn't seem to allow for more than one. The books seemed to get slightly better, but Rick didn't. Sometime about his fifth or sixth load, Nathaniel began to smell him — a scent of mixed physical ruin and astringent chemicals. He finally understood: The man was dying.

He wanted to ask why. If there was any hope. If he could help. But somehow the relationship they had defined long before didn't allow for such informalities.

Nathaniel hadn't had much experience dealing with death, at least not actual experience gained from something other than a book. His parents (who had never forgiven him for dropping out of college when he'd become bored with his business classes) were still alive, his grandparents had either died when he was very young or before he was born. He'd had one friend in high school who had shot himself, but Nathaniel had never seen the body and to this day — ten years later — he didn't quite believe his friend was really dead. Nathaniel had no siblings and few friends; he'd been too involved with his fledgling career to have time for socializing.

So Rick Herson — who he couldn't even say he really knew — was the first person he'd seen who was actually dying, who was approaching death rapidly. Nathaniel still looked forward to his visits, but now he feared them as well; he feared seeing what new horror had been wrought on Herson's weakening frame.

When Rick went completely bald, Nathaniel guessed it was some sort of cancer. When he could no longer lift a box from the trunk of his car, Nathaniel guessed the chemotherapy wasn't working.

Ironically, as Rick Herson died a little more, his books became fuller and richer. One trip might provide a first edition of Harper Lee's *To Kill a Mockingbird;* the next, a printing of *Treasure Island* with color plate illustrations by N. C. Wyeth.

Nathaniel paid him well for the books; truthfully, he paid more than he should have, because the books were not in fine condition.

In fact, every single book had small, neat, handwritten notes on the rear endpapers. Sometimes the pencilled notations were brief biographies of the author or bibliographies of other works, but sometimes they were commentaries on the work, which Nathaniel found fascinating. James Blake Bailey's early 19th-century account of bodysnatching in London, *Diary of a Resurrectionist 1811-1812*, held a short essay on how conditions in pre-Victorian Britain rendered corpse-selling not only undetectable but even desirable. A biography of the brilliant, American filmmaker Preston Sturges contained only the wry comment that Sturges and his comic peers probably did as much to get the U. S. out of the Depression as FDR did. Nathaniel knew he could easily have taken an eraser to the damaging writings, but somehow the metaphor of rubbing out a man's thoughts was too cruel, so he took the slight loss and sold each book "as is".

Herson's last box was small — evidently he couldn't lift more than five or six books now — but extraordinary: A first edition of Baum's *The Road to Oz,* with color plates; an 18th-century travelogue distinguished by its fore-edge painting, a tiny landscape visible only when the pages were fanned in a certain way; a huge leatherbound family bible from 1888, with decorated covers and brass hinges and ornate clasp; an early hardback printing of Kenneth Patchen's poetry; and a signed first in dust jacket of Ray Bradbury's *Dark Carnival.*

But it wasn't the box of books that initially drew Nathaniel's attention — it was Rick himself. He was walking with a cane, and his hands were covered with needle marks. His skin looked brittle, like pages from a musty-smelling pulp paperback. Nathaniel didn't believe he could live very long.

He was right; Rick Herson died two weeks later.

* * *

Of course Nathaniel didn't know that at first. Everyday that Rick failed to appear advanced his suspicion, but he'd always felt melancholy when he realized that this man would simply fail to appear in his shop again. Nathaniel would never attend a funeral or meet his loved ones, he'd never have the chance to discuss

Rick's books with him, to ask him about some of the curious annotations he'd scribbled.

Then came the afternoon when he received the phone call. The voice belonged to an annoyed-sounding middle-aged woman with a slight, unplaceable accent; she said she managed an apartment building where a tenant had just died, and he'd left nothing behind but books. The books had to be cleared out immediately; she'd called him because she found his store's bookmarks in some of the books.

They set up an appointment, then she told him where to come. After he hung up, he dug out one of Rick Herson's receipts, and felt dread clutch his spine when he saw the addresses matched.

He closed the store for the afternoon, loaded his van with boxes, and drove to the apartment building. It was nearby, a small two-story structure with a courtyard in the middle that the management believed had earned them the right to call the units "garden apartments". Rick Herson lived in a one-bedroom apartment on the lower level. Nathaniel was glad the man hadn't had to endure the additional struggle of climbing stairs, towards the end.

He met the obese, middle-aged landlady near the front, and she took him to the apartment, complaining about how quickly she must clean the unit out. Then she unlocked the door to the apartment — #4 — and Nathaniel stepped inside.

The first thing that occupied his senses was the odor — it was that miasma of sickness and chemicals that had surrounded Rick Herson for the last month, only amplified. Then he realized what he was looking at, and forgot the smell or the droning sound of the landlady's voice.

The apartment was filled with books. Literally filled, with just narrow pathways between towering walls of books. He thought 10,000 might be a conservative guess.

He turned to the stack nearest him, scanned a few titles — and felt his heart skip a beat. Even though the books were stacked in a way that virtually guaranteed damage, even though he knew that each book held the previous owner's pencilled thoughts . . . he knew he was looking at the most astonishing private collection of books he would ever see.

He reached to the top of the nearest stack, and pulled down a 1717 folio edition of Ovid's *Metamorphosis*. Below it was an 1820 edition of Poe's *Tamerlane and Minor Poems*. A few books down he saw a copy of *The Hobbit* that he guessed to be the 1937 British first edition.

At some point he realized the landlady was asking him a question, and he forced himself to focus on her voice. Were all of these old books actually worth anything?, she wondered. A rambling diatribe against crazy dying old men who filled their apartments with books followed the query.

Nathaniel assured her the collection was worth something, and he ventured further in. There was Tacitus' *The Description of Germanie* in a 1604 folio; there was a 1649 octavo by Rene Descartes; there was a first American edition of Philip K. Dick's *Ubik*.

Nathaniel knew this collection was completely out of his league; it belonged with a major auction house, or a high-end dealer in rare books. He asked the landlady when she needed the books gone. She replied, By tomorrow.

He knew it was impossible. He also knew he had to have the collection.

Going through the books one by one in the apartment was out of the question. Was there any family?, he asked, hoping to find someone other than the scornful landlady to deal with; but the tenant had no kin, leaving the apartment owners to dispose of his goods. Nathaniel told the landlady he could write her a check for a thousand right now, as a sort of down payment on a consignment deal. Her only response was to ask if he meant a thousand *dollars*?

He wrote the check, and then began filling boxes. It took eight trips, and the books filled every spare inch of his store, including the attic.

On his last trip, free from the doleful presence of the landlady, he gave in to curiosity and toured the rest of the apartment. There wasn't much to see; behind the towers of books there were a few pieces of old, badly scarred furniture. No television. A fifteen-year old compact stereo with plastic speakers. The landlady had already cleaned out the kitchen and the bedroom closets. He asked the landlady where the tenant had died, for some reason expecting the bedroom, but of course the man had been comatose in a hospital bed when he'd passed away.

Finally Nathaniel finished hauling his boxes out, and he told the landlady he would call her when the books sold; she didn't seem to care, and Nathaniel realized he wouldn't call. He didn't think Rick Herson would have wanted that woman or the faceless corporation that owned the building to have any of the proceeds from the books.

They simply didn't deserve to profit from the last vestiges of Rick's life.

* * *

Nathaniel indulged in a bottle of champagne that night. He was aching from moving the books, and was both wary and exhilarated by their presence now in his store. He opened the champagne, toasted the books, and drank right from the bottle, a deep pull that immediately melted the rough corners of his anxieties. Then he plucked a book at random, took it back to his living area, flopped down on the futon and saw he had a 1944 limited edition of Aleister Crowley's *The Book of Thoth*. It was halfbound in morocco leather, and would bring an outrageous price, even worn as this copy was. He opened the back cover, and saw Herson's neat, cramped writing. It covered not just the endpapers but the blanks at the rear of the book as well, giving a brief biography of Crowley and ending with a story about how he had once calmly bitten a beautiful girl, whom he did not know, in public.

Nathaniel finished the bottle and was asleep five minutes later, the book sprawled on the floor beside him, his small reading light still on.

Something woke him up. He didn't know how much later it was; his head was spinning from the alcohol, but at some point he had turned the light off. He lay there for a moment, listening. And heard very clearly the sound of a book being closed, from somewhere out in the main room of the store.

He sat up abruptly, tasting bile in the back of his throat, but it was now inspired by fear, not liquor. His first thought was that he had forgotten to lock up, but then he clearly recalled checking the front doors when he had left for the apartment. He thought it was possible he might have forgotten to lock the back door, however, so he rose as carefully as he could. He stood in the darkness for a moment, straining, listening, but there was no other sound.

He kept a baseball bat — an old-fashioned solid wooden bat, not one of the new aluminum ones — by the front counter, and he headed that way now, tiptoeing in stocking feet. As he reached the doorway to the main room, he edged carefully around the stacks, found the bat and felt its reassuring heft in his hand. Then he stepped more boldly into the aisles, and walked to the main lightswitch.

He flipped it on, and squinted, his eyes working frantically to adjust.

The room was empty.

He walked through the aisles carefully, checking in the bathroom and under the counter, but there was no one. The doors were all locked.

There was a book on the front counter, though, that he didn't remember putting there.

Of course there were books stacked on the counter, just as there were books stacked everywhere else in this store. But one book lay by itself, open to the rear endpapers. Nathaniel had no memory of having left the book there. He closed it and turned it to see the title: *True and Faithful Relation of What Passed for Many Years Between Dr. John Dee and Some Spirits*. It was an extravagantly bound reprint that still smelled slightly of sickness.

In fact, Nathaniel noticed the scent strongly now, all around him. When he shivered, he realized it was also cold in the room. Of course it was after 4 a.m., and he was about to suffer a considerable hangover . . . But he'd been drunk in his store late at night before, and this felt different.

He opened the book again, to the rear endpapers. This inscription was different, only one word long, phrasing a single question:
True?

He finally returned to his bed, but passed the rest of the evening with the lights on.

*   *   *

He spent the next week trying to decide how to handle the collection. He thought about passing the whole thing over to an auction house, but at last decided to catalogue it himself. He knew it would take months, possibly years of work, but it was work that would keep him alive, perhaps even allow him to finally see some black in his ledger.

And so he began, scrutinizing each book, researching values, verifying editions and dates, noting condition and defects. On a good day he could work through no more than fifty titles; on busy days — which he began to see more of — he was lucky to manage ten. In the meantime, there were no more strange sounds or misplaced books, and he forgot about the first occurrence . . . especially when the books began to sell.

The first order was for the 1934 limited edition of *Lysistrata*, signed by its illustrator, Picasso. Even though he knew the book was well worth it, actually seeing the amount written out on a check astonished him. He packed the book carefully, sealing it inside layers of cardboard and paper, and finally closed up late. He was asleep as soon as his head hit the pillow.

What woke him up this night was nothing as gentle as the soft thump of a book cover closing. It was, rather, the sounds of violent ripping and tearing.

He sat bolt upright, his heart triphammering as he listened. He didn't have to strain to hear these noises, of paper being shredded, and the distinctive shrill pitch of packing tape torn apart.

It went on for perhaps seven or eight seconds — which felt like years to Nathaniel — then stopped.

The silence was just as ominous as the sound. Nathaniel waited, expecting more, but nothing came. After a frozen moment, he forced himself up, not even bothering with clothes. In nothing but sweatpants he slowly opened the door leading into the shop. He hesitated there, listening for voices or footfalls, but nothing came.

He debated calling 911, but decided against it when he realized he didn't know what to tell them. If they told him to get out of the store, he'd have to pass through the front room anyway.

He stepped into that room, and was struck immediately by the cold and the scent, stronger now than he'd ever smelled it, even when Rick Herson was alive. He moved stealthily through the dark stacks, finding his way by heart and fingertip, breath held in anticipation of bumping against a crouching body . . . but there was no one. Finally he flipped on the lightswitch.

Nothing was out of place. There was no human intruder, no evidence, no mangled books.

He searched for fifteen minutes, but — aside from the cold and the scent, which seemed to be fading now — there was nothing. He finished and leaned against the front counter, and his arm bumped something.

It was the box holding the sold copy of *Lysistrata*, waiting to be mailed in the morning.

The box was impossibly cold to the touch, almost freezing.

He picked the box up, ignoring the way his fingertips almost burned from the chill. He turned the box over carefully, but saw his neat packing job was completely intact. Still, he had heard the sounds of packing tape tearing, of paper padding being ripped . . .

That was the first time Nathaniel Watson seriously began to consider the possibility of ghosts.

*　*　*

Over the next six weeks, there were three more "disturbances". Once, while still up and working late, Nathaniel heard footsteps in the attic. When he climbed up to look, there was, of course, no one there. Another time, he and a friend actually saw a book float three inches into the air, then set gently back down. The weirdest and last involved a pile of books he'd been cataloguing; when he awoke the next day, he saw that the books had all been moved back into the towering stack from which he'd pulled them. On these occasions, the room was cold and suffused with the acrid scent of Rick Herson.

Nathaniel was neither a superstitious man, nor a gullible one. In his mind he mocked patrons who bought from his New Age and Occult sections, and who sometimes espoused their personal beliefs at length. If asked for his opinion, he derided everything from UFO's to belief in an omnipotent being.

But there was simply no rational explanation for what was happening in his store. If the first night had been some sort of alcohol-fueled hallucination, the other incidents had been observed under sober conditions, and in one instance corroborated by a witness.

Nathaniel began to dread his store.

Before purchasing Herson's collection, Nathaniel had considered closing his shop because business was down and showed no signs of improving. Now his business was healthier than it had ever been, and he was considering closing the shop because it was . . . well, haunted. He knew he could just sell the Herson collection, that Grendel's could go back to the way it had been before . . . but somehow he didn't think that the — *happenings* would cease just because the books were dispersed.

More importantly . . . his store wasn't the only thing that was haunted.

Nathaniel devoured every book in his store that made mention of ghosts, apparitions, poltergeists, life after death, parapsychologists and supernatural forces. He read (or reread) *The Castle of Otranto*, *The Turn of the Screw*, and *The Haunting of Hill House*. The novels did their job superbly, and left him even more unnerved.

Finally he dug out a copy of his lease, and resolved to call the landlord in the morning; he knew he would be heavily penalized for breaking his five-year lease two years early, but he thought he could afford it now, ironically due to Rick Herson.

Sleep wouldn't come that night, and Nathaniel opened the bottle of tequila he touched once every few months. After a few shots his thoughts grew pleasantly unfocused, and he finally drifted off.

What woke him this time was no sound, but the vapor-producing chill, the stench, and the overwhelming presence of *something*. Nathaniel was still drunk, and was glad — the alcohol was a slight shield. He sat up and looked out towards the store; he'd left the door open, and could see a faint light coming from the main room, a mild phosphorescence.

His stomach tightened and Nathaniel was suddenly leaning over, the tequila burning its way back up his throat to spill out in a steaming froth. When it was over and he could breathe again, he staggered to his feet. Now he was drunk, he was sick, he was scared — and he was angry. He wanted to act on that most primitive of impulses, to lash out violently. He heard a hoarse, incoherent shout issue from his lips, and then was surprised to find that his feet were carrying him towards the main room. Where he had left the lease, lying on the front counter.

He entered the main room, and couldn't immediately see anything, his view blocked by columns of books; but the sensations were stronger here, the glimmer in the air brighter, and even in his drunkenness he was beginning to regret his actions. He could still turn around, go back to his little cubicle and close the door, turn on all the lights, call his landlord in the morning . . .

Or he could face his demons, figuratively and literally.

So he inched forward, slowly, stealthily, as though one could creep up, unseen, on an unreal dead thing. He shivered as he moved inch by inch, his breath vaporizing, his bitter stomach clenching on nothingness.

Then he was around a corner, and staring at the impossible.

Rick Herson stood in his store, calmly reading one of his books, even though there was no other light. At first Nathaniel was surprised at how solid Rick looked, then he realized that Rick was transparent, the stacks vaguely visible behind him. The apparition took no notice of him, intent upon its reading.

Nathaniel stood there in shock for a moment; then his heart found its pace again, as he sensed that the spirit was completely disinterested in him. He also realized something else:

The ghost of Rick Herson was beautiful.

This was neither the man who had been dying of a pathetically degenerative disease, nor was it the small, soundless customer who would have disappeared in a crowd. This Rick Herson — and it was undeniably him — was somehow fuller, even healthier. The glow seemed to pour from him as if he simply couldn't contain his own great energies. When his hand moved to turn a page, he shimmered, and Nathaniel had to look away for a moment. When he looked back, Rick was still there, engrossed.

Nathaniel watched the ghost for nearly ten minutes. Finally the shade put down the book and walked into the stacks of his library, vanishing. The cold, the smell, and the charge in the air disappeared with him.

Nathaniel stood for a long time, knowing that the ghost was unlikely to return this night, but unwilling to move yet. He was sober now, not from fear but from what he could only think of as wonder.

When he could move, he turned on the lights and did two things: The second was to file the lease back in its manila folder inside his cabinet. The first was to pick up the book Herson had been reading. He expected something ethereal, Edgar Cayce or Israel Regardie or even F. Marion Crawford.

Instead it was Lewis Carroll — *Alice's Adventures in Wonderland*.

Nathaniel laughed when he saw the title. Herson had returned from the dead not to study or be enlightened, but to be entertained. Nathaniel flipped excitedly to the back of the book, and was at first disappointed to see the blank endpapers. Then he thought more about it, and finally decided that Rick Herson simply wasn't done yet.

This time Nathaniel didn't mind the idea that Rick would be back.

* * *

He never saw Rick again, not with the clarity of that one vision, at least. He still occasionally heard the footsteps, found the misplaced books, put on an extra blanket to ward off the cold. But he found these happenings soothing now, and wondered why he'd ever found them terrifying.

He used the profits from the Herson collection to expand his store and hire real employees. He considered moving into his own apartment or house, but he didn't want to leave the books. Not yet.

Nathaniel never did catalogue the volumes that had blank rear endpapers. He had a special case built for them, and they waited in his store, untouched, pristine. Sometimes hungry collectors inquired about them; he politely declined all offers. He didn't bother to try to explain why.

The one other witness to the haunting of Grendel's Bookshop — the friend who had once viewed a book levitation — spent one long dinner trying to convince Nathaniel to write his own book about ghosts. He could make Grendel's famous, the friend argued.

Nathaniel heard him out, but finally declined the suggestion. He didn't tell his friend that he was afraid no one would believe him, because he didn't really care; he didn't even say that he didn't want to have his secret revealed, although that would have been partly true.

He finally smiled slowly, and told his friend that he didn't have any interest in writing a book because of one very simple thing he'd learned from Rick Herson:

What a writer brought to a book didn't matter as much as what the reader contributed.

Grendel's Bookshop enjoyed a long and successful life.

SHAKESPEARE & CO.

Jack Williamson

I loved my grandfather. Once I had to fight a boy who called him a mean little skinflint. I got a black eye, but I'll never forget my joy in the treasures he used to give me. A pocket knife, a neat little pocket compass, an old pocket watch that still kept the time. They were items left in pawn and never redeemed, precious now because the wheelers said civilian units did not require them.

He loved the music and magic of words. I remember the poems he used to recite when we were safely alone in the shop. Poems by writers named Poe and Kipling and Hopkins, names he repeated in tones of devotion. Their books were gone, but he knew the poems by heart.

Our town had been larger. Half the houses were empty now, windows broken and the yards grown into jungles of weeds. The monument works had closed forty years ago; I learned to swim in the abandoned quarry. Old iron rails lay rusting on the rotten ties where the trains once ran. My grandfather's shop was in a dingy red brick on the square. You could still read the faded sign over the door, SHAKESPEARE & CO., but he had painted another on the dusty window.

PAWN SHOP
SMALL LOANS

He was a spry little man, with a wide white mustache, yellow-stained along the fringe from the long cigars he chewed. He used to sit all day, hunched on the tall desk behind the counter, haggling over the value of an old kettle or clock or fiddle. He let me sweep the floor. When we were alone and he thought we were safe, I used to beg him to tell me about the world he remembered.

We lived with him in the rooms above his shop. My mother kept the house and worked the kitchen garden on the lot behind the building. My father was away, drafted before I was born. A faded photo of him hung over my mother's bed. I had never seen him, but every year at Christmas she got a printed form that commended him for his loyal service and a check for what he had saved from his pay. She cried and kissed the card and bought a bag of candy for me.

"There used to be private letters," she told me. "But the wheelers have forbidden privacy. It is a hazard to security."

My birthday gift the year I turned five was a framed picture of the Prophet. A lean, dark man in a long black robe, he had a long sad face. His eyes were black and sunk deep in his skull, so sharp they frightened me. My mother wanted me to hang it my room, but the eyes seemed to stab through me, even in he dark. I couldn't sleep that night till I got up and hid the picture under a blanket in my closet.

My brother made me play wheel and cog with him as soon as I was old enough to understand. He said he had to teach me the words of the Prophet and the Manual of the Wheels. He asked the questions and laughed when I answered wrong. He said I was asking to be recycled into agricultural chemicals.

"Who rules the stars?"

That was the first question. I had to answer, "The Supreme Machine."

"Who rules our Mother Earth?"

I had to say, "The Master Wheels."

"Who are the Master Wheels?"

"The Wheel of Liberty, the Wheel of Equality, the Wheel of Fraternity."

"What are their functions?"

"The Wheel of Liberty keeps us free to learn and obey the rules of the Prophet. The Wheel of Equality protects us from those who might forget them. The Wheel of Fraternity holds us to our ordained places to the great brotherhood of the Master Machine."

"Who gave us the Master Wheels?"

"The Prophet of the Wheels. He had lived through the Time of Terror. He created the Machine to preserve us from the terrorists — those mad wreckers who tried to destroy us all."

Feeling proud when I knew the answers, I recited them to my grandfather. "You've got them right," he said, but they seemed to make him sad.

Cigarettes were forbidden. The wheelers had decreed that the life of service did not require them, but my grandfather grew tobacco plants in a little plot hidden back in the woods. He cured the leaves in the tool shed and rolled them into long cigars he never lit because the odor might be detected, but when the shop was empty he used to sit with a dead one hanging from his lip. He slipped it out of sight when anyone came in.

Alone in the shop, he liked to talk about the past.

"I've lived a long time," he used to say. "I've seen change. Too much change, and none of it good. I grew up in a golden time. We used to call it the age of wonder. New technologies had made all of us magicians. Everything looked possible, and we never knew the price."

He used to sigh and wave the dead cigar at the cluttered items on the shelves, or sometimes sit staring at them wistfully, recalling the time when they'd been new.

"The world was wonderful then." Sometimes he smiled. "We had magic out of the labs and the skipships still carrying new colonies toward new frontiers. I felt had the urge to join them, but my parents had gone in debt to open the shop. I stayed here to help them keep it afloat. They'd both been teachers, and I learned their love of books. I stayed on after they died, and the shop did well enough till the world broke down.

"A sad time."

He paused to shake his head, staring moodily at the dead cigar.

"We'd been blind to history, but the age of wonder was already ending itself. Spreading out to the stars, we carried all our new powers, but also all the old animal traits evolved to keep us alive in the jungle."

He looked beyond me, exploring the past and speaking to himself. "Tribalism, aggression, intolerance. Too many differences in language, culture, religion. Too little love for one another. We were apes with biobombs, fighting interstellar wars for no sane reason.

"The old order crumbled. No planet or nation was secure. To save themselves, frightened peoples flocked to follow Prophet. He set up the Wheel of Man to save us from ourselves. He promised order, safety, survival. That was what people longed for. They came to worship him, and let him give this."

He spread his gnarled old hands toward the shelves and tables where books had been, piled now with yellow-tagged object left in pawn. Beneath the stained mustache, his thin lips twisted bitterly.

"The wheelers kept the hypernet to flash their commands across the stars, but kept it only for themselves. They stopped the printing presses, all except their own. They shut the post office down. They killed the private telephone. They closed the schools. They tried to stop private writing and even private talk. They said we'd poisoned ourselves with too much knowledge. They'd tell us all we needed to know.

"That was the end of Shakespeare & Co."

He stopped to shake his head and sit for a long moment staring bleakly at the piles of outworn junk nobody would ever want.

"The Prophet was a mad genius, obsessed with the fear of war and terror. People believed when he called books the enemy of peace. He condemned them, ordered books and bookstores destroyed. People obeyed. When stores resisted, the wheelers incited mobs to burn them down. The owners sometimes inside. But here —"

He bit down on the dead cigar.

"I loved books too much."

I stared, wondering at him. A tiny man in rough blue denim, he was gnarled and bent beneath a lot of years, but his pale old eyes still had a glint of cold determination.

"Weren't you afraid?"

"Of course I was." He shrugged. "But the town was small and far from anywhere. I had friends who loved books as much as I did, and the wheelers had made books precious. Nobody turned me in. I sold the books in stock, or trade them for others. Even after the mails were cut off, people heard about the us and came from far away."

His lean old shoulders tossed again.

"Till the whole stock was gone."

Yet he had saved a handful of the books he loved most. He taught me to read and gave a few of them to me. Stevenson's *Treasure Island*. Mark Twain's *Tom Sawyer* and *Huckleberry Finn*. A worn school edition of Shakespeare's *Hamlet*. A book of wonderful stories by H. G. Wells. I kept them hidden under the carpet, under a little door in the floor my father had cut to hide something of his own.

They came down from a lost time, magical to me and hard to imagine, but he had seen *Hamlet* on the stage. He liked to talk about life and times in ancient England, where Shakespeare himself had acted in his plays. He talked about far-off Scotland, where Stevenson was born, and the island where he had gone to die. He remembered his own honeymoon cruise on the far-off Mississippi, where Twain had been a river pilot. He knew the prophetic books of Wells, a canny little Englishman who had foreseen the age of technology could end in darkness.

Alone in my room, I read the books and read them again till I knew them by heart, secretly grieving for the writers and their worlds.

"Don't talk!"

He said that many times, stabbing the cold cigar at me to underline the warning.

"The wheelers have erased the past. They don't want us reading, don't want us talking, don't want us thinking. Get caught at it, and you'll be recycled."

Books had been banished, newspapers, private mail, the hypernet, radio and TV, but private talk was hard to stop. One morning my mother came back form the market on the corner with our weekly bread ration and a whispered tale of trouble out on the Polaris frontier.

"A rebel gang under a leader they call the Star Hawk. They've raided a wheeler outpost and got away with a printing press and a shipload of weapons. They're skipping now around the frontier planets just ahead of the wheelers, preaching rebellion against the Machine."

"Don't believe it." My grandfather hushed his creaky voice. "The wheelers killed the truth when they killed print and shut us off the hypernet. All we get today is a river of lies."

My mother touched her lips and shook her head to hush him. I didn't believe it, till a wheeler came to ask her unit number and hand her a card edged in black. It fell out of her fingers and I picked it up to read it.

The Master regrets to inform you that UNIT 792 354 875 is missing in action.

That had been my father's unit number. My mother cried and kissed the card when I gave it back to her. We knew no more till my brother turned sixteen. The morning of his birthday, a black-armored car came jolting over the ruined pavements from the wheeler station.

When people saw the flag of the Wheel of Man, a red cogwheel on a field of black, they scurried out of its way. It stopped in front of the shop, and a black-uniformed officer came in to demand my brother's unit number and read him another card.

Greetings from the Master to Unit No. 867 945 321 XN: You are ordered to report at once for service with the Wheel of Action. You are hereby informed that the penalty for any evasion or delay is immediate recylement.

Standing with her arm around him my mother tried not to cry, and whispered that he should be proud to serve the Machine. He kissed her and hugged me and looked back to give my grandfather crisp salute before he climbed into the car.

I was left at home with him and my mother. When he grew too feeble to tend his little tobacco patch in the woods, I did it for him. I let him teach me how to cure the leaves and roll his long cigars. He hobbled around the shop on a silver-headed cane left in pawn and spent most of his days perched on the high stool behind the counter. One morning I found him sprawled over the counter, stiff in the rigor of death. The wheelers took him away to be recycled.

My mother wanted me to run the shop, but I was no good at it. He had kept the books in his head, with no record of the loans. I lacked his sense of value and whom to trust. Yet, as long as she was able, she and I took our turns at the counter.

One clear day we heard a strange thunder. A panting boy burst into the shop ran in to tell us that something was roaring in the sky. A flying machine, my mother said. We ran outside to look. I'd played ball games on the broken runways at the old airport, but I had never seen a machine in the air.

My mother was terrified. She thought somebody had reported the tobacco patch, or perhaps the wheelers had come to look for unburned books. We watched from the street till the machine came down to the old runways. Wheeler patrol cars rushed to meet it, sirens screeching. I followed the crowd for a closer look. A wheeler roadblock stopped us a mile away, but I watched with a pair of old binoculars left in pawn. We'd seen nothing like it.

"Trouble for the wheelers?" a corn farmer said. "Maybe those rebels already here?"

"More likely trouble for us," the blacksmith muttered. "New taxes, or maybe another roundup of cryptos and rats." Uneasily, he shook his head. "Whatever happens, they never let us know."

His wife hissed and nudged him in the ribs, with a warning frown.

I made out the jet engines and the bright silver wings. A strange flag was painted on it, a big green star on a field of white. It just sat there. A dozen patrol cars stopped on the roads around it. A door opened in the side of it. Men in green came down a ramp and waited till the patrol cars moved closer and wheelers climbed out to meet them. Finally a group of them climbed the ramp and went inside.

When nothing else happened, I went back to my mother in the shop. That afternoon she was resting in the back room when a wheeler car stopped on the street outside. A tall man in a neat green uniform walked into the shop, smiling as he knew me. I stared till he spoke.

"Kim," he said, "don't you remember me?"

It had been nine years. It took me a moment to be sure he really was my brother, older, straighter, wearing a black mustache trimmed more neatly than my grandfather's had been. I stood gaping at him until he laughed and put his arms around me.

My mother had heard his voice. She came out of the back room and stood shaking her head, leaning unsteadily on my grandfather's silver-headed cane. He picked her up and set her down on an old plush love seat left in pawn long ago. The cane had fallen on the floor. I tried to hand it back to her, but she didn't see it. Her eyes were fixed on him, tears running down her withered cheeks.

"I thought — thought I'd never see you." Her voice was a husky quaver. "We never knew anything. Where have you been?"

"North," he said. "Out on the Polaris sector."

She wiped her eyes and studied him again.

"The mustache," she whispered. "You're the image of your father."

He put his arm around her. She huddled closer to him. They sat whispering together till I made him answer questions. The lander had brought him down from a Freedom Force skipship waiting out in low Earth orbit.

"The uniform?" My mother drew back to scan him again. "You're handsome in it." Anxiety edged her voice. "You've been fighting?"

"Not much." He laughed. "But we were trained as a commandos and ordered out to the north frontier on a covert mission."

"A spy?" Her arm tightened as if to snatch him back from danger. "You could have been killed!"

"I wasn't." He shrugged, with a quizzical grin. "We went out in an old cargo craft as refugees from the wheeler advance and dropped one dark night on the planet where the Star Hawk grew up. We were there a year. Time enough to get to know the colonists.

"Most of them were refugees from the breakdown the Machine was created to stop. Their answer to it had been migration farther out, but the Prophet was afraid of freedom anywhere. The wheelers had forbidden books, all except his own laws and gospels. They'd set a satellite in geo orbit overhead and built surface bases.

"And they were winning converts. The pioneer settlers were already desperate, eager for anything better. The planet needed more terraforming than they were able to do before Machine cut off the supplies and support they'd hoped to get. The climate was still ugly. They'd suffered famines and epidemics of strange diseases.

"Yet still they were still free. We came to share their love of liberty. Before that year was over we met together, voted to defect, and made contact with the rebel command. The Star Hawk heard my name and sent for me. I was taken aboard a little skipcraft hidden on an island the wheelers hadn't reached.

"I spent a day there with the Star Hawk. A woman. No longer young, she was still vivacious and attractive. I never learned her name. She showed me her collection of forbidden books. They were her passion, the literature of liberty. She'd fought her war for freedom with a printing press she carried on this ship and flimsy little pamphlets she was passing out.

"She had written and printed them herself, poking fun at the Machine and the wheelers. Themselves meat machines that had been human. Promising to restore all the freedoms the Prophet had taken away. Spreading forbidden ideas she had found in her father's library while she was still a kid.

"A surprise to me." He grinned at the hodgepodge on the shelves. "Most of the books had come from Shakespeare & Co. They'd been bought here while Granddad hung on and smuggled all the way from Earth before the wheelers got full control.

"The books she loved most were on the history of democracy. Its origins here on Earth and all the wars fought to establish and defend it. Her pamphlets had retold the story of our own American Revolution, when the patriots of thirteen small colonies united to defy the king of England and establish our new nation.

"One pamphlet reviewed the ugly lesson of the French Revolution, which began with a splendid dream and ended in an early reign of terror. The best of the dreamers lost their heads to the guillotine. Many thousand more were slaughtered in the wars of Napoleon Bonaparte.

"She said her best inspiration came from a few older books, written three thousand years ago in ancient Greece. I've brought you a set of the pamphlets. They'll change your world. They changed mine."

The smile was gone. His jaw set hard, his voice turned bleak.

"I never saw her again. In spite of the vote, our leader had used us to bait a trap for her. He lured her off the ship to meet a wheeler agent who promised to negotiate the surrender of the satellite fortress. They captured her, but her war was already won." With a grim little smile, he looked off beyond the jumbled shelves and tables. "The wheelers recycled her, but the ideas in those pamphlets were impossible to kill."

His voice changed as if reciting from them.

"Those old Greeks began as simple folk, scratching a living out of little farms among the mountains of their narrow peninsula, but they were creative. Organizing their small city-states, they invented democracy, the concept of free individuals ruling themselves. Fighting off the assaults of the vast Persian empire, they invented new ways of war. Setting down the story of that, they invented history.

"Xenophon, Herodotus, Thucydides."

He paused to savor the names.

"Xenophon was a student of Socrates in Athens. Sent into exile, he became a mercenary soldier. Democratic Greeks made far better soldiers than the slaves of Oriental despots. Greek mercenaries elected their own generals, debated strategy and tactics, shared the loot of victory. They enjoyed the rights of private property. They fought for those freedoms.

"Xenophon was among the ten thousand Greeks hired by Cyrus the Younger for his war to claim the Persian throne. They won the decisive battle for him, but he was killed when he pushed rashly on ahead to slaughter his defeated enemies. The Greeks were left in strange lands a thousand miles from home, outnumbered by the hostile tribes all around them. Xenophon's *Anabasis* is the history of their victories on the long march back to the Black Sea."

Listening, her wet eyes fixed on his face, my mother kept nodding fondly.

"Herodotus, writing his history of the Persian war, became the first real historian. Born in Asia Minor, he lived in Athens and died in Italy. He traveled widely, to Egypt and the Black Sea regions. Active in politics, he was himself an exile. He wrote with a scientific interest in facts and causes.

"He knew and influenced Thucydides, whose own great work is his history of the Pelopenisian war. Fought between Athens and Sparta, the two main centers of Greek power, it dragged on for a quarter century and left Athens defeated and Greek democracy disabled. Alexander the Great crushed out beneath his own despotism.

"Yet the dream of freedom is still alive!" Under the trim green jacket, my brother's shoulders lifted. "Better than bullets, it became the Star Hawk's weapon in her war with the wheelers. Her pamphlets scattered it all across the star frontier. It toppled the Machine."

"Already?" My mother shook head. "That's hard to believe."

"A sudden thing." My brother nodded soberly. "But the wheelers were weaker than they seemed. The Prophet had been a mad genius, but by then he was dead. His followers lacked his charisma and his zeal. Erasing history, they had erased memories of the Terror. They'd kept the hypernet alive because effective rule required it. When free men regained access, freedom spread like wildfire."

"And you are home?" my mother whispered. "Home to stay?"

"Home to stay," he told her. "I've been far enough."

There had been many causes for the Terror and the rise of the Prophet. Inequities between the rich and poor, arrogant abuse of power, neglect of individual rights, technology run beyond the wisdom to control it. Perhaps future men will read the lessons of history and steer a safer course. The Star Hawk has given them a chance.

My brother had returned with a commission from the new Free Space Republic to plant a memorial to her on the square across the street from the bookstore. It's a statue of her in some mirror-bright metal, holding a book toward the sky. Lettered in gold, the title is *Shakespeare & Co.*

All that was ten years ago. The Restoration Force set us free to rebuild civilization. We've repaved our roads. Rails have been repaired. The mail runs again. Telephones and TV are back, airports and spaceports, schools and private enterprise. The hypernet is open to everybody. People smile when you meet them on the street.

Out of uniform, my brother took over Shakespeare & Co. He auctioned off what he could sell, put a front and a new roof on the building, restocked the shelves when books came back. He has written a book of his own, a history of the Star Hawk and the Restoration. The store is thriving, and my mother seems younger since his return.

With no head for business, I've earned a degree in liberal arts from the new Terran University. I have an editorial job with a new publishing house that stands on the site of the old monument works. We published my brother's book.

BALLARD'S BOOKS

Gerard Houarner

"The problem with books," my uncle Terry used to say, when everyone was younger and still alive, "is that they always end."

"Same problem with living," was my Dad's usual answer.

Later on, of course, they both got tired of living. Living wore them down, wore them out. It wasn't the physical labor — they'd both gotten out of riding the rails as lines were bought up or went out of business, and they settled into riding chairs in offices until retirement. The war hadn't touched them much, though they'd done their duty as engineers. It was the dying that took the need to keep on living away. Mom left with cancer when I was nine, and Aunt Elisa died of asthma a little while later. Uncle Terry lost a son in Nam. My sister Evelyn was killed with her husband and two children in a car accident. And then there were the friends, neighbors and other relatives who moved away or died, same difference when no one wrote or called back. And toward the end, when I'd visit from college and catch Uncle Terry sitting on Dad's patio, both men older than their years and tired and waiting, paperback and hardcover books, old and new, piled on side tables next to glasses of lemonade, I'd hear the same bit of conversation nestled into their quiet reading, and their talk of James Cain and Cornell Woolrich, Damon Runyon and Premchand, Pearl Buck and William Beckford, Maupassant and Liaozhai, Twain and Tolstoy, Bradbury and Doc Smith and van Vogt.

The joke would finish the same as it had as far back as I could remember, back to when there wasn't a television in either brother's house, and the music from the radio wasn't so loud it would interfere with the reading. Uncle Terry would come back and say, "Of course, it's not so bad when you can pick up another book," and they'd both laugh, slow and low, like they'd just told an old joke everybody knew the punch line to, except me.

And sometimes the joke brought back clear as day a conversation overheard when everyone was young and I was even younger, on a hot summer day when I shouldn't have been home but I was because I'd walked back to the house three miles from some stupid picnic the neighborhood's moms organized so their kids wouldn't drive them crazy before going back to school. Mom had told me I couldn't bring anything to read because I had to play with other kids, but I got tired of standing around and getting picked on.

I'd snuck back into my room to finish up *The Tower Treasure* and dream about what it would be like to have a brother like Dad had Uncle Terry, and be like the Hardy Boys, instead of having a sister who didn't like Edgar Rice Burroughs at all, or classmates who stole the books you liked to read at lunchtime or beaned you with a ball when you weren't looking.

I heard a car pull up outside. It was my Dad, home early with my uncle. I kept quiet. Car doors slammed, and their voices came up through my half-open window. The air was heavy with humidity and the smell of fresh-cut grass.

"We should've looked at the biographies," Uncle Terry said, as they walked toward the house from the curb.

"What's the fun of living if you know what happens next?"

"Things are too good. There's change heading our way, like in the rest of the world."

"The world needs changing."

"I'm not arguing against changes. It's just that maybe if we'd read up on ourselves, we'd know what to do, what mistakes to avoid, to keep things going smooth."

"Every book has to end," my Dad said.

"Nothing wrong with trying to add a few good pages." They stopped at the front door. I worried I'd left it open. Nobody locked their doors back then, but they did close them. "Wish we could find that store again."

"We couldn't afford the prices then, sure as hell couldn't afford them now."

"I didn't mention buying."

"Can't really read a book by browsing, Terry. How many times we've been told, 'this isn't a library.'"

"Then there should be a library full of those kinds of books someplace. And we should've been looking for it."

"Library's not the same kind of thing, Terry. Not the same at all. Those books are everybody's books. Books from the store, from *that* store, want to be *your* book."

The storm door slammed shut. Their voices sounded through the house and rose up from the floorboards as they kept on talking. Then my Dad came upstairs, changed, went back down, and they went on to Uncle Terry's house so he could change, and then they went to the picnic and a little while later they came back looking for me and I got a good little something on my backside for scaring my Mom to death by disappearing. But it's not the beating that I remembered all these years. I even forgot the rest of their talk, until lately, when what my father said coming up the stairs came back to me, like a ghost of somebody that didn't want to be neglected. His words were muffled, but I picked them out of the air like a dragonfly snatching mosquitoes. "You can't spend your whole life looking for something that came and went, because then you won't live your proper life."

Remembering that part's made me sad, a little, after all these years, and I wish I could forget it again. I throw out an answer, "Maybe looking for something that came and went is your proper life." But no matter how hard I try to bury that memory like I buried my Dad and Uncle Terry, it doesn't want to give me rest. The smart answer doesn't work, either. There's nobody to laugh with me, slow and low, at the joke.

That part of the conversation may not have stayed with me during the time remembering it might've done me some good. But what did abide with me was the fact that my Dad and his brother had found a bookstore like no other I'd ever heard about. And they'd found special books in that store. And they hadn't told anyone about it. Ever.

I tried, over the years, to find out more about the bookstore they mentioned. Where and when did they find it? What kind of books did it have that were so special? Why couldn't they find it anymore? But neither one of them budged an inch off of wondering what I was talking about. Mom and Aunt Elisa didn't know anything about any special bookstore, and told me I didn't need to go hunt out any more books, as my Dad and Uncle were doing a fine job of that all by themselves. It bothered me, some times more than others, like when I heard them perform their 'problem reading a book' routine. But there was nothing I could do about it, so I just kept reading what I wanted to read, getting good grades and getting by.

Maybe, when we went into town, or on vacations, I paid a little extra attention to any bookshops we passed, and especially to the way my Dad noticed them. But I never saw anything more than my Dad's usual eager look, or a longing one if my Mom was in the car. I never noticed the special way I imagined he'd react if he ever saw that store he'd visited with his brother such a long time ago, the one no one wanted to talk about.

A mystery. One that took a bite out of me, and I never missed what it took. Never felt a thing.

It wasn't until college, when I was drifting through courses I had no interest in, reading books I'd already read and forcing myself to think about them in ways that went beyond the sheer pleasure of losing myself in their words and worlds because teachers wanted me to, that I got my first clue about the mysterious store.

Uncle Terry's oldest son was dead. The draft had already caught the younger one. A cousin had come back missing half a leg. The family was hurting, grieving. Everyone was telling me to stay in college, keep the deferment, stay out of the war. And it seemed a few people were angry, too, that I was in college, and out of the war. The family was breaking up, folks were moving away, and it was coming down to just the two brothers still in town. And they were getting tired.

I came home one weekend, without warning, and found my Dad upstairs, sleeping. For a minute, I thought he was dead, and my heart jumped, and tears came to my eyes, and the smell of all those old books in the house, the yellowing paper going back to the turn of the century and the leather and cloth covers and the glue and old thread stitching, suddenly choked me. I went to where he lay on the bed, dust motes floating in the beam of sunlight streaming through the window, and I thought I saw his spirit moving through the dust and the glass, to what was waiting for him beyond. I sat down next to him, raised a hand to shake him, and then I saw him breathing, and I almost laughed with relief.

The drawer next to his bed was half open. Looking inside, I saw books. I took them out, discovered they were journals, filled with neat, evenly-spaced handwriting, the kind you don't see these days because nobody knows how to put words on paper with just your fingers and a good ink pen, anymore. I went through them quickly, catching dates, skipping through books like the Time Traveler through the future, until there was only one left. A younger, less disciplined scrawl filled it, along with brittle newspaper clippings about the New York Yankees, garish *Amazing Stories* magazine covers folded in half, and careful drawings for Buck Rogers rocket ships and other science fiction devices. A piece of paper slipped out, bright and clean. I picked it up, discovering a card, beige, with shiny black lettering. It smelled new, fresh, not old like everything else in the journal, including the pages themselves, as if it had been printed the day before. The crisp stock was cool against my fingertips, and something about the typeface, the uncommon tag line and hours without an address, reminded me of the speakeasies that had preceded the decade from which these artifacts came. The card promised the illicit. The illegal. The enticing.

Ballard's Books

All The Books One Can Ever Need

11 a.m. till 11 p.m.

Daily

I took the card. Replaced the journal in the drawer, at the bottom of the pile.

Dad died after I graduated. I don't think he ever missed the card, and if he did he never mentioned it to me. I visited him in the hospital, and Uncle Terry, too, when his turn came. I asked them about the bookstore. I tried to shame them with the name, Ballard's Books, thinking that on their death beds they would relent and let me in on the joke they had shared for so long. They both gave me the same smile that said they were sorry. Sorry they couldn't say, sorry I didn't know, sorry I didn't have the luck or brains or guts to find the place for myself. Sorry I wasn't worthy. I'm still not sure which.

I buried them both.

I spent time in the Peace Corps in Africa, glad to be away from the war. I farmed, built houses, dug ditches, cut trails, taught, and I never missed the good times so many from my generation were having. At least, the ones not in the Nam. I still had books. Some of the children from the places I went caught the fever of words from me. I like to think they're still reading, holding a place in their homes for books like they sometimes did for gods or ancestors.

After the war, I used my share of the inheritance to travel. I went cheap, backpacking all the way, trading books I'd read for ones I hadn't, seeing the sights to be seen in Europe and the mid-East, even India. I had my fun with women, those I found alongside me on the road, and the ones who lived in the places I visited and found me interesting in an old-fashioned, traveling-man kind of way. I went back to Africa, then South America. In between, I caught the parts of America I hadn't seen, as well as Canada and Mexico. I taught and used the handyman's skills I'd picked up in the Corps to earn some extra money. I made the inheritance last a long time. I read a lot of books, never keeping any, and saw most of the world everybody I'd read had bothered writing about.

I never found Ballard's Books. At least, not on that leg of my journey.

I didn't realize at the beginning of my wandering that I was looking for the shop. Even after I settled into the routine of showing the card to local expatriates or tourist boards or to a bookstore owner, it didn't occur to me I was following a plan. I accepted the fact that no one could help me as part of the ritual of entering a new place. When there was no one left to ask, I took it as a signal to leave.

Every now and then, I met someone I thought might be trying to hide what they knew. But like my Dad and Uncle Terry, they wouldn't budge, no matter how I begged or what I offered as a reward.

I offered my inheritance for the shop's location. Anyone who showed interest, I soon discovered, knew nothing. For the ones who refused to even consider money, I had nothing else to surrender, and took away nothing but their forlorn smiles when I gave up.

In my forties, as the generation of young people around me partied with renewed vigor and greed became popular and ways of doing business changed, I discovered I was getting old. I also discovered I had spent the last two decades living like a character in an unwritten Kafka story, looking for something that probably didn't exist. My inheritance was almost gone. I had to get a job, to stay just over broke.

I went to work in a bookstore, offering my catalog of handyman skills and knowledge of literature both elevated and low. Computers opened a new window to the world, and I began learning how to use them. The bookstore went out of business. I found another. Learned more about computers, until that store went out of business. I followed a road of failing booksellers and growing electronic interconnections across America, until I had no choice but to either try my hand at my own store or work for the large chains. And all through this time, I kept searching for Ballard's Books, my own net cast wider across the world than all the trails I'd traveled, through the miracle of ever more sophisticated machines and communications.

I found the site during a lunch time search at a library computer center. The opening page was a precise reproduction of the card I had found and still carried, down to font, size and spacing. I stared at the screen, not believing I'd finally found a secret part of my father's life. For a moment, he was with me again, breathing softly in his chair by the living room window, his face pale with the light reflected from the open page before him, a faintly sour smell defining the aura of his presence after a day at work. For a moment, I heard his voice in the library's background noise, reading Seuss and Wodehouse to my sister and me at night, or talking about the how Pohl and Kornbluth had it right and why wasn't anyone paying attention, or gushing about a new writer he'd discovered, like Mishima, or Mahfouz, or Ellison.

He was alive again, the gate through which I passed to worlds I much preferred, where bloodthirsty pirates landed on my desert island, and Martian war machines stalked the streets, and the Cardinal's men waited in ambush around the next corner, and I knew I'd survive and emerge from the adventure better, stronger, richer in spirit.

For a moment, the hurt of being shut out from this little part of my father's life pierced me, and the ache turned and twisted in my heart.

But then I wondered, was the site a prank? I clicked on the name, and the machine froze. I had to shut down, log back on, search again. This time the search engines could not find Ballard's Books.

That had the ring of truth.

The shop had announced itself. It was close. The rest was up to me. Remembering my Dad's and Uncle Terry's smiles, I did not go back to work. Instead, I hired a cab and drove through the back streets and alleys of the town I lived in. Finding nothing, I broadened the search to nearby malls, going from one to another by bus, jogging through floors and outlying mini-malls searching for the store. In another cab, I cruised slowly past strip malls along local roads and highways.

Night came. I returned to the town where I'd settled for that year, wandered its streets. I was desperate, as hungry and frantic and dangerous as the worst addict on the meanest street of the most cruel city ever imagined. The few other people I met avoided me. A police car flashed its lights on and sounded a siren as it came after me, but I slipped away in the night, through yards and fields and ditches.

I walked deeper into the night, away from the town, from any house light or traffic, until the road I walked on changed from tar to dirt, and the stars overhead vanished behind overhanging trees. I walked until the insect songs and animal calls stopped, until the breeze no longer rustled through leaves, and even my footsteps made no sound.

I walked until I wondered why dawn wouldn't come, if I'd died, if I'd ever even existed at all.

That's when I found the cabin. A single oil lantern hung by the door, announcing its roadside presence. The light illuminated a neat, hand-carved sign below the lantern: Ballard's Books. I stepped up to the porch, reminded of old-time juke joints my father told me about, when Mom wasn't around, where he and Uncle Terry went with gandy dancers after working the rails before and after the war. The porch roof had holes in it, and wood creaked under my weight as if ready to break. I jumped at the sudden sound, reminded I was alive, and probably not alone. The cabin looked like it had been left standing since the 20's or 30's, untouched except for time and weather. Mold and wood rot was in the air.

I opened the door, went in.

I was almost ready for what was inside. I'd read about this kind of place enough in my lifetime, from Wells to Sterling and even Corville: the magic shop, where hearts' desires are found. My first, quick glimpse of the interior's stunning vastness, impossibly contained by the shabby cabin's walls, was dizzying, and as I stumbled across the threshold I was afraid I'd fall, and keep falling, forever through a hole to the center of the universe. A cool breeze gusted into my face, bringing with it the crisp smell of fresh paper, and suddenly my fear transformed into the pleasure of opening a new book.

"Come on in, sir," a voice said, drawing my attention to a man, about the age of the son I never had, standing behind an old-fashioned mechanical cash register on a mahogany counter a few steps from the door. He smiled cheerfully and added, "Glad you could find us." His hair was too long for his face and the bald patch atop his skull, and he needed a shave. He wore black pants and a T-shirt, also black, and pressed, with 'Ballard's Books' printed over the left side of the chest.

The door closed behind me. The wooden slam reminded me of the storm door to my old house closing on that day when I was home to overhear my Dad and uncle talking.

I headed for the counter, slowly, taking in as much as I could, senses slipping like a drunken man on ice. Past the entry, with its low-ceiling and counter, an aisle bordered by shelf after shelf of books two stories high stretched further than I could see directly before me. The few figures browsing the shelves diminished along a warped perspective, as if an infinite distance had been compressed into a nearly infinite corridor. More aisles opened to either side, progressing steadily like columns from an ancient temple, until they reached two walls looming like mountains over a valley. Winding, metal staircases connected balcony piled upon balcony hugging the walls, each also filled with shelves and books and dotted by an occasional figure, the highest disappearing into a ceiling of mist, implying more tiers climbing to celestial heights. Head spinning again, I looked to the marble floor, and found stairwells on both ends of the counter, with steps spiraling down into cellars and sub-levels I couldn't imagine. More stairwells lay open along the wall behind me.

My father's bookshop. A *magic* bookshop.

"Can we help you with anything?" the clerk asked.

"I . . . don't know. My father visited this place along time ago, and his brother, too."

"We're happy for the return business."

"He never said — I didn't know —"

"And that's all as it should be, sir. Is there any particular kind of book you're interested in?"

"Any kind?" I laughed, came up to the counter, leaned on it with both elbows. I was suddenly very tired, and I wasn't quite sure where I was, or how I'd gotten there. "Fiction. The kind that's a story, not the kind that's about college professors in mid-life crisis."

The clerk didn't change expression. "We have an extensive fiction section in the upper galleries, sir, categorized by the popular genres, of course, and language, and by collections burned, and banned, and lost. Do you have any favorite writers? Living or dead, it doesn't matter. We're dealers of exclusive editions of unknown works by all writers in the Library of Congress catalogue, and all works by unknowns who have yet to write a single word, or who never wrote in their lifetime." Arching an eyebrow and leaning slightly forward, the clerk whispered, "Our most popular seller for the past three years is the great American novel, by Ruth Mayberry, called *Southern Angel*. Her father was lynched before she could be conceived." Resuming his former posture, the clerk continued. "The literary and popular output of every nation and tribe in their original language is, of course, available, as well as in numerous translations into every other written language ever used by humanity." Again, he leaned forward, put a hand on the counter as if the polished wood was my forearm. "The edition of Dostoevsky's *Crime and Punishment* in Middle Kingdom 18th Dynasty hieroglyphics is quite a *tour de force*."

He knocked twice on the counter, sniffed, took a step back, half-turned to face the nearest aisle. "On the way up to the fiction tiers, of course, are the plays, and the poetry, including the Alexandria collection. Quite popular, that one. But frankly, fiction is not one of our most requested sections. We stock extensively, of course, because we pride ourselves in full service to the customer. But perhaps we can interest you in other works that might prove more valuable. Of course, you can always browse." He turned back to me and lost his smile. "Browse, but not read, sir. This *is* a bookstore, not a library."

That's what he said. Every word. It's like he typeset them in my brain, and I can open up that memory and re-read his entire sales pitch at any time.

What I said is easy to remember. "I don't understand."

"Of course you don't, sir. Few people do. I certainly don't, and I *work* here." The smile returned. "We cater to the customer who needs particular books. Books that should've been written, or were lost, or might someday be written but, chances are, will never actually exist. Books a customer used to, or wished, they owned. Books that tell them what they want to know, that give them the feelings they need to feel. Books that confirm their perspective on reality, that tell them secrets no one else could possibly know or understand. Those books are all here. Every last one of them. And more. Somewhere. It might take a while to find the specific edition required but, after all, that's part of the fun in visiting a store like this, isn't it? The thrill of the hunt!"

"I . . . can't even begin to imagine what I might want out of a place like this," I said.

"Well, I must admit biographies are our best sellers. Right down this way," the clerk said, indicating an aisle a few rows beyond the one I faced, "between Politics and General Reference.

People look for their own, and for other people's, as well. They like to catch details they've forgotten, or find someone else's secrets. Or they want a taste of the could've's, should've's, would've's, those sweet and terrible might-have-been's imagined and enacted, here and there, then, now, to be. Or not to be. Historians, in particular, love to congregate there. Always trying to crib references. Then there's the self-help and how-to sections, down there," he said, pointing to one of the stairwells, "with instructions and manuals and guides to make and fix just about everything, from the perfect gumbo to the perpetual motion engine. I do *mean* everything." He shook his shoulders and half-closed his eyes. "Good thing our competitors haven't paid us a visit. Anyway, down in that basement," pointing to the stairs at the other end of the counter, "are the Science and Philosophy departments. Theoretically, anyway. I suppose you'd have to actually go down there and look at it to know it exists. And if you're interested in spirituality, you'll find every tract, treatise, declaration, proverb, letter containing scripture from and about every entity ever conceived, or, to be quite correct, who ever conceived of us, down those stairwells by the entrance. I must warn you, however, institutions and organizations like the Vatican and any number of Jihads have accounts with us, and their representatives are quite aggressive in their pursuit of works supporting their point of view. It would be dangerous to squabble with them if you happen to be perusing a volume they declare crucial to their tenets. These groups are quite respectful, however, of the works themselves, even when they represent other beliefs and forms of worship. We hardly ever find books in that section out of place, or hidden between the racks, or tucked behind rows, anymore. And we never, ever find any texts defaced or in any way harmed. At least, not since we threatened to close down the accounts of that section's most frequent users."

"Do you have any cards?" I asked, knowing it was a stupid question, but I couldn't think of anything else to say. My years of reading fiction had not prepared me for the magnitude of this discovery, and I can only excuse myself by saying I'd spent too much time lately working in chain stores.

The clerk took out a pile of cards identical to the one I had found in my father's childhood journal. I took a handful, absently, and as the clerk raised an eyebrow, I said, "No, I meant those greeting cards with the pictures and paintings suitable for every occasion, but without anything written inside." As if I knew anyone to whom I could send such a card. I was babbling.

"Sir," the clerk said, facing me squarely again and glancing over my shoulder at the door to the outside, "we are a bookstore. We *sell* books. I am certain there is a history of greeting cards somewhere on the shelves. In fact, I can guarantee there are a healthy number of volumes on the subject tucked away in some corner or other, fully illustrated. But no, we do not sell . . . greeting cards."

The conversation between my father and uncle returned, in pieces, like confetti, and I grabbed hold of a few stray words. "The biography section? Where is it again?"

The clerk thumbed the direction and watched me walk towards the aisle he had indicated, as if I was a thief.

I was grateful to escape his scrutiny when the shelves cut us off from each other. I took two steps. Rows of books loomed over me, and sped past. I glanced over my shoulder and found the opening to the aisle far behind me. I felt as if I had exchanged my ragged sneakers for seven-league boots. I took another step. The head of the aisle was invisible. Two more, and I came upon another customer, startling her into nearly dropping the book in her hands. She fumbled with her glasses, then pulled at her skirt. Our gazes bumped into each other, fell away. Surrounded by words, we had none for each other. I walked another three steps, quickly, before I realized I had better figure out what I was looking for.

I pushed aside the idea of looking up my own biography, thinking it would be more noble, and interesting, to look up my father's and mother's histories. What had they really been like? What had my father found in this shop, years ago, along with Uncle Terry, that had held such power over the both of them? The names of bullies I wished dead, and girls I wished liked me, authors I admired, teachers who guided me to treasures, all sparked my curiosity.

But in the end, I couldn't resist my ego. I had to know who I was. I quickly scanned the shelves, found my bearing alphabetically, and moved on through the aisle, pausing every now and then to check my progress by sighting the nearest shelf tag indicating the shelf's biographical subject. I seemed to walk for half a day, though I wasn't hungry or sleepy, and I didn't feel the need to go to the bathroom. I doubt the bookstore even has such a facility. Finally, I found my name.

My heart jumped; my palms were instantly damp. I was hoping to pull down my parents' and my own biography at the same time, since we all shared a name, but I was stunned by the number of books dedicated to me. As far as I could see on either side, and above me, the shelves had my name on them. What had I done, what was I going to do, that was so important?

I grabbed the nearest volume, appropriately brief, opened to the first page, and discovered I had died in a car accident with my sister. The book was closed and back on the shelf before the idea found the depth of my sister's memory. I had another book in my hand, more substantial, before I felt her loss, again, and read that I was a writer of a popular detective series. Another said I was a war hero, and yet another, a baker at a high-end New York pastry shop. Book after book revealed alternative histories, possible roads I might have taken: policeman, murderer, garbage man, circus clown, psychiatrist. The options appeared endless.

I methodically examined every book, ignoring the titles that ranged from *The Twilight of Stars* to *A Hard Day's Work*, skimming the opening paragraphs to confirm the book was indeed about me. In each one, I was born in the same town, from the same parents, on the date and at the time I'd been told. Most followed what I knew to be true, until grade school, when I began to make my own choices. Then the histories diverged.

In most, I married and had my own children, and there were references to multi-generational biographies of not only my ancestors, but my progeny, as well. In most, I seemed to have lived a good life. But the details eluded me. I couldn't hold any book for more than a minute or two, or retain specific names, dates, places. The weight of so many more possibilities dragged me through the shelves, drove me to put one volume down and pick up the next. I gorged myself on the possibility of possibilities, plunging into one book after another, and in the back of my mind, I recognized the idea I had about getting old was actually a seed, and in Ballard's Books, that seed was growing into regret.

My roller-coaster ride through the funhouse reflections of my life slowed when I began identifying familiar events and places later in my life. The books I picked up and put back came closer to my own, true history, at least the way I could recall it. The urge to put down each book lessened, and in fact I felt compelled to linger, to stare harder, deeper into a reflection made harsher by its truth.

Finally, I opened a book to a page where I was reading my own biography in Ballard's Books, and without thinking I went back to the first page, leaned against the bookcase and settled down to read.

"This is not a library, sir."

The clerk was behind me, and when I turned I was as surprised by his sudden as by his physical appearance: his face was clean-shaven, his long hair was tied neatly into a pony tail, and the mechanical expression of good humor had melted into a frown. "What? I'm sorry —"

"Are you interested in that particular edition?"

"Yes, well, I think I am. How much is it?"

Something tugged at my insides, like a tilt-a-whirl's centrical force. "You may not be able to afford it. I would have to speak to the owners. Should I bring the book up to the counter and make inquiries?" The clerk held both hands out, as if a baby was about to be transferred.

"No," I said, putting the thing back, "please, let me shop around some more." The clerk was gone when I looked back. There was no sign of him at either end of the aisle, at least as far as I could seek, and certainly not from overhead. I stamped the floor once, to make sure. Solid.

I tried to pick out the exact same book I'd just had, but all the editions on that part of the shelf looked the same. I went to the end, this time. Found out when I died. When I'm going to — when I'm supposed to die.

Regret blossomed into loneliness.

I went back to the books I'd looked at earlier. The ones that sounded happier. I started checking the last pages.

"Have you found something more to your liking?"

The damned clerk, again. "I haven't made a decision, yet."

"These others are definitely out of your price range, sir."

"How do you know?"

"It's my business."

"Do you take credit cards?" I don't honestly know where that came from. I have one, of course. I never let a balance run. The bank keeps increasing my limit. But I've never bought anything big on it. I've never wanted or owned anything costing a lot of money.

"I would have to inquire, sir."

"Give me some more time to decide."

In a blink, the clerk was gone. I tried to imagine my Dad and uncle coming here as kids or teenagers. Did they buy anything? If they did, what did they give as payment? If not, did they regret not buying, or being able to buy? What book did they pick? Had they wanted to find the store again, go back inside, shop some more? Why hadn't they told anyone?

My fingers danced along the book spines. I thought about all those bright, fresh pages containing my life. My lives. And then I thought about what the clerk said about competition among religious factions downstairs. I wondered about the prosperity of some faiths, particular those putting value on the written word, and how so many others vanished. I considered the account of souls, or spirits, or whatever it was the store took out of a person as payment, available to the faiths with larger followings, so that they might be able to take out of print certain volumes inconsistent with their beliefs as well as purchase those illuminating them with new glory.

Survival of the fittest. Adapt to the environment, or change it.

Change. If you don't like the story or the ending, change it. I could change my life through manipulation of the shop's stock, just as, perhaps, some religious leaders had, at one time or another, steadied the course and progress of their faith by a judicial pruning of heretical and rival sacred texts on the shelves of Ballard's Books. Certainly, the same had been done in the world outside the shop, from ancient times to present, by conquering armies and seduced kings and missionaries possessed by righteousness.

Obviously, changing the written word or somebody's truth or story isn't a new idea. How many times have you read a book and said, I could do better than this? Or, I didn't want that character to die, or the story to end this way? I never bothered trying to do better, or changing stories I'd read for my own pleasure. Too much fun reading. Too much work writing the damned things. And for what? Do you know how little those guys get paid? Well, the fiction writers, anyway.

It's not like scholars and academics and journalists and even prophets haven't interpreted facts and dates and circumstances to prove the point they wanted to make. It's not like everything in books, in non-fiction books, is absolutely true. What is truth, anyway? Is it there if you look, like that Science and Philosophy section, then gone when you turn away? That's why I prefer fiction. I know for sure it's all lies.

So it didn't bother me to take out a pen. Pick out one of those copies of my biography that held close to the way things have gone. Cross out the death date. That was a start. My head was full of ideas, but I needed time, first.

It was a funny feeling, being an editor. Or a copy editor, at least.

"Sir!"

I dropped the pen.

"What are you going?"

"I want this one," I said, holding the book out to the clerk. My hands were shaking. The clerk was a blur in front of me. Ears ringing, face flushed, I felt like a kid again, caught by Mr. Whitmore stealing coverless copies of E.C. Comics from the used bins at the back of his candy store.

"You're writing in the book. That's not allowed."

"I'm going to buy the book," I said, not looking at him but at the book in my hand, at rows after row of books about me, at the floor, back at the book. "I want this book. I have enough to buy it. You said so, right? It's practically mine. Hell, it's *about* me. People can write in the books they own. They do it all the time. They make notes, underline passages, make comments, argue with what's written. They dedicate them to lovers and friends and family. It's not a crime to write in a book."

"Defacing the store's property is not allowed," the clerk said, snatching the book from my hands. He whisked it back onto the shelf, took hold of my arm, shoved me down the aisle.

I felt like I'd been strapped to the nose of a 747 and launched on a trip around the world. The clerk definitely knew shortcuts through the stacks, because we dipped and leapt and slipped through impossibly thin cracks, passed through dark, dank places under floors and between back-to-back shelving units, and we were back to the front of the store in moments instead of hours. Breathless, I fell against the smooth, polished counter top, looked up, and hardly recognized the clerk. Oh, it was the same one. He had the eyes, the turn of the lips. But now he was bald, except for gray tufts around his ears. And chubby. And not smiling. It didn't look like he'd smiled in many, many years.

"I must ask you to leave the premises, sir," the clerk said, crossing his arms over his chest.

"What? I'm sorry. But I want to buy that book. It's about me. I damaged it, I'll buy it from you. Whatever you ask. Just let me have it."

"Shop policy forbids sales to customers who do not respect the merchandise. We have lost accounts over this matter, sir. Please, do not force me to ask you again to leave."

"Wait. Stop. Isn't there a manager I could talk to? Someone in charge? The owner?"

"I represent management on this matter. There is no higher authority on the issue." He gestured at the door.

I found myself stumbling away from the counter, gliding towards the door as if the clerk's hand was on my neck pushing me out. "Hold it. My father was here, a long time ago, but he never told me. Why? If I'd known, if I'd been able to find you earlier —"

I crashed against the door, which opened to the night. I held onto the frame, searching for things to say while waiting for an answer. "The shop has rules," the clerk said, directly into my ear. "They are simple rules. Rules common courtesy and decency accommodate without mention. And there is a rule of discretion, for those customers who leave with the grace of a purchase, or a simple visit. Our customers cannot speak of us, on pain of never returning. That is why your father never spoke of his visit to you."

"What the hell kind of rule is that? Don't you want to attract business?"

"We have been in business for a very long time. Longer than most nations. We are not desperate for custom. True seekers, our best clientele, find us. The rest, the ones who buy greeting cards, we do not need."

"But that's crazy. How can you possibly know if someone mentions you out in the world?"

"Don't you think we read our own books?"

I lost my grip and was thrust into darkness. I tripped, flew through the air, landed on hard dirt and bristly brush. The door slammed behind me, an echo of another door closing long ago. Dazed, I looked up. Saw stars through overhead branches. The air was cool, and I smelled green things growing and decomposing. The little shack was gone.

I've never been able to find it again.

Which is why I've gone to the trouble of telling you this story.

I can't ever go back. But you can find it. Here's their card. Just do me a favor. For introducing the idea to you. For giving you clues on how to find it. For showing you an opportunity to do something significant in your life. To your life.

When you find the shop, go the fiction section. Find my name. It'll be on a docu-drama account of my life, a fantasy-autobiography, so to speak: *The Wind At My Back*. It's not about my real life, but it's the life I wished I'd lived. I have things in there like my Dad taking me to Ballard's Books when I was young, instead of hanging on to his stupid fantasy with his Hardy Boy brother for all those years. My Mom lives a long time. I get a brother, to go along with my sister, who doesn't die until her grandkids get old. You can get a print-on-demand copy through Amazon.com, but don't worry about that. Take a copy you find in the shop, tuck it under your arm, keep going, maybe pick one or two more books. If the clerk asks what you're doing, tell him you're shopping and you haven't made your final selections yet. Whatever you do, don't mention greeting cards, boxes of candy, espresso bars, house decorations, or anything else you might find in one of the big chains. Then go to the biography section. Find the books about me, the ones that sound like the story I just told you. Open up to any page, you'll see right away. At the end, the bad ones say I die in a couple of years. Most of them had blue or black spines, half-an-inch thick hardcover, three-quarters of an inch soft-cover, with titles like *Life in the Shallows* or *Steps Not Taken* or *What My Father Didn't Leave Me.*

Take one, maybe two. Replace them with the book I wrote, the one you took out of the fiction section. Walk around some more. And then lose those biographies.

Mis-shelve them. Put them in fiction. Behind the rack, between the stacks. Find out if the shop has a bathroom and put a copy behind the toilet tank. Throw them into the boiler — I think I saw a few on my jet-ride through the store. Anything, just make them disappear.

I don't know if this plan will work; if I can alter my fate — edit my life — by changing books on a shelf in a bookstore that's more hallucination than reality. I don't know if I'll live longer, or remember things differently, or have a better life from the moment enough of those bad biographies get taken out of circulation. I know, it's kind of magical realist, isn't it. All I've got to go by is a conversation I overheard as a kid, and what that clerk implied about his customers in the religious department.

I think it's worth a try.

The problem with books is that they always end. Yes. My book — the book of my life — is ending. Very soon. There's no sequel. There aren't any other books to pick up. And I'm not tired of living. It's been a long time since anyone's been close enough for me to feel losing them.

It's like my Dad said: "You can't spend your whole life looking for something that came and went, because you won't live your proper life." What came and went in my life was a mystery. It took a piece out of me, and like Ahab, I've been chasing it ever since. That's not a life.

I want a different book. It's probably too late to revise the whole damned thing, and I know, the book has to end sometime. All I want is a shot at making it last a little longer. And having it come to a good end, instead of a sad one.

Just, whatever you do, don't let the clerk catch you.

BOOKS

David Bischoff

The old-fashioned wood sign had five letters carved deeply into it, charcoal against weathered walnut:

BOOKS

It hung from a pole on a chain in a yard by a large Victorian house, shaded by oaks. This kind of house, Teddy Beacon reflected, would be cut up into apartments back in Palo Alto. Here though it was pretty well intact — although obviously someone had turned it into a bookshop.

Teddy pulled his rental car off the little road and parked. There was a Thunderbird and an old Chevy Station wagon already in the lot. Sheesh, the kind of old junkers you saw here in the Midwest! The rental Lincoln was bad enough but the pieces of crap that rattled around on the highways and the old byways of Indiana were not only eyesores, they were dangerous.

In fact one of the reasons he was in this small town of Goshen, Indiana now was that an old Ford truck that had to be forty years old if it was a day had cut him off, forcing him to a shoulder and nearly off the highway. He'd been rattled enough to want to take a break so he'd pulled off at the first exit to look for something to eat. Oddly enough instead of a McDonald's or a Denny's he'd found a small town just a few miles off the thruway with a nice little

179

diner where he'd tucked into the best damned cheeseburger and ice cream soda he'd ever eaten.

Well, it wasn't like the guys he was going to see were eager to see him. A couple hours off his schedule wouldn't hurt anything. He'd fleece them in any case. Always had, always would. Teddy was post-modern and predatory with a vicious take-no-prisoners attitude in business that had allowed him to swim with the silicon sharks. Life where all the values were in dollars and cents was so much easier than all that religious claptrap his parents had tried to hang on him. "Son, if you'd only take some time to read and reflect — you'd see the moral gravity of things!"

Reading, though, had always been hell for Teddy. And there's been so many other heavenly diversions in his busy life.

He got out of his car, not bothering to lock the door. With his own car — a beautiful red Jaguar — he'd lock the door, you bet, even in the podunk town. Hell, if he'd had his Jaguar, he wouldn't *be* in this podunk town — he'd easily have scooted around that truck and sprinted off toward his appointment. Oh well. It was a nice place, if kind of stupid, this Goshen, Indiana. What kind of name was Goshen, anyway? Indian?

As he walked closer, Teddy could see that the old Victorian was not in the best repair. Its red paint was peeling and leaves from last fall hung out of the gutters. It had an old comfortable feeling and what with the nice spring breeze and the smell of dandelions and new-mown grass in the air it made him feel okay.

On the stairs headed up to the porch was a big wood box, labeled QUARTER BOOKS. DICKERING WELCOME.

Inside, were just a bunch of damaged old paperbacks. Teddy saw an old Alfred Hitchcock collection on top, lots of men's adventure, some westerns, a *Twilight Zone* collection, a couple of science fiction books and an anthology of stories by a man named Roald Dahl. He recognized them not because he read books but because of his grandfather who had been a book reader and had tried to pass the tradition onto his grandchild. Yeah, right!

Still, because of Pop-pop, and a more specific reason, Teddy Beacon knew a little bit about old books. Just enough, in fact.

There was an old timer on the front porch, deeply engrossed in a big old collection of Shakespeare plays. By him on the rocking chair was a glass of lemonade sparkling in the afternoon sun. The old-timer picked it up, and the ice cubes tinkled.

There was a faded old oriental rug right before the big door of the entrance. Above this was a plaque that read ATHERTON AND SON — BOOKSELLERS. A big glass knob turned easily, a bell rang and as Teddy entered, the smell hit him.

The smell was of leather and ink, aged and mellowed. The smell was of other ages. Of reflection. Of thought and language and pulp and deep, deep time unbordered by anything approaching "now". It was a rich smell, and Teddy hated it. But he'd smelled it before and he well knew that he got used to the musty, fusty odor soon enough.

Classical music drifted through the place quietly. Although Teddy had never been a classical music fan, he recognized that it was Mozart. What Mozart piece, though, he had no idea. But being a computer guy in the thick frenzy of Silicon Valley, busy scratching after his first million, he didn't have much time to waste with cultural flotsam and jetsam.

An old man with a shock of white hair smiled at him from a desk teetering with piles of books.

"Good day, sir." The pronunciation was brisk and crisp, but friendly. The man had remarkable features. A jutting jaw, an aquiline nose and blue eyes somehow simultaneously mild and piercing. However, it was the eyebrows that leant the greatest effect to the man's face: They were bushy and black.

In the man's hands was a slim hardback entitled *Nightlife of the Gods* by Thorne Smith.

"Hey," said Teddy. "Nice place?"

The man nodded graciously, with a reserve that was both elegant and regal. "We like to think so. Are you looking for anything special?"

"Uhm. You got any used Nintendo games?" Teddy had noticed that sometimes these kind of rat holes had just about everything, and as his personal hobby was computer games, he figured he might as well check. That was why he was here — plus one more major reason.

"Nintendo?"

"Yeah. You know. Japanese things. Control pads. Shooters.

Golf. Mario Brothers. Nintendo games and Playstation games, you hook to your TV?"

The man's face went a little sour. "No TV here, I'm afraid."

"Uhmm. What about . . . uhm . . . baseball cards?"

The man shook his head. "No. No, I'm afraid that the sign outside tells no lies. We only sell books." The smile brightened: a footnote smile. "And, of course, magazines."

The old man set down the book in his hands and picked up another volume. It was another old book entitled *The Twonky and Other Stories*, by Lewis Padgett.

"Oh. Sure."

Teddy sighed. He looked at his watch. Well, he had an hour or so.

"Okay. I guess you have mysteries then."

The man took a moment to assay the book in his hands. Then he carefully scribbled in a price in number 2 pencil on the right side of the first page, and carefully set the book on a pile.

"My personal favorite, sir," said the man with rolling intonation. He picked up another volume. The title was *I and Thou*, by Martin Buber.

He regarded the book for a moment and then fixed Teddy with his gaze, which suddenly seemed alarmed.

"I've never seen you here before."

"I'm from out of state. I'm here for a business meeting with some colleagues," said Teddy. "I had lunch here and was just driving around. Saw your sign."

The man said nothing. He regarded Teddy blankly for a moment, and then pulled out a box from the side.

"You'll need a name tag."

"Excuse me."

The man smiled amiably. "I believe I can analyze your accent. You are from California . . . ah . . . the Bay Area, I should think."

"That's right."

"You must excuse us old fogies here in Goshen. We go way back. Back to a time when everyone knew each other's name. I like to continue that tradition here in my store. When you run into another browser or reader, please say hello, and use his name. It makes for such a pleasant environment."

Teddy shrugged. "Sure."

"Oh good. Your name?"

"Smith. John Smith."

The man's eyes sparkled. There was a little kink to his smile. "What a pleasant name. So easy to remember. I'll just write down 'John'. Is that all right?"

"Yeah. Yeah, that's fine."

The old man took a big black magic marker. He wrote the name JOHN in flowing letters on a card. Then he placed the card in a plastic holder and handed it to Teddy.

Teddy pinned himself.

"The mystery room is on the second floor. You go up those stairs and take an immediate right and walk to the end of the corridor. There's a big sign on the door. I think you should find it all right."

"Second floor?" Teddy said with disbelief. "You've got a lot of books!"

The man finished pricing the book in his hand, then picked up another one. It was *End of Eternity*, by Isaac Asimov.

"We're a bookstore, sir, and we've been here a very long time indeed. Happy browsing!"

Nice guy, thought Teddy as he started toward the steps. But still he kind of gave him the creeps. These old guys, they just weren't in step. They weren't on the cutting edge. They had their cerebellums in history's cellar and just couldn't see what was coming up on the wired horizon.

As Teddy wended his way through the cluttered stacks of books and books and books, books and books and books, smelling deeply of paper graveyards. He allowed himself to feel vastly superior. Sheesh, now that there were E-books and Rocket-books and Tomorrow Books, you really didn't need musty, yellowing paper. Of course, it wasn't that Teddy ever read fiction — he'd read the word-bites of news sometimes and of course he could program. But he left things like documentation to other people.

Plenty of people could write in English. So few could write in the computer languages that allowed them to program and create the kind of games that Teddy Beacon created. Fun, intelligent shooters like *Blitz* and *Kill! Cat! Kill!* and *Kennedy Hunter* he'd already worked on, and now he was doing a start-up, with the help of those chumps he was on his way to see down the road.

They were a couple of brothers who were ace *Blast the Quaker III* fans who had some cool ideas and didn't know squat about business. Teddy intended to front them some Diet Coke, pepperoni pizza and a few thousand bucks (a few thousand bucks! Chicken-feed in Silicon Valley!) and get himself a cookin' game that would get him way out of Ego Software and well into his own company — MiliPhartz.

Ha! Then maybe he'd find some other stuff out there. Maybe start up a new operating system and outbillionaire Bill Gates.

Of course, he needed venture capital for all this, and of late there wasn't as much as there used to be. But hell, he'd scratch it up. There were always chumps out there, eager to lay down some money on a hot brainy guy with a Plan like himself.

Teddy found the stairs. They were not easy to navigate. There were piles of books on both sides. He had to be careful as he went up, or he'd topple a stack, and the domino effect — well, it would be pretty damned awful. As he prepared himself for the tricky enterprise, Teddy noticed a beautiful volume to his right. In gorgeous gilt letters, it read. *Dante's Divine Comedy*.

Divine Comedy. What kind of book was that?

A Jesus and God joke book?

What did Jesus say to St. Peter?

Hey, Pete? Heard any good blonde jokes lately?

Hmm. Nope. That one didn't work, but it gave Teddy a neat idea.

A new computer game.

Jevovah Hijinks.

You're God in the Old Testament looking down and you blast bad Israelites for putting up idols.

Extra points for plagues on Job.

At the top of the stairs was a landing, and on this landing was an old couch. On the old couch sat a woman. She looked to be middle aged, with an old style of hairdo for her greying hair. She was plump and the smell of rosy perfume was a pleasant switch from the stench of books, books, books.

On her name tag was the name PHYLLIS.

"Hello," Phyllis said, looking up from her book. Teddy could see that it was an old paperback called *I, The Jury* by Mickey Spillane.

"Hey," said Teddy.

"Beautiful day, isn't it?"

"Oh. Yeah."

"Are you finding what you're looking for?"

She had a cup of tea on the table beside her. The cup was a beautifully designed delicate tea cup, absolutely exquisite. Teddy knew a little bit about china because of his grandmother and he could see that the teacup was of top grade.

"Well, actually, I was looking for the mystery section."

The woman's eyes came alive. "Oh dear. I know it well! That and the romance section. My two main weakness, although I must say that I can read just about anything as long as it's well-written." She smiled emphatically and lifted up a fingernail, delicately painted pink, pointing the way. "Just down this corridor and then to the right."

"Thanks. I'm from out of town. Never been here before."

"Oh! I thought you were new, John. We love new people here. Plenty of lovely books. I'm Phyllis of course." She giggled, because that was obvious from her name tag. "Phyllis Brown. I lead the mystery discussion group every Wednesday evening. If you'd like to join in, please do, It's in the Methodist church Sunday School social hall about half a mile toward town."

"Oh, I'm just passing through. Thanks anyway."

The woman folded her book on her lap. She was wearing half frame spectacles and she tilted her head to look at Teddy. The cord around her neck wobbled like outlines of dewlaps.

"Ah. Passing through . . ."

She didn't quite know what to make of the concept.

Then she giggled. "Oh dear me. You must excuse me. I am such a silly twit sometimes. Of course! Passing through! And why not?"

"Well, I'd better be going. I'll see you on the way back."

"Happy book hunting. This place looks chaotic, and I suppose it is, especially the books in stacks which are pretty trashy. But the actual book racks are alphabetized. There's a mystery hard-back section. And there's a mystery softcover section. I believe there even a few signed editions mixed in. And oh! Do you fancy mystery pulps?"

"Pulps?"

"Old fiction magazines. I suppose they were mostly detective mysteries. *Black Mask*. Things like that. There never was an *Agatha Christie's Mystery Magazine*, I'm sorry to say. And *Ellery Queen's* — well, that was mostly digest. That and *Alfred Hitchcock's* of course."

All these names!

They all went right over Teddy's head.

"Actually, I'm just looking for paperbacks."

"Oh? Might I enquire who your favorite writer is?"

"Well, actually they're for a friend. Richard Stark's the name."

The woman's eyes glittered.

"Oh well, it's a good thing you met me! Those books were actually written by Donald E. Westlake. So they'll be in the 'W's."

"No kidding!" Teddy grinned. "Thanks!"

"My pleasure!"

She waved him a toodle-loo. "Oh, and Mr. Westlake's other books are very amusing. Although once in a while, as you can see, I do like my mysteries rough and hard-boiled."

"Thanks again."

Teddy hurried along before the woman could say anything more. Jesus, these folks in the Midwest moved like Bay Area traffic at rush hour! The guy at the malt shop just about chewed his ear off and there'd been only one subject: the weather.

As promised, the room containing the mystery books was topped with a sign. When Teddy walked in, he was stunned by the size of it. It must have once been a master bedroom. Now bookcases lined the walls and bookcases formed floor to ceiling columns. Shelves and shelves and shelves.

Books and books and books!

The sheer numbers were almost suffocating. Teddy felt a little bit claustrophobic as he picked his way carefully through the narrow aisles formed by the stacks. He found the paperback section easily enough and then speedily located the 'W's.

Willeford.

Williams.

Westlake!

Yes, Donald E. Westlake.

Teddy perused. *Busy Body. Hot Rock. Smoke.* Hardcovers. Paperbacks. Good grief! There were like three shelves of Donald E. Westlake books. He looked closer and yes, there — Richard Stark. They were mostly the Fawcett books from the 60's, with some hardcovers — but there were also a few of the AVON editions, as Jack had said to look for as well.

Teddy picked out one of the earlier editions. He didn't know much about paperback books, but it didn't take an expert to realize that this book was in really good shape.

The ones in good shape are worth way more, Jack had said.

Teddy looked inside for the price. Penciled on the top of right hand side was '$.50'.

He felt a surge of excitement. These books were worth serious money . . . and there were lots of them. Fifty cents each? Oh my God. Would he be able to carry them all?

He was looking through the hardcover Richard Starks when the thought hit him.

Sure, he didn't read books. But he'd taken English courses. Number one, books were kinda going out of style with most people. The New York corporate publishing industry was in a tailspin. Small presses really hadn't caught on, and to tell the total truth, who the hell wanted to read books on computer screens after they stared at screens all day at work?

Old books were getting popular and even more collectable than ever. And the already valuable books —

Telling himself to keep calm, he put the Richard Stark book back in place and walked down the corridor.

Mrs. Mystery was still engrossed in her book. Teddy cleared his throat.

She looked up at him and smiled.

"Hello, John. Did you find what you were looking for."

"Yeah! Thanks! This is an amazing collection of . . . stuff!"

"Oh, it's heaven! Just heaven!"

"I thought I'd buy my Dad some books too. I was wondering where the general fiction books were. You know . . . like classics?"

"Oh, on the third floor dear. Takes up the whole floor."

"My. Thanks."

Teddy made his way up more steps, careful not to knock down any of the teetering books.

The third floor was, as promised, filled with general fiction. There were scads and wads and nests of paperbacks of all sorts, clearly more modern and not in particularly good shape. It didn't take long to find the hardcovers and soon he found what he was looking for.

Here were the Hemingway books.

He didn't know Hemingway from a hole in the ground, but his grandfather liked him and he was famous. This was as good a place as any to start.

At random, Teddy selected a good looking copy of *The Sun Also Rises*.

Scribners.

First edition.

Clean, mylar encased — a little yellowed, but otherwise in really good condition.

The price marked was ten dollars.

How much was this thing worth? Hundreds? A thousand? And he'd picked it at random.

Damn! Who else did he know about from those lit classes? He tried F. Scott Fitzgerald.

The Great Gatsby. First Edition.

Ten smackeroonies.

William Faulkner. *The Sound and the Fury*.

Ten small ones.

There was a chair in the corner. Teddy went and sat in it. Trying to keep calm, he looked around the vast, packed room.

This was like a ancient Egyptian tomb of books!

And here it was, buried in the vast plains of the forgotten Midwest.

Sheesh! Forget about start-up money. Forget about a company! He could get rich just buying books here and then selling them!

Then, from the dim corners of his mind, a memory emerged.

After taking a series of deep breaths, Teddy got up, steadied himself and walked back down to the Mystery Woman.

"Hi there," he said.

Pleasant as ever, Phyllis looked up. "Hello, John. Did you find your Richard Stark book?"

"Yeah. Thanks. Wow. My friend is going to be very, very happy."

"Perhaps you should introduce him to Ngaio Marsh. Now there is a fine writer."

"Oh. Okay. I'll have a look. I was thinking though — all these books here. One of my favorites is Stephen King. Where would he be?"

"Mister King? Why, he's a horror writer. That would be in the cellar, of course," the woman beamed proudly. She spoke in a rather condescending tone, as though Teddy should have been able to guess that, and easily.

"Okay. Thanks. I'll have a look."

Teddy started down the stairs.

His first instinct had been to grab an armful of the Starks. But then, there was so much more at stake here. No, Teddy pal, he told himself. You've got to play it cool.

On the first floor, the old guy was still hard at work, going through books and pricing.

"Cellar?" asked Teddy.

"I thought you looked like a horror aficionado," said the man in rolling, amused tones. "Yes. You just go through the history section over there, and then around past the rest room and you can't miss it. There's a sign there with a quote." The man's eyes twinkled. "You can't miss it."

The man was working on a book named *The Wanderer* by Fritz Leiber.

"Oh. You say you're looking for horror now? It just so happens that I've just priced a book that just came in. Now where is that thing?"

The white-haired man peered around at the stacks thoughtfully.

"Ah!" he said. "Here it is."

He managed to pull out a hardcover book and hand it over to Teddy.

It was an old book. "*Dagon and Other Stories*," said Teddy, "by H.P. Lovecraft."

"First edition, Arkham House," said the old man. "I've got a few, so I'll give it to you for five dollars?"

"Lovecraft? Never heard of him. Actually, I'm looking for Stephen King."

"Oh yes. Plenty of Stephen King in the cellar. Can't remember exactly what —"

Teddy was already on his way. "That's okay. I'll just go down and check."

This was fun, but a little bit overwhelming. Already Teddy's mind was churning. How could he truly capitalize on this? Hell, maybe he could just offer to buy the whole place. But of course, he'd need venture capital for that. Better just buy this and that first, show what kind of books were here — and get the money together that way.

As advertised, there was a sign marked DARK FANTASY above a thick oak door.

This door was closed and securely bolted with no less than three old fashioned bolts.

Sheesh, though Teddy. There must be really valuable stuff down there!

One by one, he opened the bolts. As he pulled the door open, the hinges squeaked horribly. A subterranean smell — must and darkness and mold — bloomed up. Below were shadows and dimness.

Teddy laughed.

Cool.

How atmospheric.

The steps were old and creaky, but solid enough. Even as he descended, Teddy could feel the cool air envelope him. It felt nice and soft and welcome, and it relaxed him. It had been a little warm and close upstairs, he thought.

Downstairs was a large room with old bookcases that disappeared into the dimness. Teddy fancied that he could see curls of mist back there.

Before the stacks of books, though, was a couch.

A man lay upon the couch. He was reading an old yellowing magazine. The man seemed engrossed in the magazine (which Teddy could see was an old pulp magazine named *Weird Tales*. It had a picture of a slinky, half-dressed woman and a demon on it) that Teddy thought he's just avoid him, but as he walked past, the man looked up from the magazine.

"Good day!" said the man cheerfully.

"Oh. Hello."

"Horror fan, I take it? Or are you just looking for the john?"

The man had a round face with a sharp nose. His hair was short and he looked to be in his sixties. On his tag was the name ROBERT.

"Sure. Looking for Stephen King."

"He's not here yet."

Teddy shook his head. "No. No. I don't know what you're talking —"

"Although I look old, I'm young at heart. In fact, I have the heart of a young boy. I keep it on my desk in a jar."

The man's eyes twinkled.

"Stephen King. You know. Like, *Carrie* and *The Shining* and stuff like that."

"Oh books! I love that craft!" The man smiled slyly. "Yes, I believe you can find those particular books over yonder."

Teddy went over and had a quick look. There was a whole wall of Stephen King books. He quickly selected one at random. *Salem's Lot*. Doubleday Books. First Edition.

On the title page was an inscription.

"To Kirby. Come up to Maine when it snows. Best, Stephen."

The cost, neatly penciled in the front, was "$5.00".

He walked back to the man.

"This is really some place," he said. "I've never seen so many great books. Where do they all come from?"

"Books? Printing presses, initially, I suppose."

"You know what I mean."

"Ah. Well, maybe this is just sort of a book graveyard. Actually, books tend to go where they are wanted, don't they?"

Well, he was getting nowhere with this guy. Hopefully he'd be gone next time he came back, Teddy thought.

"Thanks."

He started back up the stairs.

A slithering sound echoed in the distance.

The trouble was, which books to grab first? Teddy knew there must be priceless stuff in here that these bozos didn't know about. Trouble was, he didn't know about it either.

What he'd do was to call Jack. Jack would know.

Then he'd come back, buy a few books. Sell 'em. Then come back with a moving van!

The old guy had stopped marking books. Now he was reading a book.

"Pardon me. Where's the nearest pay phone?"

"Up at Hank's garage, I believe. Not find the book you want?"

"There's so many good ones here, I can't decide what I want. I thought I'd call a friend and ask for recommendations."

The man nodded. "Good idea. I could give you some, if you like."

"I'm sure you'd have some good ones. But my friend and I . . . We have similar tastes."

And they tended to have pictures of dead presidents on the front.

"Ah. I see. Well then. I wish you luck."

The man turned his attention back to his book.

Teddy went out the door and walked over to his car. He felt a vague coldness and a shiver swept over him. He looked back at the house. Yes. No dream. There it was. Solid, old and dominating the sky.

Teddy shrugged. He found his keys and got in his car.

It was a fortunate day that he found this place.

He'd better act fast, though, before some other hustler found it.

Teddy turned the key.

Nothing.

He frowned. He turned the key in the ignition again, and got the exact same result.

Damn! What a time for the battery to die! And in a rental car? This never happened!

Teddy took a deep breath. Well, it wasn't like this was South Chicago or Detroit or anything like. Help was just a quick phone call away.

He went back inside.

When he got in, the man from the basement was standing, holding a pile of books. Beside him was Phyllis, the Mystery Woman. Finally, the man behind the desk had a big pile of books as well.

They were all smiling at him.

"We've taken the liberty of finding a few books for you to read," said the old man with the white hair. "I'll have them delivered to your room."

"Room?"

"Well, yes. Where you'll be staying."

"Huh? What are you talking about? And how did you know my car wasn't working. What's going on here?"

The old man looked puzzled. Then he brightened. "Ah. Well that explains it."

"Explains what?"

The sharp nosed man shrugged. "He hasn't guessed."

"I wonder if he's in the right place?" said Mystery Woman.

"There are no mistakes. The ways of the cosmos are subtle and rich," said the old man. "Well, well, in any case — you're here for a reason. Welcome. I think you'll find things comfortable enough. Alas, your room has no computers or television — none of that stuff here I'm afraid. So you'll have to make some adjustments to your lifestyle —"

"You guys are nuts! Where's the garage? I just need to get my car fixed!"

"Well, that would be quite the task!" said the guy from the basement. "Quite the task indeed!"

"What are you talking about. The battery's just dead. That's —" Teddy looked around.

His car sat where it had been, although now it presented an entirely different picture. The front and side looked as though some giant had mistaken it for an accordion. The front window looked like a crystalline spiderweb in which a splash of blood dwelled.

". . . all," finished Teddy in a whisper, said he turned to the others.

"Here's a book you might enjoy," said the man with the white hair. "My gift to you. To make you feel comfortable."

Numbly, Teddy held out his hand and soon found himself holding a first edition copy of *For Whom The Bell Tolls* by Ernest Hemingway.

ESCAPES

Nina Kiriki Hoffman

"**W**here are the books where you write your own ending?" the girl asked me. She was pale and bedraggled; her shoes were scuffed, and so was her face. The shoulders of her long brown coat were sopping from the rain outside the two-story building that housed Brannigan's Bookstore. The brown leather satchel strapped across her chest bulged at her side, its clasps broken and outside pockets gaping to display a selection of her underwear, mostly white cotton. I wondered if I should ask her to check her bag. I didn't think she could shove anything else into it, though, even if she *wanted* to shoplift.

"The Choose-Your-Own-Adventure books?" I glanced toward the kids' section. Choose-Your-Own-Adventure books were from my childhood. I didn't know if anyone still published them. I'd only been working at Brannigan's for a week, though, and I didn't know the stock yet. Every time I straightened a section, I found all kinds of books I'd never heard of in my previous incarnation as a bookseller at a big chain store in Seattle.

David, the supervisor on duty, handed a little old lady a copy of the latest *Witches' Almanac* and came to the cashwrap. "Hey, Sylvia, need some help?" he asked.

Everybody at Brannigan's was really nice. They didn't trust me yet. Every time I tried to answer a customer's question, somebody swooped up and checked on me, which was probably a good thing, as I usually had the wrong answer, apparently. It was as if my eight years in book sales didn't mean a thing.

They were watching me as though I was a baby chick in a hen yard. It was nice. It was also driving me nuts.

I wasn't ready to protest, though. I needed this job. I couldn't go back to Seattle. Peter was terrifyingly there, with all his friends, not all of whom I knew, but all of whom knew about me. The three earlier times I had tried to escape, Peter had tracked me down with his friends' help and punished me for abandoning him. To actually escape, I had had to leave everything behind, change my name, my hair color, and my behavior.

I liked my new town, Tonkit, somewhere in the middle of Washington State. So it was small, and I was lonely; at least I had my own place. I could go home without worrying that Peter would be waiting in the apartment for me with another suitcase full of things he called toys.

Well, that wasn't true. I always worried. The change was that even though I worried, nobody was there when I got home, and the tension that twisted my guts relaxed.

I loved selling books. Books had saved my life time after time when I was a teenager and there was no way I could leave home except by reading. Hell, they had helped me survive the time I spent with Peter. I got a rush helping other people find the perfect escape.

I was lucky Brannigan's had hired me. Brannigan's was not an easy place to get a job. Some of the clerks had been there fifty years. Nobody ever quit unless they were moving or they died. I still wondered why I had gotten the job, but I didn't want to lose it. I was still on probation.

I could survive being helped too much.

"I'm looking for the books where you write your own ending," the soggy girl said in a soft voice to David.

"Ah," said David. "Follow me." He didn't head for the kids' section, but back into the stacks where new and used books rubbed shoulders.

Parts of each section were set up based on the special knowledge of the clerks. Elizabeth, the owner, had asked me after I was hired what I had special knowledge of, and she'd set up a shelf just for me. "Stock all your favorites here," she said, "the books you can sell because you've read and loved them." So far I'd ordered a hiking guide, three plant identification books, my favorite biography of Houdini, an illustrated book about the goddesses of India, three historical mysteries, four kids' books, and eight fantasy novels.

Maybe David was taking the soggy girl to his own section?

Miki, another clerk, was nearby, talking to the bookstore cat, Tetisheri. "Watch the front?" I asked her.

"Sure."

I followed David and the customer. I wanted to know where everything was, and I hadn't heard of this book category before.

Against the back wall between the sections on Self-Help and History, there was a bookshelf I hadn't noticed, with a fold-down desk and a collapsible metal chair below it. The books on the shelf were covered in various fabric colors and designs, and none of them had titles.

"What kind of story is it?" David asked the soggy girl.

"It's about a runaway."

David tsked his tongue against the roof of his mouth, scanned the book spines. He picked one covered in faded blue denim, opened it, skimmed a couple of pages, handed it to the girl.

She turned to the first page. She read a paragraph, then glanced up at David. Her smile was like a shaft of sunlight coming through a cloud. "Thank you."

He held the chair for her. She sat at the desk, the book open in front of her. He handed her a pen.

"Thank you," she whispered again, her gaze already fixed on the words. David nodded, then took my arm and led me back to the cashwrap.

"She's going to write in that book?" I asked. "A book she hasn't even paid for?"

"She'll pay later."

"That's a category? Books where you write your own ending?"

David smiled. He was an older man, slight and wispy, with iron framed glasses and a retreating hairline. He dressed in blues and grays, soft sweatery shirts and vests and nondescript slacks. He had a V-shaped smile that changed him from invisible into something cunning, sparkly, and almost dangerous. I had been trying to train myself not to back away when he smiled, but I still stepped back. His smile widened. "We have special customers for that section. Let me know if anybody else asks. It takes a while to learn those books."

"Okay."

I was helping a kid track down a book about dragon hunting — Miki told me to check Juvenile Non-fiction — when the soggy girl emerged from the stacks. Her clothes had changed: her full-length coat was lavender and waterproof now; her leather satchel had turned into a big black suitcase with wheels, and clasps that actually held it shut; her scuffed shoes had become elegant high-button boots. Her face had filled out. She smiled as she paid David, using a shiny new credit card.

Okay, my only clue that she was the soggy girl was that she was buying the denim-covered book. I took a couple steps toward the cashwrap, longing for a better look at her, but the boy tugged on my arm. "They don't have a picture of the dragon I want," he said, waving the *Illustrated Guide to Dragons* at me.

I knelt beside him and helped him look through the descriptions of the dragons. He was right; there was no black-and-gold dragon the size of a baseball in the book.

This was Brannigan's, so I checked the shelf again, and found two more large books with full-color illustrations. We searched them and finally found the information he wanted. He read it carefully. He asked me how much the book cost.

"Thirty dollars," I said.

His face turned red. "I've only got three bucks," he mumbled.

"That's okay." I rose and re-shelved the books. "I bet this book will be here when you come back, if you still want it. Want to find something else today?"

He bought a used paperback about mummies. By that time, the soggy girl was gone.

On my mid-afternoon break I went into the back office where we did the bookkeeping, kept the overstock, and received new books. It was a dark, cavernous room with shelves up to the ceiling on every wall and no windows. It had a dark pink carpet that reminded me unpleasantly of the surface of a tongue.

Piranella, the store's used book buyer, had her own desk there where she repaired used books, covered them with mylar dust jackets, and priced them. The rest of us sat at Elizabeth's desk when we were on break, below the small oil portrait of the store's founder, Elizabeth's great-grandfather Samuel Brannigan. Elizabeth's desk was an antique monster with lots of drawers in it, most of them locked. We were all taught the combination to her file drawer, where the female clerks kept their purses during their shifts.

Miki was in the back room, sorting new receiving into categories on three rolling carts.

I got my lunch and the current book I was reading out of the tote bag I had brought. I settled to eat at Elizabeth's desk. "How long have you worked here?" I asked Miki.

"Six years."

"No kidding? How old are you?" She looked about sixteen, though she was Japanese, so it was hard for me to judge.

"Twenty-four," she said.

"Wow. So do you know every section in the store yet?"

Miki laughed. "Nobody knows every section. Don't let them fool you. Yesterday I saw Clifton find a shelf he'd never seen before."

"Gosh." Clifton was the senior clerk. He'd been at the store for fifty-three years, longer than Elizabeth had owned it. "What was on it?"

"A set of encyclopedias from 1879. Just what somebody was looking for. A dollar a volume for a set of twenty-four. They'd been there so long we don't even know who priced them; maybe they'd been there since they were published."

"Did you know they were there?"

"I'd seen them before. I'm the only one who uses a duster, remember? I've touched more books in this store than anybody else."

"I just saw David show somebody a section of books where you write your own ending. Do you know about those?"

The tip of Miki's tongue stuck out of her mouth. She took a stack of books out of a box and stuck them on the New Age section of the cart. "I've seen people shop that section once in a while. I get the wanders when I head there."

"The wanders."

Her black eyes glanced at me, then away. "You know. When the store pushes you another direction?"

"Um?"

"You haven't gotten the wanders yet? Relax. They'll come. It's very helpful. When I've forgotten where something is, I get these little nudges from the store. Listen to your feet. The floor's telling them where to go. You'll wind up in front of the right shelf."

"The wanders." I opened my yogurt and stirred the fruit.

"Or maybe you won't get them." Miki shrugged and opened another box of receiving.

"I'd like to. Sounds helpful. I just never had them at my other store."

"Your other store." Another shrug.

I ate my yogurt and banana and let the conversation wilt, the way my shoulders were doing. I guessed everyone who worked at independent bookstores hated the chains. I'd heard stories about how the big chain bookstores built stores in locations specifically to kill independent stores. It hadn't happened in Tonkit, of course. Tonkit was too small. In fact, it was surprising that Brannigan's survived. We were close enough to draw Canadian book buyers over the border, and even though Tonkit wasn't on any tourist route, we seemed to pull in a lot of out-of-towners. The first day I worked here I had talked to people from Paris, Tokyo, and Cairo. Each had found books in their own language, too. I wasn't sure how I would straighten the foreign language sections if they were ever assigned to me. How do you alphabetize Arabic when you can't even read it?

I checked my watch. My fifteen-minute break was up. I disposed of my trash, put my book in my tote bag, and headed back to work.

For a minute there, I'd thought maybe Miki and I were making friends, and I'd felt hopeful. Sure would be nice to have somebody to rent videos with (Tonkit was too small to have a movie theater). Microwave popcorn was as haute as my cuisine usually got. I seemed to have soured my chances for friendship somehow, though.

As I crossed the threshold between the office and the store, the pink rug rose up and licked my leg just above my hiking boot and below the cuff of my black jeans. I stumbled into the wood-floored store, slipped, and fell on my seat.

I glanced over my shoulder at the rug.

Perfectly flat, totally quiescent.

The wide black door shut. The lock clicked. Had Miki followed me to the door and locked me out? I had the office keys; all the employees did. Maybe she was making some kind of point. Whatever it was, I didn't get it.

"Are you all right, Sylvia?" David held out a hand and helped me to my feet.

"You ever get the feeling that office is a great big mouth?"

"Of course, but it never swallows, only tastes. Would you like to straighten the self-help section this afternoon?"

"Love to," I said.

The self-help section was back by the shelf where the soggy girl had been. When I got there, the desk was folded up into the wall; the chair had been collapsed and slid into a little alcove just the right size to shelter it. No wonder I'd never noticed the desk before. I reached for one of the fabric-covered books. They were part of our inventory, and I wanted to know more about them. There was a turquoise one that particularly intrigued me. Before I touched it, though, I turned around and headed for the beginning of my section.

I spent two hours alphabetizing by author as hard as I ever had. By the time I'd reached Wegscheider-Cruse/Williamson/Zukav, my shift was over.

*   *   *

When I went to the office to collect my purse, tote bag, and jacket, I noticed two things: the office was warmer than the rest of the store, and the air smelled faintly of peppermint. Miki had finished all the receiving and was out in the store shelving new books. I hesitated before I went to the computer to clock out.

The room acted like a room.

I logged off, got my belongings, and stood in front of the door.

Then I turned and went to the corner past the safe and the file cabinet, where there was a little alcove. I dropped my things and sat down, placed my palms on the furry pink rug. It felt rough but not wet.

"Well," I said.

I stroked my hand across the ridged and nubbly carpet. I leaned against the wall. I patted the carpet again. I thought I felt a faint vibration under my hands, a distant purr.

I was imagining things.

My imagination was the best friend I had.

"Guess I should go home," I muttered. It wouldn't be as warm at home, of course, and I would have to do what I did every evening, stand in front of my apartment door while my stomach tied itself in knots, steel myself to unlock the door, and go in and look around, gripping the blackjack I had bought before I left Seattle. I had no idea if I could actually use it on another human being. After a check of the apartment, I would fix a little dinner and a big pot of tea, settle down with the current book, read, maybe, all alone. . . .

My eyes drifted shut. I slid down, curled up with my cheek against the rug. The store was open until eleven p.m. and it was only seven now. Nobody would mind if I —

"You don't mind if I nap here?" I asked Samuel Brannigan. He was a sturdy man in old-fashioned clothes. He had wild red hair parted in the middle, and elegant handlebar mustaches. His eyes were bright blue, and his cheeks were ruddy.

"Not at all. All part of the process. Bit sooner than usual, though."

"I'm so lonely."

"They all are when they first arrive, Lexi. Don't mind if I call you that, do you? Sylvia's just not right."

I laughed. Then I sobered. "But you won't call me that in the waking world, will you?"

"Couldn't if I would, love. I'm not in the waking world. I died quite a while back."

"Not all the way, huh?"

He laughed. "That's right. The body's gone, but there's lots of me left. How do you like my establishment?" He held his arms out and looked around the room. The walls melted and we saw through them into the store, where books hung in the air on invisible shelves, each one alive with stories and information, gifts and salvation, waiting to help.

"I love it," I whispered.

"Are you in this business for life?"

"That would be my dream come true."

He stared at me. He took my hands and peered into my eyes. "Give us a kiss, then."

I'd never kissed a ghost before. Oh well. It had to be better than kissing Peter. I stood on tiptoe, and aimed my lips at his. He put his arms around me and pulled me up against him. His kiss was gentle, searching. After a long time, he lifted his head. "You're a strange lass, Lexi."

"Too strange?" My heart thudded. Had I done something wrong here too, and soured all my chances again?

"Oh, no. No! Don't worry, love. We'll keep you on."

I kissed his hand.

"Sylvia? Sylvia, wake up. What are you doing still here?"

I rubbed my cheek against Brannigan's shirt, which felt rougher and scratchier than it had looked.

I opened my eyes and looked up into David's face. I pulled my dreaming self back into place. "I'm sorry. I fell asleep."

"Strange. You've only been here a week."

"I know." I sat up and yawned against the back of my hand.

"You're still in the first stage of the review process. Er — or maybe you were just tired?"

"That's right." I stroked my cheek. Rug burn. "Please don't fire me."

A book dropped from a high shelf to land open beside my hiking boot. I flinched.

David and I leaned forward.

"You're not going anywhere," said the first line on the page.

"Oh," I said. "All right. Thanks."

"Hmm. I guess the review period is over. Won't be official until Liz says it is, but welcome to Brannigan's, Sylvia." David chewed on the first knuckle of his index finger. "Are you going to spend the night?"

"I don't know." My stomach growled. There was a bathroom here, of course, with lots of bookseller humor on the walls, but there was no shower that I knew of, and I didn't have any more food with me. Still, I would spend the night if I was supposed to.

Pages of the book flipped. They stopped. "Go home," said the line at the top of the page.

"Okay. Thanks." I blew the carpet a kiss and stood up.

"You worked at one of the big chains before," David said.

"Yes."

He shook his head. "Surprising. Of course, your references didn't check out, but nobody's ever do. See you tomorrow."

"Yes. Good night." I left David to his bookkeeping and headed out through the dark and silent store. I trailed a hand along the bookshelves, touching something more than wood, paper, cloth spines and leather. I made it to the front door without tripping over anything and paused to stare out at my new town through the glass.

Rain drifted down, slicking the pavement of Main Street and capturing puddles of reflected light from the few signs lit at eleven at night: next door, Daylight Doughnuts' sign was on; they stayed open until two a.m. Across the street, the sign for Mabel's Diner was dark. At Tucker's Tavern next door, beer neon flickered in the small high windows, sparking colors from the water on the street. The door to Tucker's opened and someone staggered out.

I gripped the door handle and turned it. Time to go home. Tomorrow ought to be different. I could ask them to call me Lexi now, maybe.

My apartment was only a block away from Brannigan's, upstairs from the Greasy Spoon, a tiny cafe with only a counter, no tables. Kash, the breakfast cook, served the best home fries I'd ever eaten. I had them every morning.

I climbed the outside staircase, reached into my tote for the blackjack, running on automatic. I felt sleepy and jubilant. It didn't matter whether Miki liked me; the store had chosen me. I had a future now.

I gripped the blackjack and opened my front door.

Peter grabbed my arm before I could raise it, twisted my wrist until I dropped my weapon, pulled my arm up behind my back until pain screamed through me. He dropped my arm and snapped something around my neck before I could catch my breath.

"Hey, Lexi," he said in his purring voice, the one that stroked you like a feather. "You're supposed to get home at seven-ten. Why are you so late?"

My right arm felt like it had been torn off. I checked. It was still attached.

I walked into my apartment and dropped my tote bag, then lifted my left hand to the collar he'd put on me.

"Want to see how it works?" he asked.

"No," I whispered. It *worked?* It wasn't just a humiliating fashion statement.

Well, of course it worked. This was Peter.

"You need to know," he said.

I turned toward him. Fire shot through my neck. I felt like I had been decapitated, only the pain went on and on. When it was over, I found myself curled up on the floor.

"Sit on the couch, Lexi. Don't be such a slob."

My muscles still worked, though they were spasming. I levered myself up and went to the couch. Peter held a remote control. His familiar suitcase lay on the coffee table. He came and sat beside me, took my hand, played with my fingers. "Shall we talk about how frustrated I am?"

"Anything you want." My voice was back to its old monotone, though a little harsh.

"You were very hard to find this time. I had to pay strangers for information."

"Why. . . ," I whispered.

His finger hovered over the red button on the remote, then dropped to the side. "Go ahead. Ask."

"Why did you follow me? Why did you find me? Why won't you let me go?"

"I love you, Lexi. There's something so — perfect about you. You're the best woman I've ever owned. It's like somebody built you just for me."

Yes. Father had done that, taught me many lessons in the basement after Mother died. So much of what Peter enjoyed was similar to what Father had enjoyed. Living with Peter had felt uncomfortably comfortable.

Then one day I read a book. It was a book I'd read before, but this time some of the words rose up off the page and pounded into my brain. Sandy, the waitress at the coffee shop where I ate lunch, noticed which book I was reading, and said she had read it too.

We talked every day for a while. She helped me pull my courage together enough to run away from Peter that first time.

"Besides, I can't let you escape," said Peter. "It sets a bad example for the others. They're watching me. They'll expect to see that I've punished you properly for all the trouble you've given me." He leaned forward and spun the combination lock on his suitcase, flipped the top up. Polished metal gleamed. He had added to his toy collection. "Hmm. What shall I start with? I know. Your favorite. Take off your shoes, darling."

"No," I whispered.

He touched the red button on the remote.

When I could see straight again, I took off my shoes.

* * *

"I have to say good-bye to my new boyfriend," I whispered the next morning. I had no voice left.

"A new boyfriend? I've had someone watching you for a while, and nobody mentioned that detail." Peter had packed everything he'd brought but the remote. He had only to move a finger and I would do whatever he wanted; he had trained me all night.

"He's at the bookstore."

"These workplace romances. So risky. Are you sure you want me to see this person? You know how jealous I am."

"I'll just leave a note."

"Wouldn't it be better to just leave? No. Now that I know, I have to see him. Who could you prefer to me?" He knelt at my feet, slid fresh socks up over my bloody soles, smiled as I winced. During the night, following Peter's instructions, I had packed everything I had acquired since I left Seattle. He opened one of my suitcases and took out a pair of moccasin slippers. "Or would you prefer your tennis shoes?"

I didn't say anything. I would prefer never to walk again.

Peter handed me a jacket. "Better put this on. Your forearms are a bit obvious. I'm glad I saved your face for later. Fresh bruises are more frightening to the others. Isn't this nice? Your new lover will see you and think you're still just fine."

He left me on the couch while he loaded his suitcase and mine into the trunk of his car, then returned to escort me downstairs.

Knives sliced into my feet with every step I took. The first steps were the worst. After a little, I remembered old skills; I dialed down the intensity of pain and walked almost normally, with only a phantom wince each time I put my foot down.

"You're early, Sylvia," Elizabeth said when she saw me. Today her silver hair was up in ponytails that sprouted from above her ears and sprayed down across her shoulders. She wore a purple kaftan and a red fleece vest and six of her best giant, jewel-encrusted rings. Another thing I would miss, seeing what Elizabeth was wearing *this* time.

"I've come to quit," I whispered.

"You can't quit. David said you passed review."

"I'm sorry. I have to leave."

She came out from behind the cashwrap. "Are you all right, my dear?" she asked. "You don't look well."

"My fiancée just had a touch of wedding nerves," Peter said from behind me. "She's led me a merry chase. Imagine." He patted my shoulder. I couldn't prevent a wince. The burns hadn't even had time to scab over. "She can't stay here, ma'am. I need her back at home."

"Introduce me to your young man, Sylvia."

"Peter Montrose, Elizabeth Brannigan. Elizabeth, this is Peter, the one I ran away from."

"I see," she said slowly.

The floor pulsed under my feet, sending fire through all the new cuts. I cried out, only my gasp was ragged, torn from a voiceless throat.

"Lexi says she has to say good-bye to her new boyfriend," Peter said.

"Ah," said Elizabeth. "I'd like to give her a farewell present as well."

"What sort of present?" Peter asked.

"A book, of course." She darted away from us.

"Where's the sweetheart?" Peter asked me.

"In the office."

"Show me."

I took out my keys. Carefully I opened the key ring and pulled my office key off of it. I limped down the aisles past the shelves to the wide black door of the office. Peter followed me.

What could he do? What on Earth did I imagine the ghost of Samuel Brannigan could do?

I could imagine lots of lovely things. My imagination was as far as events like that usually got.

I unlocked the door and flicked on the light. The room was just the way it had looked the night before, minus David.

"There's no one here," Peter said, staring in from the store.

"I'll leave a note." I stumbled to the desk and took a piece of stationery out of Elizabeth's middle drawer. *Dear Sam*, I wrote.

Peter came silently up behind me and leaned over to watch me write.

I have to leave now. I'm so sorry. All I want to do is stay here with you.

The pink carpet snapped up and wrapped around Peter. He screamed and dropped the remote. The carpet wrapped tighter until all that was visible of Peter was his head. A corner of the carpet stuffed itself into his mouth.

David came in and handed me a book bound in turquoise cloth. "From Elizabeth," he said. He glanced at Peter's head, then at the remote. "Hmm."

Peter stared at David, his eyes wide and angry.

I tugged at my collar. "Can you see how this comes off?" I leaned forward, pulling my hair in front of my shoulders.

David's cool fingers brushed the back of my neck. "It's not immediately obvious. Can it wait? I need to show you something."

I straightened.

"This is your book," David said. "You must write the ending. It works better if you dip your pen in blood. This is a blood sampler." He handed me a thing that looked like a fat, angular pen, with a button and a slide on its side. "You cock it like this, and when you press the trigger, a lancet pops out of this tip and digs a hole in your finger. It's less painful if you lance the sides of your finger, up near the fingernails, rather than the fingertip. Understand?"

"I think so."

He laid a pen on the desk in front of me, patted my shoulder. "I'll leave you to it, then."

After he left, I opened the book to the front.

"Where are the books where you write your own ending?" the girl asked me.

I flipped ahead to where the writing ended. The last sentence was, "After he left, I opened the book to the front."

I thought for a little while. I glanced at Peter, whose face was so red I wondered if he'd die of suffocation or heart attack, releasing me from everything. Maybe Sam was killing him for me.

But that wasn't fair.

I lanced the middle finger of my left hand and dipped the pen into the upwelling blood. Then I wrote:

Lexi's father rose from the grave with only one mission in mind. After all he had done to his daughter, he needed to make amends. He needed to make her safe, to free her from all the things he had taught her.

He stepped into the office —

The hair on the back of my neck prickled. The room, which had been warm, cooled to the temperature of ice. I didn't turn around.

— went to Peter and picked him up. Peter was helpless to do anything in the father ghost's grasp. "Come on, son. I'd like to show you my basement," said Lexi's father.

(Even as I wrote, I heard the words being spoken beside me.)

Lexi's father walked away through the wall, taking Peter with him. He did not stop until he reached the basement which had no windows nor doors, but was full of all the toys Father had collected across the years. "Ah, my son," said Father. "I'm glad you're here. I have so much to teach you."

Lexi never saw Peter or Father again. She lived happily ever after in Tonkit, working at Brannigan's Bookstore.

I closed the book, set down the pen. When I looked up, Peter was gone. I lay down in the little alcove beyond the filing cabinet. I closed my eyes.

Samuel Brannigan smiled at me in my dream.

"Thank you," I said.

"Of course."

"You're not like them, are you?" Had I just exchanged my first two prisons for another?

"Only a little," he said. "And you can rewrite that part if you like."

I hugged him. He didn't smell at all like Father, or Peter for that matter; he smelled like pipe tobacco and bay rum and horses. "What did he do to your feet?" asked Samuel. His lips rested against my forehead for a long moment. "Great jumping Jehoshaphat. What's he done to the rest of you? Holy leaping lords, child!" He laid me down, then rushed off somewhere.

I rubbed my cheek against the rug. Why had I thought it was rough? It felt warm and soft and welcoming as water. I could sleep here without being laced tight by tension.

I opened my eyes sometime later to find David sitting on the carpet near me, my book open in his lap. Warm and drowsy, I watched him read. At last he closed the book, and smiled when he realized I was awake. His smile didn't remind me of Peter's anymore. "Elizabeth's called Dr. Ambrose. We'll take care of you."

I closed my eyes. It didn't stop the tears from leaking out.

"Hey, Lexi. Welcome home," said David.

"I AM LOOKING FOR A BOOK . . ."

Patrick Weekes

9:00 AM

Gorhok the Immitigable looked carefully at the freshly-painted doors, and after a moment of indecision, he straightened his dark and foreboding shoulders, pushed on the door grandly, discovered that he was actually supposed to pull it, pulled it, stepped through the theft detection panels, and made his way over to the cashier.

"Excuse me," he said, using a bare fraction of his presence for fear of destroying the poor fragile mind of the mortal behind the register, "but wasn't this once a small used bookstore?"

The cashier kept pressing buttons for a moment. A little display facing Gorhok read, "Logging in." Finally, he looked and said, "What? Oh, yeah, that old place? Yeah, we bought that shop out a few months ago."

"And now, this is . . .?" Gorhok kept his voice level, and refrained from disemboweling the cashier. The mortal was a pale man of indeterminate age. With his slender frame and long, pony-tailed hair, he could have been an appeasing virgin. Well, except for the arm hair.

"Boundaries Bookstore," said Wade the cashier. "Now proudly serving the community. I can't believe this town only had one of them until we came along."

"Ah," said Gorhok. "Yes. But you still have all the old inventory, yes?" He leaned in closer and let the flames in his eyes smolder just a bit. "If there were a particular item of power that one needed to procure by, say, the rising of tonight's full moon, that would still be doable?"

"Um." Wade blinked. "I'll have to check with my manager."

"No matter," Gorhok declared, and spun on one army-crushing heel. His black cloak flared out as he turned. "It is still here. The prophecies were quite specific." He walked off, chuckling to himself in a tone that drove priests and sensitive children to madness.

9:14 AM

Gorhok the Immitigable came back to the cashier, taking care to still look quite impressive. "Where are the books?"

The cashier looked at him carefully. "Well, sir, we do have quite a selection. Was there something in particular . . .?"

"No. Look, I moved toward the most concentrated source of mortal attention in this store, the nexus of thought. I imagined I would find myself surrounded by tomes of power. Instead . . ." He held up a thin square of plastic.

"The music section. Oh." The cashier nodded. "Yeah, CDs and music pretty much take up the north section. You've got some travel stuff over on the left, and there's employment guides and wedding planning over there on the right."

Gorhok grit his teeth. "Okay. Ah . . ." He looked at the cashier's nametag. "Wade. Where would I find old books?"

"What, like, used?" Wade the cashier leaned in and lowered his voice. "Actually, Congo-dot-com is better at getting those, but we're not supposed to talk about —"

"No. No, in here. Where are your old books? Books on . . . religion. Philosophy. Dark secrets of the metacosmos."

"Second floor, between computers and self-help. You know," Wade added pointedly, "I'm sure that the Information Desk can help if you have any further questions."

"I will not require further assistance," Gorhok said, biting the words off as if he could chew them and drink lovingly of their blood. "Thank you."

9:42 AM

Gorhok the Immitigable found Wade the cashier in the coffee shop.

"How can you be on break already?" he demanded. "It hasn't even been an hour!"

"Sir, was there something confusing about the whole Information Desk concept?" Wade looked up from his cup of coffee and fixed Gorhok with a bleary stare. "It's the kiosk over there under the back of the stairs."

"In the small used bookstore," Gorhok said, "there would be one small, decrepit bookkeeper to lead me to the tome I seek."

"Look, ask for Callie at Information. I'm sure she'd be happy to help you." Wade held up a plate upon which rested a crescent of vague brown starch. "Would you like a caramel-raisin biscotti?"

Gorhok had been known to make jerky from the skins of those who doubted his almighty wisdom. He was still nonplussed by the biscotti. "Your confections shall not sway me from my task!" he declared, and turned boldly.

After a moment, he said, "Again?"

"Small kiosk, under the back of the stairs."

"Thanks."

Callie was a slender woman with short, spiky blue hair, a gold-studded nose piercing, and a T-shirt that left her midriff bare. "Hi," she said after a moment, with no real enthusiasm. "Welcome to Boundaries. Would you like to hear about our email newsletter?"

"I, er, no." Gorhok was thrown momentarily, but recovered. "No. I need to find a book. An item of great power."

"Title?" Callie stared at her computer terminal, violet fingernails poised over the keyboard and ready to strike.

Gorhok coughed. "I don't actually have the title per se . . ."

Callie hit a button. "Author?"

"A prophet or madman, no doubt, driven from his wits by the enormity of the darkness his meditations uncovered . . ."

Callie hit another button. "Keyword?"

Gorhok rallied. "Death, destruction, apotheosis, transcendence, rising, scourge . . . Those should all be good."

Callie typed rapidly. "You want me to Boolean those?" She glanced at him. She was actually quite pretty, but then Gorhok was into piercings, provided they were of other people. "All of the above or any of the above?"

"Oh. Any is fine."

Callie clicked once more, and then turned around and ripped off a page that was spitting out of the printer. Her jeans were hip-huggers. They went well with the shirt. "Here you go."

"Thank you, lovely mortal," Gorhok said, and took the sheet from her. "When the rivers of black blood bubble up from the crust of the dying Mother Earth, I shall not forget you."

9:52 AM

Gorhok the Immitigable sidled over to the Information Desk and gave Callie an embarrassed smile. "How are these organized?"

"Alphabetically," she said, not looking up from her terminal.

"Ah, okay. Thank you." Gorhok turned and left.

9:57 AM

"The thing is . . ."

"Welcome to Boundaries. Would you like to hear about our email newsletter?"

"No, I was just here. The thing is, they're not."

"What?"

"Organized alphabetically." Gorhok the Immitigable held up two books. "This book begins with a 'T'. This one begins with a 'C'. And yet they are next to each other."

"Alphabetically within subheading," said Callie. she glanced at the books with a dispassionate eye. "That one's at the end of Shamanism. This one's at the beginning of Taoism."

"Ah. Ah, yes." Gorhok nodded sagely. "And how are the sub-headings organized?"

"Alphabetically."

"Of course. Yes." Gorhok turned away, then turned back. "Is there any way you could maybe just walk me to the books?"

Callie looked around perfunctorily. "I'm really not supposed to leave the Information Desk unattended."

"But . . ." Gorhok gave what was meant to be an explanatory gesture at the stout, unblinking woman who was perched on a stool next to Callie, face down in a book of unicorn-themed poetry.

"Trainee," Callie said. She went back to her terminal, the conversation apparently over as far as she was concerned.

"I'll just hunt them down myself, then," said Gorhok, and rolled out his shoulders. "Not a problem."

12:17 PM

"Finding everything okay?"

Gorhok the Immitigable jumped and nearly dropped his book. "No! No, I was looking at nothing!"

Wade the cashier leaned in and looked at Gorhok's book. "*To Ride a Golden Broomstick*," he read, "by Sylvana Ravenheart?"

"Not what I was looking for," Gorhok said quickly, "but nevertheless, it has some fascinating insights into living the modern pagan lifestyle."

"Plus," Wade said, "the woman on the cover in the off-the-shoulder dress."

"Hadn't noticed."

"Way off the shoulder."

"Look," said Gorhok testily, "is there something you want?"

"I just got off break," said Wade. "I saw you were still here. Wanted to see how you were doing."

"Fine," Gorhok said shortly. "Though momentarily stymied, I am certain that the object of power shall reveal itself to me with plenty of time."

Wade looked around. "You're sure that what you're looking for is in the New Age philosophy section?"

"Callie said it was," Gorhok said a bit petulantly. "And it is a book of most potent knowledge and enlightenment."

"Hmm." Wade shrugged. "Well, good luck." He turned to go.

"Wait," said Gorhok. "You just got off break? It's been . . ." He glanced at his watch. "It's been two hours."

"Yeah, I'm not really a morning person," said Wade, and wandered off.

Pathetic, Gorhok thought. And yet . . . "And yet, you give me an idea, little mortal. I shall expand my search." The book should reveal itself to his senses, and it was obviously not in the New Age section. He would search the bookstore from top to bottom. And he would find the source of power.

And then there would be much wailing and gnashing of teeth.

2:38 PM

Gorhok the Immitigable cleared his throat and shifted his weight back and forth until the writing group in the Military History aisle looked up.

"I need to look for something," he said, and after a moment of silence added, "on the shelves."

The four women clustered in overstuffed chairs around the low table gave him narrow-eyed looks of disdain. "Are you sure it's in this area?" one of them demanded, as if moving their puny mortal frames were too great an inconvenience.

"Yes," he said. "Yes, definitely." They continued to stare at him. "I'll just be a moment," he added.

Finally, with much sighing and muttering that Gorhok thought he was actually supposed to overhear, the writing group struggled to its feet and let him by into the aisle. Gorhok stepped in and began scanning the shelves, attuning his senses to the unholy essence that he knew would burn like a beacon amongst the other books.

"If you're looking for *Guns, Germs, and Iron*, it's on the display case," said the writing group leader. Her tone implied that any idiot who came to this section was looking for *Guns, Germs, and Iron*. "Or the new one by that general. That's on the display, here."

"No," Gorhok said shortly. He doubted that the book of power would be one of twenty or thirty on display.

"They're thirty percent off," said another of the writing group. "That's pretty good, for hardcovers."

"The book I'm looking for is very particular," Gorhok said, and went back to looking. The unholy presence burned somewhere in this bookstore. He was certain of it.

"So, anyway," one of the women said quietly, "I thought it was really an inventive idea. A lot of great imagery. It must have been really difficult to write something from the cat's point of view. It's such an original concept —"

Gorhok snorted, despite himself. After a moment, he became aware of the silence, and the piercing stares.

"It doesn't seem to be here," he said, and shuffled around the chairs.

"Have you tried the Information Desk?" the leader asked acidly. "It's right under the stairs —"

"Yes, yes, sorry to disturb you," Gorhok said, and hurried off.

4:19 PM

"You will give me food that I may feast upon it," Gorhok the Immitigable said, "and drink to quench my unslakeable thirst."

The man behind the coffee counter had a nametag that said, "Sirus." He was a young black man with a great number of piercings. They were not nearly as tantalizing on him as they had been on Callie. Currently, Sirus looked nonplussed. "Dude, I don't think unslakeable is even a real word."

"You know," Gorhok said, "there was an ancient Egyptian god called Osiris. His brother ripped and tore him into many pieces. His wife found nearly all of him and put him back together, but she never actually found his —"

"So," Sirus said, tone unchanged, "one mocha. Size?"

Even Gorhok's victories felt hollow. "Large."

Sirus turned around and looked at the menu board. "Wait, large is Fortissimo, right? Or is it Pianissimo?"

"Large. Mocha," Gorhok said again. A blood vessel behind his right eye was pounding, and he had a nasty headache coming on. He had looked through a lot of books. It had been a long day. the source of cosmos-shattering power still eluded him.

Sirus finally hit some buttons. "Would you like an addition with that?"

Gorhok growled. "The fresh-flowing blood of the next insipid servant to vex me with his questions."

"I'll just mark that down as 'Soy'," Sirus said.

4:25 PM

"Is it ready yet?"

"Oh. Oh, yeah. Did you want that nonfat?"

4:32 PM

"Finally. Wait, wait . . . This has whipped cream on it."

"Well, you didn't say that you didn't want whipped cream."

"Look, the whipped cream only goes to the top of the cup.

There's like an inch and a half of space filled with whipped cream that could have had mocha in it."

"Oh, right, you've got that unslakeable thirst thing going."

"Look, just forget it," Gorhok the Immitigable muttered, and stalked away.

7:30 PM

"Attention Boundaries Bookstore customers. Our store will be closing in two and a half hours. Please bring your final selections to the register at this time."

Gorhok the Immitigable hurried over to the Information Desk. "You're not . . . you're not Callie!" he said, and then hunched his shoulders defensively when Wade raised an eyebrow.

"Callie got off in the late afternoon," Wade said.

"You work the cash register."

"Slow night."

"And you've been here all day."

"I take a lot of breaks. You're not hung up on Callie, are you?" Wade shook his head. "I don't think she's really your type."

Gorhok scrambled for a different topic. "Why are you announcing that the bookstore will close in two and a half hours?"

"I thought you might like to know," said Wade.

"But all it does is add to my immortal stress! It makes me grind my infant-rending teeth!"

"It raises your hellish blood pressure?" Wade tried.

Gorhok thought. "Yes, that too. But no matter. I am almost through the mystery section."

"Really? Find anything good? Have you looked at our employee recommendation list?"

Gorhok glared at him. "I'm in the cat series right now. 'The Cat Who Found an Old Book and Wrenched Open the Gates of Heaven and Eviscerated the Cashier.'"

Wade never stopped smiling. "That caramel-raisin biscotti I offered? Whenever you want. My treat."

Gorhok walked off, muttering to himself.

8:45 PM

"Attention Boundaries Bookstore customers. Our store will be closing in one hour and fifteen minutes. Please bring your final selections to the register at this time."

"Screw you, screw you, screw you," Gorhok the Immitigable chanted under his breath. "*Accepting the Inner You. The Child Inside. Our Parents, Ourselves.*" He was making steady progress through the self-help section, and it was almost enough to make him question why he wanted supreme rulership over all of mortality anyway.

"*You Are Special. Learning to Love. Where Did the Cheese Go?*" Gorhok blinked, rubbed at his eyes. The book was still there. It wasn't the prophecy book. He had just been certain he'd misread that. . . . That can't be a real title. *Where Did the Cheese Go?* They're trying to distract me. Ha!"

9:36 PM

"Attention Boundaries Bookstore customers. Our store will be closing in twenty-four minutes."

"Not listening! Not listening! La-la-la-la-la!"

"Please bring your final selections to the register at this time." It was as though Wade had somehow known to wait until Gorhok took his fingers out of his ears.

Gorhok shook it off and kept reading. "*The Promotion to Wife. Planning a Wedding that will Make your Friends Sick with Envy. Mothers-in-Law, a Survival Guide.* It's just a wedding! How many books do you need?"

A pretty young woman with a shiny new ring looked over at him, wide-eyed, and started to cry.

"Sorry, sorry," said Gorhok the Immitigable. "I've had a very long day."

10:00 PM

"Attention Boundaries Bookstore customers. Our store is now closed."

"NOOOOOOOOOOO!"

Wade thought that Gorhok the Immitigable took it pretty well, all things considered. He found the man on the floor in the music bibliography section with the new Brandy Lance's autobiography clutched to his chest, rocking back and forth slowly.

"It had to be here," he was saying over and over again as Wade approached. "It had to. All the prophecies. It had to."

"It was," said Wade. "But those prophecies are pretty widely read. You think you're the only person who can hack through provincial Sumerian? By the way, the full moon just rose. You're out of luck." He worked out a crick in his neck, pulled his ponytail free of its hairband, and shook his hair out until it billowed around him like a chestnut cloud. "We're closed, by the way. You have to leave now."

"What was it?" Gorhok said, unresisting as Wade helped him to his feet with a thin, pale hand.

"The source of power? Oh." Wade coughed. "Remember that caramel-raisin biscotti thing?"

Gorhok looked at him. "That's wrong."

"Well, we were going more for ironic."

"That's just wrong."

"Okay. I think we both have good cases. We can meet somewhere in the middle." Wade held up a small plastic rectangle that dangled from a chain. "Here, put this on."

Gorhok looked at it. "Cory?" he asked.

"Well, what else are you going to do? You lost your chance at ultimate power." Wade clapped him on the back. "Maybe you'll like it here." He slipped the nametag around Gorhok's neck.

"Is Callie seeing anyone?" Cory asked as Wade led him to the break room.

"Not at the moment. But she tends to mutilate and devour her lovers."

Cory the Trainee nodded thoughtfully. "I think I can deal with that."

THE GLUTTON

Melanie Tem

The viewer paints the picture,
The reader writes the book,
The glutton gives the tart its taste
And not the pastry cook.
— Author Unknown

Phoebe liked to think that everything joyous and everything hideous that had ever happened to her, every transcendent moment, every horror, every revelation and epiphany and sin, had come out of her love of reading. The fancy added a uniqueness and grandeur to her life, which otherwise would have been quite small and banal. At night in the bookstore, drifting alone among crowded shelves, casting no shadow and leaving no fingerprints and making no sound, Phoebe would sense herself in the company of her victims as if they were beloved characters in favorite books.

The old friend who'd become a nun right out of high school, confessing over dinner her encroaching doubts. Drawn and agitated, enfeebled by spiritual desolation, she'd been easy to entice next door where Phoebe had known just where to find a seductive piece on the dark night of the soul.

The teenage boy exhilarated by his alienation, who'd taken to sitting in an armchair in the dimmest corner of the bookstore for entire afternoons when he should have been in school, feet flat on the floor, book on his lap not even open as though he could absorb its holy contents right through the cover, and Phoebe had no doubt that he could. When everybody else had gone and Phoebe sat at his feet to read Whitman and Jimmy Santiago Baca to him, he trembled with rapture and anguish. His head writhed under her stroking fingers, and he leaned against her side.

The bitter old woman she'd introduced to Sappho. The sweet old man she'd led to Nietzsche and the Marquis de Sade. The pair of little sisters writing their autobiographies for school, shyly presenting them to her and running off so she'd have to summon them back for more, which, of course, she was glad to do.

Richard.

Images of Richard came bidden and unbidden. Snatches of dialogue between the two of them no less authentic than when it had been composed: "I love you." "You give my life meaning." "Oh, my love, tell me more." Scenes. Themes. Figures of speech that said more than he ever had.

Richard. Richard. Richard of the soft belly and whiskered neck. Richard of the childlike tears so endearing from such a big stolid man. Richard, who recounted and otherwise revealed to her enough of his many stories that she could make up the rest. She had gratefully used what he gave her and much more, taking and taking what she needed, and she needed a great deal.

Richard had been the proprietor of the store when Phoebe had first floundered in off the street sobbing and soaked with rain and barbecue sauce which he mistook for blood. "Good God, are you all right?"

She'd stopped just inside the door, not wanting to make a mess. Although there wasn't much contrast between the gray light outside and the brown interior of the store, her eyes hadn't adjusted yet, but she could smell the books. His instinct was to come to her aid, and she liked that, but he didn't come too close.

"No, I'm not all right! Those mean little bastards! I didn't do anything to them! It's not fair! It's not right!"

Out of the rain and cold now, sheltered enough to tell and embellish the story, she had found herself shaking. She'd held out her bags to show him what had been done to her, or what might have been. "Did they get my books? Are my books okay?"

Richard had regarded her with what she would learn was a

characteristic expression of befuddlement and wariness and intense interest. "Who? What? What are you talking about?"

"I was just sitting at the bus stop, waiting for the bus, in the rain, and this car full of teenage boys went by and they were laughing at me and calling me names, I'm used to that, happens all the time, but then one of them threw a jug of *barbecue sauce* at me, and it got in my hair and all over my clothes. Why would anybody do that?"

Together, eagerly, they began to create back stories, any one of which could be true. The boys were skinheads, abused children or spoiled brats with a sense of entitlement, who told themselves that a bag lady sitting at a bus stop in the rain deserved public humiliation. The boys had just robbed a 7-Eleven and were high on Ecstasy and adrenaline. One of the boys, showing off for his girlfriend, experienced an epiphany and would be an unusually kind person for the rest of his life.

"Did it get on my books? *Did it get on my books?*" Herself not daring to look, she shook the bag of books at him for his inspection. The handle in the plastic broke. Both of them gasped as books tumbled. Both fell to their knees. She saw how reverently he touched her books.

After a moment he looked up, his face radiant with relief. "It's okay. There's no damage to the books. You had them well protected."

"Oh," she breathed, already wondering what stories he had in him, what his name was, how he came to be in this time and place with her, what would happen next.

He sat back on his heels. His hands were big and broad, on big broad knees. "You've got quite a mobile library here. Dostoevski? Aristotle? Toni Morrison? Simone de Beauvoir? Pretty impressive."

Then she knew she'd hooked him the way a writer hooks a reader in the first paragraph; he wouldn't leave her until the story was done. The sting of the barbecue sauce in her eyes and the stench of it, the sting and stench of the gratuitous little cruelty itself, had not abated. But the hunger was stronger than any of that. She hadn't had a decent meal in weeks, since the drunk who'd once been a philosophy professor had opened himself to her over a loaf of day-old French bread and a bottle of Mogan David and his life's work, an exquisitely-reasoned, incandescently-expressed, incomprehensible four-hundred-page manuscript about the meaning of suffering.

Richard had brought her a towel and supervised her drying off. Finally he'd pronounced her fit to enter. "Okay. Come on in."

"It smells good in here."

"Coffee and brownies. There's a reading this afternoon, and I always feed people." She didn't tell him she'd been referring to the luscious scent of books. "Are you hungry?"

The question had taken her aback. In fact, she'd been starved, for words and ideas. "Yes."

"Help yourself."

During their love affair, Phoebe had been more than faithful; she'd been satiated, sometimes deliciously, sometimes to the point of dangerous torpor. Eventually she had used him up, as she'd known she would. There had come a time when nothing was left of him to read, she had absorbed all his stories, the business had gone bankrupt, he'd wasted away, and Phoebe had taken up secret residence in the musty attic above the closed and then brightly-reopened bookstore.

Now, seasons later, Phoebe's grief was still acute, but even more than mourning Richard, who might well have been the love of her life, she needed to lose herself in someone else's story, written or told. So before one city dawn she descended to the park across the street, which was deserted and only hinted at the stories it surely contained. The bookstore opened at ten. As usual on a weekday morning, business was slow. Phoebe forced herself to wait until she would not be the first customer of the day.

The woman behind the counter had determinedly dark hair, fingernails and toenails like perfect oval seashells, and ruffles on her cuffs. This was Misty, the new owner. Phoebe had watched and listened to her in astonishment. "Good morning," Misty sang out now before the bell on the door had finished tinkling, "How are you today?"

"I'm fine." Phoebe restrained the impulse to smooth her hair and straighten her clothes. "Thank you."

"Oh, *good*. That's what we like to hear. And are we looking for any particular book today?"

Touching for courage and sustenance a stack of gaudy hard-covers, but careful not to set them sliding, Phoebe managed to say, "Actually, I'm looking for a job."

Misty's rosy face registered disappointment and then absolutely emptied of interest as she turned away. "I'm sorry, we're not hiring."

"Oh, I didn't mean a paid job. I'd like to volunteer."

"Volunteer? In a bookstore?" Misty was incredulous, suspicious.

Phoebe nodded, trying not to seem desperate. "I'd just like to be around books." Misty regarded her blankly, and Phoebe realized with a chill that the bookstore proprietor did not love books, and that seemed so bizarre that she thought there must be a story behind it. "I — used to work for Richard," she offered, in self-defense, but Misty wasn't interested.

Misty turned out to be older and less perky than her name and demeanor implied, and for a while Phoebe was curious about that. It took many long days alone together in the store when there were no customers and after hours devising strategies for attracting them, many days working events and stocking shelves and making displays, many nights listening for some sign of habitation downstairs before Phoebe could bring herself to accept that this woman lived an utterly unexamined life, told herself no stories, had no stories to tell. And did not read.

At first Phoebe thought that must be a story in itself and set herself to discovering it. Misty wasn't secretive; it wasn't hard to get her to chatter about her family, her hobbies, her childhood. But she gave no details and used no descriptors that couldn't have been attached almost anywhere. Her husband was nice. She had good kids. She lived in a pretty house. She liked her parents. She liked the soaps. Among all her words there was nothing to hang onto, and despite her intentions Phoebe's mind kept sliding into the stories, one after another, in the folklore books she was organizing, even though she had read them all.

"Tell me about yourself," Misty invited, but Phoebe knew she was just being polite, and it didn't take much effort to divert her attention.

Increasingly frustrated, Phoebe picked up snippets of stories from the world at large. On the bus, in the grocery store, on talk radio in the middle of the night, she scrounged, and, though she didn't find much of substance, managed to keep herself going. A conversation behind her in a ladies' room line about recent abortions gave her something, but neither of the young women would engage with her anywhere near enough for her to really read them. She read with great hope and interest a newspaper story about a woman who'd fled to this country to escape genital mutilation and then been kept in an INS prison camp for months, but, although the woman's face in the photo was open and urgent and the story was written with at least the illusion of intimacy, she was and always would be thousands of miles too far away to read the tantalizing understory. Kisses in the park between two nubile young girls somewhere on the border between exhibitionistic and free-spirited made her circle them for a hot afternoon, but beyond that they weren't interested in exposing themselves to each other, let alone to her.

Starving. She retreated to the classics and did find nourishment there — Othello had more stories than even Shakespeare knew, and Millay's autumn woods ached and cried with more than color. Passing by, Misty demanded airily, "why in the world would you read something more than once!" and didn't wait for an answer.

More and more often, as Misty's flimsy attention wandered, Phoebe worked by herself. When there were customers, she kept them around as long as she could, chatting, drawing them out, helping them find or order the books they thought they wanted no matter how rare or ridiculous. Every once in a while Misty dropped by — mostly, it seemed, to hang around Phoebe since, for all her fluttering and babble, she seldom did anything herself.

When she was alone, and sometimes even when Misty was there, Phoebe read. She'd conceived a plan to read every word of every book in the store, starting in the southeast corner and working back and forth, keeping meticulous track of any new stock. By September, when for a few days she did her best to fill the reading lists of high school students costumed in gaudy disrespect and slightly more literate college students, she had worked her way through romance and, light-headed and queasy as if she'd gorged on cotton candy, was relieved to be starting to cleanse her palate with horror, about which Misty wrinkled her nose and said, "Eeuw!"

Engrossed in a new erotic horror anthology, she was startled by the autumn sunshine when the door opened, and then again by how thoroughly it disappeared when the door closed. There was the brief glow of backlit white hair, a bulky shadow. The person who entered with a quick, heavy step was wearing something flowing and purple, and a strong musk.

"Hello. Can I help you?"

"Just browsing." A husky voice, bespeaking smoke in the lungs and whiskey in the throat, maybe years of singing, certainly laughter and screaming and tears.

The big woman lumbered around the store, breathing heavily, causing the floor to creak and some of the narrower shelves to sway. Able to reach much higher than most people but having trouble with the lower shelves because of her girth, she took down book after book that hadn't been looked at for a long time, standing huge and solid to read, now and then grunting in what might be appreciation or disdain.

Phoebe judged the woman to be in her mid-sixties, though she could have been ten years older or younger than that. The white of her thick curly hair was under- and overlaid with intricate patterns of pale and darker gray. A filigree of lines through the flesh of her face and neck spoke of joy and sorrow and adventure. The hands that held book after book bore intriguing spots and scars, each of which, Phoebe was sure, had a story behind it. She would have those stories.

Now that rich, ragged voice was reading from a book Phoebe had never seen before. Phoebe stood transfixed and gluttonous, taking in a story about love and loss complete in itself but also suggesting — promising — a multitude of others.

After a moment of silence, the woman offered her the open book. Phoebe took it with caution born of barely controlled desire. "Would you consider carrying my book?" the woman asked.

It took a moment for Phoebe to realize she wasn't asking her personally to carry the book in her hand or close to her heart, but wanted the store to stock it.

Somewhat dazedly, she examined it. On the gray cover was an abstract design of reds and purples, under the clear white words *Stories by Angela Winquist.*

Phoebe looked up from the book into complicated gray eyes and stammered, "I don't — we try to honor the request of our patrons," a principle she doubted had ever entered Misty's uncluttered mind. "*Your* book?"

She had to reach up to take the proffered hand. The grip was firm and practiced; this woman had grasped many things in her life. "I'm Angela Winquist."

"Read something to me."

"Really?" Angela had already taken her book back and was flipping through it. Phoebe was thrilled to realize she must be looking for her favorite among the stories, or one that seemed to suit this particular moment.

"I love —" Phoebe swallowed and began again. "I love to hear people tell their own stories."

A slightly condescending laugh rippled the expanse of violet fabric, making the intricate embossed designs gleam. "Don't confuse fiction with autobiography. These aren't my stories. These are my characters' stories."

"But you wrote them," Phoebe insisted. "You created them. It's your energy and your vision. They came from you." There was a pause, and then a massive shrug. For just a moment as Phoebe came out from behind the counter, she was close enough to Angela to have a visceral sense of her bulk and body heat.

Phoebe led the way and Angela followed her to the cluster of furniture in a clearing among bookshelves, where writing classes and readings were held. Taking the most comfortable chair, Phoebe motioned Angela onto the loveseat, which, though it accommodated her size, looked dubious as to whether it could bear her weight. "Please," Phoebe said. "Read to me." Angela settled herself and began reading.

That first afternoon, then, overflowed with pieces from Angela's book. There were mysteries, fantasies, historicals, a space opera, a fairytale, a vampire story. A tale of desperation and intrigue in a southern town caused the cadence of Angela's speech to slow and her accent to broaden. Another told in the voice of a lost alien child sounded heartbreakingly alien and heartbreakingly familiar in Angela's slightly skewed delivery. No other customers came in.

For nearly a week after that Angela didn't come in, and Phoebe worried that she'd gone too far too fast with this one. She began to notice a brash young man in a wheelchair who'd been frequenting the store lately, ready at the slightest provocation to talk about himself with no apparent need for anyone else in the conversation, but his stories were callow and reading him too easy to engage her for long. She missed Richard. She missed Angela.

Misty stopped in one day and shooed Phoebe out of the store for a rare lunch break. Twenty minutes later when she hurried back, Misty was tending in her unfocused, chipper way to half a dozen customers. One of them was Angela, musky, dressed in a Hawaiian-print muumuu. Misty was gushing, "It's so *exciting* to have a real writer in the store!" in a tone that surely a writer of all people could tell was insincere. Swaying, Phoebe caught herself on a floor-to-ceiling shelf of heavy used textbooks, which swayed, too.

When Angela saw her over Misty's shoulder, the broad face lit up. "Your star employee here is the reason I keep coming in," she said to Misty while looking at Phoebe.

Half-turning, Misty looked from one to the other and back again. "Oh," she said, sweetly snide. "I didn't know."

Angela scowled impatiently. "I don't think you know what a treasure you have in Phoebe. Her passion for reading is what every good bookstore needs."

When Misty more than willingly let herself be pulled away by another customer's question, Phoebe said quietly, "I do have a passion for reading. Thank you."

Angela nodded. "This time I'd like you to read to me."

Alarm made her stomach churn. "Oh, I don't have any stories of my own."

"Of course you do. Everybody has stories." Thinking of Misty's vapidity as well as her own, Phoebe started to protest. Angela held up a hand. "Would you read mine?"

"Read your stories to you? Why?"

"I'm having trouble with the new novel. It's structured as a cycle of interconnected stories, and I keep losing track of the over-arching narrative. I think if I could hear it in somebody else's voice, I could get myself re-oriented."

Phoebe didn't know what all that meant, exactly, but evidently she was being invited to partake of not just the telling but the creation of stories, the reading of a work in progress. She took a deep, grateful breath. "I'd be honored."

Day after day after day, then, night after night, Phoebe read Angela's stories to them both. At the beginning it was always a sweet and somewhat unnerving surprise when Angela appeared, manuscript in hand, frazzled and unkempt or possessed of a rich, almost preternatural calm. Sometimes she'd be waiting in the morning when Phoebe eased down the back stairs and around to open the door as if coming to work from her home somewhere else. Sometimes she'd barge into the store while Phoebe was with a customer, to ensconce herself on the loveseat and struggle some more with the writing or admire it, luxuriate in it.

Having gladly assumed that Angela, like so much else, had slipped from Misty's notice, Phoebe was taken aback when, happening to be in the store one day when the writer loomed outside the window, Misty remarked conspiratorially, "Now *that's* disgusting."

"What is?" Phoebe set her jaw.

Angela was at the door now, waving, beginning her ponderous entrance. Misty murmured, "That. How can you even stand to be around it? I'd rather die than look like that," and then called vivaciously, "Good morning, Angela! You're looking especially lovely today!"

Senses filled by Angela's musky fragrance and the iridescent green of her wide-sleeved shirt, Phoebe whispered, "She's gorgeous," but Misty wasn't listening.

Autumn that year was particularly spectacular, aflame with leaves turning like perfect paragraphs imperfectly read and about to be forever unreadable. Gradually a routine developed. Angela would arrive just after closing, and Phoebe learned to wait for her, at first without seeming to, after a while openly. There came a night when Angela didn't leave, a morning when on the way downstairs to open the store Phoebe had to step around her. They'd read much of the night, and Phoebe was exhilarated by exhaustion and near-satiety. Angela had collapsed in sleep on the floor, laptop still on beside her. Phoebe paused and bent closely over her; when she couldn't quite read her dreams, she smiled indulgently, covered her gently with a blanket, and tiptoed out. There was plenty of time, and in this one remarkable woman a vast reservoir of material.

As the nights grew longer, Phoebe allowed herself to fancy that Angela's creativity might even be limitless, and the more stories that emerged the greater her hunger for them grew. Every night she had a new one, about characters she would not otherwise have conceived doing things she never would have thought of in places she hadn't known existed for reasons that would have been quite beyond her if not for Angela saying so.

"This is incredible," Angela kept saying, shaking her head in wonder over the rapidly filling disk and manuscript box. "Maybe you're my muse."

The elastic in Phoebe's waistband was creasing her flesh. A few months ago when she'd found these pants at the clothing bank, they'd ridden low across her jutting hipbones, the smallest size she could find and still too big. Running her fingers inside the elastic to relieve the discomfort, she marveled at how different she was starting to feel inside her clothes, inside her skin, and said, "I'm a reader."

"No kidding. You look positively radiant. I myself, on the other hand, am having a nervous breakdown." Angela laughed a little. "The novel's not getting any closer to being finished, but stories are coming to me faster than I can write them down."

"Tell me," Phoebe said slyly, "where do you get your ideas?" Not infrequently, she'd heard the question at a reading at the store, and writers never knew how to answer it.

This time they both laughed in genuine amusement. "I don't know." Angela rubbed her eyes. "They're everywhere. Clamoring."

Phoebe said, "Yes." There were stories in the streets, pungent and crisp. The air smelled wistful, like tales not quite told, or told and not received. Light slanted as if across the pages of a book.

Mornings, the store sang when Phoebe let herself in, almost always now with a freshly-printed manuscript she carefully folded and stapled and shelved. Soon the stories she and Angela had read and written and read were everywhere — slid between science fiction hardcovers, inserted among the pages of young adult novels, doubling the thickness of poetry volumes, adding destinations to the travel books with their bright illustrations. By winter, Phoebe had begun to suspect that some of the little chapbooks were in places she'd forgotten or never known about, and she reveled in the sensation of being surrounded by stories.

"You sure are looking pretty these days." Misty cocked her head. "Have you done something with your hair?"

In the cold, wet weather the attic space became uninhabitable, and Angela and Phoebe all but took up residence in the bookstore itself, sleeping on the floor between bookshelves, using the curtained-off toilet behind the counter, washing up in the leaky sink that had only cold water, sending out for pizza. Although they weren't especially clandestine about it, Misty showed no sign of knowing. As the winter wore on, Angela became more and more driven. Rarely did she get through anything — a conversation, a meal — without interrupting to write something down. Awakening to the muted click of computer keys or the scritch of pen on legal pad against the backdrop of nighttime street noise, in the faint streetlight wash through the store windows seeing Angela's intent disheveled bulk — somewhat diminished these days; less obese now than solid, ample — Phoebe would fall back asleep feeling safe and provided for.

Angela, though, was wearing out. "I'm obsessed," she complained. Trembling lips made it hard for her to get the words out. "I'm possessed. Ideas keep coming. The stories won't leave me alone."

"I think it's wonderful," Phoebe told her. "The creative process in action." Angela groaned, winced as another inspiration struck her, and flung herself at the keyboard.

Misty was coming in less and less often, staying for increasingly brief periods of time, paying next to no attention to anything but the business aspects of the bookstore and that only cursorily. She didn't like to come into contact with the books because of the dust. If a customer happened to show up, she pretended to be a browsing customer herself and let Phoebe handle it. Whatever it was that she'd hoped to get out of running a bookstore, she clearly wasn't getting it, and the grim thought occurred to Phoebe that the place might be sold out from under her. Misty's cheery announcement late in frigid January that she was going to the Bahamas for at least a month to work on her tan felt both ominous and liberating. "I'll pay you, of course," Misty chirped, and named a ridiculously low compensation that Phoebe accepted without hesitation in order to avoid talking to Misty any more than necessary.

The first postcard arrived less than a week later. The picture showed gaudy beach and sky and women with a great deal of shiny skin, shot through with the word "Bahamas" in fulsome script. On the right half of the back were Phoebe's name and the address of the store, and a blurred postmark.

The message on the left was, she was amazed to realize, the opening of a story. In fact it was titled "Story," with Misty's name underneath followed by two short paragraphs, all that would fit in the space. It was not very good. Besides several errors in spelling and punctuation and a general awkwardness about the prose, the characters and situation and story line were obvious and trite already in these first fifty words. Just what Phoebe would expect from someone as callow as Misty.

But she couldn't deny that the format was interesting. The fact that Misty was writing a story at all, had sent her a card like this at all, was interesting. This seemed to be a story within a story, a story about a story, meta-fiction. Her pulse raced.

Angela came in then, struggling, evidently under the weight of a bag of sandwiches from the deli on one forearm and the laptop slung over the other shoulder. Phoebe slid the postcard into her pocket and hurried to help. Out of breath, Angela collapsed onto the loveseat. "I just don't have any strength anymore. I don't know what's wrong with me." After a moment Phoebe moved behind her to massage the thin tangled hair and flaccid neck, doing her best to calm and reassure them both.

A postcard arrived every two or three days after that, a serialized story in miniature. The narrative itself continued to be clumsy, the viewpoint character stock, the use of language uninspired. But very soon Phoebe found she could hardly wait for each installment.

She'd just checked again for the mail, which was late that day, when from among the religious and spiritual books on the back wall a customer pulled one of the hidden manuscripts. "What's this?"

Glancing at Angela, preoccupied with writing on a long legal pad at the end of the counter, Phoebe said, "That's a great short story. My friend here wrote it. Angela Winquist. A name to remember. You should read it."

The young woman already was reading it, having moved out of the dimness at the back of the store into the diffuse light from the front windows. Phoebe watched her. Someone came in looking for a book about gargoyles. Someone else wanted Chaucer. A middle school English teacher called inquiring about Harry Potter and Jane Yolen. Angela kept writing furiously.

The customer looked up. "This is good." She spoke to Phoebe but looked at Angela, who still paid no attention to her. "This is really good."

"It's even more amazing when you hear it read." Phoebe laid her hand on Angela's broad back, noting that it was not as fleshy as it used to be. Angela flinched. Creative energy coursed through her and through Phoebe like blood. To stand on tiptoe Phoebe braced herself against the writer's tensed, quivering shoulder, startled at first by the shoulder blade she could clearly feel under the brown shirt, at first thinking it an injury or a disease. On the screen she read a few sentences and, with a transfusing, transforming thrill, knew what the rest of the story would be.

Wordlessly the young woman offered the manuscript and Phoebe took it although she knew the story by heart. It was only for appearances that she kept her eyes on the printed words and turned the physical pages as she read aloud. The customer stood rapt. Others gathered until there was a little crowd, a small dense mass. Angela kept writing. When Phoebe reached the end of the story there was scattered applause. She went on, making no pretense now of needing visual cues, resting a hand on the writer's wrist, not much bigger now than the circle of her thumb and forefinger, and closing her eyes and *reading* the story Angela hadn't yet written but was in her to tell. Reaching the conclusion before Angela did, Phoebe stood with bowed head, thinking how Richard would have loved this, while the crowd sighed and exclaimed and dispersed. It was a few minutes before the small noise of the keyboard stopped and Angela let out her breath.

It became an ongoing event, performance art in chapters and scenes, the sort of draw Misty had had in mind though she never would have thought of this, wouldn't understand it if she saw it happen. Angela wrote and Phoebe read. Phoebe read and Angela wrote. Part of its popularity seemed to come from surprise, so there was no set schedule; people began coming into the store several times a week or a day in case they might catch a reading.

Phoebe was on fire. The postcards from Misty kept coming every few days, telling the obvious tale and suggesting many others. In everyone who came into the store, everyone she passed on the street or with whom she shared a bus, in voices on the phone or on the radio, she read stories; whether or not they were factual, they were true. She started over reading every book in the store, and discovered subtexts she'd missed before. She never let Angela out of her reach.

In between performances Angela sat blank-faced on the loveseat, legs splayed under billowy, dusty dresses, lips and hands trembling; or she lay like a burial mound on the faded oval rug. She hardly spoke, as if she had no extra words. The bookstore opened earlier now than it ever had and stayed open later; some days it didn't close at all.

Spring came in February, a surprise warm spell that didn't end. Snows from the short, heavy winter melted quickly, bringing gobs and rivulets of mud into the store and making clammy pages stick together. The postcards came less frequently now, the standard climax having occurred and the standard denouement now winding down to an ending Phoebe dreaded for its inevitability but watched for every day.

Dressing for the warmer weather, Phoebe and Angela found they could wear each other's clothes. Phoebe's were a bit too tight for Angela, sleeves and pantlegs too short, and Angela's hung loose on Phoebe, but the fit was close enough that it ceased to matter whose clothing was whose.

Sometime around the vernal equinox, Angela wrote her last story. For several days she'd been alarmingly weak, hardly able to get up off the floor, not eating or drinking much of anything. The scenes and sentences she wrote were only loosely connected; Phoebe still managed to read stories out of them, but with much greater effort and far more precarious results. On a balmy Tuesday afternoon at the end of March, with quite a few customers in the store, she began and couldn't finish a reading; Angela's fingers stopped moving on the keyboard, then began typing random letters and symbols. Phoebe extemporized an ending for the tale but it was quite unsatisfactory, and the audience coughed and murmured in displeasure. On Friday evening, when she tried it again, only four people showed up, and Angela couldn't get past the opening.

It was over. Phoebe knew it was over. Whatever this magic had been, it was spent. With a wan, scattershot desperation she tried everything she could think of: reading aloud the stories in Angela's book, leaving the beginning of a scene or a provocative bit of dialogue up on the screen in hopes Angela might be inspired, sitting beside her in the dark or in the spring daylight and recounting every myth and narrative poem and soap opera plot she could remember. She even tried telling stories of her own, but found, still, that she could not.

None of it worked, of course. Angela didn't respond to any of the prompts. By the middle of April she seemed almost comatose, and from one minute to the next Phoebe was sure she was going to die. For days on end nobody came into the store, and there was no mail.

Phoebe was driven out again to forage for stories to sustain herself. She spent hours in the library, thinly comforted by the reminder that it would take a long time to get through all those books. She forced herself to check out the new titles in the chain bookstores. Searching online bookstores brought her ephemeral reassurance.

One flowery evening she stumbled back to the store to find Angela gone and Misty returned. Phoebe was aware of the absence first, because she'd been expecting it, and had hunted for and not found half a dozen of the hidden manuscripts before Misty spoke her name. She started but didn't turn.

"Phoebe." Misty was right behind her. "Where've you been? That writer friend of yours, that Angela, was passed out on the loveseat when I came in. Scared me half to death."

"I — I just went out to — get some Ibuprofin. She said she had a bad headache."

"Good heavens, Phoebe, you know better than to leave a customer alone in the store. Although she was too sick to do any harm."

"Where is she? Is she all right?" Phoebe knew the answer.

"She was unconscious and I couldn't rouse her. I also couldn't move her. She's, you know, heavy." Misty laughed. "I called the ambulance and they took her to the hospital."

Phoebe caught her breath, thinking she'd found one of the folded and stapled stories. But it was only a flyer advertising a reading that someone — disgruntled, probably; cheated — had randomly stuck on a shelf.

"She made a mess on the furniture and on the floor. That loveseat will have to be thrown out." Misty had entered Phoebe's field of vision enough that she could see her wrinkling her nose.

"I'll help you clean up."

On her knees scrubbing at the spots on the floor and rug, Phoebe missed Angela already. Misty had gone back to get something from behind the counter. "Looks as if you did okay while I was gone."

Phoebe cleared her throat and managed to answer, "Business was pretty good for a while there."

"I guess!" The voice and the smile were bright and empty.

"It's fallen off lately, though. I — don't know why."

There was a pause. Then, shyly, Misty asked, "Did you get my postcards? Knowing she should have said something by now, Phoebe could still only nod. "Well, for goodness sake, what'd you think?"

"I — was surprised."

"Didn't know I had it in me, did you?"

"Everybody has stories," Phoebe said, and bowed her head in sudden grief and gratitude for Angela.

Misty sat back on her heels. "Do you like it?"

Relieved she hadn't asked for a critical opinion, Phoebe could answer honestly, "Yes. I looked forward to every postcard. I've been waiting for the ending."

"I need your help with that."

"I'm a reader, not a writer."

"Phoebe, please." Both of them still on their knees, Misty

crawled close enough to put her hand over Phoebe's. "Please help me. I can't finish it myself. I don't know how it ends."

Trembling, Phoebe leaned back against the loveseat which bore residue of Angela and less visible traces of Richard. She closed her eyes, turned her hand over to lace her fingers with Misty's, and allowed thoughts to gather. There were many possible endings to this story and many possible beginnings to the next. After a moment she began to tell one of them to Misty, who sat wide-eyed, open-mouthed, hollow at her feet.

IN THE BOOKSHADOW

Marianne de Pierres

I thought of the shop as a halfway house. A place in the shadows for people of the shadows. Strangely enough it was its most dangerous in the height of summer. When the outside world was hot and sharp, the shadow people sought blur.

I arrived every morning on the eight-fifteen train, pressed awkwardly between the already perspiring bodies of commuters, and trudged along the subway that led from the station, under the roadway, into the back of the arcade. The arcade had been recently renovated and the air conditioning circulated air at a pleasant nineteen degrees, cool enough to make me shiver at the transition.

The surfaces of the main food hall gleamed with the smart light of expensive marble tiling. The sushi bar was clean and crisp, the chef polishing his knives. The florist fussed, tethering balloons to floral arrangements.

Along one subdued arm of the arcade, in the coolest, darkest corner, was the bookshop — a place only likely to be discovered by a combination of luck and an afternoon's aimless wandering. The window was well dressed, full of bold-covered new release books. Inside was a smorgasbord of Crime, Horror, Science Fiction, Fantasy and all those in-between stories that had no home.

The clientele were mostly dedicated regulars. A blend of young, straggly intellectuals, middle-aged free thinkers and some genuine freaks. Occasionally bright, young office workers flaunting ironed shirts and nose rings stumbled in, quickly snatching up a light romance or a murder mystery — but the shop lived and breathed by its hard core.

Mostly I worked with Sean. He was a charming, urban boy with a knack for selling to anyone who could hold a half decent conversation.

I specialised in the 'Others'.

'Others', like Mink, the tragic, drug-fucked street poet, a one time writer raped by the publishing world and cast adrift. Or Duro, the compulsive shoplifter, a small, furtive man who survived on what he could steal, when he wasn't in jail. Then there was Grace, a withdrawn spinster who rarely spoke, and had lived all her life with her alcoholic father. And Seb, the homeless, disturbed teenager. And Celestial with the hideously disfigured face.

I'd gradually learned their whims just as I'd pieced together their life stories. Now I could pick the days Duro was likely to steal, and the days where he would have a handful of coins in his pocket, enough to buy a SF classic in cut price format.

I learned to read Celestial's lips despite the spittle that gathered in the corners and forced her to dab at them furiously. I learned when Grace wanted help choosing something with her pension money, and when she was likely to slip a pocket knife from her purse and thrust the blade at me if I interfered with her browsing. I sensed when Seb's abusive mother had given him money; whether it was safe to recommend a hard-boiled crime novel, or if he was likely to forget himself and practise stalking techniques on the girls from the bank. I knew when Mink could stand a sad ending.

Sean watched me with contemptuous laughter as I petted and chivvied my 'Others'.

"Why do you waste your time? We don't want them in here," he complained one day as I chased Duro out of the shop for slipping a Zelazny Omnibus into his baggy, thief's trousers. "They've got no money. Not like Peter or Sharyn."

Dr. Peter Lowe and Sharyn Graystone were two of our best customers. Voracious readers with eclectic tastes and ready incomes. Sean coloured pheremonal when they called in.

"This place anchors them," I explained, not expecting him to understand. "It's somewhere to come. Things don't change here. They feel safe."

I understood because I was really one of them disguised in my shabby sales assistant's clothes.

Sean was young, vibrant, capable. Life hadn't even begun to digest his hope.

He shook his artfully blonde hair impatiently. "You should be working in a crisis centre not a bookshop. *This* is a *business*."

"Yes," I agreed. But it was 'other' things as well.

Sean turned away in irritation.

Some days, I could tell, he loathed me.

The 'other' things weren't just my curious human clientele.

It began when Sean was on his lunch breaks, increasing slowly to whenever he was out of the shop at the bank or the post-office or wherever else he scurried to during his outings.

The first time, one appeared on a publisher's display stand — nine pockets of new books by one author, an epic fantasy of the type that were numbingly popular — a mere flickering in my corner sight. I glanced up from my invoicing thinking a customer had entered quietly — probably Duro sneaking in while I was busy.

It was not Duro, or any other customer.

It resembled a bat. A large, shadowy, evil, unblinking creature with wings and talons that pierced the cardboard on which it perched. The air in front and around it rippled as if I was watching through slow moving water.

"What —?"

Before I could move or properly speak, the door to the shop opened and Grace entered. I called excitedly to her and pointed.

"Grace. Do you see that?"

She shrank back at my forthright approach and I worried for a moment she might leave. I tempered my voice to a gentle cajoling.

"On the new book stand? Can you see that thing?"

Reassured, as a nervous animal might be, she stepped around a shelf of True Crime to oblige my question.

The creature was still there, silently malevolent, unmoving.

Grace froze. Her thin, withered face drained of all colour.

"You see it, don't you Grace?" I couldn't control the shrill in my voice.

She stared at the creature. After a long moment she fished in her bag and produced a chain which she slipped around her neck. Not a cross but a misshapen medallion.

The door banged open again. Sean entered chewing on the remnants of his lunch. "Sorry, got caught . . . something wrong?" He stopped, bemused, his head pivoting between Grace and I.

Grace hissed.

I looked back across to the stand. The creature had disappeared.

As I stood gaping, Grace saved me from idiocy.

"Sick," she grasped her belly. "Need air."

"I'll help Grace outside, Sean," I croaked, recovering.

We stumbled outside together.

I touched her arm. "What was it, Grace?"

She drew her thin arms around herself until she appeared shrunken. Her hand slipped into her bag and retrieved her knife.

"Keep away."

She said it in a firm voice, not frightened or hysterical, as I felt. It was almost as if . . . this event was not peculiar.

I shook the notion from my head and let my hand fall.

Grace edged quietly back into the main people-stream of the arcade and disappeared.

I returned to the shop. It was thick with a putrid odour.

Sean was unpacking books. "That woman needs to wash."

I nodded absently. The smell, I knew, had nothing to do with Grace.

I took the book home that night and read it. It was one of those tragically, detailed fantasy stories full of boring routine imagery and cliched prose. Yet, feeling an urgency to explain the vision Grace and I had shared (had we really shared it?), the book seemed the only clue.

But the reading gave me no comfort and I lay restlessly awake late into the night.

As I left my apartment for work the next morning, tired and nervous, I noticed a drunk asleep in the gutter. The sight itself was not uncommon near my stingy rental, yet something in the cast of the body, perhaps the gaudy pseudo fur coat, captured my attention.

Mink? Is that you?

I called to him softly.

The pile of papers and ragged clothes moved, standing shakily.

"Mink? This is not your . . . your patch?" I said astonished.

His glassy, green eyes stared wildly at me. He seemed agitated. Strung out?

I stepped closer, enough to taste his fetid breath, but he backed away whispering in his hoarse once-performer's voice;

"Suffer their vainglory."

He shuffled away out of sight.

From there began a nightmare of days and nights. I ate little and slept less. I began to dread Sean leaving the shop, for the visions came regularly. Sometimes in the shape of wild, fearsome, fantastic animals, sometimes just nebulous glowing patches of density. The latter were worse, almost, for it seemed that the less form the vision took, the stronger its emanations of raw malevolence and fury.

Sometimes I would be entirely alone in the shop when it happened, at other times, amidst a handful of customers, I would be the only one aware of the shrieking demon, renting flesh from the limp form of a corpse.

One time, as I served Sharyn Graystone, a vision of an angry man with two knives appeared behind her. He reached one to her throat and one to her belly. It cost me everything to stop from crying out. Yet I must have lurched awkwardly — even violently — towards her.

She did not flinch, but I saw fearful speculation in her eyes.

"Is there a problem?" she asked politely.

Yes, I was desperate to scream, behind you, about to gut you, slit your throat . . .

The door opened, a distracting movement, rescuing me from an outburst of paranoid insanity.

Seb prowled in and began roving up and down the shelves. He glanced repeatedly at Sharyn Graystone and myself at the counter, his hands fluttering in little circular movements, his lips moving silently. Praying. I was sure. I was also sure he could see the vision — as Grace had done weeks before.

Slowly, the vision faded.

Sharyn Graystone collected her purchases and coolly left. Her calm did not deceive me, though. I knew she would speak quietly to Glen, and I would now be scrutinised, my performance more closely monitored.

Seb came to the counter.

"Did you . . .?" I began, but he slapped a vintage J.G. Ballard on the counter as if to chop off my words.

I took the book in my hands. It was a tale of psychological and physical survival. A thrilling introspective masterpiece in its own way. Not the sort of story Seb would normally buy.

"Safest," he mumbled, and left.

The visions heightened.

Daytime nightmares.

I battled for perspective — for a reason.

I sought help with a psychiatrist. With a smoothing of her carefully pinned hair, she began to make immediate confinement plans for me, whispering coded messages into her audio diary.

I gave her a false address and cancelled my next appointment.

Sean watched me, only leaving the shop for ten minutes at a time. It should have been a relief. Instead each day became dotted with short, intense bursts of violent visions. Guillotines, hangmen's nooses or presences pulsating with envy, jealousy and hate.

The 'Others' haunted the shop too.

Through a haze of misery I saw them, though I had ceased being able to pander to their wants.

Their appearance became almost routine.

Grace or Celestial in the mornings. Seb or Duro in the afternoons. None of them speaking or buying, just prowling the shelves like freakish guardians.

Grace stroked the spines of crime and passion stories as

though they were her longed for lovers. Celestial poured over book covers of ravishing heroines with a corporeal yearning. Seb handled fantasy sagas like they were siblings, reciting whole passages out loud, and Duro stole bookmarks.

Had I been myself, the sight of their emotional impoverishment would have wrenched my insides.

Shining Sean hastened to wipe and dust when they left, as though their touch had debased things.

I also noticed Mink, living permanently on the street outside my flat. I recognised the coat. We didn't speak but his presence gave me strange comfort.

Somewhere my life had unwound.

By their presence alone, the 'Others' were lending me a thing I had once sought to afford them.

Celestial dropped the first clue. Through dribble and spit, she whispered three words from her disfigured mouth.

"Fear the writer."

Then she scuttled to the back of the shop amongst the darkened shelves and took up her patrol.

As if I had been dangled a rope with which to pull myself from quicksand, I clawed back towards sanity. I pondered over Mink's few words, spoken weeks before.

"Suffer their vainglory."

Who's vainglory?

When the next vision came, a severed limb draped across a customer's shoulder, I breathed deeply and concentrated on the sale. The book they were purchasing was a thriller; a type that championed blood and cheap fear.

Soon I began to see a pattern. The visions accompanied what I had always considered, 'ugly' books, where the writer had churned out careless words, driven by their desire to compete in a voracious industry. As I saw them, "Soul-less books".

"Fear the writer!" Celestial had told me.

Feverishly, I read author biographies and studied their photos. Behind the grainy black and white portraits on dust covers I began to see dark images. Shapes of evil lurking behind posed smiles and faraway stares.

A comprehension, totally fanciful, settled across my mind. I resolved within me, that the tortuous visions were escapees from books. Greedy, dark, writers' animas. Souls that had sold.

What a fantastic conception! But right — I felt it. Knew it.

It brought little solace.

Why was *I* plagued with their presence? Why not shining Sean, with his pert sales talk and invincible, taut flesh?

I stewed on my misfortune, building an anger so intense that it burnt away my fear, scoured my confusion. I came to work charged with energy and ragged truculence.

I began to wage a battle.

"That is a terrible book," I told customers, "not worth the paper. Wasting your money."

I sold only the books I believed in. The books in which I could detect an intact writer's soul.

Who set me in judgement?

I did.

Survival can teach you anything. Make you anything.

But the visions worsened still, materializing whether Sean was present or not.

Cuts, bruises and unexplained burns started to appear on my body like I'd been performing small self-mutilations. Sometimes invisible fingers pressed at my throat making it impossible to breathe.

Sean began hushed, behind-his-hand phone calls, discussing my deteriorating appearance and behaviour with the shop's owners. He took care not to touch me or come close.

I noticed he began to hang a heavy bunch of keys from his belt loop.

On the last day, Dr. Peter Lowe came in. As was his custom he began to harvest books from the shelves. Some visits he would choose twenty or more. Sean fussed around him, relegating me to the background.

I lurked like one of the 'Others', amongst the shelves; pretending to unpack books, a Stanley knife tight in my grasp. I ran the knife along the taped edge of a box, listening.

"Something light, Sean. Something easy, full of . . . thrills," he said. "I'm on holidays. A trip to the mountains and then a week at the beach."

"Take me! Take me!" Sean flirted as he piled "soulless" upon "soulless" novel onto the counter.

Visions exploded around the pair as they joked. I saw grotesquely murdered bodies that smelt of fresh death and a long, bloodied sword wielded by a skeletal knight.

Rage mounted so fast, it rushed my crumbling control. I felt the battle line roll over me.

"No, put them away!" I yelled "It's not safe!"

I lunged at the skeleton knight, meaning to wrestle its sword away.

But the knight was stronger.

Bearing me forward like a mere decoration on its hilt, it stabbed — not in a clean swipe, but with hacking moves — roughly severing Lowe's head from his neck. The sound of it roared in my ears. The gush of blood choked my nose, spattered my face, ran into my mouth. Lowe's flesh, slippery in my fingers.

Sean ran, screaming, screaming. High pitched and girlish.

I called out after him to explain, but my tongue was thick, saturated with the taste of warm metal . . .

The 'Others' entered some time later.

Duro, Grace, Mink, Celestial, Seb. All of them. They formed a circle of protection, wiping blood from my face and hands. They moved Lowe's body with practised ease, placing it out of sight behind the counter.

Mink's green eyes were calm. Celestial's mouth was dry of spittle. Grace was smiling. Duro patted my arms. Seb placed a misshapen medallion around my neck.

I knew them now.

Discarded characters from books, self appointed Guardians of the soul.

Like me.

Cajoling, caring, they steered me out onto the streets . . . to safety.

NON-RETURNABLE

Rick Hautala

-1.-

Manda knew it meant trouble as soon as Jason, the manager of the Borders where she worked, asked to see her right after the Monday morning staff meeting before the bookstore opened for the day.

No way it could be good news.

It never was.

After finishing her coffee and the donut she had left from yesterday, she walked into the back room, thinking this might be it.

She might actually get fired.

Jason was standing by the returns station, leaning with clenched fists against the desk as he stared at something on the computer screen. A faint, bluish glow underlit his features, making his skin look ghastly pale.

Manda walked around the full pallet of boxes that no one had bothered to open last night and stopped a few feet from him.

How bad could it be?

She didn't have long to wait. She saw the book — *the special order* — on the desk in front of him and instantly stiffened.

"If you're not gonna buy this," Jason said without looking away from the computer screen, "then you should return it. Today."

He seemed to be trying to maintain an "all-business" tone, but she caught the glint in his eyes. It might just be the reflection of the computer screen in his glasses, but it sure seemed like he was enjoying the hell out of this.

249

He always did.

Holding the book out at arm's length, he carefully studied the front and back covers. There was no dust jacket. Just a fake black leather binding with the title and author stamped in faux gold leaf. The left corner of Jason's mouth kept twitching. Finally, unable to hold back a sniff of laughter, he opened to the first page and read the title out loud.

"*Psychic Black Holes.*"

His voice dripped with derision, and he cleared his throat before continuing to read the subtitle.

"An exploration of the 'event horizon' and mental abilities."

Glancing at Manda, he repeated the words, "Event horizon," before dropping the book onto the workbench. "I don't blame you for not buying it — especially for eighty dollars."

"There'd be the employee discount," Manda said, not quite daring to look her boss in the eyes.

"Not on special orders, there isn't," Jason snapped automatically. Straightening up, he turned and glared at her, the overhead fluorescent lights glinting in white bars off his glasses. "You don't really believe this crap, do you, Manda?"

Manda tried not to wither under his steady glare, but she couldn't help it. She didn't like her boss, and she knew he didn't like her. Especially since she turned him down when he had asked her out last winter.

Still, there was no reason to be so mean to her. She tried to look past the glare off his glasses and into his eyes instead of staring at the floor and feeling like she had done something wrong.

"Not really," she said, her voice hushed. "It's just . . . kind of interesting." She shrugged. "I like to keep an open mind about things."

"I'd rather see an open wallet, so if you don't have the eighty bucks, get the book out of the inventory. 'Kay?"

Manda thought — not for the first time — that she should pop the book into her backpack and walk on out of here, but she would never do something like that. She couldn't. It was bad *karma* to steal from work, even though she knew several employees who had lots of books and CDs on "permanent loan." And anyway, now that Jason had made an issue of it, she knew he'd be watching her.

Without another word, Jason dropped the book onto the returns table and strode past her. Seething with resentment, Manda watched him go out onto the sales floor. He wasn't such a bad guy, she thought. Underneath it all, there might even be a human heart, but he was such a hard-line, corporate dickhead. As if eighty dollars was going to make or break the inventory.

Music suddenly blared from the overhead speakers. The Beatles' *White Album*.

Good choice, Manda thought as she hummed along with "Birthday" and started straightening up her work area. Someone had left a teetering stack of books on her chair. Glancing at the computer screen, she saw that Jason had been looking at the returns information for Swann Press, the publishing house that had sent her the copy of *Psychic Black Holes*.

"Thanks for the help . . . dickweed," she muttered.

The back room door slammed open as Chris and Billy came out to get a load of books for their sections. On most days, Manda would have taken a few minutes to talk with them, but she was still fuming about Jason as she turned to the shelf beside her desk where she kept an assortment of padded book bags for returns.

"Goddamned cock swallower," she whispered as she grabbed a bag that would fit her book. When she pulled the envelope down, her hand scraped against the rough edge of the wooden shelving. She cried out in pain as a splinter of wood sliced her wrist open as cleanly as a razor blade.

Billy looked over and asked if she was all right.

Holding her wrist tightly with her other hand, Manda nodded as she stared at the wound. It wasn't as bad as it had felt, but tiny drops of blood were beading up along the thin, two-inch gash. It had a little sting to it.

"Yeah. Just caught a splinter," she said.

"Whoa! Workman's comp time!" Chris called over his shoulder. "You'll be sitting in the sun, sucking down beers, and watching HBO."

Manda sniffed and looked carefully at the wound to make sure there weren't any splinters in it. It looked clean, and she decided not to bother cleaning or bandaging it. After wiping the blood on her pants leg, she turned back to her worktable.

"What the —" she muttered when she noticed the tiny drop of blood on the cover of her special order. She reached out to wipe it away, but before she could, the tiny red dot disappeared, absorbed into the slick, pseudo-leather cover and gone without a trace.

"Did you see —" she started to say as she turned around to her co-workers, but Billy and Chris had their handcarts full and were already heading out onto the sales floor. By this time, the Beatles were halfway through "Dear Prudence." Manda had a mountain of returns to send out, so she put the whole thing out of her mind.

- 2 -

"Hey you," Manda's boyfriend, Rob, called out as she stepped into the apartment and closed the door behind her. She latched the dead bolt, even though they had never had any trouble in the two years they had lived on Munjoy Hill.

"Hey me," she replied automatically as she slumped out of her jacket and hung it on the peg by the door beside Rob's sweatshirt. "How was your day? How'd the writing —"

She caught herself as her gaze shifted down to the faded, peeling linoleum floor of the entryway. The braided rug her grandmother had given her as a high school graduation present was gone. She glanced into the closet by the front door, but it wasn't there, either.

"Hey, Rob? . . . Where's my rug?"

She stayed where she was, unable or unwilling to move until she found out what had happened. The rug had been special to her. It was the last hand-braided rug her grandmother — who had died almost six years ago — had made.

The scuffing sound of Rob's bare feet on the floor drew her attention. He appeared in the doorway, a crooked half-smile on his face.

"Rug?" he said, cocking his head to one side and looking like a dog who was listening to a high frequency whistle.

"Yeah. My rug."

Manda was fighting back the urge to shout at him. It had been a hard enough day at work. The cut on her wrist still stung, and she didn't need this right now.

"The one my grandma made for me. Remember . . .?"

Rob gave her a blank stare. No longer smiling, his mouth hung open, making him look stupid.

"The blue and gray one . . . with three roses in the middle . . ."

Rob looked at her expectantly as though prepared for the punch line of a joke.

"Come on, Robbie. Stop teasing. What'd you do with it?"

Rob took a tentative step forward, then halted as though not feeling entirely safe too close to her.

"I have no idea what you're talking about, Manda."

He looked past her, focusing on the wall for a moment, then shifted his gaze back at her.

"Jesus, Rob, I've had it in front of the door since before you moved in. You can't tell me that you don't . . ."

Her voice trailed away as she studied Rob's confused expression. Maybe he had been smoking pot instead of writing today and was putting her on. His eyes seemed clear enough, but she could never tell for sure.

"Tough day at work, huh?" he asked as he came forward and gave her a hug and kissed her lightly on the cheek. He placed one hand on the back of her head and pulled her close.

"Uh-huh." Manda's voice was muffled against his chest. "A real bitch! That bastard Aceto started in on me first thing this morning, and he didn't let up all day."

"I'm telling yah. You should charge him with sexual harassment or something. That asshole's been making your job . . . What's the legal term for it? An unsuitable work environment. Yeah. He's making that place an unsuitable work environment for you."

"To hell with him," Manda said, waving her hand as she broke off their embrace and walked into the living room. Letting out a low groan, she eased herself onto the couch and just sat there, staring blankly out the living room windows. In the corner of the room, away from the distracting view of the city outside the window, was Rob's writing desk, cluttered as always. The desk light and computer were on. It sure looked like he had been working.

Manda jumped and let out a little squeal when Muggins, her

overweight tiger cat, jumped up onto the couch and started rubbing his head against her thigh.

"Hey, guy," she muttered, reaching down and scratching the top of his head. Muggins flopped onto his back and began kneading her leg with his claws. Within seconds, the room filled with his motor-boat loud purring.

Manda leaned back and closed her eyes, lost in the comfort of her cat. She gave only a moment's thought to what Rob might be doing. At least he wasn't writing. Maybe he was looking for the missing rug, but she couldn't believe him, pretending that he didn't know what she was talking about.

Silence settled, broken only by the Muggins' steady purring and the muffled sounds of traffic through the closed windows. Before long, Manda slipped off into a deep sleep.

- 3 -

The rest of the week went about as well as Manda could have expected, considering Jason was on her case about every little thing he could think of. He criticized her for the way she handled a cash return with a particularly rude customer; he threatened to write her up for taking too long a break on Wednesday; and he complained several times in one day that she hadn't gotten all of the returns boxed and shipped fast enough.

She didn't care.

Even if he fired her, she was sure she could find another job — a much better paying job, too — without too much effort. If Jason gave her any more grief, she was ready to quit on the spot. What she wasn't ready for was when *Psychic Black Holes*, which she'd returned to Swann Press on Monday, showed up in Thursday's mail.

"Christ on a crutch," she muttered as she regarded the padded book bag stamped *"Return to Sender"* in bright red, front and back. She had been shift leader for three hours yesterday because Tim, one of the assistant managers, had called in sick. There were mountains of returns she hadn't scanned out of the system, so her first response was to toss the package onto a shelf until she could get to it. Maybe it'd still be there when she got the nerve to quit. The next person in charge of returns could deal with it.

But she hesitated, hefting the package in one hand, knowing it contained a book she *really* wanted. Hesitantly, she placed it on her desk beside her now-cold cup of coffee. The back room was deserted, so she sat down at her desk. Sighing, she leaned forward and cupped her chin with both hands, staring long and hard at the package.

"Who would know?" she muttered, glancing around the vast, book-cluttered room.

It would be so easy to slide the book into her backpack and walk out with it. If Jason noticed that the return credit never showed up, she would suggest that the book had gotten lost in the mail, or maybe claim the publisher was screwing the store out of the money.

Either way, she'd have the book, free and clear . . . clear, that is, except for her conscience.

"Yeah, damn it." She huffed as she reached past her cold coffee and picked up the package. A terrible sourness filled her stomach. Her hands were clammy as she wedged her fingertips under the stapled flap and ripped it open.

She let out a cry when the up-raised prong of a staple sliced the underside of her forefinger. Dropping the package to the desk, she shook her hand to relieve the sudden stab of pain, then held her finger up and inspected the wound.

It wasn't so bad.

Not even an inch long.

But the staple had cut deeply. The wound spread open like a tiny eye slit with a bright red bead of blood for an eyeball. Placing the wounded finger in her mouth, she gently sucked on it. The faint, metallic taste of blood teased her tongue.

When she pulled her finger from her mouth and looked closely at the cut again, she decided that she didn't even need a *Band-Aid*. Her breath caught in her throat when her gaze shifted down to her desk. A corner of the returned book stuck out of the padded envelope, and two drops of her blood glistened like miniature rubies on the edge of the black, faux-leather cover.

As she reached to wipe the blood away, something peculiar happened. Later that day, Manda all but convinced herself that it had been a trick of the light, or maybe something wrong with her eyesight; but as she stared at the book, the rich, black tone of the leather darkened and swelled. A wave of dizziness swept over her, and before she could react, she saw the fake leather absorb the two tiny drops of blood. Once they were gone, a hint of deep, dark red swirled inside the textured black cover.

"That is *weird*," she muttered, taking a quick step back.

"What's weird?"

The man's voice, speaking so suddenly behind her, startled Manda. She let out a squeal and spun around to see Billy, crouching beside his book bin next to a cart stacked with books.

"How long have you been here?" Manda asked, gasping.

Billy grinned and shrugged and shot her a lopsided grin.

"Whaddayah mean? I'm just loading up my cart." He hesitated, then added, "All right. You caught me. I was reading." He held up a book, but Manda couldn't see the title. "Promise you won't turn me in."

"Yeah — sorry," she said, "I was just . . ." Her voice drifted off, and she chanced another quick look at the book lying on the table. "You startled me, is all."

"I do that to a lot of people." His charming grin spread across his face. "It's what Tiggers do best."

Manda couldn't help but laugh at his Tigger impersonation. It was actually quite good. She always found Billy amusing, even when he was cracking jokes that several of the female employees found offensive. It was because of him, she realized, and a few other employees that she hung onto her job at the bookstore.

Just then, the backroom door slammed open, and Jason strode over to the returns station. His gaze immediately landed on the returned book. He glared at Manda.

"I thought I told you to return that book."

Looking past him, Manda caught Billy's eye. Jason's back was to him, and Billy was twisting his face into a mocking, sour expression.

"Yeah, I — I'll do it today," she muttered, avoiding eye contact with Jason because she knew, if she looked him in the eye, she would either start laughing hysterically or else run, screaming, out of the store.

- 4 -

Later that evening, once she got home from work, Manda did scream. She had worked an extra hour, trying to catch up, and as a result had missed the bus she usually took home. Almost two hours later than usual, just as the sun was setting, she got back to the apartment and discovered that Rob wasn't there. She found a *Post-it* note stuck to the refrigerator, informing her that he had gone out to Gritty's for a few beers with Marty and Sheena. She should join them, if she wanted to.

"As if," Manda mumbled as she crumpled up the note and tossed it toward the trashcan. She missed, and she left it where it landed, between the wastebasket and the refrigerator. Opening the refrigerator, she scanned the shelves for something to eat. When her gaze alighted on the half-opened can of cat food covered with *SaranWrap* on the bottom shelf, she realized that Muggins hadn't greeted her at the door. Turning quickly, she scanned the darkening apartment.

No dark blob on the couch where Muggins usually slept . . .

No silhouette on the windowsill, looking longingly out at the city lights . . .

"Muggins . . .?" she called out, her voice twisted as she stepped into the living room. She couldn't ignore the icy clenching in her stomach.

"Muggsie . . .?"

No answering *meow* from the bedroom . . .

She glanced at the floor by the window where she kept Muggins' litter box. The litter was undisturbed, exactly the way she had left it this morning before rushing off to catch the bus to work.

"Damn, if that jerk let Muggsie get out . . ."

Manda stomped to the front door, undid the deadbolt, opened the door, and glanced up and down the dimly lit hallway.

Of course the cat wasn't there. Muggins was an indoor cat. In the city, he had to be, but Manda knew if he ever managed to get out, he'd be off chasing pigeons and rats, or wandering the alleys. A dull, burning sensation stung the back of her eyes. Her vision blurred as tears gathered.

"Muggins . . .?" she called out softly, looking up and down the corridor once more, then drawing back into the apartment and closing the door.

"Oh, *Jesus!* Oh, *fuck! Goddamn!*"

She clenched her hands into fists and pounded her upper thighs in frustration. It'd be just like Rob to space off something like this.

Muggins had probably slipped out without him even realizing it. Probably darted between his feet and bolted when he was leaving to meet up with Marty and Sheena.

Or maybe that's why Rob had gone down to *Gritty's* . . . because he knew Muggins had gotten out and didn't want to face Manda's wrath when she got home and found her cat was *A.W.O.L.*

So mad she was sputtering, Manda strode over to the portable phone by the couch, grabbed it, then fished the telephone book out of the drawer, looked up the number for *Gritty's*, and hurriedly dialed. A woman answered on the third ring. Manda asked if she would check to see if Rob Rusch was there. The woman wasn't very helpful. She said they didn't have a PA system, but Manda said it was a family emergency, so the woman said she'd check.

Crossing her arms tightly, Manda stalked back and forth across the living room floor while waiting for the woman to return. She was surprised to hear Rob's voice above the background din of the pub.

"Hey, what's up, babe? You comin' down or what?"

"Where's Muggins?" Manda snapped, so suddenly and loudly it sounded like a bark over the phone.

After a short pause during which all she could hear was the background noise of the crowded bar, Rob spoke up.

"Huh?"

Manda exhaled loudly, imagining for a moment that her breath was a ball of dragon's fire that could melt the mouthpiece of the phone.

"Muggins! My goddamned cat, you moron! You didn't let him get out this morning, did you?"

There was another pause, longer this time. When Rob finally spoke, he sounded confused and tentative, like maybe she was playing some kind of joke on him.

"I — ah, look here, Manda." He didn't sound at all sure of himself. "I have no idea what you're talking about, 'kay? A *cat?*"

"Jesus, Rob! Yes! A cat! *My* cat, Muggins! He wasn't here when I got home from work. If you let him get out, I swear I . . . I'll . . ."

Her voice trailed away because, in fact, she had no idea what she would do. Probably end up plastering PET MISSING posters on the telephone poles in the vicinity of the apartment building. Over the years, she had seen plenty of missing pet posters around town and had always thought it a touching but futile gesture.

What were the odds that a missing pet would ever show up?

The city had more than its share of stray cats and dogs, and if a pet was really valuable, chances are it had been stolen to be resold.

But Muggins was no prize. As much as Manda loved him, he was just a "mutt cat," as she lovingly called him. If Muggins was gone and missing, it meant only one of two things — either he was wandering around scrounging for food . . . or he was dead, maybe flattened by the city bus she had taken home from work that day.

"Manda? . . . Honey?" Rob said.

Manda could barely hear him above the background noise of the bar. She took a steadying breath, trying to focus.

"Muggins . . . is . . . missing," she said, enunciating each word so there would be no mistake. Tears spilled from her eyes and ran like drops of heated oil down both cheeks. "If you know what happened, just tell me. Even if you fucked up and let him get out or something, just fucking *tell* me! Otherwise . . . otherwise . . ."

"I haven't got a clue what you're talking about, babe," Rob said. Manda detected a slur in his voice and guessed that he had been at the pub for a while. "As far as I know, we — you don't even own a cat." He sniffed with laughter. "You always told me you were allergic to them, remember?"

"Wha —"

Manda's voice choked off. She had no idea what to say to that.

Is Rob nuts?

Am I?

What the hell is he talking about, no cat?

She glanced over her shoulder at the refrigerator. Moving swiftly, she walked to it and flung the door open. Bending down so fast both of her knees made loud popping sounds, she started to reach for the can of cat food on the bottom shelf when her hand suddenly froze.

It wasn't there.

The cat food was gone.

The only thing on the bottom shelf was Rob's twelve pack of beer and something that looked like either very old meat or very new cheese.

"Where'd it go?" she whispered into the phone. Her voice were like metal filings, rubbing the inside of her throat.

"What's that babe?" Rob yelled. "I can't quite hear you."

Manda backed away from the refrigerator, pausing in the doorway to glance into the living room to the corner where she kept Muggins' litter box.

It wasn't there.

Moving slowly, she walked over to where the litter box should have been and stared down at the threadbare carpet. Even if Rob had taken it out and emptied it, which wasn't very likely, and then forgotten to put it back, there wasn't even a trace of litter in the corner from when Muggins scratched the fake sand to cover up his poops.

"What is going on?" Manda mumbled, no longer aware that she was still talking into the phone. "Jesus *Christ!* What the *hell* is going on?"

"You coming down or what?" Rob asked. His voice buzzed like an insect in her ear. Manda didn't even try to understand what he had said. Her hand was suddenly heavy and numb as she lowered the phone from her ear, switched it off, and let it drop. When it hit the floor, it sounded like the plastic casing cracked.

Leaning against the wall, Manda covered her face with both hands and sobbed as she slid slowly down the wall into a sitting position. Bending her knees and leaning her head forward, she cried as the apartment grew steadily darker with the descending night. And when the thought hit her that Muggins was gone — *really gone!* — she didn't have the strength to scream as she stared into the dense darkness that filled the living room.

- 5 -

As it turned out, Rob had too much to drink at *Gritty's*, and Sheena ended up calling to say that she and Marty were taking him back to their place to sleep it off.

What difference does it make? Manda wondered after hanging up the phone. It's not like he had a real *job* to go to in the morning. All he was doing with his time was writing and, judging by the scant pages she had read so far of his "novel in progress," he wasn't doing much of that. In the morning as she got ready for work, she kept one ear tuned toward the front door, hoping she would hear ole' Muggins meowing to be let in after a night out on the town.

But he didn't show up. Tears filled Manda's eyes as she eased the apartment door shut behind her and started down to the street to catch the bus for South Portland. She considered calling in sick, or at least showing up an hour or two late so she could look for her cat, but that could mean her job. With Rob not pulling in his half of the rent, she couldn't afford to lose her job, such as it was.

Things only got worse when she got to work and found the package from Swann House propped up on her desk. A bright yellow *Post-it* note was stuck to the front. It read:

"I TOLD YOU TO RETURN THIS! ! ! — Jason"

Manda crumpled up the note and dropped it to the floor. She couldn't tear her gaze away from the package. One of the last things she had done yesterday was repackage the book, check to make sure the publisher's address was right, and sent it out with the last mail pick-up.

And here it was, back on her desk with RETURN TO SENDER stamped in bright red letters on front and back.

She started to reach for the package but jerked back, not daring to touch it. Leaning closer, she stared uncomprehendingly at the postmark.

How could it have come back so fast?

It had gone out late yesterday afternoon, but here it was with a postmark canceled in Des Moines.

Still not daring to touch the package, Manda leaned close, her nostrils widening as she sniffed the air. She caught a faint whiff of . . . *something*. She wasn't sure quite what. Maybe a hint of . . .

"Burned hair," she muttered, wincing as she pulled back quickly. Before she could catch her breath, the backroom door slammed open. She turned around quickly, expecting to see Jason glowering at her, but saw that it was only Jesse, from the cafe, looking for a carton of napkins. Manda watched him, waiting until he got what he was after and left. Then she turned back to the package.

Her impulse was to toss it into the trash compactor behind the store. So what if the return credit never showed up? As long as the thing was out of her life forever.

Like Muggins, she thought as a chill teased between her shoulder blades. *Out of my life . . . forever . . . like he'd never even existed.*

Manda knew that, one way or another, she had to get rid of the book before Jason saw it. She could just imagine his reaction.

"Wait a second," she whispered, snapping her fingers and nodding as a thought took shape. "That's what's going on . . . Jason's doing this . . . He took the package out of the out-going mail and put it back on the desk just to mess with me. That's *got* to be it!"

She was tempted all the more to toss the book into the trash to be rid of it, but then a better idea struck her.

If Jason was playing with her mind, why not play back?

Grabbing a box cutter from her desk, she sliced open the back of the envelope. The new blade cut quickly and cleanly through the padded stuffing, exposing the black cover of the book. For a second or two, Manda didn't even notice that the blade had also sliced into her hand, just above the heel of her thumb. It wasn't until a large, red drop of blood landed with an audible *plop* on the back of the book that she cried out in pain and surprise.

"Mother-*humper!*" she screamed as she reached for a tissue from the desk dispenser and pressed the wad against the fresh gash. Dull, stinging pain spread like poison up her wrist and down into her fingers, bringing tears to her eyes. Within seconds, the tissue was saturated with blood. She grabbed another to staunch the flow, then blotted the tears that were streaming down her face. After a moment, once she had regained her composure, she lifted the wad of tissues and inspected the wound.

Surprisingly, it wasn't as bad as it felt, but she thought she must have sliced open a vein because the blood flowed so freely.

"Son of a bitch," Manda muttered as she leaned back against the table and pressed the tissue hard against her wrist. Her pulse throbbed in her hand, and she wondered about the possibility of infection. After a minute or two, she peeled back the tissue, glad to see that the blood flow had stopped. She heaved a sigh of relief, turned, and looked down at the package on the table.

The returned book was lying title side up. Manda couldn't look away from the fake-leather cover. The textured black surface caught the overhead lighting just right, making it swirl with an inward-turning whirlpool of light flecked with a deep, rich red intermingled with dense, light-less black.

Reaching blindly behind her, Manda took down a padded book mailer. All the while, the black book cover held her gaze. The longer she stared at it, the more she could feel herself being pulled into it. The subtle interplay of light and shadows, of black and deep, clotted red danced across the cover like the windruffled surface of a pond at twilight. Waves of vertigo swept through her. She was falling . . . falling as she leaned forward and stared, gape-mouthed into the rippling black surface. She was only vaguely aware of the crazy thought that — somehow — she could see *into* or *through* the book into . . .

— *What?*

She snapped back to reality when the backroom door burst open, and McNealy and Cindy, two coworkers, entered, engaged in an animated conversation. Manda turned her back to them so they wouldn't see her tear-stained eyes.

"Yo, Manda," Chris called out. "You still planning to come tonight?"

"Tonight?" Manda asked, still not turning around and busying herself with the new padded envelope. In spite of the cut on her wrist, she wanted to do what she had thought of.

"Billy's gig. At Free Street. It's tonight. Remember?"

"Oh, yeah. Sure," she replied, nodding automatically. She had forgotten all about Billy's gig and was totally focused on getting *Psychic Black Holes* sealed up and addressed to Jason Aceto's home.

"That'll show him, lousy son of a bitch!" she muttered.

"You say something?" Chris asked.

"Huh? Oh, no. Nothing . . . Just talking to myself."

- 6 -

"Rob . . .?"

The air in the apartment sounded curiously muffled as Manda closed the door behind her, making sure to lock the deadbolt and the security chain.

The silence within absorbed both her voice and the sound of her footsteps. No lights were on. Only the soft, blue glow of the streetlight outside their building filtered through the unwashed windows, casting a powdery haze over everything.

Is Rob even home? she wondered, moving forward. *Maybe he's in the bedroom, taking a nap.*

Manda's hand brushed over the wall switch. The sudden glare of light stung her eyes. Unconsciously, she felt the bulge of the bandage that covered the cut on her left wrist.

"Robbie . . .?" she called out, louder now, as if defying the darkness to stifle her voice.

She walked boldly to the bedroom door, swung it open, and snapped on the light.

The bed was empty, undisturbed, just the way she had left it that morning. She knew Rob well enough to know that he would never have remade the bed if he had come home any time during the day. Chances were, he was still at Marty and Sheena's.

Manda listened to the hungry grumble of her stomach and decided to eat something before calling Marty and Sheena and telling Rob to come home. Billy's gig didn't start until 9:30, but she wanted to get there early enough so she could hang out. After the last few days at work, she needed some serious R&R. Tomorrow was the last day of her workweek, and on Monday, she and Rob had plans to go kayaking with some friends on Sebago Lake.

Her feet whispered on the threadbare rug as she walked from the bedroom into the kitchen. Along the way, she snapped on every light she could reach. She wasn't sure why. Rob always left lights on, and she always complained about it because she had to work to pay the bills while he just hung around the apartment, pretending to be working on his novel.

Tonight, for some reason, she wanted to feel safer, and leaving as many lights on as possible seemed to help.

A little, anyway.

She entered the kitchen and hesitated, glancing over her shoulder to where Muggins' litter box used to be — *should have been* — in the living room. She still had no idea what was going on with that, and she was anxious to find Rob so she could ask him about it.

Why had he acted like she was crazy or something, thinking she had a cat?

Of *course* she had a cat!

She'd had Muggins since before she and Rob met, long before they moved in together. So what was this about her not having a cat? And why was Muggins' litter box missing? Was Rob trying to mess with her mind at home the same way Jason was at work?

Manda tried to ignore the wave of paranoia that swept over her, but she couldn't. Maybe that was it. Rob and Jason were in on this together, trying to make her lose her mind or something.

But why?

Rob barely knew Jason, and the few times they had been together, they hadn't exactly hit it off, probably because Jason had made it quite clear to Rob that he wanted to sleep with her.

Manda heaved a sigh as she opened the refrigerator and inspected her prospects for at least a half-decent meal. They weren't very good. A wave of helplessness swept over her when she stared at the bottom shelf and — still — didn't see the half-full can of cat food she *knew,* she just knew was supposed to be there.

"Fuck it," she whispered as she eased the 'fridge door shut and turned around. Her voice sounded oddly strained in the eerie quiet of the building. For the first time in a long time, she wished Rob was here with her. Usually she didn't always appreciate him hanging around, but tonight — for some reason — she really wished he were home.

Fighting back the undefined fear that trembled in her gut, she walked into the living room and picked up the cordless phone. After dialing Marty and Sheena's number from memory, she waited as the phone rang on the other end once . . . twice . . .

"Damn," she muttered when it rang a third time, and she cleared her throat, preparing to leave a message. Just before the fourth ring, Sheena's sleepy-sounding voice answered, "Yeah?"

Manda's first thought was that she had interrupted her and Marty making love.

"Yeah, uh, hi. It's me," she said simply.

"Manda. How's it going? Long time no hear."

"Okay, I guess," Manda said. "I was just wondering if Rob was still at your place or if you know where he was."

After a tense moment of silence at the other end of the line, Sheena cleared her throat and said, "Rob?"

"Yeah. Last night you called and said he was gonna crash at your place. I just wondered if he'd left and where he might've gone, 'cause he's not here."

There was another, longer stretch of silence at the other end of the line. Manda's face flushed. Her pulse started beating fast and feathery in her neck.

"I was heading down to Free Street for Billy's gig and was hoping I could catch him and tell him to meet me there."

"Ahh . . . Have you been drinking or something, Manda?" Sheena asked.

It was impossible to miss the concern in her friend's voice.

"What? No, I — What are you talking about? Of course I haven't been drinking."

Manda let her shoulders drop and exhaled sharply, hoping to relieve the tension that was building up inside her.

"Look," she said. "Just tell me if you know where Rob is, okay? I want to hook up with him so he won't have to come all the way back here and then have to walk down to Free Street."

"Manda. The only other person I know named Rob is my cousin who lives in Pennsylvania," Sheena finally said. "If you mean that guy you were dating, he died two years ago in a car accident. You don't remember?"

"What are you talking about?" Manda said, almost choking. "My boyfriend — Rob . . . Rob Rusch. You and Marty were out drinking with him last night, and you called to tell me he was staying at your place. I just need to —

"Whoa, girl. Get a grip, why don't 'cha," Sheena said. "I don't know what you're on, but you'd better watch it. You don't sound so good.

"No. No, I'm *not* good!" Manda shrilled. Tiny, ice-cold fingertips were clawing at the inside of her throat. "I most *definitely* am not good. Not if you're gonna be fucking with me, too!"

"I'm not *fucking* with you, Manda. Honest."

Sheena's voice remained low and calm, but it did nothing to stop the rushes of fear inside Manda. There was a hot pressure behind her eyes as she glanced around the apartment. Outside, the evening sky had darkened, taking on a curious depth of black. Her legs were as stiff as sticks as she walked over to the window and stared at the night sky above the city. Darkness shifted against darkness like a living thing. High above the city, a curious cloud formation swirled as though driven by a harsh, cold wind. At first it was almost impossible to see, but the longer Manda stared at it, the clearer she could see that the cloud had taken on an odd dimensional effect. A huge spiral turned and shifted in upon itself, swallowing itself and the surrounding blackness into an ever deepening blackness. Within the spiral, elongated flecks of deep, dark red twisted and merged like thick clots, then separated and merged again as they were sucked into the spinning vortex.

Manda was transfixed. The telephone dropped from her nerveless hand to the floor. She didn't hear it hit, and she was only distantly aware of Sheena's high-pitched voice, twisted with worry and fear, calling out to her so loudly it rattled the tiny speaker in the handset.

- 7 -

"It figures," Jason muttered as he glanced at the morning crew gathered in the break room for the opening store meeting.

"What figures?" asked Craig, the assistant manager.

"Manda's late . . . as usual." Jason shielded his mouth with his clipboard as he spoke. "Fifth time this month. She probably won't call, either." He made brief eye contact with Craig and smirked. "So I guess that's it for her. Company policy is company policy. I'm gonna have to fire her ass . . . if I ever see her again."

Craig glanced at him, stone-faced, not revealing his thoughts. Jason either didn't notice or didn't care. He cleared his throat to get everyone's attention and began the meeting. After he ran through the store announcements and news from the home office, Billy went to the front desk and popped a Beatles CD into the music system, and everyone got to work.

Jason closed his office door and plunked down in his chair. Staring past his computer at the wall in front of him, he drummed his fingers on the chair arms, seething that Manda hadn't called in before not showing up. After all the times gone to bat for her when he knew he should have fired her.

But this was it. He had to follow store policy.

As much as he wanted to be rid of her, though, he also didn't want to be rid of her. He still harbored what he knew, deep down, was a futile hope that — given time — Manda would realize how better for her he would be than that poseur writer she was living with. He had a mountain of e-mails and paperwork to go through, but he pushed back from his desk, stood up, and went out to the cafe to grab a cup of coffee.

The day passed slowly for him, and by noon, he was toying with the idea of calling Manda's apartment to see, if nothing else, if she was all right. She might be sick or hurt. Maybe helping her out would be a way to get into her good graces.

But the day's responsibilities piled up, and his workday was over without finishing half of everything he had hoped to finish. With a sharp feeling of remorse and resentment, he left the store a little after five o'clock and got into his car and headed to Manda's apartment.

By the time he pulled up to the curb in front of the building, daylight was bleeding from the sky. Rafts of clouds spread across the western horizon like purple-stained fingers trying to tear through the thin fabric of the sky. Pinpricks of starlight appeared overhead, barely visible through the glare of city lights.

For five minutes or more, Jason sat hunched over his steering wheel, peering up at the darkened windows of Manda's apartment. Several times he thought he caught a hint of motion — something dark and indefinable — moving behind the glassy reflection; but when he strained to see if it was Manda, he realized it was only the reflection of the clouds, shifting across the window.

"Go home . . . Just go the hell home and forget about her," he whispered to himself, and several times he gripped the key in the ignition, preparing to start the car and drive away.

But he couldn't bring himself to do it.

He knew — he could sense that Manda was up there in the gathering darkness.

Maybe she really was sick or hurt . . .

Maybe she wasn't able to get to the phone to call work or a doctor.

As much as he tried to deny it, Jason knew he was going to go up and knock on the door just to make sure Manda wasn't in any danger.

"Damn it," he muttered as he drew the key from the ignition and swung the driver's door open. As he stepped out into the street, a brief gust of cold wind raked chills across his back. Hunching up and tucking his neck into the collar of his jacket, he walked up to the front door, pressed his face against the glass, and peered into the foyer.

There was no one in sight.

The dim, bare light bulb cast a nut-brown glow over the dust and grime-caked floor and stairway. His teeth were chattering, and his hand trembled as he pressed the doorbell for apartment 7-B. From deep inside the building he heard — or thought he heard — a faint buzzing sound. He took a breath and held it as he waited for Manda to buzz him in. All he could hear were the sounds of the city behind him.

"Jesus . . . Jesus . . . *Jesus!*" he whispered, watching his breath fog the front door glass and then dissolve. The reflection of the city lights was distorted in the door glass, and for just an instant, he thought he saw a dense, black smudge reflected over his left shoulder. Grunting with surprise, he turned and looked, but there was nothing there.

His anger rose as he gritted his teeth and pressed the buzzer button again, harder this time. He held it while slowly counting to five, then released it.

Still no answer.

She probably isn't even home, he thought.

Most likely, she had skipped work without calling in because she was just as sick of her job as he was sick of her bullshit. She was probably off for the day, having a grand old time with her loser boyfriend the writer, and hadn't gotten home yet.

"'Scuse me."

The voice, speaking so suddenly behind him, made Jason jump. He turned to see a young man standing close behind him.

"Sorry . . . Sorry," Jason muttered, stepping aside so the man had room enough to insert his key into the front door lock. The man barely acknowledged him, but as he stepped into the foyer, Jason braced the door open with his hand. The man regarded him with undisguised suspicion.

"Forgot my keys," Jason said, knowing how lame he must sound. "My girlfriend's in the shower and can't hear me buzzing."

"What apartment you in?" the man asked.

"Seven-B," Jason replied with a flick of his head to indicate the upstairs.

The men glared at him in silence for a second or two, then nodded and proceed inside without another word. Jason watched him walk down the corridor to a darkened doorway on the left at the far end of the corridor. After the man let himself into his apartment and shut the door, Jason exhaled. He was going to go upstairs to Manda's door, but something to his right caught his attention.

The apartment mailboxes.

He wasn't sure why, but Jason experienced a jolt of recognition when he saw a padded manila book mailer on the floor in front of the row of glass-fronted boxes.

"Son of a bitch," he muttered as he walked over and, bending down, picked it up.

The package had been sent from the bookstore. The store's return address was clearly stamped in the upper left-hand corner on the front along with a carefully hand-lettered address:

Manda Simoneau
325 Congress St.
Apt7 B
Portland, ME 04401

"*Goddamn! I knew it!*"

Jason hefted the package. He could tell, just by the feel, that it was a book, and it didn't take Sherlock Holmes to figure out which book it was.

It had to be the one Manda had special ordered and then not been able to afford. Instead of returning it, like she had been told, she had mailed it to herself.

Jason's hands were trembling as he slid his forefinger under the stapled end of the package and ripped it open. As soon as he did, he yelped in pain as a staple sliced into his forefinger just above the knuckle. A bright streak of blood ran down the side of his finger, smearing the book cover as Jason withdrew the book from the package.

"You sneaky little . . ." he whispered when he saw the black, fauxleather cover and read the title out loud: "*Psychic Black Holes.*"

Snorting with laughter, he slipped the book back into the padded bag and tucked it under his arm. Without thinking, he brought his hand up to his mouth and sucked the blood from the wound. The metallic taste made him wince.

The cut's not so bad, though, he thought. *Probably won't even need a Band-Aid.*

As he left the building and walked down to his car, he couldn't help but smile to himself. He'd bring the book to the store tomorrow and return it to the publisher himself, and that would be the end of it. But not before he confronted Manda with it and fired her under the threat of prosecution for theft. That'd make her think twice about trying to rip off him or the company.

Before getting into his car, Jason glanced up one last time at Manda's apartment windows. The flat glass mirrored the black, velvet night sky with a cold marble gloss. The clouds swirled in reflection, spiraling inward on themselves.

"So I guess that's it for you, Manda," Jason whispered.

His breath came out a gray puff of mist in the chilly night air, and then the gentle breeze silently swept it away into the gathering shadows of the night.

THE CHEESE STANDS ALONE

Harlan Ellison

Cort lay with his eyes closed, feigning sleep, for exactly one hour after she had begun to snore. Every few minutes he would permit his eyes to open to slits, marking the passage of time on the luminous dial of his watch there on the nightstand. At five a.m. precisely he slipped out of the Olympic pool-sized motel bed, swept up his clothes from the tangled pile on the floor, and dressed quickly in the bathroom. He did not turn on the light.

Because he could not remember her name, he did not leave a note.

Because he did not wish to demean her, he did not leave a twenty on the nightstand.

Because he could not get away fast enough, he pushed the car out of the parking slot in front of the room and let it gather momentum down through the silent lot till it bumped out onto the street. Through the open window he turned the wheel, caught the door before the car began rolling backward, slid inside and only then started the engine.

Route 1 between Big Sur and Monterey was empty. The fog was up. Somewhere to his left, below the cliffs, the Pacific murmured threats like an ancient adversary. The fog billowed across the highway, conjuring ectoplasmic shapes in the foreshortened beams of his headlights. Moisture hung from the great, thick trees like silver memories of time before the coming of Man. The twisting coast road climbed through terrain that reminded him of

273

Brazilian rain forest: mist-drenched and chill, impenetrable and aggressively ominous. Cort drove faster, daring disaster to catch up with him. There had to be more than the threat of the forest.

As there had to be more to this life than endodontics and income properties and guilt-laden late night frottage with sloe-eyed dental assistants. More than pewter frames holding diplomas from prestigious universities. More than a wife from a socially prominent family and 2.6 children who might fit a soap manufacturer's perfect advertising vision of all-American youth. More than getting up each morning to a world that held no surprises.

There had to be disaster somewhere. In the forest, in the fog, in the night.

But not on Route 1 at half-past five. Not for him, not right now.

By six-thirty he reached Monterey and realized he had not eaten since noon of the previous day when he had finished the root canal therapy on Mrs. Udall, had racked the drill, had taken off his smock and donned his jacket, had walked out of the office without a word to Jan or Alicia, had driven out of the underground garage and started up the Coast, fleeing without a thought to destination.

There had been no time for dinner when he'd picked up the cocktail waitress, and no late night pizza parlor open for a snack before she fell asleep. Acid had begun to burn a hole in his stomach lining from too much coffee and too little peace of mind.

He drove into the tourist center of Monterey and had no trouble finding a long stretch of open parking spaces. There was no movement along the shopfronted sidewalks. The sun seemed determined never to come up. The fog was heavy and wet; streaming quicksand flowed around him. For a moment the windows of a shop jammed with driftwood-base lamps destined for Iowa basement rec rooms solidified in the eye of the swirling fog; then they were gone. But in that moment he saw his face in the glass. This night might stretch through the day.

He walked carefully through the streets, looking for an early morning dinette where he might have a Belgian waffle with frozen strawberries slathered in sugary syrup. An egg sunnyside up. *Something* sunnyside up in this unending darkness.

Nothing was open. He thought about that. Didn't anyone go to work early in Monterey? Were there no services girding themselves for the locust descent of teenagers with rucksacks, corpulent business machine salesmen in crimson Budweiser caps and Semitic widows with blue hair? Had there been an eclipse? Was this the shy, pocked, turned-away face of the moon? Where the hell was daylight?

Fog blew past him, parted in streamers for an instant. Down a side street he saw a light. Yellow faded as parchment, wan and timorous. But a light.

He turned down the side street and searched through the quicksilver for the source. It seemed to have vanished. Past closed bakeries and jewelry shops and scuba gear emporia. A wraith in the fog. He realized he moved through not only the empty town and through the swaddling fog, but through a condition of fear. *Gnotobiosis*: an environmental condition in which germfree animals have been inoculated with strains of known microorganisms. Fear.

The light swam up through the silent, silvered shadow sea; and he was right in front of it. Had *he* moved to *it* . . . had *it* moved to *him*?

It was a bookstore. Without a sign. And within, many men and women; browsing.

He stood in the darkness, untouched by the sallow light from the nameless bookshop, staring at the nexus. For such a small shop, so early in the morning, it was thronged. Men and women stood almost elbow to elbow, each absorbed in the book close at hand. *Gnotobiosis*: Cort felt the fear sliding through his veins and arteries like poison.

They were not turning the pages.

Had they not moved their bodies, a scratching at the lip, the blinking of eyes, random shifting of feet, a slouch, a straightening of back, a glance around . . . he would have thought them mannequins. A strange but interesting tableau to induce passersby to come in and also browse. They were alive, but they did not turn the pages of the books that absorbed them. Nor did they return a book to its shelf and take another. Each man, each woman, held fascinated by words where the books had been opened.

He turned to walk away as quickly as he could.

The car. Get on the road. There had to be a truck stop, a diner, a greasy spoon, fast food, anything. *I've been here before, and this isn't Monterey!*

The tapping on the window stopped him.

He turned back. The desperate expression on the tortoiselike face of the tiny old woman stiffened his back. He found his right hand lifting, as if to put itself between him and the sight of her. He shook his head *no*, definitely not, but he had no idea what he was rejecting.

She made staying motions with her wrinkled little hands and mouthed words through the glass of the shop window. She spoke very precisely and the words were these:

I have it here for you.

Then she motioned him to come around to the door, to enter, to step inside: *I have it here for you.*

The luminous dial of his watch said 7:00. It was still night. Fog continued to pour down from the Monterey peninsula's forest.

Cort tried to walk away. San Francisco was up the line. The sun had to be blazing over Russian Hill, Candlestick Park, and Coit Tower. The world still held surprises. *You're loose now, you've broken the cycle*, he heard his future whisper. *Don't respond. Go to the sun.*

He saw his hand reach for the doorknob. He entered the bookshop.

They all looked up for a moment, registered nothing, the door closed behind him, they dropped their gazes to the pages. Now he was inside among them.

"I'm certain I have it in hardcover, a very clean copy," the little old turtle woman said. Her smile was toothless. *How could there be fog in here?*

"I'm just browsing," Cort said.

"Yes, of course," she said "Everyone is just browsing."

She laid her hand on his arm and he shuddered. "Just till a restaurant opens."

"Yes, of course."

He was having trouble breathing. The heartburn. "Is it always . . . does it always stay dark so late into the morning here?"

"Unseasonal," she said. "Look around. I have it here for you. Exactly."

He looked around. "I'm not looking for anything special."

She walked with him, her hand on his arm. "Neither were they." She nodded at the crowd of men and women. "Yet they found answers here. I have a very fine stock."

No pages were turned.

He looked over the shoulder of a middle-aged woman staring intently at a book with steel engravings on both open pages. The turtle said, "Her curiosity was aroused by the question 'How was the *first* vampire created?' Fascinating concept, isn't it? If vampires can only be created by a normal human being receiving the bite of a vampire, then how was the first one created? She has found the answer here in my wonderful stock." Cort stared at the book. One of the steel engravings was of Noah's ark.

But wouldn't that mean there had to be *two* on board?

The turtle drew him down the line of stacks. He paused behind a young man in a very tight T-shirt. He looked as if he had been working out. His head was bent so close to the open book in his hands that his straight blond hair fell over his eyes.

"For years he has felt sympathetic pains with an unknown person," the turtle confided. "He would sense danger, elation, lust, despair . . . none of his own making, and none having anything to do with his circumstance at that moment. Finally he began to realize he was linked with another. Like the Corsican Brothers. But his parents assured him he was an only child, there was no twin. He found the answer in this volume." She made shoo'ing motions with her blue-veined hands.

Cort peered around the young man's head and hair. It was a book on African history. There were tears in the young man's eyes; there was a spot of moisture on the verso. Cort looked away quickly, he didn't want to intrude.

Next in line was a very tall, ascetic looking man carefully holding a folio of pages that had obviously been written with a quill. By the flourishes and swirls of the writing, Cort knew the book had to be quite old and very likely valuable. The tortoise woman leaned in close, her head barely reaching Cort's chest, and she said, "Sixteenth century. First Shakespeare folio. This gentleman wandered through most of his adult life, and decades of academic pursuits, tormented by the question of who actually wrote *The Booke of Sir Thomas More*: the Bard or his rival, Anthony Munday. There lies his answer, before his eyes. I have such a superior stock."

"Why doesn't he . . . why don't *any* of these people turn the page?"

"Why bother? They've found the answer they sought."

"And there's nothing more they want to know?"

"Apparently not. Interesting, isn't it?"

Cort found it more chilling than interesting. Then the chill fastened itself permanently to his heart, like a limpet, with the unasked question, *How long have these browsers been here like this?*

"Here's a woman who always wanted to know if pure evil exists anywhere on the face of the earth." The woman wore a *mantilla* over her shoulders, and she stared mesmerized at a book on natural history. "This man hungered for a complete list of the contents of the great Library of Alexandria, the subject matters contained on those half million handwritten papyrus scrolls at the final moment before the Library was torched in the Fifth Century." The man was gray and wizened and his face had been incised with an expression of ancient weariness that reminded Cort of Stonehenge. He pored over two pages set so closely with infinitesimal typefaces that Cort could not make out a single word in the flyspecks. "A woman who lost her memory," said the turtle, indicating with a nod of her tortoise head a beautiful creature festooned with silk scarves of a dozen different colors. "Woke up in a white slave brothel in Marrakech, ran for her life, has spent years wandering around trying to discover who she was." She laughed a low, warm laugh. "She found out here. The whole story's right there in that book."

Cort turned to her, firmly removing her withered claw from his arm.

"And you 'have it here for me,' don't you?"

"Yes; I have it here. In my fine stock."

"What *precisely* do you have that I want? Here. In your fine stock."

He didn't even need her to speak. He knew exactly what she would say. She would say, "Why, I have the answers you seek." And then he would saunter around the bookshop, feeling superior to those poor devils who had been standing here God only knew how long, and finally he'd turn to her and smile and say, "I don't even know the questions," and they would both smile at that one—he like an idiot because it was the most banal of clichés, she because she'd known he would say something dithering like that — and he would refrain from apologizing for the passing stupidity; and then he would ask her the question and she would point out a shelf and say, "The book you want is right there," and then she'd suggest he try pages such-and-such for exactly what he wanted to know: that which had driven him up the Coast.

And if, ten thousand years later, the karmic essence of all that's left of Sulayman the Magnificent, blessed be his name, Sulayman of the potent seal, Sultan and Master of all the djinn, of each and every class of *jinni, ghūl, ifrit, si'lā, div* and *iblis*; if that transubstantiated essence comes 'round again, like Halley's comet comes 'round again; that transmogrified spirit circling back on its limitless hegira through crimson eternity . . . if it comes 'round again it would find him, Cort — Dr. Alexander Cort, D.D.S., a Dental Corporation — still standing here elbow-to-elbow with the other browsers. Coelacanths outlined in shale, mastodons flash-frozen in ice, wasps embedded in amber. *Gnotobiosis*: forever.

"Why do I have the feeling all this isn't random?" Cort said to the old turtle woman. He began edging toward the door behind him. "Why do I have the feeling all this has been here waiting for me, just the way it was waiting for all the rest of those poor fucking losers? Why do I get the smell of rotting gardenias off you, old lady?" He was almost at the door.

She stood in a cleared space in the center of the bookshop, staring at him.

"You're no different, Dr. Cort. You need the answers, the same as the rest."

"Maybe a little love potion . . . a powerstone . . . immortality . . . all that good jive. I've seen places like this in television shows. But I don't bite, old lady. I have no need you can fill." And his hand was on the doorknob; and he was turning it; and he yanked; and the door opened to the ominous fog and the unending night and the waiting forest. And the old lady said, "Wouldn't you like to know when you'll have the best moment of your entire life?"

And he closed the door and stood with his back against it.

His smile was unhealthy. "Well, you got me," he whispered.

"When you'll be happiest," she said softly, barely moving her thin lips. "When you'll be strongest, most satisfied, at the peak of your form, most in control, bravest, best-looking, most highly regarded by the rest of the world; your top moment, your biggest surge, your most golden achievement, that which forms the pattern for the rest of your life; the instant than which you will have no finer, if you live to be a thousand. Here in my fine stock I have a tome that will tell you the day, hour, minute, second of your noblest future. Just ask and it's yours. *I have it here for you.*"

"And what does it cost me?"

She opened her wet mouth and smiled. Her wrinkled little hands fell open palms up in the air before her. "Why, nothing," she said. "Like these others . . . you're just browsing, aren't you?" The limpet chill that ossified his spine told him there were worse things than deals with the devil. Just browsing, as an example.

"Well . . . ?" she asked, waiting.

He thought about it, wetting his lips — suddenly gone dry now that the decisive moment was at hand. "What if it comes only a few years from now? What if I've got only a little while to achieve whatever it was I always wanted to achieve? How do I live with the rest of my life after that, knowing I'll never be any better, any happier, any richer or more secure; knowing I'll never top what I did in that moment? What'll the rest of my life be worth?"

The tiny turtle woman shouldered aside two browsers — who moved sluggishly apart as if turning in their sleep — and drew a short, squat book from a shelf at her waist level. Cort blinked quickly. No, she hadn't drawn it out of the stacks. It had slid forward and jumped *into* her hand. It looked like an old Big Little Book.

She turned back and offered it to him. "Just browsing," she said, moistly.

He reached for it and stopped, curling his fingers back. She arched her finely-penciled eyebrows and gave him a bemused, quizzical look.

"You're awfully anxious to get me to read that book," he said.

"We are here to serve the public," she said, amiably.

"I have a question to ask you. No, two questions. There are two questions I want you to answer. Then I'll consider browsing through your fine stock."

"If I can't give you the answer — which is, after all, our business here — then I'm sure something in my fine stock has the proper response. But . . . take this book that you need, just hold it, and I'll answer your question. Questions. Two questions. Very important, I'm sure." She held out the squat little book. Cort looked at it. It *was* a Big Little Book, the kind he had had when he was a child; with pages of drawings alternating with pages of type, featuring comic strip heroes like Red Ryder or The Shadow or Skippy. Within reach, the answer to the question everyone wanted to ask; what will be the best moment of my life?

He didn't touch it.

"I'll ask, you'll answer; *then* you got me . . . *then* I'll do some browsing."

She shrugged, as if to say, *as you choose.*

He thought: As you choose, so shall you reap.

He said: "What's the name of this bookshop?"

Her face twitched. Cort had the sudden rush of memory from childhood, when he'd first been read the story of Rumpelstiltskin. The turtle woman's face grew mean. "It doesn't have a name. It just is."

"How do we find you in the Yellow Pages?" Cort said, taunting her. It was obvious he was suddenly in a position of power. Even though he had no idea from what source that power flowed.

"No name! No name at all! We don't need a name; we have a very select clientele! It's never had a name! We don't need any names!" Her voice, which had been turtle smooth and soft and chocolate, had become rusted metal scraping rusted metal. No names, I don't got to tell you no names, I don't got to show you no stinkin' badges!

She paused to let the bile recede, and in the eye of the silence Cort asked his second question. "What's in this for you? Where's *your* fix? Where's the bottom-line profit on your p&l? What do *you* get out of this, frighty old lady?"

Her mouth went tight. Her blazing eyes seemed both ancient and silvery with youthful ferocity. "Clotho," she said. "Clotho: Rare Books."

He didn't recognize the name, but from the way she said it, he knew he had pried an important secret from her; had done it, apparently, because he was the first to have asked; had done it as *anyone* might have done it, had they thought of it. And having asked, and having been answered, he knew he was safe from her.

"So tell me, Miss Clotho, or *Ms.* Clotho, or Mrs., or whatever you happen to be: tell me . . . what do *you* get out of this? What coin of the realm do you get paid? You work this weird shop, you trap all these fools in here, and I'll bet when I walk out of here, poof! It all vanishes. Goes back to Never-Never Land. So what kind of a home life do you have? Do you eat three squares a day? Do you have to change your Tampax when you get your period? Do you even *get* the menses? Or has menopause already passed you by? Immortal, maybe? Tell me, weird old turtle lady, if you live forever do you *get* change of life? Do you still want to get laid? Did you *ever* get laid? How's your ka-ka, firm and hard? Do weird old fantastic ladies who vanish with their bookstore have to take a shit, or maybe not, huh?"

She screamed at him. "You can't talk like that to me! Do you know who I am?"

He screamed right back at her. "Fuck no, I don't know who the hell you are, and what's more to the point, I don't *give* a righteous damn who you are!"

The zombie readers were now looking up. They seemed distressed. As if a long-held trance was being broken. They blinked furiously, moved aimlessly; they resembled . . . groundhogs coming out to check their shadows.

Clotho snarled at him, "Stop yelling! You're making my customers nervous!"

"You mean I'm waking them up? C'mon, everybody, rise and shine! Swing on down! How ya fixed, destiny-wise?"

"Shut up!"

"Yeah? Maybe I will and maybe I won't, old turtle. Maybe you answer my question what you were doing waiting for me specially, and maybe I let these goofballs go back to their browsing."

She leaned in as close as she could to him, without touching him, and she hissed like a snake. Then she said tightly, "You! What makes you think it was *you* we wait for? We wait for *every*one. This was your turn. They *all* get a turn, you'll *all* get your turn in the browsing shop."

"What's this 'we' business? Are you feeling imperial?"

"We. My sisters and I."

"Oh, there's more than one of you, is there? A chain bookstore. Very cute. But then I suppose you have branches these days, what with the competition from B. Dalton and Crown and Waldenbooks."

She clenched her teeth; and for the first time Cort could see that the old turtle actually *had* teeth inside those straight, thin lips. *"Take this book or get out of my shop,"* she said in a deadly whisper.

He took the Big Little Book from her quivering hands.

"I've *never* dealt with anyone as vile, as *rude*," she snarled.

"Customer is always right, sweetie," he said. And he opened the book to precisely the right page.

Where he read his finest moment. The knowledge that would make the remainder of his life an afterthought. An also-ran. Marking time. A steady ride on the downhill side.

When would it come? A year hence? Two years? Five, ten, twenty-five, fifty, or at the blessed final moment of life, having climbed, climbed, climbed all the way to the end? He read . . .

That his finest moment had come when he was ten years old. When, during a sandlot baseball game, a pick-up game in which you got to bat only if you put someone out, the best hitter in the neighborhood hit a shattering line drive to deepest centerfield where he was *always* forced to play, because he was no good at baseball, and he ran back and back and stuck up his bare hand and *miraculously,* as he, Little Alex Cort, leaped as high as he could, *miraculously* the pain of the frazzled hardball as it hit his hand and stayed there was sweeter than anything he had ever felt before — or would feel again. The moment replayed in the words on the page of that terrible book. Slowly, slowly he sank to earth, his feet touching and his eyes going to his hand and there, in the red, anguished palm of his hand, without a trapper's mitt, he held the hardest, surest home run line drive ever hit by anyone. He was the killer, the master of the world, the tallest thing on the face of the earth, big and bold and golden, adept beyond any telling, miraculous, a miracle, a walking miracle. It was the best moment of his life.

At the age of ten.

Nothing else he would do in his life, nothing he had done between the age of ten and thirty-five as he read the Big Little Book, nothing he would do till he died at whatever number of years remained for him . . . nothing . . . nothing would match that moment.

He looked up slowly. He was having trouble seeing. He was crying. Clotho was smiling at him nastily. "You're lucky it wasn't one of my sisters. They react much worse to being screwed with."

She started to turn away from him. The sound of him slamming the Big Little Book closed onto the counter of the showcase stopped her. He turned without saying a word and started for the door. Behind him he heard her hurrying after him.

"Where do you think *you're* going?"

"Back to the real world." He had trouble speaking; the tears were making him sob and his words came raggedly.

"You've got to stay! *Everyone* stays."

"Not me, sweetie. The cheese stands alone."

"It's all futile. You'll never know grandeur again. It's all dross, waste, emptiness. There's nothing as good if you live to be a thousand."

He opened the door. The fog was out there. And the night. And the final forest. He stopped and looked down at her. "Maybe if I'm lucky I won't live to be a thousand."

Then he stepped through the door of Clotho: Rare Books and closed it tightly behind him. She watched through the window as he began to walk off into the fog.

He stopped and leaned in to speak as close to the glass as he could. She strained her weird little turtle face forward and heard him say, "What's left may only be the tag-end of a shitty life . . . but it's *my* shitty life.

"And it's the only game in town, sweetie. The cheese stands alone."

Then he walked off into the fog, crying; but trying to whistle.